The Yoga

MW01017484

By Mohan Ashtakala

Print ISBN: 9781771456579

Books We Love, Ltd.
Calgary, Alberta
Canada

Dedication

To my spiritual teacher H.H. Bhaktisvarupa Damodar Swami.
Thank you for all your blessings!

Chapter One

New Delhi, The Present (Beginning of Kali Yuga)

The bus to Badrinath leaned badly over to one side. As the doors opened, a sea of pushing, shouting passengers got on and half an hour later, upon departure, another wave of travelers bullied their way aboard while hawkers of all descriptions announced their assorted wares in the crowded bus before scrambling to get off. It puzzled Jack that no one got left behind, run over or pushed off in the overwhelming bedlam. With much grinding of gears and many perfunctory lurches, the bus wound its way out of the Interstate Bus Terminal in the middle of New Delhi. It was only six-thirty in the morning but beads of sweat already clung to his forehead.

His older brother sat next to him. Steve Goode clasped his long, artistic fingers together, as if hesitant to allow them to express themselves. Jack's fingers, strong but always restless, tapped steadily on the seat as if looking for something to do. He sighed. Steve's silent treatment tested his patience.

"Why didn't you just stay in Kansas City?"

Steve glared back. "I used the last bit of my student loan to join you on this expedition to nowhere."

"Well, don't be a martyr about it."

The reproach had its effect. "I'm sorry. I didn't mean that." Steve reflected for a second. "I didn't want to spend the money but I always wanted to visit India." He returned to his guide book about Himalayan pilgrimage towns, making notes in his small, ever-present pocketbook. A light gray jacket, a plain white shirt, dark brown slacks and sensible black loafers comprised his outfit.

5

Jack restarted the conversation. "When the hell'd you shave?" he queried, scratching his own scruffy chin. He sported a black T-shirt promoting some long forgotten band tour, tight blue jeans, and grubby white tennis shoes.

"I woke up at four-thirty. Being prepared, you know."

Jack snorted. "Where'd you get the book?"

"At a bookstore in Connaught Square. Yesterday."

Just like Mom, thought Jack, *both book lovers.* He stretched and stared out the window as the bus slowed through the slums in North Delhi. Small, unkempt children played in open gutters. He shook his head. *Poor kids, they'll never get a chance. Never get a chance to go to college, play football or attend concerts.* He had dropped out of Missouri after discovering that university demanded scholarship and gave no credit for having a good time. Not because he was stupid—no, everyone told him he was intelligent—but not a single course held his interest. After two years of the college grind, he quit.

But still, he had his choices and these people didn't. The crowded hovels, the poverty, the dust and the heat hit him in the gut. *How the hell did I end up here,* he wondered, *in the middle of a noisy bus crowded to the gills with humanity, on a trip to God knows where?*

* * *

They had arrived in New Delhi two weeks earlier and engaged in the usual tourist things: a visit to the Taj Mahal, the Purana Quila, the Parliament buildings and the Delhi Zoo. Disregarding the warning that May is the hottest month on the Indian subcontinent when only the proverbial mad dogs and Englishmen roam in the midday sun, they wilted after a couple of weeks. They approached their hotel manager for advice.

"Too much terrorists in Kashmir," stated the man. On a small shelf behind him sat a picture of Lakshmi Devi, the goddess of fortune, garlanded with fresh jasmine. Fair-skinned, she sported four arms, wore a red sari and sat crossed-legged on a white and pink lotus. An incense stick burned in front of her.

"Hey," enquired Jack. "Where would you go?"

"Me?" retorted the manager, with surprised eyes. He reflected. "My father went to Badrinath in Himalayas. My grandfather, same thing. In my life, I pray for chance to have darshan of Sri Badri Narayan, the temple Deity."

Jack knotted his eyebrows.

"Darshan means to have audience with, vision of, the Deity."

"Okay, okay. How do we get there?"

The hotel manager arched his eyebrows. "No. Not a tourist place. Only pilgrims go. Very difficult."

"Hey, you only live once," countered Jack. "Just give us the directions."

The manager shrugged his shoulders and threw a bus schedule on the counter. "You go by the bus. Only part way. Then you climb on the foot."

Jack grabbed the brochure and as he turned to go, he glimpsed, out of the corner of his eye, Lakshmi Devi winking at him. His eyes widened, he held his breath and turned around. She stared back, impassive. He shook his head. Maybe the heat got to him.

* * *

Jack looked out the window. If a game inside the city, traffic resembled war outside, with every highway a battlefield. The casualties littered the roadside: huge lorries lay flipped over at depressingly regular intervals, along with broken cars and an occasional dead goat.

At night, the traffic became even more hair-raising. Making no concession to darkness, navigated by fatalistic drivers with no fear of death, the trucks, with six or eight headlights blazing, their sides painted with fierce female divinities carrying swords and axes, careened down dusty country roads at breakneck speeds. But the next morning, away from the large metropolis, came scenes of great beauty: hills garlanded with shimmering green rice fields, snow-capped mountains reflecting in their blue waters. In the evenings, they rested in tiny villages where small wiry men of the hills returned home from fields, their lives following the timeless, primordial cycle of seasons, rains and crops. Stopping in these hamlets, he sensed the simplicity of the inhabitants' lives. Despite the poverty of their possessions, they showed little anxiety. Genuine warmth filled the evenings: the villagers shared songs and what little food they had unhesitatingly. *What does it take to be like them*, he wondered. *What makes them happy with what they have?*

Though constantly broke, Jack somehow always coughed up enough money to impulsively travel to various parts of the world. He spent last spring in Paris; the previous winter, snorkeling in Mexico. He traveled at every chance, but each trip ended in disappointment, always finishing where he had started—with no idea what his life was about. Maybe India would inspire him, unlike his previous adventures. He shrugged. Mom constantly reminded him that he had to stop wandering and become serious. She no doubt insisted on his big brother coming to watch over him, as if Steve was his father or something.

He caught himself. That wasn't quite fair. He had to admit, his brother rescued him from some tight spots over the years—once Steve drove all the way to San Antonio and bailed him out of jail after he got drunk and punched out a guy in a bar. Or last year, when Steve pulled together the money to retrieve his impounded vehicle. Jack laughed. *That's me,* he figured—*a hellraiser just like Dad.* He understood why Mom wanted him to settle down; she didn't want him to turn out like his father. *It's in my blood,* thought Jack, *I have to keep moving.*

And the other thing that Mom always harped about: girlfriends. He liked the chase, the thrill of getting a woman, but as soon he established a relationship, he'd lose interest. Jack rubbed his chin. Damned if he knew why, but it happened every time. It led to some awful scenes, with hurt girlfriends slamming doors behind them, but he couldn't help himself. If there were no feelings left, he moved on. *I can't be blamed,* he supposed, *it's better to be honest about these things.*

Jack suddenly felt depressed. He took a deep breath and caught himself. *Forget about the past,* he reminded himself. *It's just an empty place and there's no point dwelling there.* He exhaled and pushed out all the negative thoughts and felt better. *Just live for the moment. That's my philosophy.* He looked down on the floor and grinned. *If that's what you call a philosophy.*

Chapter Two

Badrinath, the Present (Beginning of Kali Yuga)
Their route took them to Haridwar, where the Ganges
flows from the mountains to meet the plains, and then up to
Hrishikesh in the high hills, famous for its many yoga
ashrams. When they reached Hrishikesh, the temperature
became bearable, even cool at night, and they reluctantly
had to buy thick green woolen sweaters at a roadside stand.

The three-day bus journey ended at Hanuman Chatti,
where they left the rest of the passengers. Grateful to
escape the claustrophobia, and with much stretching of
cramped muscles, they headed on foot along the pilgrim
trail following the blue-green Alakananda river. They
climbed for two days, straining under heavy backpacks,
with the night spent in an unnamed village: a cluster of
brown stone huts with grey slate roofs, a stranger to both
electricity and indoor toilets, clinging to the leeward side of
a high ridge, surrounded by forests of silver-green
Himalayan pine.

By the time they arrived in Badrinath, the sun hung
low in the west. Steve took the backpack off his weary
shoulders and dropped it on the ground at the edge of the
trail. His brother stood next to him. Exactly six feet tall,
Steve, twenty-seven, measured a hair shorter than his
younger brother and featured dark brown eyes and a mop of
pale brown hair curling over his forehead. Jack had sharp
blue eyes, an oval face, an aquiline nose, a handsome chin
and, at only twenty-three, boasted broad shoulders with
long black hair, which women found irresistible.

Slowly bending his aching knees, Steve rested his thin
frame on a large boulder and gazed at the town below. The
Alakananda river, fast moving and fed by melting snows,
split the town in two. Several buildings, mostly shops and
restaurants, occupied the near side of the river while sweet

pine-wood smoke wafted along the cobblestoned streets. The trail enlarged into the town's main road, running right through its center, across its only bridge and ended at the front steps of the shrine, while mountains loomed beyond it. The whole place gave off a sense of impossibility, as if arising from the rocky ground rather than having been crafted by human hands.

Steve referred to his notebook. "The great Indian philosopher, Adi Shankaracharya, originally established the temple almost twelve hundred years ago." An aura of great antiquity permeated the town's every nook and corner, from the ancient weathered stone buildings to the rough-hewn granite temple, which looked as if it had been there forever. Even the dust that blew in from Tibet seemed ageless.

Steve continued. "The famous Tapta Kund, hot springs encircled by terraced stone steps, renowned in antiquity throughout India and China, lies close to the temple. The Kund is older than the temple and according to legend, built by the Pandavas, five legendary brothers whose names are mentioned in the five-thousand-year-old *Mahabharata*, the history of ancient India."

He recalled his readings from the bus: that Badrinath rested at an elevation of about 11,000 feet above the vast Gangetic Plains. No inhabitants lived permanently in this isolated area as no agriculture, industry or trade could take durable hold; rather, it existed only as a place of pilgrimage and, for six months of the year, when the winter snows closed the mountain passes, the whole town shut down and the carved stone Deities icons of the temple were relocated to a lower elevation.

In the fading sunlight, Steve straightened, looked down and spied several small eateries.

"I'm hungry."

"Hey, I'm famished," added Jack.

They scrambled down and found the Ajanta Hotel, which followed the Indian custom of calling a restaurant a hotel. They climbed a flight of stairs to an expansive open-air room and chose a hefty, bare wooden table with rough-hewn benches overlooking the bridge leading to the temple. Several large hissing kerosene lamps hung on the walls. The setting sun lent a golden hue to the snows on the mountain tops and from across the river came the tinkling of temple bells.

A thin, dark-skinned, middle-aged man dressed in a long white shirt extending down to his knees and a clean white-cotton toga-like garment, wrapped around his waist and covering his legs, approached them. He parted his black hair, slick with oil, neatly down the middle and peered at them through round, dark-rimmed glasses. Reminding Steve more of a scientist than a restaurant owner, he precisely poured a tall glass of water for each of them.

"Yes, sir," he pronounced. "You want to eat, no?"

"What do you have?" Steve asked.

"Yes, sir. I have very good food. *Iddli* and *dosa*. Also *dahi*, *sambar*, and coconut chutney. Everything vegetarian only."

"Nothing with meat?" questioned Jack.

The man adjusted his glasses. "No sir. No non-veg. This is temple town. It is sacred place. No killing of animals here."

Jack shrugged. "Whatever."

"What do you suggest?" Steve inquired.

"I will bring everything," the man replied and abruptly disappeared.

"What's he wearing?" asked Jack.

"You mean that white robe wrapped around his waist?"

"Yeah."

"It's a *dhoti*. It is the traditional dress of India for men, just like the sari is for women. And that long shirt is called a *kurta*."

Ten minutes later, the man returned with plates filled with food, introduced them and detailed their ingredients. "This is iddli, is made with rice flour and steamed and put in sambar." The iddlis resembled large white dumplings floating in bowls of sambar, a richly-spiced golden broth

12

with an assortment of vegetables. Steam, redolent with the scent of fresh spices, rose and disappeared into the chill evening air. Steve sliced warily into an iddli with his spoon. It tasted light, almost feathery, with a slight sourdough taste.

"Sambar, it is made with lentils, spiced with curry powder, roasted cumin, poppy seeds, and garam masala," the man recounted. Bits of red tomatoes, fresh green chilies, and coriander leaves floated on top. It was spicy, spicier than Steve expected, but the heat drove away the cold blowing in from the open walls.

More food came, and they ate hungrily. "This is dosa. Is made with rice flour and urad dahl." The man waited for a moment. "Urad dahl, is kind of small white lentil."

Steve pulled over the dosa, a thin, almost translucent, crepe rolled into a long cylinder, golden on the outside and stuffed with spiced, herbed potatoes. A side dish of coconut chutney accompanied it. He broke off a piece of the crispy crepe and tasted it. The dosa almost melted on his tongue.

"I first peel potato," explained the man, "then I chop, only a little I boil it, and then I fry in the pan with oil, herbs and spices. It becomes crispy and tasty. " The dosa sent a warm glow from Steve's mouth all the way to his stomach. A small taste of the coconut chutney, seemingly containing equal parts of fresh, green chili and raw, scraped coconut, seared his tongue and left him grabbing for water. He concentrated on the dosa.

The man pulled up a chair and sat down beside them. "*Angrezi?*" he asked.

"No, we're not English," Steve replied, recalling coming across that word in New Delhi. "We're American. Where are you from?"

"Yes, sir. I am from South India. I am speaking very good English!" He smiled proudly. "I am owner of hotel. My name is Iyer."

It explained the English, more familiar in the South, remembered Steve.

"Why you are coming here?"

"To see the temple."

"*Achha?*" enquired Mr. Iyer, obviously puzzled that two young Americans would be visiting.

"I just graduated from college," explained Steve, "majoring in languages." The countless hours spent in the library at the University of Missouri left him with a permanent crease around his eyes, giving him the air of a university professor. "I even completed two courses in Sanskrit and Indian philosophy. So coming to India is in some way a fulfillment of my years of study. I enjoyed learning the philosophy of India."

Mr. Iyer beamed.

"So what else is there to see besides the temple?" asked Jack

"The temple is the town. There is nothing else."

"Maybe we can trek in the mountains."

"The Valley of the Rishis is up there," offered Mr. Iyer helpfully.

"What's that?"

"The word *rishi* means 'sage' or 'seer'," answered Steve. "They're basically like yogis who spend their lives in meditation."

"In that valley are many rishis," added Mr. Iyer. "Some been meditating there for hundreds, maybe thousands of years!"

Jack straightened up. "Thousands of years?"

"Some rishis been there since *Satya yuga*, the golden age, thousands of years ago. They been meditating in cave or under tree all this time. Because they are so much meditating and so much yoga doing, their brain is able to keep the *Vedas*, the holy teachings of wisdom, and carry it from one *yuga* to next."

"Wow!" exclaimed Jack. Vedas? Yuga? Humans living for thousands of years?

Mr. Iyer pushed two small clay bowls containing plain yogurt toward them. "*Dahi*. Eat."

The cool, creamy yogurt perfectly ended the meal. It removed the heat left on the tongue from the spices and admirably relaxed the stomach without eliminating the pleasant warmth enveloping the body.

14

"So if we go to this valley, we can see the rishis?" asked Jack, his eyes lighting up.

"*Ji. Ji,*" replied Mr. Iyer. He moved close to Jack, peered into his eyes, raised a finger and shook it professorially. "But only if you have spiritual vision."

Jack grabbed a pencil and paper out of his backpack and looked expectantly at Mr. Iyer. "I'm into yogis meditating in caves. Tell me more."

Steve stared apprehensively at his brother. First of all, even Jack must know that there are no thousand-year-old yogis meditating under any trees. Besides, what guidance could any yogi, ancient or not, give him? The best advice could only come from those closest to him and what his little brother ought to be doing is to get an education or a real job.

Sometimes he just couldn't understand Jack. Jack always ran around without any stability in his life. When Dad died, Steve automatically got a job—Mom needed the help. Life forced a disorderly existence on Steve and academics became his refuge. Reading, writing and spending time with books turned out to be something he controlled, regulated; a place just for him.

The thought of studies brought out his latest dilemma. He stared out the window at the waters flowing under the bridge. He especially liked languages, but could he pursue it as a career? Or look for a job unrelated to his major? That was a tough one. Not many jobs appeared in his field, especially ancient ones like Sanskrit. But working for a company for the rest of his life? That was a big commitment. Yet it seemed inescapable: getting a steady income would help everyone. He exhaled, glad in coming to India—he needed to think things through.

He shook his head and fixed his gaze at his brother furiously writing on a piece of paper. "What are you doing?"

Jack, his sense of adventure piqued, hardly heard him. Outside, the moonlight shone silver on the Himalayan peaks while the distant chants of pilgrims making their way back from the temple and the rushing sound of the swollen

15

river echoed in the open room. The kerosene lamps illuminated Jack's face and threw deep shadows in every corner. He positively glowed. In this wondrous setting, anything seemed possible.

"Don't worry," retorted Jack. "I know what I'm doing." Steve sighed but kept quiet. When Jack got an idea stuck in his head, nothing could be done.

"Sometimes you've got to go with the flow, with your destiny," said Jack. "Anything is possible. Is it by accident that we're sitting here tonight, in this restaurant, getting instructions on how to get to this hidden valley?"

Steve yawned. "How about getting instructions on where to sleep?" Jack stared back sheepishly. It was late.

"The *dharmashalla*, the pilgrim's hostel, is just down the street from where you came," said Mr. Iyer. "Go now if you want a place." They paid their bill of a hundred and fifty rupees, about three dollars, picked up their backpacks and walked briskly down the winding, unlit street.

The dharmashalla had very basic amenities—a place to sleep on a hard wooden floor and not much else. No electricity. No running water. The freezing river provided water for a bath and an outhouse leaned up behind the building. But a place in the dharmashalla was a much sought-after prize: it cost nothing and constituted the only shelter in town as neither five-star hotels for the wealthy nor youth hostels for the adventurous existed. Everyone, young and old, Indian and foreigner, believer and non-believer, piled into it in the evening, connected by one of the most basic of human needs: a safe place to sleep.

In one corner of the huge room they found a couple of thin reed mats and pillows, spread their sleeping bags on top of the mats and quickly fell into a deep, restful sleep. The next morning they heard, but managed to sleep through, the noise of the pilgrims who rose by five o'clock, bathed and wandered to the temple. By the time they woke at seven-thirty, the dharmashalla had almost emptied. Jack rose bounding with energy, ready for a day of action and adventure. Steve, too, felt bright and well rested.

They gathered their backpacks and tagged behind the few remaining stragglers to the river bank. They stripped, wrapped themselves with thin cotton towels called *gamchas* and poured buckets of freezing water over their bodies.

Thoroughly numb, his fingers barely functioning, Steve somehow managed to change into fresh clothes. Then, following the pilgrims and, according to custom, they first visited the Tapta Kund, the hot springs. At first the heat felt unbearable, but after several minutes, the water loosened Steve's muscles and dissipated the numbness in his body. Women bathed on the opposite side, separate from the men, fully clothed in their draping saris yet fully wet, displaying a certain grace and sensuality. He noticed Jack staring at them.

After a long time, they dressed and headed for the shrine. The temple was not large, maybe fifty feet high, and positioned itself in the middle of an enclosed courtyard whose stone walls contained many ancient carvings. Standing in line outside, they awaited their turn to have darshan of Sri Badri Narayan, as travelers ahead of them stepped into the inner sanctum of the temple and rang large bells hanging from the ceiling.

As they strode inside, Steve tugged Jack's shirt. "The canopy covering this inner sanctum is made of pure gold," he whispered, consulting his notes.

"Wow," replied Jack.

Upon approaching the Deities, the pilgrims immersed themselves in their private devotions. With palms held together in supplication and prayers on their lips, they stood one by one in front of the carved stone Deity of Sri Badri Narayan, who was dressed in a yellow silk dhoti, a blue silk shawl embroidered with trees and colorful birds, and a golden crown encrusted with numerous jewels. The priest waved a lamp in front of the Deity.

"What's he doing?" enquired Jack.

Steve consulted his notebook. "This, I believe, is called *arti*, a ceremony of worship. It consists of offering a lamp filled with clarified butter in which cotton wicks are soaked and lit. The Deity is also offered flowers and water and, finally, fanned with a whisk made of yak-tail hair."

"Far out!" exclaimed Jack.

The pilgrims bent down from their waists, touched the Deity's feet with both hands and patted themselves on their heads in a gesture of receiving blessings.

"I don't know about this," whispered Jack. "I could never bow down in front of anyone or anything." Steve nodded his head. He hadn't seen much devotional expression in his life, and certainly not this type. He wrestled with conflicting feelings. The pilgrims' obvious, genuine, piety certainly impressed him but it also jarred his American sensibilities. Yet he came to India to witness exactly this kind of thing.

"Are you going to request something?" joked Steve.

Jack glanced back questioningly. "You think I should? I mean, I don't know if I believe in any of this stuff. It's a little weird, you know."

"Well, it can't hurt. We need all the help we can get."

"Yeah, maybe I'll ask for a brand new Corvette. Or to win the lottery."

"How about an answer to a really big question?"

"Like what?"

"Like your purpose in life?"

"Oh that." Jack shrugged but when his turn came to stand before the Deity, he inexplicably folded his palms together and with the straightest face he could muster, requested Sri Badri Narayan to reveal to him his destiny. Steve laughed quietly and, upon approaching, carefully noted the Deity's appearance, the garments, the priest's actions, the pilgrims' movements and silently walked away.

Exiting the temple, Steve eyed his watch. Eleven o'clock. He looked up just in time to see Jack walking up a path toward the mountains.

"Wait," shouted Steve. "Where are you going?"

"To the Valley of the Rishis."

"Are you crazy? We need to pack food, make plans, and check directions. You know, prepare to leave for Delhi tomorrow."

Jack stopped. "That's not going to take all day."

Steve slowly shook his head. Jack was right; it wouldn't take the rest of the day, but that wasn't the real objection. His brother was chasing rainbows again.

"Loosen up, Steve," Jack continued. "Trust me. Everything's gonna be fine."

Steve dubiously put his backpack over his shoulders and followed his brother up the narrow trail.

Chapter Three

Badrinath, The Present (Beginning of Kali Yuga)
Jack sat in the restaurant playing with his curried vegetables and rice. Last night, in the same place, the mood had been magical. Tonight he felt exhausted, angry, his face drained, and his eyes barely open. A waiter they didn't see yesterday served them. Mr. Iyer seemed to be hiding in the kitchen.

They had spent the afternoon tramping around the mountains following Mr. Iyer's inscrutable instructions, which described a passage not of this world. After five hours of climbing, a black granite boulder, the size of a modern apartment building, roughly triangular in shape and as smooth as glass, stopped the trail dead in its tracks. They found no way over, around or through it and when the sun started to set and shadows darkened the trail, they admitted defeat and trekked hastily back to town.

"Hey, thanks for taking notes on our route out," Jack finally remarked. "Otherwise we would have been completely lost."

"See," declared Steve humorously, trying to cheer up his brother. "If I didn't plan things, we wouldn't have made it back."

"Yeah," uttered Jack glumly, "And if I wasn't spontaneous, we wouldn't be here in the first place."

"What's the problem? You really didn't expect to discover those old yogis, did you?"

"I don't know. We've been in India for almost a month and instead of mysticism, all I've encountered is misery. I'm ready to pack it in and go back home. I guess I'm looking for something that just can't be found."

Steve smiled. "So why did you come?"

20

Jack grimaced. Steve always needed a reason, a purpose, a plan, for everything. "Just to have fun," he replied. "And you?"

"Well, I came to think about my future," mumbled Steve, "and Mom asked me to keep an eye on you."

Jack rolled his eyes.

"Come on," Steve said, cocking his head. "Don't give up. Maybe you were right last night. Maybe we aren't here by accident."

"I don't know. This is probably just a big mistake. This place sucks and so does the rest of this country." After leaving New Delhi, coming to the mountains and visiting the temple, what next? Except for a few brief moments, the whole trip disappointed Jack. Maybe the fault lay with him. He came expecting something. Answers, maybe? But answers to what? They paid the bill, picked up their gear and headed out the door.

Although still early evening, a crowd filled the dharmashalla. The brothers went to the corner of the room, searching for the mats and pillows. None were left and a very disagreeable old man, smelling like he hadn't seen a bath for a whole month, slept in the same corner they had occupied the previous night. Bare-chested, he wore a ragged old dhoti and a loop of string running over his left shoulder, across his chest and around his back,

"Now what?" demanded Jack. "I'm too exhausted to deal with this."

"Let's just find another place to sleep." They located a couple of spots near the door, but another problem arose. Jack emptied his backpack but his sleeping bag had disappeared.

"Did you remember to pack it this morning?" asked Steve.

Jack looked around. There, under the thin cotton sheeting covering the old man! His sleeping bag!

"Hey!" he shouted, "Give me back my sleeping bag." The old man made no effort to get up. "Hey," Jack shouted even more loudly. "I want my sleeping bag."

21

"Stop!" admonished Steve, grabbing his brother. "You can't do that here."

Jack looked around. A few travelers murmured in Hindi. He backed off silently but glared angrily at the decrepit old man.

"Just drop it," warned Steve. "In India, people always defer to their elders, even if they are in the wrong."

The man opened a baleful eye and surveyed the two young Americans from about ten steps away. He smirked, revealing two yellow teeth on the top of his mouth and three brown ones on the bottom. He sat up, retched loudly and spoke in a high-pitched, thick accent. "So you two fools went looking for the rishis? What will you do tomorrow, look for God himself?" He turned around and made a comment in Hindi. His neighbors laughed. Jack's face flushed red. How did he know? Of course! It must have been that Mr. Iyer!

"Let me tell you a secret," the man confided. Jack and Steve both ignored him. "Idher aow," coaxed the old man. "Come here."

The others looked up expectantly, motioning them to come. The brothers glanced at each other and then at the old man. Slowly, hesitantly, they approached.

"Closer. Come closer," he prodded. Jack grimaced. The old man's thin face remained unshaven, his gray hair disheveled, his head balding and his nostrils flared wide open. A foul smell wafted up from his sweaty, unwashed body and through his shabby clothes. He sat up and put his mouth next to Jack's ear.

"I am Gautama Rishi himself," he shouted, referring to one of the ancient sages. The room exploded with laughter. Jack jumped and glared back angrily. He felt exhausted, his neck stiff from carrying the backpack all day and his calf muscles throbbed painfully. A hard anger coiled in the pit of his stomach. Steve tugged at Jack's arm.

The old man bent over in laughter. "Why did you idiots come here? You fools are either looking for God or hashish. Are you on a holy trip or a hippie trip? Maybe you want some ganja?" The old man whispered. "I can get some cheap. Very cheap. Twenty rupees." A young man next to him grinned broadly, held up both hands and rubbed his fingers together as if rolling a joint. Jack peered into the old man's red eyes. He seemed to have smoked a lot of cheap ganja already.

Jack's temper exploded. *"Pagal!"* he shouted angrily, one of the few Hindi curse words he knew, his finger pointing at the man. His blue eyes blazed and he pulled his dark hair behind his ears. Steve pulled him back, but Jack refused to be restrained. "Crazy," he shouted again.

The room stilled. The old man fell silent. He dropped his gaze to the floor. "Yes," he admitted softly, "I'm crazy." He regarded them with sad, tired eyes. "I studied engineering at Jawaharlal Nehru University in Delhi. Then I became a *pujari* here in Badrinath. I worshiped Sri Badri Narayan daily. I had everything a Brahmin could ask for. I served God directly, but I threw it away." Jack's eyes widened. Obviously, being a priest at this shrine stood to be a prized position and the education explained the man's English.

"What happened?" probed Jack gruffly. "How did you lose your position?"

"By committing too many offenses against God," replied the old pujari. "What exactly, what does it matter? Now look at me, begging like a useless man, living on the charity of strangers."

Not charity, concluded Jack, more like thievery.

"I don't want to talk anymore," announced the man abruptly and, belching one final time, turned his body away, closed his eyes and covered his head with the sleeping bag.

Jack and Steve resigned themselves to sleeping on the bare floor. Their backpacks served as pillows and they shared the single sleeping bag. In spite of the warmth from the huddled bodies in the room, cold seeped in through the floor and the walls and they lay shivering, occasionally nodding off in fitful sleep, waiting for morning to start back to Delhi.

The commotion started well past midnight. The old man first moaned intermittently, then shouted in Hindi, refusing to calm down. Children woke up crying. One by one, the pilgrims arose, some lighting candles, others turning on their flashlights, moving over to the pujari. They found a large candle and planted it on the floor next to him. The light illuminated his face contorting in pain, wavered on the pilgrims gathered over him, and cast flickering shadows on the ceiling and on the bare walls.

"Now what the hell's the matter with the old man?" Jack complained.

But the pujari's moaning got worse. A crowd gathered and an animated conversation followed. They consulted amongst themselves and came up with different suggestions, but nothing helped. Jack felt queasy; something felt seriously wrong. The young traveler sleeping next to the old man approached them.

"The pujari is too much sick," he informed Steve. "You go get doctor."

Steve's eyes widened. He pulled the sleeping bag close. "Why me? I don't speak Hindi."

"He is saying you to help him. No one else."

The young man looked up. "Please, please get doctor."

"Why? Why me?"

"I...I have no money," cried the old pujari. Tears of helplessness flowed down his face. "If you give him, he will come."

Steve arched his back. "How much?"

"Only five hundred rupees!"

Steve hesitated. More tears rolled down the man's cheeks.

Jack jumped up. "Hey, that's only ten dollars." He pulled out the money and handed it to Steve. "If it saves the old geezer's life and we get some sleep, it's worth it."

"Please," pleaded the pujari. "He lives at the end of the street. He knows me. Go now."

The personal appeal felt impossible to ignore. Steve grabbed his sweater, wrapped it hurriedly around his waist, and rushed out.

24

The man waited for Steve to leave before signaling Jack to come closer. With his thumbs, the pujari made a massaging motion on his chest.

Jack jumped back. "Hey man," he exclaimed, "No."

"Help me," pleaded the pujari. "Please." Jack hesitated. The old man's antics tested his patience, but undeniably, he appeared seriously ill.

"I will pray to God to bless you. I will die without your help."

Jack grimaced. He reluctantly approached the old man and rubbed his bony chest.

"Yes. Yes," the man gasped, finally getting some respite from the pain. But the let-up didn't last long. His breathing became more rapid, more shallow. The pujari quickly forgot what little relief the massage provided when the next wave of pain washed over his thin body. "It's no use," he finally panted. "What is destined to happen will happen. Tonight, I will die."

"The doctor will arrive soon," reassured Jack.

"No," replied the pujari with conviction. "It's too late." He reached into the folds of his dhoti and pulled out a paper, folded many times over. "Take this."

With knotted eyebrows, Jack opened the old yellowing parchment. Line upon line of Sanskrit text filled it. His eyes opened wide and he looked up in surprise.

"What is this?" he exclaimed.

"It's named the Yuga Shastra."

"What? What'd you call it? The Yoga Zapper?"

"Please take it. Very, very important. You have to take it."

Jack felt embarrassed. He hardly knew this man and yet, on his deathbed, he was gifting him an obviously prized possession. The Yoga Zapper? What did that mean?

"No. No, I can't...." started Jack, handing it back. The old man refused it and made an extraordinary effort to sit up, gasping in pain. Sweat rolled down his forehead, his thin arms shook uncontrollably, his face paled and his eyes rolled unsteadily.

"No. No. You have to take it. I cannot explain...." he whispered, pulling in a long, wheezing breath. The candle glimmered on his skull-like face and cast deep shadows on his eye sockets. "You do not understand. This *shastra* is more valuable than you can ever know. Your life, the future of the entire world depends on it. You have to take it. Only you. No one else!"

Jack looked questioningly at the delirium old pujari. The man coughed violently and his frail body shook uncontrollably as he lay down. He gazed pleadingly one last time, silently begging Jack to keep the scripture. As the light slowly escaped from his dulling eyes, he gasped fiercely for air one final time, lay straight on his back and with all the bones in his body rattling, died in front of the assembly.

"Raam! Raam!" exclaimed the gathered pilgrims, hoping that the pure name of God entered the old man's ears before death took the soul.

"Jesus Christ!" cried Jack, looking away, witnessing death for the first time. His stomach churned. He sucked air into his lungs, forced the vomit back down, bent over, clung to his knees, wobbled and fell to the floor.

"Damn! Damn!" he shouted. He swallowed hard, impelling the nausea out of his gut, through his extremities and into the air. He put his hand on the floor, shifted unsteadily back to his feet and stood next to the dead man for several moments, gathering his senses.

Steve rushed into the dharmashalla. He had brought the doctor just a minute too late.

"Let's get the hell out of here," yelled Jack.

Chapter Four

Kansas City, The Present (Beginning of Kali Yuga)
They landed early that June Sunday morning at the
Kansas City airport with nowhere to go. Out of habit, they
returned to their old haunt, the university area, and to an
old church near the campus. Jack sat on its cement steps,
his well-traveled knapsack at his feet, rubbing his eyes,
suffering from the ten and a half hour time difference.
Steve slumped beside him, nodding off.

"Where do we go from here?" Jack asked, nudging his
brother.

Steve forced his bleary eyes to open. "The way I see it,
we have two options: live with mom, or look for work, save
money and apply for grad school. Or at least I can apply if
it is not too late." Jack didn't take offense. He accepted
Steve being the accomplished student as a matter of fact.
But how could his brother get enough money for grad
school? And flipping burgers for the summer would be the
ultimate letdown.

Living with Mom remained out of the question; she
barely managed on her pension. Besides, she let Jack know
that he was wasting his money on this trip. Despite her
general disapproval, less exotic destinations didn't draw
complaints but, for some reason, India provoked stiff
resistance. It happened to be just too foreign. The last thing
he wanted now was her 'see, I told you so.'

He stopped listening to her when his father died. "The
only one who can tell me what to do is Dad," he informed
her years ago and he meant it. He loved her well enough,
but they exhibited such different personalities. Her solid,
Midwestern sensibility cast an unmoving deadweight on his
spirit for a long time and, while he bore it well enough as a
child, it stifled him after Dad's death.

He had been just fourteen. Everyone remarked at their resemblance. Yeah, he did inherit his father's good looks and, he grudgingly admitted, some of his bad qualities as well. Dad had a wandering heart—after all, he wore an army uniform. Growing up meant an interminable exercise in smothering a burgeoning, boundless energy and wanderlust. Jack couldn't wait to become old enough to travel all over the world. Kansas City developed into a prison, a blip on the map, swallowed up by a thousand miles of featureless prairie. And Mom, bless her heart, remained at the center of this bottomless inertia.

Jack glanced behind him. The red brick walls of the church stared back. Originally built by the Baptists in 1935, the Hare Krishnas bought it forty years later when the congregation moved from the city to the suburbs and the church lost its base. The old building graced a corner lot on a quiet street and served as a hangout for students who fancied themselves spiritualists. Early mornings saw students in yoga postures on the front lawn and the Krishna devotees engaging visitors in long discussions on intricate points of Indian spirituality.

"Hey, you remember this place?" he enquired.

"Yes, we came once for a Sunday program. Besides, I visited a few times for research for one of my religion classes."

"Hey! I've got an idea," exclaimed Jack. "Why not stay here? We can work in exchange for room and board."

"What do you mean?" Steve questioned, his eyes wide and eyebrows knotted. "Become one of them?"

"No," countered Jack. "Maybe they take boarders. I'm sure we can stay here till the end of the summer."

"You've got to be joking!"

"No, no," responded Jack, his eyes bright. "Let's find out."

"No way! Mom would be shocked."

"She's already shocked. Besides, we don't even have enough money for a deposit on an apartment, never mind jobs."

"But the Krishna temple?" probed Steve. "This sounds like another one of your crazy ideas! Wasn't India enough?"

"Hey, it's worth a try. Let's just find out. No commitments. If we don't like it, we leave."

Steve hesitated. "I don't know...."

"Do you have any ideas where to spend the rest of the summer?"

Steve shook his head silently.

"Okay then, let's go!" declared Jack, pulling him up by the hand.

* * *

Dhaneswara dasa, Dhana for short, the temple president of the Kansas City Krishna center, sat behind his desk looking at the two young men in his office. The place smelled faintly of incense and pictures of Hindu divinities and saints lined the walls. The temple needed cleaning, the vegetables required cutting, the pots and pans lay unwashed and seventy or eighty guests would arrive at five o'clock for the weekly Sunday evening program of music, chanting, philosophical discussion and free vegetarian feast.

He shifted his gaze and looked at the ceiling, fingering a chain of wooden beads on which he silently chanted Hare Krishna. He had just turned forty. The hippie revolution came and went and the interest in Indian spirituality, though strong in some pockets, did not arouse the same curiosity as when he joined the fledgling movement in the sixties.

Dhana eyed the two young men, remembering them as occasional visitors from the university. Jack helped out with chores the one time he visited while Steve had participated in philosophical discussions. Jack sat strong and proud. Dhana didn't care for the attitude—he didn't regard him as a serious candidate for spiritual life. Unfortunately, these kinds of men, he reflected, learn only by hard experience. He remembered Steve asking some especially intelligent questions at a discussion once, but his approach to the divine seemed purely scholarly. Dhana remembered what his guru once stated: that an academic approach to spirituality is like licking the outside of a jar of honey. To really understand the sacred, one had to open the container and actually taste the sweetness.

He pondered their proposal. They appeared honest enough, but how long would they stay? He wasn't running a hotel and had no interest getting stuck in a long-term commitment.

"Okay. Let's make an agreement until the end of the summer. That's two months. But you must follow our rules while staying here. That means no smoking, no drinking, no gambling, no meat-eating since we are religious vegetarians, and as you are unmarried, no girlfriends. We are like monks and these are our principles. While in the temple, you need to wear your dhotis. And you must do a minimum of five hours of service each day, such as washing the pots, cleaning the temple and other things." They nodded, still half asleep.

"Make yourselves at home then," he concluded. "Some *prasadam*, some food, is in the fridge just outside the kitchen." He didn't wait for more discussion. He got up, walked to the door, stopped and looked behind. "And when you're finished, start cutting the vegetables."

"Well, that was easy," mumbled Jack, somewhat startled. The consent came quickly, unexpectedly.

It also left Steve slightly nonplussed. "Should we go through with this?"

"Yeah, well, in eighteen hours on the plane, we couldn't come up with a better idea. So here we are."

Chapter Five

Kansas City, The Present (Beginning of Kali Yuga)
Steve felt a cool early-morning breeze blowing in from the open window above his desk. The sparse furniture, probably salvaged from some long-forgotten yard sale, reflected the renounced mood of the devotees. Across the room, a bunk bed pushed up against the wall and in its front sat a long, low table. A couple of dressers and chairs completed the furnishings.

The temple, a quiet place, suited the devotees well. Their lives revolved around their spiritual practices. Gracious hosts, they welcomed guests and students who dropped in but, by and large, they led rather insular lives, unaffected by university politics, dorm parties, television programs or other disturbances swirling around them.

Besides Dhana, a veteran Hare Krishna, Steve acquainted himself with Nimai, the head pujari and his wife, Daya, both natives of the island of Madagascar. A quiet, retiring, bookish sort of man, Nimai spent many hours every day poring over texts of astrology. His wife, refreshingly forthright, had a fiery character. Of Indian descent and favorites of the local Indian community, the couple busied themselves performing various religious rituals, upon births, deaths or marriages. Two young unmarried American women, both recent entrants, one named Lori and the other Christine, rounded out the crew. Once their strange appearances and lifestyles wore off, the devotees reminded him of anyone else—they maintained their individualities, their quirks, their likes, and dislikes.

And they did not force their beliefs on them, though one morning, about a week after his arrival, Lori eagerly showed Steve her string of wooden beads. "This *mala* has a hundred and eight beads," she explained. She held a bead between her thumb and middle finger. "On each of these

31

we chant the *Maha-Mantra*, the sixteen syllable recitation: Hare Krishna, Hare Krishna, Krishna, Krishna, Hare Hare, Hare Rama, Hare Rama, Rama Rama, Hare Hare." Steve nodded. "Once one round of 108 beads is finished, we start all over again, until a total of 16 rounds are chanted every day. This is called *Japa* meditation." He tried his hand at this practice but never finished the prescribed rounds of daily chanting.

Jack barged into the room, swinging the door shut behind him. He walked around a few times and slumped on the bottom bunk, running his fingers vacantly through his hair.

Steve smiled. "Restless already?"

"I'm throwing myself into everything the devotees do—like chanting on the streets, distributing books and handing out vegetarian food to the needy near Union Station on Fridays."

Steve cocked his right eye. "Is all this enthusiasm real or are you trying to impress the unattached women?"

Jack didn't smile. "I don't know how they do it. The devotees do lead different lives but still, it's mostly contemplative. I may get used to it, but certainly not now. The devotees, after all, have a routine. And the routine was always the same." He rubbed his forehead. "I'm bored." Steve laughed.

Jack suddenly straightened up.

"What is it?" remarked Steve.

"Look. My backpack," he exclaimed. The unopened backpack hid behind the door as if, in all this time, Jack hesitated in confronting his ignominious retreat from India by opening and sorting out his things. Sighing, he pulled it up, opened the zipper and emptied the contents on the table. T-shirts laden with the dust of India, a map of Delhi and old bus schedules all poured out. As he arranged the assorted debris of his travels, he noticed a small yellow parchment, all folded up.

Steve immediately perked up. "What's this?"

"That old pujari in Badrinath, you know the one who died, handed it over when you went to get the doctor. It completely slipped my mind. He called it the Yoga Zapper."

"The Yoga Zapper?"

"Yeah," affirmed Jack. "Something like that. I can't remember exactly."

Steve laughed. "I like that. The Yoga Zapper."

Jack asked the obvious question. "Can you read it?"

Steve examined the document with rising excitement. "Sanskrit is a phonetic language. It's easy to read, but much harder to understand. Sanskrit words can have multiple meanings and a slight alteration of grammar can change the entire meaning of a sentence." His hands trembled slightly and a broad smile lit his face. "I have to study it thoroughly. Fortunately, I have a lot of time and we're in the right place to do this."

Over the next week, using every spare minute, Steve pored over the ancient text. It felt good to be intellectually engaged, to be in his element. He made comments in his notebook, constantly revising his translations. Jack came often and noticing the slow progress, walked around the room restlessly and left. The news of the Yoga Zapper spread quickly through the small temple community, becoming a favorite topic of discussion during the shared breakfasts.

The following mid-July Sunday morning was a beauty; the sun rose warm and early but with none of the humidity associated with the Midwestern summer season. Jack and Steve sat on the bunk bed while Dhana and the Nimai settled on chairs across from them. Steve placed the Yoga Zapper on the low table between them, picked up his notebook and spoke.

"The Yoga Zapper, as we call it, is 62 lines long. The first ten lines describe a certain phase of the moon, the position of the stars and constellations."

Nimai immediately perked up and picked up the parchment.

Steve continued. "The next twelve lines are more interesting. They refer to yoga, but not the exercises we Americans think of when we hear the word. More precisely, the text refers to a specific a yogic power, called a *siddhi*—one of traveling between yugas." Dhana immediately straightened up.

Jack stared uncomprehendingly. "What are yugas?"

"Wait a minute," Dhana interrupted. "Tell us the rest."

"These twelve lines also describe a ritual, technically called a *yajna*, to be performed for achieving this siddhi."

Dhana interjected again. "What does the rest of the document say?"

"The last forty lines of the Yuga Zapper is a mantra, which is untranslatable and actually, not meant to be translated, but rather, to be chanted, without deviation, in the original Sanskrit. By reciting this mantra, the practitioner attains the power of the yogic siddhi."

Jack's confusion was evident. "I'm lost. Can you repeat that?"

Steve started with the description of the position of the moon, the sun, and the stars; the depiction of the yogic siddhi of travel between yugas, and the exposition of the ritual to be enacted. He ended by reciting the forty line long mantra. He read it a third time. Some things fell in place.

"So, what do you make of this?" asked Jack, to no one in particular.

"Basically, one can travel between yugas by performing the ritual and chanting the mantras at the astrologically appropriate time," replied Dhana dasa.

"Exactly," agreed Steve.

"Ok, so this mantra confers the power of travel from one yuga to another. But what's a yuga exactly?" questioned Jack.

"A yuga refers to an age, an eon," answered Dhana. "According to the Vedas, the original books of spiritual wisdom revealed to the rishis in India, time is divided into cycles of four ages: *Satya yuga*, the first age, *Treta yuga*, the second, then *Dwapara yuga*, and finally *Kali yuga*. After one cycle of these four yugas ends, another cycle starts."

"So time is circular?" asked Jack.

"Yes."

"So what separates these yugas?"

"Satya yuga, the golden age, lasts for one million, seven hundred and twenty-eight thousand years."

"That's a stretch!" exclaimed Jack.

"And Treta yuga lasts for one million, two and ninety-six thousand years; Dwapara yuga, eight hundred and sixty-four thousand years; and Kali yuga takes only four hundred and thirty-two thousand years." Jack chuckled. It all seemed impossible.

"These are not just time periods. Each has distinct spiritual or moral characteristics," Dhana continued. "For example, in Satya yuga, spiritual principles such as honesty, morality, and humility exist in full. Life is devoid of anxiety, worry and division in human society. At the conclusion of this age, one-quarter of these principles disappear. By the end of Treta yuga, the second age, they lessen by half; when Dwapara yuga finishes, they diminish by three-quarters; and finally, at the conclusion of Kali Yuga, they become totally absent."

"So where are we now in this big picture?" enquired Jack.

"Five thousand years into Kali yuga," replied Dhana, "an age of strife and worry."

Jack considered this. If his own life at all reflected Kali Yuga, maybe this wasn't so outlandish an idea after all.

"So by chanting this mantra, it is possible to travel from through time?"

"Yes," replied Dhana, "but it is not so simple. Several things must work correctly for a mantra to have effect. Just repeating it is not sufficient. The level of consciousness, or should I say, the spiritual advancement, of the person repeating the mantra, is also important."

"Well, that rules me out," stated Jack.

"Not necessarily," countered Dhana. "Your spiritual qualifications remain unknown. But if Krishna desires, He can make things possible even for the unqualified. The impossible is achieved through His grace."

Jack pumped his hand up in the air. "All right," he exclaimed impulsively.

"What are you doing?" demanded Steve, his eyebrows raised. "You don't really believe all this, do you?" A purely an intellectual project, the translation was now a closed subject. It felt pretty thrilling to translate an original Sanskrit text, but it was time to move on to reality, though, Steve recognized, it would make a good paper for graduate school one day.

Jack smiled mischievously. "You know me, I'll try anything once."

Dhana continued. "There are other factors to take into account."

"Like?" asked Jack.

"Like ensuring the proper alignment of the stars."

"And performing the yajna, the ritual," added Steve, "and chanting the mantra properly."

"Right," declared Dhana.

"Geez. It sounds pretty complicated to travel through time!" remarked Jack.

They all laughed earnestly, suddenly realizing the absurdity of the whole scenario. Traveling through thousands of years by chanting mantras! Steve put his notebook away.

Nimai, completely quiet all this time while holding the Yoga Zapper, looked up. "I do a lot of astrological work," he stated. "The naming of a child, a marriage or buying of a house, among others, is done on astrologically favorable dates. Thus, I am quite familiar with the first part of this scripture." Jack, who had slouched back on the bed, sat up again. Steve stopped.

"According to this description, in exactly one week, that is, next Sunday, the moon, the planets, and the stars will be in the prescribed alignment. You can do the yajna, chant the mantra, and if Krishna allows, gain the power to travel to the various yugas. So if you are at all serious, make up your minds now."

Steve looked at Nimai dasa intently. Did he really believe in all this astrology stuff? He must.

"Shall we perform the yajna then?" asked Dhana, looking at Steve.

Steve surveyed the devotees in the room. "Maybe in my next life," he joked. They all laughed, got up and left.

Chapter Six

Kansas City, The Present (Beginning of Kali Yuga)

The following week, Steve turned his attention to the immediate task at hand; figuring out his next steps. Though late, he could apply for graduate school, assured, with his academic record, of acceptance at any of the first-rate schools in the country. But that seemed the last alternative. Even with a master's degree, the job prospects weren't particularly bright. He looked at his watch. It indicated one-thirty, and the rest of the Friday afternoon remained unplanned.

He closed the door to the room and sauntered to the foyer of the main chapel, spotting Jack talking to Christine, turning on the charm as she smiled, following his facial expressions. Steve arched his eyebrows. He interrupted and pulled Jack aside.

"I'm going to see Mom," he said.

"I promised the devotees to help them distribute prasadam at Union Station," Jack replied, glancing back at the young woman.

"Come on. We haven't seen her in ages."

"I don't know. Mom just gets on my case. You know the drill—find a job, get married, have kids and live in Kansas City for the rest of my life like one big happy family. Hell, when I hear that, I run for the door!"

"What will you do, hide here for the rest of your life? Besides, you didn't even see Mom before we left for India!"

"I'll be over. Just not now."

Steve persisted. "So when *will* you visit?"

"Maybe tomorrow."

"Are you sure?"

"Look, I'm not talking about this anymore," hissed Jack, his voice tinged with exasperation. He ran his fingers through his long locks. "I'll do my best. Dammit, Steve, quit bugging me." He strode back to Christine. Steve rubbed his forehead, sighed and walked out of the temple and down the street to the bus stop.

The ride took hardly twenty minutes. The second house from the corner on Hope Street bore Marjorie Goode's name. A split-rail fence ran around the ranch-style home with its large front verandah and flower beds lining the path to the front door. How many times had he run down those steps from the verandah, along the same flower beds, and out to the street when he was young? He went up to the door and rang the bell. His white-haired mother appeared on the other side of the screen door.

"Steve! Come in. I've been waiting for you!" She hugged and kissed his cheek. "How are you doing?"

"I'm fine, Mom." He followed her into the kitchen and sat down at the table as she poured a cup of coffee.

"When did you get back?"

"About three weeks ago. We would have spent more time in India, but things didn't work out."

"So where are you staying? You and Jack didn't renew the lease for the apartment, did you?"

"We're staying at the Hare Krishna temple near the university."

"What!" she exclaimed. "The Hare Krishna temple?"

"No, Mom. It's not what you think," interjected Steve quickly. "It's free and it's a nice quiet place. Trust me. We didn't join them."

"It's Jack! He dragged you into that place, didn't he? Is he one of them now?"

"No, Mom," he reassured her. "It's nothing like that." Given what Steve knew of them though, it wasn't such a bad option for his younger brother.

"Where's Jack?"

Steve bit his lip. "He agreed to come tomorrow."

"Are you sure?"

"I don't know." A pause ensued.

"You know, it's good that you and Jack are so close. He listens to you, even though he won't hear a word I tell him."

"I don't know about Jack listening to me."

"Maybe. He's just like your father was when I first met him."

Steve looked through the large, glass patio doors and into the back yard. Mom talked often about how Jack adored Dad. How Jack took so much after his father; his sense of adventure, his wild ways.

"It took a long time to get your Dad under control. For years after we married he hung around with his army buddies until all hours of the night."

Steve smiled. He couldn't imagine that she, with her interest in literature, could fall for a hard-drinking, hard-living army man. It was love at first sight, she confided, but he never understood what brought the two together in the first place. *There's no figuring out parents,* he thought.

"Steve, Jack needs guidance but don't get me wrong. You don't need to look after him for the rest of your life. At a certain point, you must think of your own future." Yet, she continued, "please talk to him. He's got do something with himself. And if he doesn't…well, move on."

Steve examined his mother. The worry in her voice, whenever she spoke about Jack, felt familiar. But now he sensed an urgency, something deeper. "We can talk to each other most of the time," he stated, "but Jack usually does what he wants. He thinks taking someone's guidance makes him less of a man."

"No, Steve. You don't know how important you are to him. At his age, he is too hotheaded to listen to me. If he heeds anyone, it's you."

"We'll, maybe you're right." He gave her the benefit of the doubt. After all, he had curbed some of Jack's wildest impulses. He shuddered. Where would his brother be without his bringing Jack to his senses once in a while?

His mother reached out and touched him. Her hand shook slightly.

"You know I'm getting on in years. The good Lord knows I've had a difficult life. You two are the only ones I have left."

"What is it, Mom?" asked Steve. She never wanted to bother them.

"I'm worried about Jack."

"You're always anxious about Jack."

"But it's different this time. I'm not getting any younger. Sometimes I wonder will happen after I'm gone."

"What do you mean?" asked Steve, his voice tinged with alarm.

"Well, son, I do think about your futures when I'm not here. In fact, more so now than ever."

"Mom!"

Her eyes glistened. "Jack's got no career, no ambition. He never finished his studies. He's not settled, he just goes from one thing to another. What will he do with his life? I'm afraid he'll end up in a bad place."

He looked into her old, worried eyes. At this stage, she had only him to trust. He held her hands tightly. "Don't worry! Mom, I'm making a promise to you right now that I'll look after Jack!"

"No. No. You don't have to."

"Don't worry. It's a guarantee."

She drew a deep breath of relief. "Thank you for your promise. I already feel better."

"You know what?" he continued, "We'll move back. The temple's served its purpose." He hoped to somehow convince his brother—at least Jack always loved Mom's cooking. They walked back to the front door.

"And please tell Jack to call me tomorrow. I really miss him and want to hear his voice."

"Of course. Bye, Mom," he said, opening the door and stepping out on the verandah. "See you soon. Love you."

The late afternoon sun streamed down on her face through the screen door. Her age covered her like a worn out blanket. She never looked older, more fragile. "I love you too, son."

Steve looked out the bus window and witnessed the tall trees lining the wide streets, the broad sidewalks, the magnificent buildings, the immensity of the city, the spread of human creation, the infinity of the sky and the sun and the clouds on the limitless horizon. His emotions blurred. What did Dhana say concerning the temporary nature of this world, the mortality of all living things, the amazingly strong illusion of solidity, the eternality of things? That everything created is bound for dissolution? Caught in the web of actions, he never before considered such things. Sitting in the bus, watching the material creation stream by, constantly changing and yet remaining the same, a profound realization of the ephemeral nature of reality overcame him.

He sighed deeply, broke the contemplation and remembered one of Dhana's instructions; on the importance of doing the right thing— that while still alive, duties remained inescapable—a lesson learned from the *Bhagavad Gita*. He recalled the promise to his mother. Jack had a stubborn nature. But he had to try.

He went to his room and discovered his brother asleep already. Steve climbed into bed, pulled up the covers and closed his eyes.

* * *

Marjorie Goode sat on her favorite chair on the verandah, watching the sun set slowly. She enjoyed most this time of day, when the heat and humidity evaporated and dusk heralded the cooling breezes off the mighty Missouri and Kansas rivers. She woke up at seven that morning, as she did every day. When she graduated from high school and started working at the local library at sixteen, she stopped using an alarm clock.

She sighed, remembering her teenage years. With long golden hair, blue eyes and a pretty face, she gained the lengthy looks of her male classmates, but painfully shy, never reciprocated their admiring glances. Maybe growing up an only child on a farm in Kansas, at least until the dust, drought and Depression forced her family to quit the homestead and move to the city explained her reticence. She never forgot her humble, farm girl origins and, instead, developed a life-long love of the written word, and when offered the job at the library right out of high school, she gladly accepted.

She worked there for forty-nine years but the last few years at the job were difficult. It wasn't enough to love books. At the end, the new kids working in the library came armed with university degrees, and the City asked her to accept a lesser position at the Children's Library on the other side of town. Rather than accept the humiliation, the lower pay, not to mention the inconvenience of the hour-long bus ride back and forth, she accepted early retirement. That and her late husband's army pension allowed her to live frugally and to send, at a regular and sometimes unexpected basis, money to her two sons.

The old house became difficult to manage. Or maybe she lost interest. It felt easier to take care of just her bedroom and the kitchen. Her living space, like her life, shrunk to the demands of necessity. She rarely went into the basement and the boys' rooms stayed as undisturbed as when they left to live in that apartment near the university.

She wriggled into her slippers, returned the kitchen and put the coffee on. The long day and the heat tired her. She had nothing to do and took comfort in that. She turned the TV on, waiting for the water to boil. The drone of the voices reassured her though she didn't pay attention to anything said. She lost interest in TV shows about ten years ago when strange people with stranger problems showed their faces with increasing regularity during the daytime hours.

She got up, brewed herself a cup of coffee, put off the television and went out to the verandah. She wondered about the change in her life once the boys returned. She knew, of course, that in a short while, once they accepted good jobs, resumed studies or married, the house would empty again.

They're both good kids, she thought, and nothing could have been done differently. She never controlled her life. Her husband and children did as they pleased and she kept things together, picking up the pieces.

She remembered the first time she saw Jim, a few years after the war. He resembled every schoolgirl's dream with his neat, handsome uniform and dark eyes set in a strong-jawed face. She wondered at his presence in the library and when she glanced at the title of the book he handed over, she had blushed. He took that as an invitation and asked her out. Not even aware of her actions, she agreed, and by the end of the month they married.

It was probably the only rash thing she ever did, and its unforeseen, inescapable consequences spread through her life, like the Missouri does through innumerable streams, gullies and creeks when it floods. Jim liked to drink and many times in the beginning he didn't come home for days on end, leaving her lying awake at night with fear and dread, mixed with anger and jealousy at his neglect. He always gave the same excuse: out drinking with his army buddies. She tolerated this for years until finally one day Jim took Steve, only six, out on one of his all-night drinking parties, leaving her alone with the baby. He had skipped from bar to bar and, though Jim denied it vigorously, she had no doubt that he bought the boy more than one cheap beer that night. The episode so infuriated her that he arrived early the next morning to find all of his possessions packed neatly in several suitcases by the front door. She snatched her inebriated son and slammed the door in her husband's face.

He slunk off like a rat into a hole and returned the next day with an apology and a dull realization that he had to grow up and become a man. The transformation shocked and filled her with a wonder that he could, after all, become a real husband, and she thanked her lucky stars that she would not end up a ditched woman living in a trailer park at the edge of town.

And then, several years after things started going well, he had to get himself killed. Jim took the family car on a cold winter morning in February to the base on the same road he had driven hundreds of times before. The road may have iced over or maybe he fell asleep at the wheel, but it made no difference now. He smashed head-on into a military truck coming from the opposite direction and death was instant.

The army buddies came, held a wake, but after everything ended, she was left alone at home with her children. Fortunately the pension, and not to mention Steve's job at the restaurant, helped her raise her children, but since that moment, she knew with a deep and unnerving clarity how really alone she was and how false is the sense of security in an inherently insecure universe.

She fought desperately against this primal sense of fragility for the rest of her life, or rather, struggled to protect her children from the inevitability of defeat at the hands of fate. She succeeded somewhat at this futile task: Steve, old enough when Jim died, understood her distress. He viewed destiny with a sense of respect; that by following the rules of society and morality, that fate, while not defeated, could at least be thwarted or deflected. At the very least by being disciplined and honorable, Steve kept the furies at bay.

The good son—he made her proud. His studies, his love of books, all came from her and his success at college made her heart almost burst with pride. She didn't want to admit it, but he was a mama's boy. *Nothing wrong with that*, she hastily thought, *but Steve needs to get out of his shell. The world could offer so much if he just accepted it.*

Jack so much reflected his father. Jim was Jack's buddy, a dashing romantic figure frozen in the glow of childhood, devoid of all frailties and flaws. Unsurprisingly, Jack embodied all of his father's great abilities, and now, more and more, his abundant flaws. Smart, stubborn, restless, good with their hands and perpetually in trouble, they charmed women off their feet. Yet, Jack, like Jim, displayed another side; a courageous heart, great generosity, a championing faith in the underdog and the loyalty of a true friend. If only he learned to trust, to take advice. In many ways, he was his own worst enemy.

The prodigal son, she smiled wryly. *Still, he resents me. He thinks I'm stopping him from doing what he wants.* Jack would rather fight with fate, take it head on and think of actually winning. His youth, his immaturity, prevented an understanding of the heavy and unexpected blows life directed at people. She suddenly panicked. A premonition of the suffering he would endure filled her with dread. Would he end up all alone in a trailer park at the edge of town, condemned to a life of loneliness and dull boozing? *Deserted*, she thought, *like me.*

She shook herself out of her reverie. Night fell softly and she realized it only when she heard the crickets chirping incessantly in the grass. She got up, entered and walked down the hall. Once these rooms were filled with husband and children but one by one, they left prematurely, leaving her as bereft as the emptiness she walked past every day. She sighed and trudged into her bedroom and changed into her robe. *Funny*, she thought, *I haven't eaten a thing all day.*

She tucked her slippers under the bed, climbed between the thin flannel sheets, pulled the blanket over herself, turned off the bedside light and closed her eyes. A vast darkness greeted her. Sometime, in the middle of the night, without once waking up, Marjorie Goode died.

Chapter Seven

Kansas City, The Present (Beginning of Kali Yuga)

Steve awoke late the next morning and discovered Jack's empty bed. He rubbed his forehead and remembered the usual Saturday chanting party—they most likely left early. He showered, dressed and according to custom, removed his shoes before entering the chapel. Charming paintings of peacocks and elephants lined its walls, stretching from the floor, half-way to the top. The domed ceiling created a large, hushed space inside which a worshipper sensed the presence of God. The altar, built on a plinth a couple of feet above the floor, was adorned with flowers, and a couple of incense sticks burned in a holder in front of the Deities. He sat down.

Of carved white marble, Krishna, tall and strong and dressed in a golden dhoti and a peacock feather adorned purple turban, smiled mischievously while holding a flute to his lips, displaying the strength, grace and charm of a youth in full bloom. Steve easily imagined Krishna sauntering along a dusty path in the pastoral village of Vrindavan, in India, where he grew up, playing a bamboo flute and leading his cows to pasture.

Radha rani, Krishna's eternal consort, stood to the right. Lovely in a long flowing red gown, intricately decorated with sparkling green embroidery which blended with the flowers and leaves on the altar, she displayed pink-colored cheeks the hue of lotus blossoms, large green eyes and beguiling long black hair. Dhana once stated that Radha rani, being the female energy of Krishna, is considered to be the same, yet different, from him. Steve remembered an analogy from a morning discussion: that Krishna is the sun and Radha rani the sunshine; one emanates from the other, yet both are different.

Suddenly a long-stemmed rose fell right into his lap. He peered up, astonished. Radha rani smiled back, compassion showing in her eyes. He noticed the basket in her hands. The flower must have slipped from it.

"Hello there." Steve turned around. Dhana greeted him.

"Look," exclaimed Steve, "This flower just dropped from Radha rani into my lap!"

Dhana laughed. "I'm not surprised. Many devotees have interesting pastimes with Radha and Krishna."

"What do you mean?"

"Krishna plays all sorts of games with his devotees. They're called his *lilas*."

Steve stared at Dhana wide-eyed.

"Krishna is famous for his transcendental pranks. His lilas are beyond our comprehension."

Steve shook his head. The idea of playful, mischievous god struck him as startlingly different from his image of a formidable, jealous old man who made His creation and then, Steve concluded at one point, totally abandoned it. The concept remained too far removed from his Western sensibilities. He changed the subject.

"I need to talk with you. I visited my mother yesterday."

"How is she?"

"Well, she's old. But I've decided to move back. She needs help, at least for a little while."

"How about Jack?"

"I'll talk to him. I don't know if he's the type to live long in this place."

Dhana laughed. "I think you're right. When will you leave?"

"Sometime this week, if it's okay with you."

"Sure. And good luck."

"Thank you. I'll call my mother and let her know."

"You know where the phone is," Dhana responded, leaving.

"Yes, of course." Steve breathed a sigh of relief as lightness entered his heart. He glanced once more at the kind, smiling faces of the Deities and their gentle, loving expressions. Things were finally working out. He got up and walked over to the lobby to use the phone.

* * *

The moon shone brightly and the night air cooled Jack's skin, a welcome contrast from the mugginess of the day. The female devotees drove the car back after the downtown chanting, leaving Jack and Nimai to stretch their legs and saunter leisurely back to the temple. Night lights burned in upstairs bedrooms and blue illuminations from television sets streamed through front windows. Streetlights shone at street corners, little puddles of brightness in the sea of blackness, and water sprinklers circled on some lawns, with little rivulets flowing into the gutters. Occasional dog barks echoed from anonymous back yards.

He listened to Nimai quietly tapping a rhythm on his *mridanga*, a two-headed drum held by a long strap hanging around his neck. They talked little, yet relished the companionship. Deep furrows lined Jack's forehead. How could he inform Nimai that the interlude at the temple soured into another dead end, despite all that he liked about them? Would it be fair to stay half-heartedly? He knew the pattern. He would eagerly get into things but, sooner or later, had to move on.

It started when Dad died. He was just eleven years old. He woke up that morning to hushed conversations, his mother's soft tears and Steve's long, sad face. A whirl of unfamiliar sounds, strange people, and inexplicable rituals filled the rest of the week and, only weeks later, he finally understood that his father had gone forever.

For months afterward he had the dreams: always searching for his father but never finding him. He recalled the very first dream. The summer sun shone warmly on the school bus returning home in the afternoon. He sat on the front seat, peering through the windshield and spied his father standing at attention on the verandah, wearing his

49

military uniform, his dark hair cropped short, pants creased crisply and a cap perched on his head. His father smiled broadly; Jack saw him from a mile away. After seemingly forever, the bus stopped in front of his home. He jumped off and ran through the open gate, up the path, past the blooming roses and daisies but when he reached the verandah, discovered, to his shock, that his father had disappeared. A desperate search began. He hunted through the garden, around the back yard, inside the house and all over the upstairs, but without luck. The dream ended only when he woke up, shivering.

Another, more regular, dream occurred outside of the home. He tramped alone in the woods near the base on a cold, cloudy, winter's day, lost like a little child, looking for what he did not know. Somewhere deep in the forest, he came across a patch of blood on the snow and, next to it, a set of boot prints. He stopped, thoroughly shaken. They were Dad's! He trudged and trudged, following the tracks through the forest for miles and miles, panting with exhaustion. No matter where he searched; behind tree trunks, bushes or rocks, no sign of his father surfaced. The tracks continued forever and he woke up drained, at the point of collapse.

The dreams panicked him, but worse, when he awoke, an image of his uniformed father hung in the air above his bed. He clamped his small hands over his eyes, trembling in complete confusion. Only after he desperately pushed that figure out of his mind did he sleep again. During the waking hours, he continued the pitched battle with his mind. Whenever his dad appeared, he consciously drove him out with teeth-gritted determination. The battle continued for months until all remembrances of his father finally stopped.

Though the dreams ended, the sensation of being left alone, of being abandoned, of something missing, never left. It penetrated deep into his psyche, and since then, he never once felt completely whole or fully satisfied, knowing something got taken out and never restored.

He finally stopped thinking of his father and, after a couple of years, even forgot his appearance. He hardly talked about him unless Mom or Steve brought up the memories. They remained in the past and dredging them up served no purpose. 'Live for the present' became his motto.

At about that time, he started arguing with his mother. Growing up, being a teenager, explained part of it. In high school, his hormones raged and drinking, partying and girls became staples of his life. As recollections of his father receded, he replaced them with just having fun. A blur of passable grades, a gaggle of girlfriends, gin and coke, grass and so much more defined those years. Predictably, his mother reacted to this behavior by worrying and nagging, and worrying and nagging some more, until he responded to her clinging by distancing himself.

Travel caused further disagreement. He remembered his first set of wheels and the unforgettable freedom and deliverance it brought from the deep pit that Kansas City had become. He drove that used, baby-blue Datsun everywhere—he took it to Chicago the junior year of high school and in the summer of his senior year, all the way to El Paso. The stories that car could tell! From then on, wandering became an obsession, almost a compulsion. Again, Mom reacted with fear. She tried to argue him out of his wanderlust by curtailing his freedom. That just pushed him further away and, after moving out and starting college, he hardly saw much of her.

But being dismissed unceremoniously from university shook him deeply. Not that he was ever serious about studies. Everything came easily in high school and he received passable grades without ever trying. At Missouri, however, real competition threatened, something he was not prepared for. After dropping out, he worked odd jobs and travelled, but over the past year, a strange feeling he could not put his finger on, of something missing, of something being not quite right, overcame him.

He remembered Laura, his last girlfriend. He broke up with her just before the India trip. With long, curly black hair, ivory skin and green eyes she was not just beautiful, but exotic. At first, she showed no interest, but he turned on the charm, his easy smile, and the funny jokes and after a couple of months of pursuit, she surrendered. The chase enlivened him and brought passion and adventure and every day felt fresh as he put his whole heart into the hunt. But strangely enough, after conquering her, he quit. She bored him; he had to move on. She made an awful scene, crying, cursing and throwing things, but he couldn't help his feelings.

He felt the need to spread his wings and, in some way, to find himself. That might explain the India trip. He never thought of that country before, but its mystical side attracted him, although he never previously expressed an interest in the mystical. And what did mystical mean, anyway? While he appreciated Steve and all his help, the idea of becoming more independent surfaced.

He rubbed his face in frustration. A familiar darkness descended, like a curtain covering his mind, blotting out all thoughts. It felt claustrophobic, suffocating, like the world closing in and he had to escape. He knew the feeling; he reacted this way every time he reached a dead end. He hated it and, sometimes, hated himself. He shook his head vigorously and pushed the feeling out—time to move on.

"What's the matter?" asked Nimai.

"Oh nothing," replied Jack, "nothing at all." He sighed. It was useless to lie or delay the inevitable. "I...I'm sorry, but I don't think the temple is the place for me."

"Really!" remarked Nimai. Was there surprise or hurt feelings? The devotees became, over the past month or so, not just strangers sharing a roof, but actually friends. A genuine sense of community and an unpretentious accepting of each other characterized their relationships. After all, they took a couple of strangers, welcomed, fed and sheltered them. Jack started disliking himself.

"I'm really sorry, but I need to move on."

Nimai kept quiet. Jack felt bad, guilty. He grabbed his wallet and offered some cash. "This is a gift. Just to show how much I appreciate everything you and the others have done."

Nimai gasped. "No! I can't accept this."

The vehemence surprised Jack. Embarrassed, he returned the money to his wallet and rubbed his forehead. Why did he reject the gift? Of course! He had put Nimai in an awkward situation by approaching him directly. Jack felt worse. They continued walking, their steps echoing in the night.

"Look," said Nimai, after some time, pointing to the sky, brilliant with stars. "Look at the *Saptarishi*."

"What's that?"

"That constellation composed of seven stars. Each of the stars is the home of a great rishi. Once a year, it is said, they descend from their dwellings in the stars and meditate on the shores of Lake Manasarovar in Tibet."

"Really," inquired Jack, engrossed by the tale.

"Yes," continued Nimai. "Their *tapasya*, that is, their austerities, lessens the karmic burden of the earth. Humankind is so sinful that if karma is allowed to accumulate unchecked, the earth would sink into the netherworld." He pointed again to the constellation. "There, do you see it?"

Jack peered intently. "Oh! You mean the Big Dipper!"

"Yes, the Saptarishi." Nimai stopped and faced Jack. "You know, tomorrow, the stars and the constellations will be aligned in exactly the way described in your Yoga Zapper."

"I forgot about that!" Jack exclaimed. An idea suddenly occurred.

"If you conduct the ritual described in the Yoga Zapper, will you accept the money?"

"Well, I don't...." started Nimai.

"Not for you personally, but as a donation for the temple."

"Maybe." Nimai hesitated. "Are you sure? Don't take these things frivolously!"

"Hey, what are you talking about? In all your years as a pujari have you ever seen anyone flying across the yugas?"

"No, but...."

Jack interrupted again. "Steve spent a lot of time translating that thing. Let's take it to its conclusion."

"Well...."

"Well, what? You're a pujari. Will you get a chance to do anything like this again?

"No."

"So let do it!" Jack took the money and thrust it into Nimai's hands. "Don't worry. You and I know this stuff will never work."

"So why do you want to do it?" asked Nimai finally.

"Curiosity," laughed Jack. "Plain dumb, stupid, curiosity."

Chapter Eight

Kansas City, The Present (Beginning of Kali Yuga)

Jack caught a glimpse of someone sitting in the dark on the temple steps. It was Steve! The moon shone directly overhead, way too late for anyone to be waiting up, especially tomorrow, with the Sunday feast program, promising to be a busy day. Nimai nodded to Steve, glanced at Jack, walked inside and shut the temple door behind him.

"What's going on?" Jack probed. Steve avoided looking at him. "Come on, Steve," pushed Jack. "Tell me. Something's wrong—I can read it in your face."

Steve glanced up, eyes glaring. "Mom died," he whispered harshly.

Jack turned white. It couldn't be true! The sound of the wind, gentle all this time, roared into his ears. The surrounding darkness rushed into his body, shaking him.

"How?" he mumbled. "How did it happen?"

"She died last night," murmured Steve, tears filling his eyes. "I called home this morning and receiving no answer, went right away."

"I'm...I'm sorry. I...I can't believe it!"

"Believe it," shouted Steve. "I just got back from the hospital. The paperwork is finished. Mom is gone."

Jack felt the world swirling. How he wished to express his regret at not seeing her when he had the chance, but no words came. Nothing justified his behavior.

"You know," continued Steve. "When I saw her yesterday, she kept asking about you."

"I'm sorry," repeated Jack. "I'm sorry."

Tears formed in Steve's eyes. "You could have come with me. But for you, everything was more important than her."

"I had no idea...."

"It's not just today. You've behaved like this for years. You've treated her really selfishly for a long time!"

Jack wiped his tears. "I...I don't know what to say...." He held his hand out. Steve slapped it away.

"I hate you," screamed Steve, completely out of character. "I never want to see you again!" He bounded up, entered the temple and slammed the door behind him, leaving Jack stunned and shivering in the dark.

* * *

"Come in," said Dhana. "We're waiting for you." Jack said nothing.

"You're going ahead with this, aren't you?" questioned Nimai, somewhat doubtfully.

"Yeah, this better work," cracked Jack without humor. "That's my last fifty bucks."

The devotees smiled uncomfortably. Jack told no one about his mother, but Dhana sensed a new edge in him. Was it the upcoming ritual, which no one quite knew how to approach?

They strode to the chapel's middle where stood a low platform of bricks on which sat a square copper tray about a foot long on each side and of equal height.

"This is the *havan*, the place of the ritual," stated Nimai. "You will find, on your side, several bowls containing various grains and spices. I have the same and, in addition, firewood and a pot full of *ghee*—that is, clarified butter." The Indian community, the main beneficiaries of these rituals, donated handsomely for the services, usually several hundred dollars at a time, which helped immensely with the temple's maintenance.

"Sit down," instructed Dhana. Jack, attired in a clean dhoti and a long-bodied, long-sleeved cotton kurta, took his spot across the havan from Nimai.

"What about your brother?" questioned Dhana.

"What about him?"

56

Dhana glanced uncomfortably at Jack. "Didn't you tell him?"

"No. I don't want to deal with him right now. I'll let him know when it's over."

"Maybe you're taking this too lightly," cautioned Dhana.

Jack tapped his fingers. "Listen. Let's get this over with."

Nimai tried again. "Are you sure?"

Jack ran his fingers through his hair. "Hey man, I paid good money for this and I want it done." There was no joke about the money in his voice. Dhana shrugged his shoulders.

"Okay. Okay, as you wish," answered Nimai resignedly. "This yajna is scientific in its technique and precision—it demands meticulousness and the proper following of steps. It releases the power residing in the syllables, in the very sounds, of the mantra. Once the yajna is completed, fix your mind as to the yuga of your choice, as thoughts determine the destination. So let's start and leave the result in Krishna's hands. Okay?"

"Let's go," demanded Jack.

The pujari lined the edges of the havan with a dozen sticks of smoking incense, placed a few pieces of wood in the metal tray, poured a couple of ladleful's of ghee on top and dropped a burning match, causing the clarified butter and wood to immediately catch fire.

Nimai first recited the *Guru Pranam*, the invocation to the spiritual master:

Om agnana timirandhasya jnananjana salakaya
Caksur unmilitam yena tasmai sri guru vena namah

Next came the entreaty to the spiritual lineage, the Mangalacharana, and other mantras. He sang the verses in a rich, sonorous rhythm, obeying the protocols clearly defined in the *Agamas*, manuals of procedure for such rituals. Having effect only if chanted accurately, the mantra required proper pronunciation and correct meter. The pujari coordinated the singing with the offering, in the exact sequence, of grains, spices, and ghee to the growing flames.

"Let us now deliver the mantra from your shastra."
Jack perked up. Nimai recounted the verses in a sure manner, intoning the word '*Svaha*' after each line, drawing out the last syllable into an exclamation.

"This word is very important as it addresses the energy of the fire, which is feminine, and ensures the proper functioning of the ritual," explained Dhana. At each pronunciation of 'Svaha,' Dhana and Jack followed Nimai's example, throwing grains and spices into the fire.

The smell of the smoldering spices encased the small chapel with a sweet, acrid fragrance. It stung Jack's nostrils and overpowered his eyes. He actually tasted those spices, transporting him to warm, tropical climates where winds carried the scent of nutmeg and jasmine to ships sailing out at sea. As the flames billowed higher and higher, he hardly saw the others' faces as they concentrated on the yajna, repeating the mantras with utmost absorption. Other devotees entered the temple and observed the proceedings from a distance.

He heeded Nimai's instruction: to deeply concentrate on his destination. Where would he go? The beginning or end of time? Either Satya Yuga or the end of Kali Yuga— only these two choices crowded his mind.

The incessant chanting increased in frequency and urgency. The crackle of the ghee and the popping of the grains exploded in volume and number until he heard, felt and saw nothing else.

Then suddenly the intonations stopped.

"Did you decide?" asked Nimai.

Jack nodded.

"Stand up."

* * *

Steve rubbed his eyes and stared at his watch. Eight o'clock! He'd slept late! All at once, his mother's death overcame him. Marjorie Goode no longer existed in this world and tears rolled down his cheeks. He looked up at

Jack's empty bunk. He already felt bad about last night; he needed to apologize. Despite his attitude, his brother undoubtedly loved Mom as much as he did. And more than ever, they needed each other.

Steve walked down the hall and into the men's bathroom. The rules were clear: the kitchen, considered to be as sacred as the altar, required cleanliness before entering. This meant taking a shower and wearing a clean dhoti and kurta. He bathed, dressed and walked into the unusually quiet kitchen. A large bag of carrots lay on top of the cutting table and, locating a peeler, he started working. Half an hour later, Daya, Nimai's wife, walked in.

"What are you doing here?" she exclaimed.

"Getting ready for the Sunday Feast, what else?"

"Don't you want to see the yajna?"

"What do you mean? Where is everyone?"

"You idiot!" yelled Daya. "We're all in the temple watching your brother do the ritual from your Yoga Zapper!"

Steve dropped the peeler. The color drained from his face as he ran out. Upon entering the chapel, the intense, fragrant, astringent smell burned his eyes. Stunned, tears streaming down his face, he stumbled toward the havan, where Jack stood erect with eyes closed, concentrating deeply.

* * *

"Decide your destination and take one step toward the fire," ordered Nimai.

Steve saw Jack shift his weight to his left foot, moving toward the sacrificial blaze.

"Jack! Stop!" screamed Steve. He couldn't explain it, but a terrible sensation of losing his only family member overcame him.

"Take your step now," commanded Nimai again.

Steve ran, arriving at the havan at the exact time Jack stepped forward.

A strange, distant, unearthly flat note, rising and falling in pitch, gusted into the hall. Dhana recognized it as the sound of conch shells blowing, but what did it herald? And who trumpeted them?

A sinuous green flame, like a verdant vine emerging from a flaming pot, rose from the center of the havan. The green stem arched and curled slowly up, glowing incandescent with heat. Dhana gasped, his hair standing on end, rubbing his eyes unbelievingly. The burgeoning vine stopped and a large pink bud blossomed on top, expanding larger and larger, flashing like a sun suspended in the hollow space inside the dome, radiating enormous amounts of light and heat.

Slowly, this glistening, burning blossom opened up. One by one, enormous hot pink petals spread up and out, the sizzling color burning into Dhana's pupils. He shivered violently at the sight of the unearthly flower, unable to move his frozen legs. Beads of sweat swelled instantly on his head and ran down his neck.

As the fiery lotus flower stretched and swelled, leaves of burning green flames curled out from under it and bristled down the walls of the chapel, surging into every nook and cranny. The smell of charred plaster filled his nostrils and the ripping sound of peeling paint burst into his ears.

An immense roar, an overpowering thunderclap, as if the universe itself split, shuddered the building. The blast shook the devotees out of their open-mouthed stances. Dhana and Nimai scrambled madly to the altar, followed by the other screaming devotees, who bounded into the alcove where the Deities stood and huddled, trembling, at their feet. Despite the torrid heat, the altar remained miraculously cool and unaffected; a small oasis in the midst of the raging storm. His arms trembling, Dhana held on to Krishna's feet with both hands, eyes barely open.

"Krishna!" he yelled. "Please protect us!"

Suddenly, from the middle of the flower burst forth a whirling globe of silvery fire, shedding brilliantly shining sparks. As Dhana watched with horror and disbelief, the blinding ball flew down and, whizzing around at enormous speed, enrobed Jack and Steve. Capturing them, it flew straight up.

The fiery lotus flower instantly disappeared as a wondrous purple, blue, red and yellow cloud of smoke streamed rapidly out of the havan and quickly surrounded the iridescent orb and spun around it at incredible speed, resembling a multi-colored planet with an incandescent core. Suddenly, a tremendous ear-splitting clap sounded and the sphere, along with the two young men, disappeared in a flash of smoke and fire.

Instantaneously, unexpectedly, the noise, the flames, and the heat all disappeared. The chapel cleared and a summer breeze, feeling absolutely cool on Dhana's skin, wafted through the open windows along with the sound of chirping sparrows. A palpable silence enveloped the temple. The whole incident took maybe half a minute but, for him, felt like a lifetime.

The devotees stood on shaking legs. The chapel's walls and ceiling still smoked, sand and hot bricks lay strewn about, but the temple remained otherwise unharmed. Dhana examined the altar. The incense sticks continued burning in their holders, the fresh flowers yet stood in their vases and Krishna still sported his mischievous little smile.

Chapter Nine

The Village of Mahavan, End of Satya Yuga

Steve walked along a soft, red dirt path on top of a hill. The knoll contained meadows and pastures filled with sweet-smelling grasses and profusely growing flowers. Tall greenery, feathered with seeds on top, lined the edges of the trail. He picked up a handful of the rich soil and smelled it. Moisture hid in the earth just at his fingertips—obviously, it had rained earlier in the day or perhaps the previous night. The showers released an aroma of sweetness held fast deep within the soil. Did this earthy scent, clinging dew-like to the sweet air, perfume his every breath and did the atmosphere, so delicately scented, flow over his body like a fresh mountain stream?

He closed his eyes and inhaled. With each wave, the soft wind rinsed away all concerns. Each breath, each step, sucked all worries, all anxieties away. Images of warm summer days spent playing in meadows full of flowers, of a carefree childhood filled with light and laughter crowded his mind. He noticed a tree with an enormously distended trunk, standing comically like a stiff sentinel on top of the hill. He laughed like a child, the joy coming long and deep from inside and for no reason at all. He dashed along the path toward the tree, laughing happily, uncontrollably, his lungs devouring great big gulps of heavenly air.

The deeper he breathed, the more his body wanted. He couldn't recall when his mind felt more clear and content. As a child he'd wake up completely refreshed after a night of restful sleep, but never before had he experienced anything like this—his entire body alert, full of energy and vigor. This place removed mountains of burdens from his shoulders; weights so accustomed to bearing, he had never noticed them before.

He stopped running, lay on his back in the grass beside the path and stared into the absolute blue of the atmosphere. Only a few soft white clouds danced in the firmament, metamorphosing endlessly into fairies and angels, knights and castles. He sensed himself merging into that infinite, unending horizon.

An intense, wonderful tingling sensation, as if his nerves themselves became alive, tickled his toes and his fingertips. The sensation grew more pronounced and ventured into his torso, where individual nerves and muscles playfully wrestled with each other. Unable to bear their blissful combat, he laughed, roared, and grabbing his stomach, rolled over the field, his clothes and hair ensnaring grass and flowers.

After a long while, he calmed and a pleasant, tired feeling overcame him. He noticed the sun—that warm, yellow globe—lay only midway on the eastern horizon. He lifted his arm and examined his watch. At first he couldn't see the hands; they whirled in an indistinguishable blur. A momentary fear overcame him. The watch suddenly felt ugly, alien, like an evil manacle on his wrist. It ticked softly, ever rapidly and, to his suddenly sensitive ears, sounded deadly—innocent-looking on the outside, but full of a complex, murderous technology inside. He tore that black, strange, thing off, threw it as far as possible down the hill and immediately experienced a sense of great relief and boundless satisfaction. *So that's what's been tying me down all this time,* he thought.

He felt happy, carefree again. He bounded up on his feet and jogged over to the fat-bellied tree. It was the strangest thing he ever saw. Curiously small leaves crowned tiny branches extending from the top of its trunk. He walked up to it, arms extended, but his embrace came nowhere close to covering even a quarter of the trunk. The fat-bellied tree looked down and smiled, as if to chastise him for being so foolish.

Large roots, like thick brown waves, emerged at intervals out of the rich, red earth. He sat on one and peered into the valley. Tall, broad-leaved forest covered the entire area. The dirt path tumbled down the side of the hill, ran through several hundred yards of dense, cool woodland, and stopped at the bank of a fast-moving river at least two stone throws across. It flowed towards him from low-lying hills in the far north, and beyond them stood tall, magnificent mountains, filling the entire horizon, their regal crowns dusted eternally with pure, pristine snow, silently surveying their kingdoms below. Ethereal, transcendental, as if unconnected to the earth, they stood shimmering blue and white on the far-away, unreachable skyline.

He shook his head, got up and walked around the tree, eyeing the river curving around the hill. The waterway turned and spread out into a large, shallow pool crowded with water lilies and lotuses, the large flowers shining white and pink. On the near shore lay a small, sandy beach, bordered by a large flat expanse of grassland. And on it, close to the river, perched a small village composed of several dozen thatch-roofed huts.

So he was not alone! Relief washed over him. The sight of human habitation raised a hundred questions. *What am I doing here? Who lives in that village?* His memory, his past, flooded back. He remembered everything: his brother, his mother's death, the fire ritual and the Yoga Zapper. He stared at the village again. *Could Jack be there?*

The community surrounded a large stone building, square at the bottom and tapering twenty feet high, set in an enclosed courtyard. From its crown rose a bronze pole with a shining metal disk on top, with stylized flames emanating from its edges. Steve surmised that it must be a place of worship. Large tree branches extended over the stone walls, their canopies shading the compound where several inhabitants, wearing white or orange dhotis, practiced *hatha yoga*. Some sat in *padmasana*, with their legs crossed, backs straight, arms extended to their knees with thumbs touching their forefingers, while others stood in *vrikshasana*, with one foot tucked up at the knee of the other, their hands stretched overhead with palms together.

Next to the temple grew an enormous banyan tree, composed of several trunks, creating the effect of a small grove, affording both shelter and community to the inhabitants. Steve saw children playing among those tree trunks and women sitting under the shade, engaged in conversation. The young ones noticed him and started waving and Steve smiled at their innocent gesture of friendship and signaled back. Soon, the adult members of the village became aware of his presence and gestured, urging him to come down.

Steve trekked down the path. At the base of the hill, he encountered a footpath meandering along the banks of the stream, shaded by tall trees on one side while rushes and long grasses grew along the shore. The sparkling blue waters, cool and inviting, sped downstream, tumbling among large rocks.

Striding on the path, and following the bend of the river, he passed the pool brimming with lotuses and lilies before stopping at the village's entrance. The entire community had gathered to meet him. The women, lithe and supple, formed two rows and small children stood peering curiously from behind the shelter of their mother's saris. Behind them, men positioned themselves, their strong bodies clothed in cotton dhotis, either white or saffron, and at the end stood an elderly man with a long white beard, holding a garland of flowers.

On the ground at the village's entrance lay an intricate design created with some sort of white powder. The care and effort going into its creation suggested more than mere decoration and it occurred to Steve that not only was he entering the village, but also crossing into the special cosmology, the different world, represented by the drawing.

Baffled, he stopped at the center of the design and several women rushed forward with brown earthen pots. Bending down, they poured water and washed his feet with strong hands. He recoiled, being greatly self-conscious, but his sensitivity remained totally unnoticed by the women who glanced at him shyly and with amusement. As soon as this part of the greeting ended, a lady applied a large round spot of red powder directly to the center of his forehead. Obviously, this was their customary way of greeting visitors, but why did they receive him, a complete stranger, with such affection and familiarity?

After the women moved away, Steve strode between the parallel lines of inhabitants as, at every step, they threw flowers, quickly smothering him with sweet-smelling petals. When he reached the end, the old man, smiling broadly under his thick beard which, combed around the edges of his mouth in a manner as to give the impression of a continual smile on his lips, stepped forward.

Despite his age, the old man displayed a strong, tanned body. Skin hung loose on his arms and chest, but his eyes remained dark and clear. His gentle and kind demeanor revealed the nature of someone who, having lived a long, fruitful and satisfying life, retains nothing but goodwill toward all souls. He stared intently into Steve's eyes, as if examining the contents of his heart, all the while maintaining an affectionate regard on his face. He slipped the heavenly garland, fashioned of lotus blossoms, each huge and aromatic, the long, thick petals gleaming white, their tips pink, over Steve's head and rested it on his shoulders.

"Namaste," said the old man, bringing his palms together. "Welcome to the village of Mahavan," he continued in Sanskrit.

Chapter Ten

Kallington, End of Kali Yuga

Jack rolled on the ground like a drunkard. An awful, pounding headache radiated from each temple and penetrated deep into his brain while a nauseous, hard anxiety knotted his stomach. He gingerly balanced on hands and knees and rested like a sick dog, his tongue hanging out. He crawled around for several long minutes before finally lifting his head and looking around.

The small square measured not larger than three hundred feet on each side and besides a few patches of dry weeds, rags, plastic bags and dust blew around. Open sewers lined its edges and the air reeked of urine and feces. He saw neither lamp posts nor street signs. Around the square, ramshackle houses, built of brick and corrugated iron roofs, stood cheek to jowl, along with others constructed of nothing more than plastic and cardboard. Though fires glowed dully in a few habitations, most remained dark. The odor of cooking meat wafted from these cooking blazes, but the stench differed from anything that Jack recognized. And a vague, dark, outline of a man materialized at the far end of the square.

Jack examined himself. A clean, white cloth wrapped his hips and legs while a long, white shirt draped his chest. Where did he get these clothes? Their cleanliness certainly contrasted with the dust and debris surrounding him. With great effort, he wobbled up on his feet, drawing in short, gasping breaths, but immediately sank to his knees—his stomach heaved but nothing came. While it relieved his nausea, it did nothing for the anxiety. In fact, the panic worsened, radiating out of his stomach and into his arms and legs, shaking his hands and chattering his teeth. Jack peered up. The sun hung low and red and clouds dangled heavy and dark, like hemorrhaging wounds in the sky.

"Where am I?" he shouted. Only silence replied.

He glanced around nervously. The man, hardly four feet tall and thickly built, with strong, sloping shoulders and compact hips, appeared much closer, perhaps only thirty feet away. He stared intently at Jack with baleful, bloodshot eyes. Patches of short dark hair covered his head, his nose bent to the left like that of a battered boxer, his unshaven and darkly tanned face looked deeply creased, his lips curled sharply downwards and small beads of spittle formed at each end of his mouth. He dressed in a torn, plain red shirt and a beltless green pair of pants, and meaty hands and gaunt arms completed his appearance. He shifted his weight on bare feet, displaying a far-away, expressionless look on his face.

Jack staggered to his feet. "Hello," he shouted, "who are you?"

The man jumped forward, picked up a long metal rod and hurled it with all his might. Before Jack could react, the heavy rod smashed into the ribs below his left shoulder. The impact tore open his kurta and hurled him into the dust. Jack grunted. He ripped off his shirt and pressed his right hand against the wound, gasping and gritting his teeth with pain as blood flowed from a deep, searing gash. Staggering up, he picked up the rod with his right hand and waved it at his assailant. The man stopped and let forth a low, guttural scream that echoed throughout the neighborhood.

Several doors opened and, from half-opened entrances and out of the dark spaces between houses, other men with beady red eyes shuffled out. They possessed similar statures: short and squat with blunt, vacant faces. Upon seeing Jack, they whipped broken bricks, empty bottles and other debris they found lying about.

A bottle smashed against Jack's forehead. He collapsed. The pain seared into his eyeballs and blood trickled down his face. More men poured out of the surrounding dwellings until a mob formed. In great excitement they shouted, baying hoarsely, like wild dogs on a hunt.

Jack got up, bracing himself for the imminent attack. He quelled the panic in his stomach and once again picked up the metal rod. The men raged forward. Jack swung hard, crashing it down on the nearest man's head. It cracked like an egg and blood spurted. Stunned, the man dropped. Immediately, a couple of attackers grabbed the fallen man by the ankles and dragged him across the square and down a dark alley. The injured aggressor screamed, desperately clawing the earth as he was hauled into one of the houses. The door slammed shut and from within, a chilling shriek rent the air.

The others regrouped and surrounded Jack like a pack of wolves encircling a helpless deer. Jack swung wildly. Suddenly, a man jumped from behind and sunk his teeth into his thigh. Jack howled in pain and fear. Emboldened, the mob rushed forward. Jack dropped the rod and pummeled his foes with bare fists and swift kicks.

Unexpectedly a long sharp whistle sounded. Brilliant white lights, circling around and around, flooded the square. The attackers stopped in their tracks. The whistle sounded again, this time much closer. Without warning, five uniformed men rappelled down from the middle of the lights and landed in front of Jack. They crouched on the ground and aimed their weapons at the retreating horde. Just seconds before, bloodlust animated the mob, but now it scattered in sheer terror. Arcs of blue energy shot forth, catching a dozen of the panic-stricken creatures. They screamed in pain, fell to the ground, their bodies twitching uncontrollably, their hollers shattering the evening, and after a few moments lay silent and stiff, letting forth gasps of intense pain. As quickly and as suddenly as the attack began, it ended. The long shadows darkened, the creatures crawled stealthily back into their hovels and doors creaked shut.

The uniformed men got up. One spoke into a radio on his collar. Following his instructions, the aircraft, composed of a dark, glassy, rubbery material and operating in complete silence, quickly descended and dropped to a height of five feet above the ground. Resembling a pyramid, it measured about fifteen feet tall, thirty feet on each side, with a round opening in its flat bottom. A ring of blinking white lights lined this aperture while blue and red lights circled at the top of the craft. With no rotors, engines or any visible mechanisms for power, it blended perfectly with the darkness and would have been entirely invisible if not for its lights.

One of the uniformed men, short in stature and dressed in blue pants and shirt, walked up to Jack. A blue beret covered his head and dark glasses hid his eyes. Thick black boots shielded his legs and, in his hands, he carried his weapon. He stood silently in front of Jack.

"Thank you!" exclaimed Jack. "You guys arrived just in the nick of time."

The uniformed officer lowered his weapon and before Jack could react, pulled the trigger. Jack screamed as the weapon's energy pulse coursed into his nerves, his entire body exploding in pain. He fell on his face, rolling and twitching wildly, gasping through chattering teeth. Bolts of energy burned into every one of his nerves and, through them, into every part of his body, exploding at their endings. It resembled no pain he had ever experienced. His eyes burned and nothing looked real, his vision becoming a glassy cobalt. Rays of light like red and white fireworks shot out of his of peripheral vision and exploded into a million stars.

"Jesus Christ," he hissed through closed teeth, "God help me!" His body stretched out as the energy pushed into his teeth and toes, from the hair on his head to the nails on his feet. After a while, he stiffened, hard and long as a board. Despite the burning, searing, pain traveling through his nerves, Jack still saw and heard clearly.

* * *

The man put his boot on Jack's body and kicked him over to his back. "Whooeee," he exclaimed in amazement.

70

"What do we have here?" asked the captain, marching over. He, too, dressed in blue but two bronze bars sat pinned on his epaulets.

"Damn if I know who he is!"

"He sure is big," declared the captain. "Much bigger than your average *Rakshasa*. He sure don't resemble your ordinary, bloodthirsty Rak. He looks more like the Elite. And if he's an Elite, what's he doing here? And look at the cloth around his waist." The captain bent down and ran his fingers along the fabric. "Nice. Real nice." He removed it, folded it up, and stuffed it into his pocket, leaving Jack in just his shorts. "It's mine now," he laughed.

The rest of the company bent down, examining Jack's hands, eyes, hair and limbs.

"All right boys, let's get going," ordered the captain finally.

The men picked Jack up, bare-chested, bare-legged and bleeding, and flung him through the open hatch at the center of the craft's flat bottom. They heaved the incapacitated Raks above their heads like pieces of wood, jumped inside and sat with legs professionally dangling out of the open hatch as the craft ascended into the gathering darkness.

* * *

From where he lay, Jack scanned the scene below, barely a hundred feet above ground. Night covered the land and vast slums spread, seemingly endlessly, in all directions. In some fortunate hearths fires burned, signifying food being cooked, but huge swathes of the slums languished in darkness. He saw their inhabitants, dull and hungry, looking through the dusty air at the passing craft from open windows and occasional street corners.

In the distance, a gigantic, brightly-lit, rectangular glass and metal building appeared, towering over the landscape as a volcano would over the plains. Half way up each side of this massive structure hung large neon signs reading 'Central Prison—Kallington.' It thrust itself up from the middle of a huge, dust-blown base at least a hundred square miles in area. Acres of grey pavement, painted with lines, signs and letterings, surrounded this colossal building as did airplane hangars, fuel depots and engineering shops. Several layers of high walls and barbed wire fences lined the complex's edges and only four heavily guarded entrances existed at the middle of each side. Bright lights traced the base's perimeter and lit its every corner.

The craft silently and quickly descended, stopping five feet above the tarmac. The uniformed men jumped out and stood in line, weapons in hand, as several green-smocked technicians with white masks, all pulling gurneys, rushed out from one of the building's bay doors. One by one, they hauled the stiff, jaw-clenched prisoners out of the craft and strapped them, hands, feet and torsos, onto the gurneys and rolled them into the building.

Despite the rough treatment, Jack, frozen stiff, couldn't protest or even make a sound as they steered him into a large, brightly-lit receiving area with clean, white tile walls and green cement floors. After a few minutes, another technician in a green tunic and a white mask came by and administered an intravenous injection into Jack's right arm. Immediately a great feeling of relief, or rather, non-pain, coursed through him from head to toe. His nerves tingled and he gasped, sucked in deep gulps of air, released his clenched teeth, relaxed his back muscles and let loose a scream of suppressed fear and pain. No one paid any attention. As sweat streamed down his face, he gathered his breath, exultant at being pain-free again. The injection drove away not only the hurt but also the headache.

For the first time since his appearance, his mind cleared but the anxiety in his gut returned, having lain quietly like a coiled snake, hiding in the grass, waiting for the appropriate time to strike. He cautiously lifted his head and looked around. A constant traffic of gurneys, personnel and hospital equipment entered and left the scene. After about a half an hour, two other green-clad men came over and spun him away.

"Where am I?" he asked, the words coming out small and broken. One of the men pointed to a sign on the wall reading 'DNA-Identification.' They stopped upon reaching a small, dully-lit room with gray walls, not much larger than the gurney. A spherical metal object, resembling a large football helmet, hung from the wall and thick cables ran from it into a steel console covered with buttons and lights. Above it, a large video screen shone from the wall. The operator in the room, wearing green pants and a white shirt, removed the round metal object, slipped it over Jack's head, retreated to the console and pressed some buttons. The screen remained blank. He walked back and replaced the helmet carefully. Again, no response showed. He lifted the gurney to a sitting position, examined the back of Jack's neck and gesticulating animatedly, left. Jack observed the goings-on, too bewildered to react, let alone process the events.

After a short while the man returned, accompanied by several other persons, some dressed in the same green pants and white shirts and others in long white doctor's coats. The crush of people startled Jack. He knotted his eyes. A sharp wave of anxiety swelled up in his stomach. *Who were they? What did they want?*

"Are you sure?" questioned one of the white-coated men. They all stood short, but this one wore gray pants, dark-rimmed glasses, flashed a shiny, partly bald head and the others flocked around him. *Obviously*, thought Jack, *the head doctor*.

"Yes," replied the operator. "We checked the equipment. There are no defects."

"So what could this mean?" asked someone from outside the door.

"We have scanned his entire brain and neck area. He doesn't have a DNA implant."

The announcement was met with intense chatter. They moved closer and peered at Jack intently. The distinct feeling of a laboratory rat being examined unnerved him.

The operator shook his head. "I don't know how that's possible. I have read reports of rebels removing their DNA implants. This may be one such case."

A murmur of assent swept throughout the crowd. They scrutinized Jack even more attentively, like zoo visitors ogling a rare caged animal.

"But even if he removed the implant, his past records should remain in the database. Everyone has a record," countered the head doctor.

"Then let's obtain a DNA sample and search for a match," replied the technician. He planted a needle into a vein in Jack's arm and extracted several milliliters of blood. Jack's anxiety turned to fear at its sight. He pulled at his tightly secured hand and legs without effect.

"Where am I?" he shouted. "What are you doing to me?" Everyone ignored him.

The man inserted the sample into an instrument in the console. Almost instantly, the monitor lit up with rows and rows of numbers and letters. After several seconds the message 'Searching Database' appeared and a few moments after that, the words 'No Match Found.' The crowd shook their heads in disbelief. They ran the test again and the same message reappeared.

"Go back to the first screen," ordered the head doctor. The white-coated men gathered around the display. "Look at this sequence here," he pointed, "and this sequence."

The doctors spent the next fifteen minutes poring over the results line by line. Jack tried following the proceedings without success. He instead forced himself to remember, back-tracking the day's events. He could only go so far as his appearance at the dusty square. He remembered only his name. Jack. He wondered what that meant. Suddenly, it occurred to him that he had no idea who he was.

"Please help me," he shouted. "Get me out of here!"

The chief doctor looked up. "Calm down," he replied reassuringly. "We are also trying to find out what happened to you." At these words, Jack let his breath go and relaxed his stiff neck.

"Who are you?" asked the man.

"My name is Jack. That's all I know."

The doctor pointed at the console. "I have never seen anything like this in my entire life."

Jack stared back blankly.

The doctor walked around. "Let me explain. At birth, everyone has a dynamic DNA chip, part of what we call the DNA implant, inserted in the neck near the brain stem area."

"What does that mean?"

"The dynamic DNA chip measures the DNA sequences of individuals, which are unique to each person. Several generations ago, the state used plain RFID implants, but those had limitations. Those implants used an external numerical identification system attached to them. For example, your implant number may have been ten thousand two hundred and one. People took out their RFID implants and swapped them with others, thus effectively subverting control. With the DNA implant, you don't need an external identification system: your identification is your DNA code."

"So what is the big deal?" asked Jack.

"The DNA implant does more than just create a fool-proof identification system. Whenever one eats, drinks, engages in sexual activity and so on, the body produces proteins which appear in the blood. The current implant measures these proteins and transmits this information."

"Where does it transmit this information? And how does it do that?'

"Well, you're full of questions, aren't you?" asked the doctor. Jack nodded. He still felt dull, but the doctor's explanations piqued his interest.

"The DNA implant is the size of a grain of rice and it has three parts. The first part, an electronic chip, collects information about the DNA and the proteins. The second part stores the information until it is transmitted. The third part is the transmitter itself, along with a battery that powers the entire unit. And as to where the data is transmitted, it is sent to the central database on the moon."

"So when you couldn't find me in the database, it's because I never had a DNA implant?"

"Yes, you are sharp. All cases so far involve someone removing their DNA implant. This sometimes happens with the rebels. But even if someone detaches his implant, the record of previous transmissions still remains in the database. Getting someone back into the system is as easy as putting in another implant. The only way someone is not in the database is if he never had a DNA implant. That's why we obtained a blood sample. However, this is very, very rare; almost inconceivable. In fact, you are the first case in my entire life."

"But I don't ever remember getting an implant."

"I don't know how that's possible. The whole system depends on everyone getting one. Not only did we not find a DNA implant or any records, but there's another twist in your case."

"What's that?"

"We look not just at people's nuclear DNA," explained the doctor, "but also at the *mitochondrial DNA*. Actually, we don't examine the entire mitochondrial DNA chain when comparing members of a population—we look at a just string of several thousand DNA sequences which we call the control region. So when comparing the control regions of the population, several DNA characteristics or mutations occur at certain points." Jack shook his head. The scientific jargon escaped him.

"Think of the entire mitochondrial DNA of a person as a huge rope, a mile long. The control region is one small part of the entire rope, maybe ten or twenty feet long. Then imagine that on this part of the rope are thousands of knots; black, red, green or blue. Now suppose we take the same small piece of rope from each person in the population and compare them, we notice certain mutations or characteristics appearing in the same places on all the ropes."

"So you are saying there is something wrong with my genes?"

"Not at all. Mutations showing up in different places are not of concern. They happen all the time. What it does mean is that the locations of your mutations don't match any others in our entire population. You are an absolutely unique specimen! In fact, you are not related to anyone in the whole world!" The doctor bubbled with excitement. He took a few minutes to gather his breath.

"You have no idea how you ended up in Kallington?"

Jack shook his head uneasily.

"You didn't just appear out of thin air, did you?"

Jack again mutely shook his head. "I…I don't know." He sensed a change in the doctor's mood. He didn't know the goal of this line of questioning and he didn't like it.

"Where were you born?"

Jack concentrated, but nothing came to mind.

"Where did you live your entire life?"

Again, Jack wagged his head. The anxiety in his stomach heaved.

"You really don't know, do you?"

"I have no idea who I am," Jack blurted. *What am I doing*, he immediately wondered. *Why am I answering their questions?*

The doctor straightened himself. "This is a matter of utmost concern for national security," he stated gravely. "We have to report this to the chief of police."

It instantly occurred to Jack that he was completely at the mercy of these people. The interrogation made it painfully clear that he remained alone, very alone, in a situation that had spun out of control. The anxiety turned to panic.

"No! No!" he yelled. "Let me go! Let me go!" He thrashed violently in his gurney.

"Control him," demanded the doctor.

The technician ran up and stabbed Jack with a needle. Within seconds, Jack's eyes closed, his awareness quickly disappearing.

Chapter Eleven

Village of Mahavan, End of Satya Yuga

"What is your name?" enquired Steve in Sanskrit. "And where am I?"

The old man's eyes widened. "My name is Parvata Rishi and you're in the village of Mahavan. Where did you learn our language?"

"It was part of my studies."

The old man smiled appreciatively.

"I'm looking for my brother," blurted Steve. "He's tall, has black hair and blue eyes. I...I need to talk to him immediately. Have you seen him?"

"Slow down," laughed the old man. "Let's eat. Then we'll talk."

Steve sighed. What could he say about the guilt he felt for his angry words, about the promise made to his mother to take care of Jack? Rushing served no purpose. The answers would appear soon enough. Yet, Steve felt pleased to hear the Sanskrit. His studies, after all, came to some use!

"Come, follow me," instructed the rishi.

They walked to the sandy beach and sat on a long white, cotton cloth, set in front of rough, unglazed, brown clay dishes. Several earthen cups and bowls completed the set.

"Shanti," called Parvata Rishi, looking at a nearby hut. "Our guest is here."

A young woman wearing a deep blue sari, the color of the fathomless horizon, partly draped over her head so as to hide her face, stepped out of the door. She neatly balanced several brass bowls, one on top of another, on her left hip and, in her right hand, clutched a large porous clay pot filled with cool water. One by one, she planted the containers on the sand and with a ladle, heaped rice and several varieties of cooked vegetables and legumes in the middle of their plates and poured sweet water from the pot into the terracotta cups.

"Please meet my daughter Shanti," said Parvata Rishi. A young woman in the prime of youth, she displayed slender arms and unblemished skin the color of freshly-pressed, golden olive oil. The silver border of her sari framed jet-black hair curling above her forehead, running behind her ears and falling loose and long on her back. Her cheeks glowed a subtle pink and large green eyes shone through dark eyelashes. A delicate necklace of bright red coral graced her elongated neck and large fish-shaped gold earrings adorned her ears. Her breasts, though small, clung full and firm on her strong, yet supple, frame. The freshness, the special bloom, of a maiden just entering womanhood glistened on her face and body.

"Hello," he mumbled. "My name is Steve."

She flashed a perfect white smile. Steve couldn't remove his gaze from the limpid green pools of her eyes. Shanti noticed his obvious stare and smiled innocently. Determined not to make a fool of himself, he forced his attention on his plate and quietly relished the sweet natural taste of the fresh foodstuffs.

After eating, the two men got up and walked towards the lotus pond while Shanti transported the empty containers back to the hut.

"I was talking about our village, but actually," clarified the rishi, pointing to the trees on the other side of the river, "Mahavan refers to the great woodland surrounding us."

"Yes, I observed the forest from the hill," Steve stated. "How big is it?"

"It extends all the way to the mountains to the north, a full month's journey by foot. It is the domain of the *Jantu*, the non-human citizens of this land. Two other forests are associated with this village—one is the *Shrivan*, the Forest of Plenty, composed of fruit and medicinal trees, planted, taken care of and used by members of this community and the other is the *Tapovan*, the Forest of Austerities, where yogis and rishis meditate peacefully in hidden places. No one disturbs its environment in any way as tampering with the natural order of things would disrupt the meditation of the sages. We truly are forest dwellers."

Steve waited for a few moments. "What about my brother?"

The rishi stopped. "I have a few questions. Did you come from Kali Yuga?"

"Yes."

"You are in Satya Yuga. Actually, I'm surprised you even traveled from Kali yuga!"

"Why?"

"Because Kali Yuga is full of anxiety, forgetfulness, and discord. One cannot have good consciousness in that age."

"What makes this age so peaceful? Is it your simple lives?"

"Simple living is a symptom of Satya Yuga, not the cause. Actually, the nature of time itself is different." Steve stared back blankly.

Parvata Rishi lifted his arm and pointed to the river. "Look at this river. See how it runs from the mountains down to the forest. Up there, its waters are clear and clean, but flowing down the hills, the current picks up innumerable grains of sand, clots of dirt and pieces of wood. You look at the current here and imagine it's clean, but hidden inside are large quantities of impurities. By the time it enters the ocean, it is heavy, dark, and swollen with residue. Like this mountain stream, time starts out fresh and pure but slowly, imperceptibly, picks up impurities until finally, it too becomes heavy and dark."

Steve reflected a moment. "What do you mean by impurities?"

"Let me explain it another way. All things require a medium, something against which to act. When we walk, our feet push against the ground. Stars move within the medium of the firmament. We are engaged in thousands of actions every day. It is impossible to be inactive. So tell me the medium in which actions take place." Steve shook his head silently, his forehead creased questioningly.

"Actions take place, one after another, in the medium of time. We know this by the symptom of actions, namely, reactions."

"That makes sense."

"Understand that when time is fresh, fewer reactions lie embedded, dormant, in it. Satya Yuga is the beginning age where time is 'cleaner' or 'fresher.' As the yugas pass, more karmic reactions accumulate until finally, in Kali Yuga, time resembles a dark, impenetrable river filled with silt, rocks, fallen trees and other dangerous objects."

"I understand your analogy," replied Steve. "But does it truly work that way?"

"Come. I'll show you."

They walked to the edge of the pond and stared into its clear waters. Parvata Rishi picked up a small pebble and dropped it into the liquid. Steve watched it sink, reaching the bottom, nestling into the river-bed.

"Imagine this pebble to be your karma. Look how clearly it is seen at the bottom of the pool. In other words, when engaged in an action, the consequences are easy to understand."

The rishi picked up a stick, reached into the waters and stirred the sand and mud. The water immediately clouded and debris swirled around the stone.

"In clear water it is easy to pick up the pebble. In cloudy waters, you will never find it even if it belongs to you. Satya Yuga allows us to delve deeply into the study of reactions to one's actions—that is, karma—as time is not burdened with the cloudiness of un-manifested reactions. In Kali Yuga, the atmosphere, dense with karmic reactions, renders it almost impossible to understand these laws."

The explanation made perfect sense. Not just intellectually, but his entire body was ridding itself of years, of lifetimes, of accumulated anxieties. His very bones shouted out these lessons.

"How did you learn these things?"

"By the practice of austerities and by renunciation, I withdrew my attachment to this world. The path of the yogi is like one of these lotuses, being of this world, yet detached from it. Natural insight is a part of life in this age. Floating above the current, I see the flow of the river downstream. That is why I am called a rishi, a seer."

"What does this mean for my brother? How can we discover what's happening to Jack?"

The rishi arched his eyebrows. "By controlling one's mind and senses. This is called tapasya, or austerity."

"And how do you do that?"

"Come. I will show you."

As they walked, Shanti joined them. Steve noticed her curious glances. He must quite be a sight with his pale skin, light hair, and dark brown eyes. He measured her. Of good height, she came up to his shoulders. The sari fell around her neck, revealing dark hair draping behind her. A small garland of jasmine flowers crowned her head and tucked itself behind her ears. To say that she looked beautiful and exotic did not do justice to her grace and femininity. He withdrew his glance and kept his eyes downcast, listening to their soft steps as they passed the two trees at the entrance to the temple's courtyard, where the villagers practiced yoga.

"To access this knowledge requires concentration and study," the rishi said. "It is a very subtle science. Kali Yuga is characterized by anxiety, hurry, and divided aims, where peacefulness, a requisite for the study of spiritual topics, is sorely lacking. In Satya Yuga, however, meditation is much easier due to time's peaceful condition. Here, the science of the yoga is truly well developed.

"Our long lives allow for the intense practice of yoga and meditation, the true *dharma*, that is, the innate occupation, for all human beings of this age. The capacity for meditation exists in every age, but the process is very difficult to access. It can be safely said that meditation and yoga exist only in shadow outside of Satya Yuga."

They found a peaceful spot under one of the trees in the temple compound. The rishi sat down in *padmasana*, the lotus pose. Steve followed his example.

"Please teach me yoga," requested Steve.

"Where did you come from?"

"From America."

"And what language do you speak there?"

"English."

"Okay," said the rishi, with a gleam in his eyes. "Teach me this Eengliz and I will teach you yoga."

Steve laughed. "That's a deal."

"Come meditate. Practice withdrawing your senses from the objects of the senses. This is the way to understand karma."

Steve glanced over at Shanti. Already deep in concentration, she showed herself an old hand at the practice.

Parvata Rishi tapped him lightly on his shoulder. "Come. Do as I do."

Steve turned his head and closed his eyes. Controlling his breath, he withdrew into himself.

* * *

Parvata Rishi arranged for Steve to spend the night at his hut. A low cot, on which lay a cushion of cut grass covered with a clean cloth, furnished Steve's small room. He fell asleep easily and awoke next morning just at dawn, completely refreshed. The calls of parrots, swallows and doves filled the air as rays of light streamed from the eastern horizon. Despite the early morning, just a touch of coolness tinged the pleasant weather. The ground, fresh and damp, emanated a fragrant, earthy scent; a product of the night rains. Shanti hung a fresh set of dhoti and kurta on a nearby branch as Steve took his morning bath with buckets of water drawn from a well, under a canopy of mango trees, behind the thin walls of a rattan blind. He dressed and greeted his benefactors at their dwelling.

"Good morning," announced Steve

"Namaste," replied the rishi, with closed palms.

"When did you get up?"

"Since well before sunrise," said Parvata Rishi. "The early *brahma muhurtha* hours are the best time for spiritual practices."

They strode to the temple where the villagers had already congregated for the arti ceremony, and with sweet, melodious voices greeted the Deities with a gentle and contemplative early-morning *kirtan*. After the ceremony, they proceeded toward the banyan tree. A three-foot high earthen platform surrounded the main trunk and Parvata Rishi climbed and sat on it with legs crossed. Following Shanti's lead, Steve sat on the ground in front of the rishi, taking notes in his small pocket notebook.

"Today, we will discuss the upcoming pilgrimage," announced the rishi. "But before starting, let me introduce our young visitor. His name is Steven Goode and he's staying at my ashram."

Steve clasped his palms against each other and saying 'Namaste,' bowed his head slightly towards the crowd. The men, mostly young, and the women, robust and handsome, glowed in the best of health. Those with children tended their young ones near the pond.

"Satya Yuga will draw to a close shortly," continued Parvata Rishi. "Already, we see omens of this. Our bodies suffer from shortness of breath, our memories are not as quick and sometimes we even forget, however momentarily, the goal of life. We live in the highest form of human society, but change will come. Those wishing to remain immersed in Satya Yuga civilization must prepare for the journey ahead. In about one month's time, sages from many parts of the world will gather at a valley in the faraway mountains to perform a great yajna."

Steve knotted his eyebrows. Parvata Rishi spoke of Satya Yuga as a highly advanced civilization, yet he saw only thatched huts and a simple way of life. What did the rishi mean?

The rishi discussed the pilgrimage: individual responsibilities, the daily routine, and the best route to take through the forest and the hills. Upon this, the villagers engaged in an animated discussion.

Steve glanced at Shanti. The morning sun, shimmering over the horizon, threw an orange hue on her hair. It warmed her golden cheeks and cast fire in her emerald eyes. She noticed him and smiled girlishly. Steve acknowledged her and smiled back. How much of her is a woman, he wondered, and how much of her still an adolescent?

The rishi got up and bowed. "Tomorrow, we will discuss further the preparations for the pilgrimage, due to start next week."

The villagers dispersed and Parvata Rishi, Shanti and Steve made their way home. Shanti went inside and brought a plate of fresh fruit for breakfast. They all sat on the ground and ate.

"Yesterday, you mentioned that people here lead long lives?" asked Steve.

"Yes," stated the rishi. "A person's lifespan in Satya Yuga is about a hundred thousand years."

Steve's eyes widened. He glanced at Shanti. "And how old are you?"

She grimaced. "I'm only eighteen thousand, eight hundred and twenty-one years old."

The rishi smiled. "Shanti is a very special young woman with a really interesting origin." Steve straightened up and looked expectantly.

"I never married," continued the rishi, "and I never asked God for anything other than to serve Him. In my youth, I spent many thousands of years in Tapovan, practicing meditation and undergoing great penances. To have darshan, the blessing of seeing God Himself in person, remains my greatest desire to this day. I don't know if it will ever happen but, if it does, it will be only due to His mercy. I spent my youth and middle age living alone in the forest, eating and drinking only what God saw fit to give me, controlling my breath so as to inhale only once every two days."

Steve's eyes widened at the narrative. Amazing, beyond comprehension, but yet, from everything he saw so far in Satya Yuga, totally believable.

85

"I spent over twenty-five thousand years this way. One day, in a small clearing in the forest, I found a *Tamal* tree with a large black trunk and long light green leaves, taller and handsomer than any other, as if placed there by an unseen force, for some unknown purpose. The tree, so singular and enchanting, distracted me from my meditation. Circling it, I discovered a large natural opening in its trunk and from inside came the sound of a baby crying. Curious, I discovered within a little baby girl swathed in delicate, heavenly, clothing—garments impossible for human hands to produce.

"I wondered who would leave this baby in the Tapovan forest, the domain of only those existing outside of human society—the sadhus, that is, the renunciates and the wild animals. I picked up the baby and to my surprise, saw clasped in each palm, a single leaf from the holy *Tulasi* plant. The little baby's special origin became immediately clear."

Steve glanced at the young woman sitting next to him. Could this be true? He shook his head.

"As I stood, a vision appeared," continued the rishi. "An *apsara*, a most beautiful divine angel, with pale green skin the color of spring's first shoots, hovered in the air above, her honey eyes shimmering in the lustrous sunlight, dressed in the same opaque, yet glistening, saffron cloth as the baby. Her dark, red hair floated behind her in the sapphire sky and with perfect limbs and delicate hands, she greeted me with palms pressed together. A large golden *bindi* adorned her forehead, diamonds and emeralds from the heavenly planets decorated her lovely neck and the words she spoke poured into my ears like honeyed poetry. The apsara informed me that the infant belonged to her and requested me to take care of it. Upon maturity, she revealed, this baby girl would bring me great honor and be the mother of numerous brave and renounced sons as well as several chaste and beautiful daughters. Saying this, she disappeared.

"The sweet little baby looked at me, smiled, and held out her arms. I hesitated on taking the responsibility. After all, as a renunciate, I'd grown extremely attached to my spiritual practices. Then I understood it as God's desire, since this baby came to me without my personally wanting her. She arrived, I realized, to teach me things that my tapasya hadn't, and raising her would also be a *sadhana*, a spiritual practice. Since then, I've lived in this village and my wonderful daughter has grown into a young woman as beautiful, as charming, as her heavenly mother."

Steve stopped and collected his thoughts. The story astonished him but, yet, Shanti's angelic parentage seemed entirely believable. He glanced at her. She draped the sari over her head and looked shyly away. Within this timid young woman, poised uncertainly at the threshold of womanhood, lay some unknown power, a future that he could hardly guess. Like the delicate flower which produces the seeds of mighty trees, none could deny her origin or her destiny. He suddenly became self-conscious. *I'm Steve*, he thought, *good old Steve, just a plain-spoken mid-western boy from Kansas City, wherever that may be now, a son of the good, strong, unpretentious soil of the American heartland.* He breathed deeply and turned his eyes to the old man.

"I have a question from your speech this morning."

"Go ahead," urged the rishi.

"You described this as a very advanced civilization. But I don't see any modern technologies, such as electricity or telephones."

"Ah!" uttered the old man. "Then tell me the goal of human civilization."

Steve pondered the question for a few moments. "I suppose civilization's goal is to create things to make life easier, longer and happier for everybody."

"Hmm," said Parvata Rishi. He slowly shook his head. "My son, the goal of human society is not to increase unnecessary wants. We can invent ever more clever machines, creating ever more things for consumption, but human desires have no end. That's the danger in serving the body and the senses. Where will it end? The real goal of human life is centered on knowledge of the eternal self, not the mortal body. If one truly understands who one is, all other types of knowledge become secondary."

The old man stared deeply into the horizon. His face turned dark and grave, lost in a faraway gaze. "In the future, human beings will move from a simple, spiritual culture connected to all things, to a complex, materialistic one which is oriented towards self-centered desires. In fact, so much so, that we may destroy our very life-giving earth."

A strange feeling overcame Steve. The rishi, though present in body, was absent in spirit. He had a sudden insight. The old man gazed not into the heavens, but far, far into the future, looking over the river of time and observing its flow, centuries and centuries from now. His statements were not mere thoughts, but factual observations. The thought chilled Steve. He shivered and took a deep breath. "I have to ask you something about my brother."

Parvata Rishi turned back his gaze. Shanti pulled the border of her sari even more fully over her head, hiding her face completely, and picked up the empty plates and strolled back to the hut.

"Yes," he said. "Go ahead."

"I don't know what to do. Jack could be anywhere, even at the end of Kali Yuga. Can you tell where he is? You are a rishi, after all."

The old man took his time. "Even though I see the future in a broad sense, I cannot trace the movements and destinies of individual persons without deeply examining their accumulated karma. It is a subtle science. This takes time."

"So karma is individual and personal?"

"Yes. It requires a concentrated study of the person involved."

"Can I do something?" inquired Steve.

"You would be the best one to gain realizations about your brother. After all, you're closest to him. The knowledge of karma is not gained from the study of books, but by deep internal meditation and a purified consciousness. It is not a mathematical formula solved with pencil and paper, but an answer revealed in the heart. It is already within you. Because of your familiarity, you will best reckon your brother's whereabouts. When the time comes, you will know."

"And how long will that be? I need to know as soon as possible."

"Satya Yuga's effects and the practice of yoga and meditation will purify your consciousness. That takes some time and until then, you won't know. Your brother may not only be in any time period, but also in any country. The realm of possibilities is almost endless. So you have to look within."

"What if he's at the end of Kali Yuga?" questioned Steve, hesitantly.

"That would pose some difficulties. Kali Yuga is characterized by the lessening of intelligence and memory. It is the age of forgetfulness. It is a dangerous and difficult place."

"What can I do?"

"Since your brother may be almost anywhere, I suggest you join us on the pilgrimage. At our destination, we will meet many great spiritual personalities from all over the world and perhaps one will have news about your brother. As well, your consciousness may be clarified enough by the time we finish the pilgrimage that you will locate your brother by yourself."

Steve nodded. The rishi's proposal made far more sense than any alternative. He directed his attention toward the hut, hearing Shanti sweeping the floor. Going on pilgrimage would allow him to spend more time with the rishi and his daughter. The plan definitely had its merits.

Chapter Twelve

Central Prison, End of Kali Yuga

Two policemen dragged Jack, dressed in an orange
jumpsuit, into an office occupying a corner suite on Central
Prison's top floor and deposited him in a chair in front of a
figure sitting behind a hefty executive desk. On it sat a sign
reading 'General Contog—Chief of Police.' They removed
his handcuffs, saluted the general, and walked out.

A big bay window, behind the desk, facing Jack,
looked over cloudy skies. Dark brown tile floors, walls
painted a utilitarian white, a grey glass cabinet built into the
left wall and pictures of the general with various important-
looking figures hanging on the right wall, completed the
large but sparse office. The clock on the wall read eleven-
thirty in the morning and a nondescript, red rug lay under
his chair. Despite the lights built into the ceiling, the office
appeared drab, even dark.

Jack felt dazed, disheveled. The general pressed a
button on his desk and a low hum filled the room. He
opened a bottom drawer, pulled out a small red tablet
computer, quickly snapped Jack's photo, punched in some
commands, immediately returned and locked it up. He
walked over and peered directly into Jack's eyes.

With rough brown skin creased like broken sandpaper,
the general's face featured bushy eyebrows, piercing dark
eyes, a sharp nose, a wide chin and a shaven head. Of
medium height, he wore a blue uniform with three stars on
each epaulet and his blue pants, with a vertical gold stripe
down each leg, were pressed crisp and straight. His thick
black shoes shone brightly. He looked to be in his fifties,
but displayed a strong chest and a clear, steady gaze.
General Contog carried himself with strength,
determination and vigor, yet with cunning, cruelty, and
ambition. His face told the story of a man who scratched

and clawed his way from the bottom to the top, and of all the scars that came with that climb.

"Who are you?" demanded the general. Again the same question.

"I don't know."

General Contog punched another button on the desk. Images appeared in the air; some sort of report. Swiping his fingers on the images, he went from page to page. "This is the report from the DNA identification unit," he said. "You have no DNA implant, there are no records of you in the database and more than that, you're a unique genetic specimen." Jack shrugged his shoulders. The general walked over, suddenly bent down, put his arms on the chair and looked directly into Jack's eyes.

"Are you a rebel?"

"What?" asked Jack, his eyes showing bewilderment.

"Are you a rebel?" shouted Contog, his eyes blazing, his face only a few inches away. Jack's heart thumped loudly in his chest.

"No!"

Contog straightened himself and walked around for a few moments. "Have you ever visited the ancient ruins?"

"Ancient ruins?" questioned Jack, his eyes blank.

The General strode back to the desk and peered again at the report. "So you really don't know anything, do you?"

"No. Please believe me, I don't know anything." Anxiety cut into him like a sharp knife.

"You're a real conundrum. You pose both an opportunity and a liability."

"What do you mean?"

"I don't know if you were sent here by the rebels. If so, you're a liability."

"But I don't know anything about a rebellion," protested Jack.

"That is why you pose a unique challenge," replied Contog. "Your ignorance doesn't mean that the rebels aren't using you. The fact that you can't be traced back to them makes you their best bet to infiltrate us." The general paused. "However, you also represent a great opportunity. You can be of use to us."

"In what way?"

"Don't worry about that," replied the chief of police, with a thin smile on his lips. The telephone rang.

"Please hold for President Kallin," announced a voice on the other end. The general stood at attention.

"General!" shouted a male voice at the other end. The speech sounded gruff, almost guttural—a voice like black Turkish coffee with unfiltered French cigarettes. It raised the hair on the back of Jack's neck.

"Yes, sir," replied Contog, saluting the phone's monitor.

"At ease, General," commanded the voice. The general relaxed. "Do you have the electronic jamming device on?"

"Yes, sir. Standard interrogation procedure." He pressed a button on his desk. The low hum disappeared.

"Who do you have?" demanded Kallin.

"I have a prisoner here. Shall I have him removed so we can talk in private?"

"Of course."

Contog called the policemen. They entered and escorted Jack out.

"What's this about your boys capturing a rebel not in our database?"

"He may be a rebel, or maybe not," countered the general.

"Then who the hell is he?" asked the president.

"We don't quite know."

"What do you mean?"

"He's a truly unique specimen."

"Can you match his DNA with anyone else's in the population?" asked Kallin.

"We can't find a match."

"How can that be? No mother, no father, brothers, cousins, nobody?"

"No. I don't know how that's possible. And neither does he."

"Then shoot the dog and get it over with," screeched the president.

"He might have some value to us."

"How?"

"He may be sent by the rebels. His lack of identity makes sure that he cannot be traced back to them. But we can play the same game. The rebels, even if they remove their DNA implants, are still in our database. What they don't have and neither do we, sir, is someone like him— that is, a complete original. We can use him against them and they wouldn't know it."

"Keep going."

"Sir, you mentioned that you suspect a mole in our administration. He can be useful to us if you understand what I mean."

"Yes, yes," agreed the president. "Damn good thinking."

"So what do you want me to do?"

"Bring him over to my country estate this evening. I want to see this motherless dog myself."

* * *

Kallin's country estate, End of Kali Yuga

In dull silence, General Contog and Jack camped next to each other on an expansive sofa while two accompanying policemen drooped on a close-by couch. Several sets of sofas, love seats and armchairs populated the large drawing room, each an island of luxury in a sea of expensive furniture. A garish green carpet spread out everywhere, over-red brocade drapes dressed the windows and marble statues stood interspersed at regular intervals. The effect of this ill-matched, ostentatious decor gave the impression not so much of luxury, but of a forced artificiality. Despite the attempt at class, it resulted in lifeless impersonalism. Several doors led out of the drawing room, emptying into different parts of the estate,

93

and at every entrance waited assorted butlers, maids and members of Kallin's security detail.

Jack and the general had arrived almost an hour ago, flying north over endless miles of monochromatic brown land. Low hills and flat plains stretched from one end of the horizon to the other, and occasionally, large industrial complexes sprouted up in the most unexpected areas. Jack saw no lakes, rivers or other bodies of water.

By the time they arrived at the estate, the sun had fully set. Jack sat bleary-eyed, having hardly any rest since his unexpected arrival in this world. The non-stop questions, the medical exams and the grilling by endless functionaries tired him. Everyone wanted to know his identity. After two days of this, he simmered.

A door opened at the other end of the vast room and a tall man wearing a shiny green suit, white shirt and a blue tie walked in, accompanied by a coterie of several men and women. The guards all jumped to their feet, saluted the man and shouted "Victory to the Hand of God!" General Contog stood up smartly and saluted. Jack rose unsteadily and looked around, baffled. *What the hell is a Hand of God*, he wondered. The man approached and examined him minutely from top to bottom. Jack felt unnerved, as if being stared right through.

The Hand of God had dark sandy hair speckled with gray and a thin white beard starting at his temples, running down his cheeks and around his chin. Hard, black, extremely observant, almost paranoiac, eyes darted to and fro, and he featured stubby hands, big but well-formed ears, and large, meaty lips. He carried himself in an aloof, even carnivorous manner, like a wolf, ever on guard, never letting anyone get too close. Obviously narcissistic like many powerful men, he projected himself as the center of all attention, which, of course, he was.

"Ha," he shouted in a dark voice, after several seconds of inspection. "You're really tall, aren't you? Almost as tall as me." He walked around. "Who are you?"

Again, the same inevitable question, asked at least a hundred times since his capture. Jack's frustration boiled over. He didn't care anymore.

"Who are you?" retorted Jack. The room suddenly chilled. The man pulled himself up. His eyes glared.

"I am the Hand of God," he shouted. "Who do you think I am?"

Jack stared right back. "Hey, I don't know," he replied loudly. "Maybe you're the president?" The green-suited man looked back with wide-eyed surprise.

"Ha! Ha!" he bellowed. The gathering breathed a sigh of relief and laughed along. He put his left arm around Jack's shoulders. "I like you, boy. You've got guts." He pointed to the others. "Unlike the rest of you sniveling idiots." They gasped. "My boy, on official business I am the president but at all other times I am the Hand of God. I am the Hand of God because God works through me. And only me." Jack opened his mouth, about to question him further. The others waited with bated breath. For once, reticence reigned. He said nothing.

The Hand of God shook his finger at him. "And don't ever question me again. Do you understand?"

"Yes sir," replied Jack. "I do." The Hand of God laughed and slapped Jack chummily on the back.

A young woman with short red hair and honey-colored eyes strode forward. "Oh, Hand of God," she commented, "he certainly is an interesting young man."

"This is Maya," President Kallin said. Maya looked straight into Jack's eyes. Jack found himself staring right back. Built like a brick outhouse and shorter than him by a good seven inches, she wore shiny black pants made of a silvery material with a matching jacket, a yellow sash around her neck and expensive red pumps. A black mole appeared above her left upper lip and dimples formed on flawless cheeks when she smiled. He looked her up and down and grinned. She beamed back, her teeth like pearls, her eyelashes flitting like tiny, black butterfly wings. Obviously she knew her way around men. Jack felt a chill. How long has it been, he wondered.

The president introduced several other members of the coterie who came by and shook Jack's hands. "This is my national security advisor," announced the Hand of God, pointing to a pale man with receding hair who observed Jack anxiously.

"So general," questioned the Hand of God, "what else did you bring?"

"President Kallin, here is the DNA identification report."

Kallin flipped through the tablet briefly before handing it to his national security advisor. "General," he commanded, "You are dismissed. I will keep this young man here." Contog saluted and quickly marched out, followed by the two police officers.

"Maya, show Jack the guest quarters," ordered the Hand of God.

"Of course, Hand of God. I will take him."

Kallin scanned at the rest of the group. His expansive mood instantly disappeared. "Why are you all hanging around? Don't you have anything to do?" he yelled. The group quickly scattered. Mumbling angrily under his breath, he stomped back to his office.

Maya led Jack through many corridors and past several intricately decorated rooms, her heels clacking on the marble floor. He suddenly became conscious of her sensuous lips, long neck, and full figure. She smiled and touched the tip of her tongue to her red upper lip.

"You have a lot of guts," she mentioned. "I'm amazed at what you said to the Hand of God."

"I'm not only brave, but also good looking," he replied, winking at her.

She laughed in amazement, shaking her head, her eyes wide open. She led him into a large, opulently decorated room with high ceilings and walls the color of clotted cream. A large white rug, black dressers, a night table, two red-brocade chairs and a chest of drawers with a wide mirror populated the room. Two large vases, each five feet tall, glazed with colorful geometric designs, stood at each side of a large bed. Two windows, narrow and high, stretched above the bedstead. She pulled back the bed cover and the blanket.

"Sleep well," she said. "Tomorrow is a big day."

Jack sat on the soft bed, breathing deeply with eyes closed, as Maya shut the door. The stress of the past few days slowly drained out of his body. His ran his hand over the satin sheets, letting the tension in his shoulders seep down his arms and out of his fingers. At last, he thought, I am in a better place. Standing slowly, he unbuttoned his shirt, removed his pants, shut off the lights and lay down. He pulled the soft blanket up over his chin and fell immediately into a thick, turgid, dreamless sleep.

The next morning, Maya knocked on his door. "Wake up," she said. "Breakfast will be in half an hour."

Feeling woozy, Jack dragged himself into the attached bathroom, quickly brushed his teeth and showered. He changed into fresh underwear, a black pair of pants, white shirt, black socks, a pair of new brown shoes, and rushed outside where a butler stood waiting. He guided Jack to the dining room.

A crowd of about fifteen people milled about. A large table, seating twenty, occupied the area and an outsized, intricate chandelier hung above. As Jack stood alone in the bustle near the door, Maya engaged in conversation with one of President Kallin's military advisors at the other end of the room. No one approached Jack, but instead cast long, sideways glances. He distinctly felt not just avoidance, but actual jealousy directed his way. Obviously, his gaining the Hand of God's favor so quickly did not sit well with them.

President Kallin walked into the room. The guests stood at attention and shouted, "Victory to the Hand of God."

The president displayed an expansive mood. "Come, come," he said, waving his hands. "Let's eat."

The Hand of God occupied the chair at one end of the table, Maya parked herself at his right and the national security advisor sat on his left. Jack found an empty seat halfway down. A tablecloth the color of antique ivory, cutlery of polished silver and plates of various sizes were displayed in his front, and despite it being breakfast, several courses would be served.

Toast with butter and jam came first, served by silent maids dressed in starched white gowns. Then arrived the hash browns. The Hand of God ate silently, keeping his eyes on the food. Some sort of unidentifiable salty, sticky meat comprised the next offering. Jack took a couple of bites and put it aside. The next course was another type of meat; small pieces swimming in gravy. It did not appeal to him either.

The diners engaged in soft chatter, their voices hardly rising over the clink and clatter of forks and knives. A subdued lot, their conversation revolved around the trivial, not much more than acknowledgments of each other's presence. Judging by the ease of their behavior, Jack realized that the more powerful members of the coterie sat closest to Kallin.

"So, Hand of God," asked Maya, "Are you going to Kallington today?"

"Yes," he replied, without looking up. "I have some business at the International Legislative Exchange."

"I'd like to come, if I may," she enquired perkily.

"Of course. I am leaving right after breakfast." Maya looked down the table, her eyes bright. Jack sensed not only her excitement for the trip but also her assertion of rank in the coterie's hierarchy.

Halfway through the meal the national security advisor's cell phone rang. He leaned over to Kallin and whispered. The president waved his hand, the man left, and butlers took away his dishes. Suddenly, a young blonde, sitting at the far end of the table, got up and occupied the empty space next to Kallin. Maya glared sharply. The blonde ignored her. Kallin kept eating, not acknowledging the woman's presence. She waited a few minutes before speaking.

"Oh, Hand of God," bubbled the young woman, her voice edged with anticipation. "I have never been to the Exchange with you." The diners looked keenly.

Kallin gazed at her. "Why do you want to come?"

"I'm your policy advisor," she replied.

"Actually, you're a policy intern," corrected Maya.

The blonde smiled sweetly back. "As you like. How can I understand policy if I don't know how the International Legislative Exchange works?" She stared at Kallin with large blue eyes. "Please. It would an educational experience for me."

"So you want to accompany me," he mused, stroking his thin beard, smiling.

"Yes! Of course."

Kallin turned to Maya. "Maya, I am going to take Jini with me this time. You can stay behind and take care of Jack." Maya turned a deep red. The blonde faced the diners and smiled. They grinned back.

"As you wish, oh Hand of God," Maya answered. She sat at the table, not eating her food. As soon as Kallin finished, she got up and left.

Chapter Thirteen

The Village of Mahavan, End of Satya Yuga

After breakfast, Parvata Rishi tended to his readings while Steve toured the community. He understood that farmers owned the majority of the huts facing the fields. Other homes, including Parvata Rishi's, lined the forest's perimeter while a few stood near the temple. It took him less than half an hour to circumambulate the village, but a lot longer to observe its inhabitants. Two hundred and fifty, perhaps three hundred souls of all types and ages, with the majority being young or middle-aged, along with a good number of children living in the utmost freedom and lovingly indulged by all members of the community regardless of parentage, lived in the place.

The village bustled; everyone worked hard, either in the fields or tending to their chores, and since their labor met their basic needs, they concentrated their spare time on the artistic, the cultural and the spiritual. The inhabitants showed remarkable honesty, sincerity and meaningfulness in their dealings and their conversations, eager to chat and commiserate with Steve on the loss of his mother and brother. Their genuineness struck Steve. No fakery, pretense or artificial emotions produced by brainless television shows crammed with canned laughter clouded their hearts.

He took lunch at the temple's priest house, welcomed by his wife and a gang of bright-eyed youngsters. The pujari, a middle-aged man with a cheerful disposition, introduced himself. "My name is Vishnuyasha and this is my wife Sumati." He looked around. "My son is somewhere around here."

As he pressed his palms together in greeting, a young boy, all mischievous smiles and youthful energy, rushed in

100

and stared at Steve, wide-eyed. The food was delicious and the company of the family, delightful.

After lunch, Steve explored the surroundings. He headed along the path out of the village, following the river bank until it came to the hill with the baobab tree and, instead of following the trail up the hill, continued along the thin path disappearing into the dense forest. Immediately, the omnipresent green fusion enveloped him. Large-trunked, broad-leafed trees surrounded him with their vast, silent fastness, observing him like ageless witnesses. Their sheer profusion, stretching out in all directions in such inestimable distances boggled his imagination. Was it possible, one day, for these forests to indeed disappear?

The path fizzled out, replaced by a barely recognizable trail. He climbed a large boulder, looked up at the canopy of leaves and thought of his distance travelled—from his family, his home and the streets of the Kansas City. They seemed so far away, so unreal. Surprised, he arched his eyebrows. Leaving the settlement and exploring the jungle by himself, let alone traveling to another yuga—this resembled Jack's persona, not his.

The thought of his brother filled his heart with a vague uneasiness. He regretted his anger, but still, Jack's treatment of Mom rankled him. He immediately pictured her, her eyes smiling through her glasses. He straightened his back, his heart pinched and tears emerged—the grief pure and untinged with any other emotion, whether regret, unhappiness, unsaid words or bitter feelings. The hurt lasted only a few seconds. Her disappearance, though final in one sense, didn't drag him into overwhelming sorrow. Mere death couldn't separate them.

He noticed something moving among the trees. He wiped his eyes. Someone was walking toward the settlement and he quickly distinguished it to be one of the women. As the figure moved closer, Steve recognized a certain familiarity in the shape, the straightness of the back and the suppleness of the limbs. It was Shanti!

"Hello Shanti," he shouted.

She strolled up to him, balancing a load of wood on her head, swaying gently to and fro. Her eyes showed slight surprise, but no hesitation or reticence.

"Hello," Shanti replied, smiling. "What are you doing here?"

"Just walking in the forest. I need the exercise."

She laughed. "If you want exercise, try collecting firewood every day!"

"Maybe I will," he answered, jumping off. "Let me carry your load."

Shanti turned red. "No! This is my service! My father will wonder what I am doing if I let you carry my firewood!"

Steve backed off.

"I've been doing this for years," she explained. "I'm used to carrying these loads."

She lifted her hands above her head and holding the bundle, swung her hips out. The wood, tied with a grass rope, came quickly off and she gently deposited it on the ground with a flick of her wrists. She leaned against a tree and faced him, arms bent back, pushing against the trunk, her hips barely touching it.

She breathed hard with her mouth slightly open. Despite the appearance of effortlessness, carrying firewood was obviously a strenuous exercise. She pushed her long hair off her forehead and wiped her face with the edge of her bright green sari. The green canopy above them, the hushed silence and the darkness of the forest created the effect of a private, personal space. He leaned against the boulder as neither spoke for a long time.

Her presence felt powerful, palpable. Though several inches shorter, she remained, nevertheless, commanding. Did a secret strength lie in her limbs, a potency hidden behind a veil of modesty, like that of the jacaranda tree which stands tall, straight and slender and covers its head with a shroud of delicate purple blossoms, yet is able to withstand the severest winds? Or did her mysterious origins now color his imagination? She seemed regal, more noticeable now that she dressed simply and lived plainly among mortals, like the sun which glows more brightly while shining through low clouds on the horizon.

Shanti finally spoke. "Where are you from?"

He realized that he, with his light skin and dark blond hair, must seem as exotic to her as she to him. "I'm from Kansas City. Wherever that might be now."

"Kansas...?" she repeated, uncomprehendingly.

"In Kali Yuga, many, many years from now, in a land called America, a very large village named Kansas City will exist," he clarified, using terminology familiar to her.

She giggled, imitating the sounds he made. "Kan...Kansas City? That's a funny name for a village!"

Steve laughed with her. "That's true. It is a funny name for a village."

"What is it like in Kali Yuga?" she enquired, her curiosity aroused.

Steve took a minute to figure out an answer. "Well, we have cars, televisions, air conditioners—you know, that kind of stuff."

Shanti kept silent. Obviously, none of those meant anything to her.

Steve changed the subject. "Do you have any brothers or sisters?"

"No. At least not in this world."

"What do you mean?"

She sighed and her eyelids flickered. "My mother is an *apsara*. She lives in *Gandharva Loka*, one of the heavenly planets. Its inhabitants lead extremely long lives, possess great beauty and are very talented singers and artists. There, she may have other children."

Steve knotted his eyebrows. Heavenly planets?

"Many heavenly planets exist," she explained, "as do many earthly planets and hellish ones. In fact, many universes are present, not just this one." Steve remained silent, absorbing the magnitude of the cosmology.

"Why did your mother leave you?" he asked, bringing the discussion to the immediate.

"From what I understand, I have a destiny to fulfill on this Earth planet."

Steve's eyes brightened with interest. "And what is that?"

Shanti's eyes clouded. "I don't know. Maybe my father does, but he hasn't told me." She looked away. "I think you are so fortunate to have a brother, to retain memories of a mother. You don't know what it's like to be an only child all these years."

Steve looked at her, surprised, taken aback by her admission of loneliness. She seemed to be so content. Thinking about it though, he realized the difficulties she faced, first of possessing such unusual origins and secondly, of sharing no siblings. Despite having such a wonderful father, young women need mothers as well. She suddenly seemed like a vulnerable girl.

"Yes," he replied. "I am indeed fortunate to have a brother." He looked down and sighed.

"Why are you sad?"

"I don't know where he is. I need to find him. And I miss my mother."

Shanti sympathized with him. "I guess we're the same. We're both missing mothers and siblings, we both come from other places and we both have destinies to fulfill."

Steve nodded his head. She very much spoke the truth.

She got up. "It's getting dark. I want to be at the temple for the Sandhya arti, the evening worship. I don't want to be late."

"Let me help you," he offered. He picked up the bundle and settled it gently on her head. Its weight, as well as the realization of the expert bodily movements required to transport it for long distances, surprised him.

They strolled to the village, side by side, happily engaged in conversation.

* * *

Parvata Rishi spent an hour each day teaching Steve hatha yoga, with its emphasis on the *asanas*; the practices and philosophy of *ashtanga yoga* and its stress on moral

104

codes, namely the *yamas* and *niyamas*; and the nine processes of *bhakti yoga*, the yoga of devotion. A few days after his arrival, Shanti asked him for help. "Do you want to do some *karma yoga*?"

"Yes," he replied hesitantly. "What is that?"

"Karma yoga is selfless service—work done without thought of personal gain."

"Okay."

"Today, we're cooking for the temple. The meal will be offered to the Deities and then to the community at lunch. Let's make some *puris*." Steve washed his hands and followed her into the kitchen. She placed a large curved copper pan half-filled with ghee on the wood stove, pulled a bowl from the shelf and poured several measures of flour into it. To that, she added salt and water and started mixing. Steve stood by, writing it all down in his book.

"What are you doing?" she questioned.

"I'm making notes on how much flour, water, and salt you added."

Shanti smiled. "You'll never make puris that way."

"What do you mean?"

"Put the book away, come here and knead the dough." Steve regarded her uncertainly and rolled up his kurta sleeves. He slowly and softly laid his hands on the dough.

"Don't be afraid of it," Shanti laughed. "Just squeeze and roll the dough." Steve kneaded it more vigorously. "How does it feel?" she questioned after some time.

"Kind of hard."

"Add some more water." Steve took a bit of water, poured it into the bowl and mixed it again. After a minute he stopped.

"What are you doing?"

"I'm finished."

She chuckled. She detached a small piece of dough and handed it to him. "Pull it apart." It tore easily.

"Kneading makes the dough elastic. Continue until it's ready." Steve grimaced. This was harder than expected. After some time, Shanti stopped him.

"Check it now," she stated. This time the dough stretched well, being soft and supple.

"Perfect," she remarked. "Let's make some puris." Following her directions, he pulled off bits of dough, rolled them into balls with his fingers, flattened them with his palms and shaped them with a wooden roller into round, flat disks each about the size of his hand.

"Excellent," said Shanti, encouragingly. "Now slip it into the ghee." Holding one of the disks at the edge of the metal pan, he slid it neatly into the hot ghee. She gently pushed it down with a ladle until it puffed up, round and smooth. Making sure to brown both sides, she lifted the cooked puri out of the pan and set it in a serving container.

"You can finish the rest."

Fascinated, Steve didn't take long to fry them and, shortly, a small mound of puris stood ready to serve. Parvata Rishi walked into the kitchen.

"Look," exclaimed Steve. "I cooked all these myself!"

"And he did it without using his book!" Shanti proclaimed. They both laughed and took the puris outside to be offered and served.

Chapter Fourteen

The Village of Mahavan, End of Satya Yuga

The big day arrived. The long hours spent in the fields harvesting crops and the toil of threshing grains ended as the bounty of the land demanded labor for only eight months of the year. Peacocks danced in the trees and wind blew fresh from the mountains. *Kartik*, the autumn season, the time for festivals, music, song, dance and pilgrimages, had finally appeared.

They awoke early and took their baths. Excitement and urgency filled the air. Steve and Shanti went over the bundles of clothes, provisions, and the parchments that the rishi insisted on taking. Foodstuffs—dried, pickled or preserved; prepared in large quantities, stood ready. Each party had grains tied in large bundles, to be transported by cows. Steve's theoretical approach to life, ingrained from living in a culture disconnected from nature, amused Shanti, as did his crude attempts at preparing food, starting fire or weaving cloth. Despite his clumsiness, she carefully taught him the practical crafts, always persevering until he got it right.

The entire village gathered at the banyan tree for the customary early morning meeting: part spiritual discussion, part worship and some scheduling of daily chores. Only fifty or so villagers would embark on the pilgrimage; the rest, for various reasons, stayed behind.

The rishi spoke. He planned to follow the course of the river as far as possible into the mountains. The journey promised to be pleasant, as forests, providing fuel and shelter, bordered the river, and the path, fairly clear of entangling undergrowth. Such a pilgrimage had not been attempted in this Satya Yuga. The journey would last at least a month, maybe more, whereas most of the other seasonal pilgrimages to the nearby holy rivers took only a week. Difficulties and hardships were expected.

"Due to the quality of time and owing to our long lives, we are able to meditate for thousands of years at a stretch," he mentioned. "As you know, the prescribed spiritual practice, the sadhana, for this age is deep meditation. In Treta Yuga, the next age, the recommended practice is the performance of elaborate yajnas, fire rituals. In the third age, Dwapara Yuga, the stipulated practice is the opulent worship of the Deity form of God in temples. Finally, in Kali Yuga, the age of degradation, the specified spiritual process is *sankirtana*, the chanting of names of God, either solitarily within the heart, or congregationally."

Steve remembered hearing this during his stay at the Hare Krishna temple.

"It is the least demanding of all practices, but surprisingly, even this simple process will prove difficult for most people. Finally, at the end of Kali Yuga, all spiritual practices will die out."

Steve raised his hand. "Why is that?"

"Because Kali Yuga is characterized by sick hurry and divided aims. Things divide as time passes. In Satya Yuga, we have only one class of people, the *brahmanas* or spiritualists, and only one culture, *varnashrama dharma*, spiritual culture. In Kali Yuga, innumerable divisions in society will appear along with an incredible number of occupations, most of them unhealthy. Humanity, once singular, will split into many competing parts, and by acting against the common welfare, destroy itself."

"How can we protect ourselves?" asked Steve.

"That's the reason for this pilgrimage. For you, this age seems free from any contamination. But for those of us living long lives, I assure you, we can feel the end of Satya Yuga in our very bodies. We could meditate for tens and tens of thousands of years, but now it is becoming difficult even for those expert in this practice.

"We are going to a sacred valley named Shambala. There, our spiritual practices will be protected and our teachings preserved. Young man, you are very fortunate to participate in something that few have the good fortune to see."

Steve stared at the roots of the banyan tree. The discussion with Parvata Rishi raised more questions than answers. Would Jack be at Shambala? A dull fear and dread suddenly arose in the pit of his stomach. He shuddered. Steve couldn't give meaning to this feeling— did thinking about Jack produce this sensation? How fortunate he was to be in Satya Yuga before the eventual unraveling of humanity! Did this cause fear, that he would be forced to leave the shelter of this time and place?

After the meeting, the villagers took a hearty morning meal and gathered at the temple where a mood of sadness, a feeling of going away and leaving behind a close, dear friend, reigned. They observed one last darshan of the Deities, considered to be the lords of the village, before setting off.

They lined up at the village's entrance, the elders first, then the single men and women. Of the families, only Visnuyasha, his wife Sumati and their son joined them, the pilgrimage in the mountains considered too demanding for children. Steve stood towards the end of the line next to Shanti. Suddenly, several men, gaunt, long-haired, with an other-worldly look in their eyes, emerged from the jungle like spirits materializing from some ethereal place. Their appearance surprised him, but the pilgrims showed genuine pleasure at their appearance.

"Who are they?" he whispered to Shanti.

"These are the yogis living in the Tapovan forest. Some of them have been meditating, standing or sitting in the same asana for over thirty thousand years. Their presence in our pilgrimage is most unusual and is a great blessing." She clasped her palms together and bowed down toward their direction. Steve followed her example.

Accompanied by the clash of cymbals and the boom of mridangas, they started at a leisurely pace. They chanted, women with trilling, melodious voices and the men with deep, commanding tones, the prayers to Narasimha deva,

God in his form as Guardian, beseeching his protection during the difficult weeks ahead.

The autumn season brought dry, pleasant weather and they followed the path along the river bank which ran between sun and shade, between forest and grass, between water and land. Steve glanced at Shanti. She walked in an unhurried, easy to maintain, measured gait, a necessity for conserving energy during the long journey. The dappled sunshine danced over her body as she moved her limbs rhythmically to an inner beat only she heard. His movements reflected hers, his arms swung just as hers did and his steps abided hers. He felt contentment at her side, as if they had spent all their lives next to each other, as if meant to be thus always. Uncomplicated and natural, her smile came readily and often, and her speech remained artless and unaffected. He only had to be himself, with no need to impress—she needed nothing, since who she was and what she had were available for everyone to see. Complete, and rather than giving or taking, she only shared.

They walked along the path, glancing sideways at each other, smiling and chatting, through the uncharted miles and uncounted days, always stepping up toward the snow-capped mountains on the distant horizon.

* * *

On Pilgrimage, End of Satya Yuga

The rishi stuck to his promise to Steve, but the early morning yoga lessons went slowly. He started with the less challenging *asanas*, but yoga forced Steve to approach his mind and body in unfamiliar ways. He took careful notes and studied them every evening, but the *sadhana* of yoga remained problematic. One evening, Shanti came by as Steve sat near a bonfire on the dry sandy river bank, puzzling through his notes from the morning's class. She glanced at his handbook, filled with sketches of different asanas, descriptions of the movements and of the muscles involved.

110

"You won't learn yoga that way," she mentioned gently.

"Why not?"

"Yoga can't be approached by the mind."

Steve laughed incredulously. "How else do you to understand things, if not with your brain?"

Shanti contemplated his answer. "Come," she said, "let's practice yoga for a while."

"Sure."

"We can start with the *Savasana*, the dead man's pose."

"What's that?"

"Just lie down on the ground, imitating a dead man."

"That's easy," he laughed.

"This asana can be the easiest or the most difficult," Shanti revealed. Steve lay down on the sand and closed his eyes. And waited.

"What do we do now?"

Shanti giggled. "It's been what, a few ticks of time?"

"Maybe," he answered sheepishly. "But I lay here like a dead man."

"No. You thought that you lay like a dead man."

"What do you mean?"

Shanti pulled her dark hair behind her ears. "The point of this asana is not to think. A dead man doesn't think. Slow your breath as much as possible, keep still and loosen your muscles. Let your energy flow out of your fingertips, your toes, your head."

"How do I do that?"

"Very easily. Listen to your body."

He knit his eyebrows, still puzzled.

"Transfer your consciousness out of your mind, where it now is, and into your toes, your fingers, your breath. This is called listening to your body." Steve regarded her dubiously.

"Go ahead. Try."

Steve once again lay flat on the ground and tried shutting his mind. Remembering her advice, he concentrated on his fingertips, loosening them, let them lie

111

flat, allowing his nerves to relax, gently pushing feeling and energy out of them. He repeated the process with his toes, then moved his consciousness into his lungs, becoming aware solely of the air being impelled and expelled from his chest. The longer he did this, the slower and more relaxed his breathing became. He continued for some time until his mind allowed no further relaxation. Once again, thoughts crept into his brain: this morning's breakfast, the sound of the river, the crackle of the fire. He opened his eyes.

Shanti smiled, her teeth gleaming in the dark, the fire reflecting on her face. "That's better," she exclaimed. "Actually, the point of *Savasana* is to transfer the mind outside your awareness. Advanced yogis can remain in this asana for hundreds, even thousands of years, hardly ever breathing, moving their consciousness completely out their bodies and into the astral plane, to return upon will."

"Wow! This asana is way too difficult for me!" he exclaimed.

"Okay. Let us just meditate." Steve got up and sat on the ground in padmasana, his legs crossed.

"That's fine. Now close your eyes and follow me." She started by controlling her breath. Steve moved his awareness into his chest, becoming mindful of the air filling his lungs, of its leaving his body, feeling the energy circulating in his heart. He continued this for several long minutes.

"Now breathe through your kidneys."

"Through my kidneys?"

"When you breathe, keep your awareness centered on your kidneys. Transfer the feeling of breathing over to them."

"Let me try," he replied, doubtfully. As he breathed, he moved his consciousness to his kidneys, feeling energy enter his organs with each intake and experiencing energy leave upon breathing out.

"Is this what you mean by listening to your body?"

"Yes. This is one way of listening to your body."

112

He opened his eyes. "Wow!" he exclaimed. "I think I'm getting the hang of this."

"Good! The more you engage in sadhana, the easier and deeper it gets."

"I can see that!"

"The key is trusting yourself. Our minds, hearts, and bodies keep telling us things but we're too busy to listen. In Kali Yuga, one connects to the world and to one's body with mostly the mind. But knowledge is not always just linear nor to be realized in only one way. Here in Satya Yuga we are much more connected not just with this world, but also to our inner natures."

"So the key is in believing myself, to trust what my body and mind are telling me?"

"And your heart," she added.

Steve had a moment of sudden realization. It was true that his heart told him something ever since he met Shanti just a few short weeks ago, something he pushed aside. He looked into her innocent eyes, her ready smile and her glowing face. Yes, she spoke the truth. He hadn't listened to his heart, not trusted himself. Now he heard it loud and clear. If he wanted her, he just needed to be himself. He didn't need to write it down, to analyze it.

Steve took out his notebook. "I won't be needing this anymore," he declared and tossed it into the fire.

Chapter Fifteen

Kallington, End of Kali Yuga

Acres of red and black stone, criss-crossed with pathways of gray asphalt, and large white fountains limply gurgling shallow basins of tepid water covered President Kallin's hundred-acre country estate. Pillars, arches, and porticos lined the outside of the faux Greco-Roman style mansion. Jack wandered about aimlessly for an hour, then rested on a stone bench under one of the porticos, leaned back and peered into the sky. The weather turned muggy and cloudy, but again, without rain, and the sun shone dully through the red atmosphere. Bored, he replayed the past two weeks at the estate, but his memory prior to his appearance made no effort to return. His past remained a secret and while it intrigued and occasionally bothered him, did not pull him into despondency. A sudden noise turned his head.

"Oh, hello," Maya exclaimed, startled to see him.

"Hello, Maya."

An awkward silence followed. She quickly gathered herself and made to leave.

"No. Please sit down." Maya hesitated, then sat next to him and crossed her knees. A tight red skirt with a big black belt accentuated the curves of her body and a sparkling, red ruby necklace lay around her neck. The sun danced on the flickering ends of her flame-red hair, burned golden on her full cheeks and shone in her amber eyes.

"You're what, nineteen years old?" he asked, winking. She laughed incredulously, lowered her head and cocked her eyes in askance. Their previous socializations included only occasional meals and insignificant conversations.

"I bet you say that to every woman," she remarked.

"What women?" he asked, with large innocent eyes.

"I'm thirty-five," she finally stated.

114

"I'm also thirty-five," he said flatly.

"Oh really?"

"Actually, no. I don't know my age," he laughed. He tapped his head as if to demonstrate its emptiness. She smiled, revealing perfect teeth, her dimples deep exclamation points on either side of her soft red lips. She looked ravishing. He couldn't help taking a risk.

"You know, you're really good looking," he stated, looking right into her eyes.

"Well, thank you," she replied without feeling, looking away, re-crossing her legs.

Jack picked up his courage. "I really like your company. I'd like to see more of you."

She stared at him questioningly. "Listen. I'm very flattered by your attention, but…."

"What?" interrupted Jack, pretending to be offended. "You don't like me?"

Maya rolled her eyes. "That's got nothing to do with it."

"So what is it?"

"I belong to Kallin. The fact is, I'm his mistress."

"I didn't know that," he lied.

Maya laughed. "You're a pretty bad liar!"

"I'm serious," insisted Jack. "But you can't fault me for trying."

Maya's smile disappeared. She got up and faced him. "I'll give you some advice," she declared. "Keep away from me."

"I'm not afraid of Kallin if that's what you mean."

Maya snorted with amazement. "You're either very brave or very stupid."

"Maybe both," cracked Jack.

Maya didn't buy into his humor. "You don't know anything about Kallin, do you?"

"Well, I do know one thing."

"What's that?"

"You may be his mistress, but you're not the only one." A shadow crossed Maya's face. "I saw how he looked at that blonde at the breakfast table."

Maya's eyes flashed. "That's none of your damn business."

"Sorry, sorry, I know. But I couldn't help notice your hurt."

Maya glanced away. Her eyelids fluttered. "So what can you do? That's something I need to deal with."

Jack jumped up and faced her. "I know I can't do anything, but I can be here as a friend." He reached out and held her arm. Maya snatched it away.

"No, you can't," she snapped. "And if you know what's good for you, you'll keep your hands and eyes to yourself."

She quickly walked away. Jack watched her backside sway as her high heels tattooed the asphalt. *I don't care who she belongs to,* he concluded. *The Hand of God is in Kallington and I'm here with her.* The situation turned interesting. He smiled. Maya would certainly be a challenge.

* * *

At the Estate, End of Kali Yuga

Maya sat alone in the living room, just after breakfast, thumbing impatiently through a magazine. Kallin left her not just worried, jealous and miserable, but also stir-crazy. Life in the city provided excitement, not the boredom of the country. Jack also showed frustration. Their social lives involved, since the episode in the garden, nothing more than meetings at breakfast, occasionally dinners and a few small conversations.

The phone rang. "Yes, hello, hello!"

"It's me."

"Victory to the Hand of God," she replied, excitedly.

"I hear you want to talk," he mentioned. She must have left at least a dozen messages. "So what do you want to chat about?"

"I...I've been here for three weeks. You've never left me alone like this."

116

A pause ensued. "You'll have to wait a little longer but, assuredly, you will come shortly."

"But...."

"Those are my instructions," stated Kallin, cutting her off.

"Of course, oh Hand of God," she agreed. "I'm extremely frustrated. With you gone, there's absolutely nothing to do."

"How's Jack?"

"He's also bored."

"I have an idea. Why don't you take our friend on a picnic? A jaunt in the country will cheer you both up."

"Okay," she replied glumly. She waited a few moments. "Is Jini there?"

"Yes, Yes," he remarked, somewhat impatiently. "She's doing a wonderful job."

Maya took a deep breath and calmed down. "That's good," she said softly. She mentally kicked herself. Why did she let that blonde outmaneuver her? She had taken care of women like her before. But this one seemed to have brains, not just a pretty face.

A female voice interrupted the conversation. "I have to go," said Kallin. "I will call you next week."

Maya hung up the phone and hunched her shoulders as tears rolled down her cheeks. Everything she had worked for lay in jeopardy.

Jack marched into the room, slamming the door behind him. "Dammit! I'm fed up," he shouted. "I don't know how long I can take this. I need to get out!" Maya turned away and wiped her face.

"What is it?" he questioned.

"Nothing. Nothing at all."

"It's that woman Jini, isn't it?"

Maya nodded her head slowly.

"Don't worry," Jack replied sympathetically, "everything will work out."

"Oh really?" she cried, her hands clenched. "How do you know that?"

117

Jack walked up to her and rested his hand on her shoulders. "Look at me." Maya hesitantly lifted her eyes. "Why the hell are you crying? Don't worry about the future."

"You don't know my situation! I'll lose everything and end up on the street."

"Look, everything can change in a moment. Kallin could ask you to come tomorrow."

Maya looked up hopefully. "You think so?"

"Of course! Live for the moment. Life is meant for fun, not worry." He pulled her up from the sofa. "If you get all serious, then you'll just become depressed." He grinned. "Be happy!"

"Thanks." Maya took a deep breath and smiled. Hope shone on her face again. "By the way, I have some good news. Tomorrow, we'll go on a picnic."

"All right!" he yelled and, in a completely spontaneous gesture, grabbed and twirled her around, her feet completely off the ground. Maya tittered, beholding him with surprise.

* * *

The transporter, resembling a big black limousine, waited in front of the mansion. The estate's security commander, a short, rough sort of man dressed in a black cap, green fatigues, and shiny black shoes, waited with the vehicle's rear door open. After Jack and Maya entered, he shut the door, walked over to the driver's side and climbed in, while two soldiers in brown combat uniforms squeezed in beside him. He turned the key and the vehicle silently raced along the driveway, floating a couple feet above the asphalt, and twisted onto the main road. Outside the estate, the countryside turned dry and featureless, a desert of blowing dust, showing no signs of rain ever falling.

Maya, stunning in a short white dress with large red polka dots and a white sailor's hat with a maroon sash around its brim, bubbled with excitement. Jack gulped.

118

They hardly saw each other for more than a few minutes a day, mostly, he realized, because she kept away on purpose. But now, she had no excuse. Jack shared her eagerness. Being with her brought fun and adventure, and exploring a new world through an attractive woman's eyes made him feel alive. He noticed small things; the manner in which dimples formed on her cheeks when she smiled, how her legs slanted together as she sat, her expressive eyebrows and the way she cocked her head when peering at him.

"We're going to have a barbecue!" she exclaimed.

"Great! I love barbecues."

As the vehicle traveled over the miles, Maya excitedly pointed out objects along the way, but after an hour her enthusiasm died down and she leaned back to snooze. The monotonous, bleak countryside lulled Jack into a dull stupor and he stared blankly out the window, unheeding the passage of time as the sun peeped intermittently through the dull haze.

The commander suddenly interrupted his reverie. "Look," he shouted, pointing excitedly at an object on a hill above the road. Maya jerked awake and peered out the window.

"Stop the car!" she yelled. The commander immediately applied the brakes. He rushed madly out, straightened his crumpled clothes and hastily opened the rear door. The two soldiers were already scrambling up the hill and Maya quickly followed. Jack peered up but saw nothing out of the ordinary.

Maya waved excitedly. "Come! Look."

He rushed up, jostled his way into the circle, and saw, for the first time, the object of excitement: an evergreen, about four feet high with a brown furrowed trunk, its bark peeling off and its needles covered by a thick layer of the omnipresent dust, struggling to gain a foothold on the side of a depressing little hill. The commander pushed his hat back and whistled in admiration. Jack didn't understand their elation—it was just another tree and not a very impressive one at that.

"Have you ever seen such a tree?" demanded Maya, wide-eyed. Jack stood dumb. The commander smiled broadly like a hunter spying a ten-point stag, basking in their admiration.

"Now, that's a tree!" he declared.

"What is so great about it?" asked Jack.

"What do you mean?"

"It isn't much of a tree. I've seen many trees over fifty feet tall."

Maya gazed at him round-eyed. The commander and the soldiers stared at each other, eyebrows knotted, then burst out in laughter. Maya joined the merriment, her teeth shining like a string of pearls. The commander slapped Jack heartily on the back.

"Sir, this is the biggest tree I ever saw. I saw one at a museum before, but this is my first catch out in the wild."

Suddenly the realization hit Jack. He hadn't seen a single tree at the estate, the countryside, nor in Kallington. Except for a few forlorn weeds, neither a single bush nor flower grew anywhere. He scratched his forehead. What made him think that trees grew so high and so densely? His eyes gave him witness: the evidence showed otherwise. Something was definitely strange.

"Pull it up," ordered the commander. The soldiers rushed forward and grabbing the tree, tugged at it with all their might. The tree's roots extended deep and though loosened, refused to yield. The struggle continued for fifteen minutes until finally the soldiers surrendered, their uniforms covered with dust and sweat.

"Enough," yelled the commander. The soldiers immediately stepped back, looking at the ground in shame.

"Get me your firearm," he ordered one of the soldiers. Subdued, the man sprinted to the vehicle and returned with his weapon. The commander cocked the bolt of the rifle and taking aim, let forth a burst of automatic fire straight at the base of the tree. The forlorn evergreen keeled over and crashed into the dust in defeat. Jack jumped back, shocked. The bizarre, naked execution of the plant jolted him.

The soldiers shouted in excitement, heaved the tree over their shoulders and ran triumphantly down the sooty hillside. They posed, one after the other, with boots on the tree, rifles in hands, taking photos. The commander snapped orders and the soldiers opened up the trunk, produced a length of rope, threw the tree on the car's top and tied it down securely, ensuring that the tree's tip overlooked the car's roof just as an arrowhead extends in front of a bow.

They re-entered the car and the commander, smiling broadly, his military cap cocked back, climbed into the driver's seat and drove off, the tree strapped overhead, looking, for all the world, like a bizarre trophy. They kept motoring through the barren, monotonous countryside for a several more hours until the sun perched directly overhead.

Jack's stomach complained. "What about lunch?" he asked.

"We'll be there shortly," Maya responded. She knocked on the glass partition. "Take a right on the next road," she commanded.

"Yes, ma'am!" barked the driver.

A few minutes later the road appeared and, immediately, a sharp odor cut into Jack's nostrils, reminding him of ammonia or laundry bleach mixed with the nauseatingly putrid stench of outhouses with overflowing septic tanks, growing stronger as the car moved on. The others noticed it, but instead of being repulsed, the smell seemed to whet their appetites. Maya perked up and licked her lips while the soldiers showed signs of impatience, their stomachs growling.

They pulled up at the doors of a very large rectangular building constructed of gray concrete, completely windowless and topped with a metal roof, set in a low depression, framed by small hills and deep gullies. As the soldiers opened the passenger doors crisply, the commander ran over and banged on the building's metal doors.

As Jack stepped out, an unbelievable, overpowering stench almost knocked him out. He fell to his knees and staggered back to the car, resting his upper body on the back seat. His head spun and he held his breath as long as possible before gasping in great big gulps of air.

Maya stepped out and took a deep breath. "Ahh," she sighed. "Isn't it wonderful to be in the country?"

The repeated banging on the building's doors produced a huge man with a very ruddy, almost pink, complexion, a large head topped with a shock of pale blond hair, small beady blue eyes, a grossly extended belly, and he looked just like a pig. Upon seeing them, he immediately stiffened and, bobbing his head up and down, obsequiously invited them into the building.

Jack's head finally cleared and he slowly staggered up and entered the building. A blast of hot stinking air, as if he had walked into a furnace, greeted him and an incredible assortment of shrieks, screams and howls filled his ears. After several long minutes, with eyes finally focused, Jack discerned thousands of small cages, one upon the other, reaching the ceiling and extending all the way to the other end of the long building, each containing a single animal. Long, narrow troughs brought food to the animals, but no mechanism removed the excrement. The beasts passed urine and dung on others below until all were completely caked with a thick layer of stinking feces.

Jack panted, held his nose, and gasped. The place resembled a scene from hell. He jumped in fright and joined the others as they walked down an aisle. The commander led the way, pointing out choice animals. One would be lunch.

Jack stopped by a cage and closely examined the animal. It resembled a large goat, thickly encrusted with excrement, shrieking and bellowing incessantly, lips raw and bruised, its wild red eyes giving a shocking setting to soft brown pupils. Jack examined its head, legs, and haunches and stopped in shock when he spied its udders, recognizable beyond doubt! This strange, unhappy beast was actually a cow! He recoiled in alarm and ran to meet the rest of the party. He angled up beside Maya.

"Did you know that these are cows?"

"Yes. And they're quite tasty."

She dumbfounded him. "But look at them. They are so small. And they stink."

Maya looked at him quizzically. "What do you mean, they stink?"

"It smells like an open sewer here!"

"Oh! I know what you mean," she exclaimed. "You're smelling their food! Kallington's main sewer runs right into this farm. They dry it, cut it into pellets and feed it to the animals."

"Don't cows eat grass?" he asked dumbly.

She glared at him in surprise. "Grass! What's grass? You are a strange man. You're always saying something outlandish. Cows eat garbage and that's what they've always eaten."

"What about water?"

"Oh, we mine that. We're forced to drill maybe seven or eight miles. It's the only sweet water left. It rains once every ten years but we can't drink that."

Browbeaten, he meekly followed her. Nothing made sense. What did cows eat? What on earth made him think that they ate grass? He didn't know the answer, but still, something felt quite not right. At this moment, he knew absolutely nothing about cows, but one thing he did know—he had completely lost his appetite.

They caught up to the commander. He'd selected an animal for the afternoon meal. The two soldiers excitedly roped the bellowing, struggling animal and led it out of the building. They marched in a line to the top of a nearby hill, the soldiers first, dragging the rickety-legged, stumbling beast, followed by the commander wielding a smile on his face and a machete in his right hand, and finally by Jack and Maya, their footsteps raising the soft dust. Arriving on top, the soldiers pulled out a few fuel bricks from their rations and set them alight.

One soldier held the back legs of the animal and the other the head. The commander raised his long sharp knife and deftly brought it down on the quivering cow's dung encrusted collar. It rolled its maddened eyes and gave an unearthly howl as its head separated from its body, ending its cruel, short, miserable life. The soldiers jumped up and down in excitement and tugged at their tight neck collars.

The commander passed his tongue over his lips, smacking them impatiently. He pushed his hand into the dead animal's neck and pulled. Much to Jack's surprise, a string of sausages tumbled out. The soldiers jumped upon them and using assorted knives or pieces of metal, roasted them over the flames.

Jack stood hesitantly. It was the strangest thing he had ever seen. "Are they all like that?" he questioned.

"No," replied Maya. "This is a sausage cow. We also have steak cows, hamburger cows, hot-dog cows, and so on."

"That's amazing."

"I suppose. A long time back, they engineered all farm animals that way. At least, that's what I've heard."

The commander looked at Jack from between mouthfuls of meat. He pulled up a sausage from the pile lying on the ground and stuck it on a large knife. He broiled and handed it over.

Jack inspected the piece of meat hesitantly. It stank horribly but didn't differ from any other piece of meat at the estate. He couldn't get the face of the pitiful, mad cow out of his mind. The sausage stopped resembling food but rather embodied the suffering of the unhappy animal.

He felt everyone's eyes staring at him. Despite the revulsion, he closed his eyes and bit off a big chunk of flesh and swallowed it. It felt and tasted like plastic and slid quickly down his throat. The commander smiled greasily.

"Aren't barbecues great?" asked Maya.

Finally, except for a thin bag of skin and bones, nothing remained of the animal. The commander rolled the remains into a square, brought it over his head and pitched it as hard as possible. It fell deep into the gully, tumbling to the bottom and finally nestled up against a small boulder, trailed by a minute avalanche of gray dust which gently buried the remains of the dead animal.

Chapter Sixteen

President Kallin's Country Estate, End of Kali Yuga
The vehicle dropped them off and Jack and Maya strolled around the building and entered the back garden. The night's cool air drove away the day's mugginess and stars sparkled in the sky. Except for the bubbling of the spouting fountains, all remained quiet.

"Thank you for your companionship today. It's been a long while since I spent a whole day with a man. I'd forgotten how nice that feels," Maya revealed, being one of those women who couldn't remain happy for long without a man's company. Being the mistress of a distant man must be a pretty lonely job, thought Jack. She catered to Kallin's desires, not he to hers. *This may be easier than I expected*, he decided.

The moonlight revealed her sad face.

"Are you still upset about Jini?" he questioned.

She sighed. "Yes. I'm frustrated, angry—mostly at myself. I have no one to talk to. It's lonely at the top and I can't trust anyone."

They came across a stone bench on a knoll overlooking the mansion. "Let's sit down," he offered. The bench retained the day's warmth. "How long have you known Kallin?"

"Almost ten years. When I first met him, I happened to be a naïve young thing. I wanted what every woman dreams of—to be with Kallin." She dropped her eyes. "In my gullibility and foolishness, I expected him to marry me but after a few years, I realized that would never happen. But at least I expected to be his number one."

"But why Kallin? Why not settle with someone else?"

She shook her head. "Why do women go after men? When I started, maybe I didn't know. But Kallin taught me a lot about men and about myself. In the end, it's about money, about prestige."

"So you don't love him?"

Maya let out a small hollow laugh. "In the beginning I fooled myself into thinking so. I grew up seeing pictures of him in my schoolbooks. His portraits hang at every street corner. I have what every woman wants, but now I realize he loves no one except himself. He just uses people."

"And you?" he questioned.

She glared at him with raised eyebrows. "You like to come to the point don't you? What do you want me to say? That I'm a calculating woman who uses men just like they use me?" Her eyes flickered. "You're right, of course."

"I'm sorry, I didn't mean it that way," he protested. He only meant to question her feelings about her situation. But she impressed him with her brutal honesty, the intelligence to see through her hypocrisy and her bravery to admit it. She made the deal with Kallin to get power and wealth and now the arrangement was slipping through her fingers, as she likely knew it would. But her rancor surprised him. She sounded like someone at the end of her rope. And maybe she was. A younger, more beautiful, and just as ambitious a version of herself was passing over her.

"Why so bitter?"

"Because of what happens to women like me in a society like this. The only way to get to the top is by using what we have, but once we get there, we're cast-off and thrown in the trash. And that's where I'm heading." Her frustration felt palpable.

"No. No," he interjected. "There's always someone for everyone. You'll definitely find someone else." He glanced at her. The attraction to this point, he admitted, had been purely physical. Now she intrigued him. He found her more complex, a lot more layered. Maybe that's what he needed. Someone who'd been around, who knew the score, who'd keep him honest. Her situation touched him. He didn't know much about this culture, but Kallin couldn't be easy to live with.

Tears formed in her eyes. "Anyway, it's not Kallin's fault. I noticed Jini since she joined our group a few months back. The moment I saw her, I saw trouble." She turned away. "Let's not talk about her now."

Jack concurred and changed the subject. "I'm wondering why Kallin has left me here all this time. He made such a fuss at first."

"Don't worry. When he figures out what he wants, he'll get you."

They sat on the bench for a long while, watching the lights in the mansion glowing softly. He pointed to distant objects and she detailed them. Savoring the closeness of their bodies in the dark night, he used his considerable charm to joke around and make her laugh until he felt her mood lighten. Maya took off her shoes and rubbed her toes on the ground with satisfaction.

When the moon glowed directly overhead, they headed back, entering through the side door, crossing the kitchen and walking down a long corridor and into the guest quarters. Jack tiptoed to his room and quietly opened the door.

"Do you want to come in for a cup of coffee?" he quizzed, winking at Maya.

"Don't spoil it," she warned him.

"What do you mean? I like you."

Maya harrumphed. "I'm sure you like me." She took her hands and slowly moved them down her curves. "All of me."

Jack reddened. "Hey, you can't blame me for trying."

"Look, for a few hours tonight I relaxed a bit and forgot about my troubles. I opened up, talked to someone for a change. For that, I'm grateful, but that's all it is. As long as I am with Kallin, nothing will occur between us. Never."

Jack didn't take no for an answer; that wasn't him. He turned Maya around and held her by both arms. She looked up quizzically. He kissed quickly her on her lips. She immediately pulled away.

"Oh God. You don't give up, do you?" She sighed. "This is my fault. I should have known better. I let my guard down and you just barged in." She folded her arms. "Listen, I don't know what you're thinking, but keep away from me. This is not a game. You'll get us both killed."

"I'm sorry," replied Jack. "I'm really sorry. I'll never do that again." Maya shook her head and walked away.

* * *

The next morning Maya knocked on Jack's door. She beamed. "Good news! The Hand of God just called. He's asking us to visit Kallington tonight."

"Really!" exclaimed Jack. "What did I tell you yesterday?"

"You were right! Maybe all is not lost."

Was it his imagination, or did she not sound all that excited?

* * *

Kallington, End of Kali Yuga

By the time Jack and Maya made their way to the city, it was almost midnight. The rooms in Kallin's apartment reminded Jack of those in the estate: luxurious enough but possessing a strange quality of lifelessness. His bed, deep and plush, easily brought sleep and he awoke early to meet the others for breakfast.

"So how the hell are you?" demanded the Hand of God, in his low, gruff voice.

"Real well," replied Jack.

"This is a big day for you, my boy. Today you'll see how great and powerful the Hand of God really is." Jack almost burst into laughter at Kallin's addressing himself in the third person, but a long stare from Maya instantly stopped him.

"Victory to the Hand of God," he shouted instead.

"Ha, ha," laughed Kallin. "I like you." He looked around the table. "This boy has some brains."

After breakfast, they drove off in a long limousine, led by three vehicles crammed with security, their blue and white lights flashing, while another followed behind. They rolled through innumerable broad avenues lined with large glass and marble government buildings. Money oozed from the very ground here, power floated through windows and influence walked through the innumerable front doors of uncountable offices. Street after street, block after block, mile after mile, gleaming white buildings stood in testimony to the might of this capital city and left no doubt that it reigned as the world government's seat. Their magnificence made Jack breathless, yet their contrast to the slums in the same city left him speechless.

For the first time, Jack understood the immensity of Kallington. Beside the huge government area with its impressive buildings in its center and the sprawling Central Prison to the north, teeming slums populated the vast metropolis.

The vehicle arrived at the International Legislative Exchange—an immense, charcoal-grey oval structure resembling a giant egg laid in the middle of a great elliptical plaza many square miles in area, dotted with hundreds of enormous black sculptures of herculean men in exaggerated masculine poses. In keeping with that mood, scores of security stations, little sandbagged mounds with large guns sticking straight up in the air and manned by thousands of soldiers, covered the area. The gigantic plaza possessed no life; no pedestrians, tourists or couples strolled the area. A four-lane, one-way, ring road circled it while occasional exits dove into the ground beneath the building. The limousine halted at one such stop and, after inspection, proceeded to the underground parking.

Inside, elevators took them, escorted by the security detail, onto a balcony overlooking an immense oval arena almost a hundred feet below. Across from them hung a huge electronic board displaying a map of the world, divided, like a jigsaw puzzle, into about a thousand small

129

pieces. Under the map ran several electronic tickers carrying innumerable signs and numbers. The pit below, from which emanated an incredible bedlam, featured innumerable computers arranged in circles. A mob of expensive-suited men flocked to these stations with tablets in hand or, alternatively, stood studying the great screen above, shouting at the top of their lungs while hundreds of identical black-suited men ran around as if in mindless panic.

They strolled along the terrace until they reached a large oval dais jutting a hundred feet over the pit, covered with lush white carpet, directly opposite the map. An immense marble table, thirty feet long and ten feet wide, dominated this platform and a large ornate chair sat its center. As soon as Kallin entered this area, a camera captured his actions and projected them on the electronic board. For a moment all action ceased and the place hushed before thousands of voices shouted out in unison, "Victory to the Hand of God."

The thunderous salutation raised the hair Jack's arms. Kallin walked to the marble railing running along the dais's edge and waved. The crowd cheered again but, seconds later, when the tickers and map reappeared, the bedlam restarted. Kallin turned around and perched himself on his throne.

Jack sat next to Maya on a chair on one side of the platform, while the security detail lined up behind them. It took him a few minutes to gather his senses. The Exchange differed so wildly from his expectations. The scene reminded him not so much of a stately, grave legislative body as that of a raucous, no holds barred stock or options market. Instead of dignified, august senators, boisterous, common men filled the arena.

"What is this place?" he asked.

"This is the seat of the world government," replied Maya. "Didn't I tell you that earlier?" Jack nodded his head but remained baffled.

"What's the map of the Earth doing on that big board? And why is it divided into all those small pieces?"

"I guess I'll to have to explain it all," she sighed. "Those small pieces are called Exclusive Taxation Areas, or ETAs."

"I don't get it."

"ETAs are bought and sold here and nowhere else. That's why this is the seat of the world government."

Jack looked at her, puzzled. "This is the world government? It looks more like a stock exchange."

"Oh, I see what you mean," exclaimed Maya. "Some time ago, the whole government became privatized."

"What do you mean, the government 'became privatized'?"

"The whole world is divided into small units. We can buy and sell those units here at the International Legislative Exchange."

Jack reflected for a moment. It still made no sense. "Why would anyone buy these pieces, these ETAs anyway?"

Maya's eyes widened. "To make money, of course!" She regarded him curiously. "What else would you want government for?"

"But how do you make money owning an ETA?" He pointed to the scene below. "And what are they doing down there?"

"When someone buys an ETA, he gets the chance to impose taxation on it. Net taxes collected become payable to the owner of that unit. Something like a franchise. That's why they are called Exclusive Taxation Areas. This Exchange determines the value of ETAs for the purpose of purchasing and selling."

"And what does Kallin do?"

"Kallin is the world's largest owner of ETAs. He also possesses the Exchange—he owns the entire government."

"What does that mean, 'own the entire government'?"

"As owner of the International Legislative Exchange, he gets a cut, a percentage, on every transaction. In effect, he collects tax on everything and everyone in the whole world!"

131

The idea flabbergasted Jack. What a set-up! It all made sense. The soldiers. The way the Raks lived. He clenched his fist. He never liked Kallin and now he liked him a lot less.

At that moment, Jini came running in with a tablet. She pulled up a chair and sat next to Kallin.

"I can't believe she did that," stammered Maya.

"Did what?"

She glared angrily at Jini. "That she pulled up a chair and sat next to Kallin. And that he allowed her to do so."

Jini smiled at Maya, batting her eyelids and waving gaily.

"I hate that woman," hissed Maya, under her breath, cheerily waving back.

"Come here, my boy," commanded Kallin. Jack shuffled over. "Pull up a chair and I'll teach you a thing or two. Let me explain: each one of these ETAs contains a certain number of ITUs."

Jack shook his head.

"An ITU is an Individual Taxation Unit."

"You mean an individual person?"

The question irritated the president. "Whatever the hell they are, they're here to pay taxes. The point is, we decide, here at the International Legislative Exchange, what taxes they'll pay."

Jack thought for a second. "How do you collect tax from these people…I mean these ITUs?"

"That's the beauty of this whole system," replied Kallin, enthusiastically. "As you know, each person is embedded with a DNA implant. My scientists tell me that every time an ITU eats, drinks or whatever, he or she produces proteins. The implant measures these proteins and transmits the information to our database. From this, we calculate and collect the tax."

Jack staggered. "That's amazing," he weakly commented.

"Yes, isn't technology grand?" asked Kallin. Jack mutely nodded his head.

"Our database and networks are also remarkable," stated Kallin. "They connect all parts of the world and they are safe from attack. In fact, our database is located on the moon!"

"This…this is incredible," stammered Jack.

"Yes, yes," laughed Kallin with pride. "The trick is to tax people just enough to keep them alive. Taxing them to death is bad for business. It's a real art and I'm its master." Jack's head reeled. He couldn't imagine the suffering of the poor people. How long had this gone on and how long could it last? Kallin walked out in front of the table and scanned the scene, like a lion surveying its domain.

"What are we doing here today?" Jack asked Jini.

"President Kallin introduced a new tax a few months back in one of his large ETAs. Today we will get the report on how it's working. If it's successful, he might sell it for a profit. It depends on how much tax revenue is produced."

"What if the tax doesn't work out?"

Jini glanced at him in alarm. "You don't want to be around if that happens."

"What tax did he introduce?"

"It's called the two-foot tax," she replied brightly.

Jack knotted his eyebrows. "What's that?"

"Basically, it's a tax on anyone who has two feet."

"You're not serious!" he exclaimed.

"Of course, isn't it clever?"

Jack reflected for a moment. "What about people who are crippled or have lost a foot?"

"We're giving them a tax credit." Jini looked at him proudly. "That's my idea."

Kallin returned to his chair, sat down and scratched his beard with impatience. He leaned over the table and pressed a button.

"Where the hell are the numbers?" he shouted. "I want those Numbers here immediately."

A minute later, three round men, looking exactly like each other, all wearing black suits, white shirts, black hats and thin black ties, came running breathlessly. They looked incredibly anonymous, almost caricatures of ideal

133

government servants: of medium height, weight, their skin a medium hue, their hair and eyes a nondescript medium brown and pants held up by identical black belts around rotund abdomens. Despite shaved chins, permanent five o'clock shadows adorned their faces. They resembled accountants or lawyers, competent enough, but somehow lacking just a little something to become partners in a professional practice.

"Who are they?" asked Jack.

"Ask them," retorted Kallin.

He questioned the nearest one "What's your name?"

The black-suited man gazed back in confusion. It glanced at its two associates. "We're not Names," it finally answered. "We're Numbers." Jack looked quizzically.

"I'm Number One." It pointed to its associates. "This is Number Two and that is Number Three."

"Actually, they're not individuals, they're clones," mentioned Jini. "We have thousands of them. They're only good for this type of stuff."

"So where are the reports?" yelled Kallin. The Numbers rushed forward and dropped their tablets on the table. The president swiped one and dozens of pages filled the air, each one filled, from top to bottom, with numbers, financial statements, ratios, and projections.

"That's the analysis on how tax much is being collected and the projections for the future," whispered Jini, breathless with expectation.

"Ha, numbers," shouted Kallin. "I love Numbers."

Number One smiled broadly. "Numbers *are* my life," it said and stared at Kallin as if it really meant it.

"Numbers are *my* life," added Number Two, with even more sincerity.

"Numbers are my *li*..," started Number Three. Number One glared. Number Three swallowed hard and kept quiet. Kallin thumped Number One on the back in a chummy mood. It smiled back nervously, unsure about the attention.

"The more Numbers I have, the more I control things," declared Kallin. "And the more I control Numbers, the more money I make." He looked at the three Numbers.

"Sound off," Kallin ordered.

"One."

"Two."

"Three."

Kallin laughed, satisfied to have proven his point. He returned to examining the reports when suddenly his mood turned. Looking directly at Number One, he pointed at a report. Number One ran up, shivering.

"What's this?" he bellowed, directly in Number One's ear.

Tongue-tied, the Number pointed to another figure on the sheet.

"Yes, I know we exceeded our expectation on the amount of tax collected. But look at this!"

The hapless Number peered intently at the offending number as if its stare would somehow erase it.

Kallin glowered. "What's happening with the tax credits? Why are your projections so wrong?" He looked around. "Who has an explanation for this?"

Number Two timidly put up its hand.

"Well?" demanded Kallin.

"They…they're cutting off their feet to take advantage of the tax credit, sir," reported Number Two.

Jack hid a gasp and shuddered involuntarily, trying to erase the image of desperate people hacking off their own feet.

"Damn them. A man can't make an honest living anymore," barked Kallin. He looked up on the board. The value of the ETA fell by twenty percent. "Whose idea is the tax credit?" he demanded. Jini, already pale, straightaway pointed to Number One.

"It's the one responsible," she immediately responded.

"Guards!" shouted Kallin. "Take it away." Two security guards immediately rushed and dragged Number One away.

"Wait." Kallin paused for a second. "And cut its feet off," he ordered. Number One perked up. Kallin glared back. "You stupid ass, you think you can fool me? You

135

want that tax credit, don't you?" He looked at Jini. "Make sure it doesn't get the tax credit."

Number One's face fell, realizing that it had lost it all. It wailed piteously, trying vainly to keep its suit straight, reaching for its briefcase while being dragged away. Kallin had already lost interest in it.

Number Two rushed up to Kallin. "Should it be the only one not to get the tax credit? Or should it be all prisoners?"

Kallin laughed and thumped it on the back. "Yes. I like that. Make it all prisoners. And throw all the people who cut their off feet in jail."

"Yes sir," said Number Two. "On what charge should they be arrested?"

"Tax evasion, what else," snapped Jini. She looked up at Kallin. "It's my idea."

Kallin nodded. "Good." He looked at Number Two. "Run those revisions through and give me the new projections."

The Number grinned, scurried away and ten minutes later, ran back with the revised figures. Kallin examined them. "Ah. That's more like it." He glanced at the board. The free fall stopped. But his ETA had lost a lot of value. He pointed at Number Two. "You are now Number One." Kallin searched for Number Three, who meekly sat on a chair in the back.

"Come here," ordered Kallin. "You are now Number Two." The new Number Two nervously tugged its tie. Just then, another black-suited, black-tied Number crossed behind the balcony. Kallin ran over, caught it by the neck and dragged the quivering creature to the front of his chair.

"Who are you?" bellowed Kallin.

"I...I...I'm One Five Seven Three Two, sir," it blubbered.

"No, you're not," shouted Kallin. "You're now Number Three." Kallin picked up the new Number Three and hurled it like a bowling ball. All three Numbers tumbled like nine pins. "Sound off."

The three Numbers jumped up.

"One."

"Two."

"Three."

The Numbers fidgeted with their ties, blinking stupidly at Kallin, not knowing what next to expect. Obviously, besides financial reports, other things, such as social situations, stumped them.

"Get the hell out of here and get to work," shouted Kallin angrily. "Damn numbers. I hate Numbers." The Numbers scrambled off in different directions. Despite the absurdity of the situation, Kallin's vehemence frightened Jack. He quickly got up, walked back and sat next to Maya.

"The previous Number One must have been pretty bad," he commented.

"Oh no. It was better than most. It lasted over six months. It's difficult to keep getting more and more income from these ETAs. And if you don't do better all the time, Kallin doesn't like it."

Jack leaned over and whispered "How do people bear it? Isn't there some limit?"

Maya's face whitened. She covered her mouth with her hand and leaned over. "Some of them are escaping civilization, living in mountains and hills or hiding in caves. Those are the rebels. Don't ever mention them. Kallin gets furious. They'll soon be caught and executed, all of them."

Jack was intrigued. So people actually lived outside the grip of this tyranny! Mindful of Maya's warning, he didn't pursue the topic.

The roar suddenly increased in the pit below. The revised projections had reached the traders. The value of the ETA rose sharply.

"Sell it," Kallin ordered, picking up a phone

They all relaxed, knowing that the day's success would keep Kallin happy. Maya however, still burned.

"Watch this," she murmured to Jack. "I'm going to put this stupid blonde in her place."

She got up and walked to the table. "Made a profit again, didn't you?" she asked Kallin.

"Of course. When don't I make a profit?"

"I have an idea."

Kallin regarded her, sharp-eyed. "Yes?"

"What if we charged them two thousand paysars to get their feet reattached?"

"Go ahead."

"It costs only one thousand paysars for the operation. So you make a profit of a thousand on each of these ITUs and you save money by keeping them out of jail."

"Yes, yes," agreed Kallin, "those poor suckers deserve a break." Maya smiled triumphantly.

"What do you think?" he questioned Jini. She grabbed a tablet and quickly pulled up a report. "According to our records, less than five percent of the Individual Taxation Units have savings over two thousand paysars. They just don't have money for operations. So it's not going to work, pure and simple."

"Excellent work," proclaimed Kallin. "You're exactly what I need around here."

Jini smiled at Maya, showing all her teeth. "Better luck next time," she said sweetly.

Chapter Seventeen

Kallington, End of Kali Yuga

After finishing their business in the International Legislative Exchange, Kallin displayed a fine mood again, slapping Jack on the back, joking with Jini, the anger from the morning dissipated by the profit in his pocket. Maya too appeared happy, though Jack suspected her lightness to be a show and nothing else. As they stepped out of the building, followed by the three Numbers and the national security advisor, Jack stopped to enjoy the cool breeze blowing in from the west. After the madness of the morning, the air felt positively fresh.

"I'm hungry," declared Kallin.

"I know," suggested Maya. "Let's go to McBaby's!"

"Excellent idea. Let's have a quick lunch before heading off to the estate."

The national security advisor stepped in. "It's at the edge of the Rak slum sir. There may be some risk."

"Who's afraid of the Raks?" countered Kallin. "They love me. Besides, our security is joining us."

Maya pushed herself next to Kallin in the limousine, but he looked out the window, avoiding eye contact while she avoided looking at Jack. Did she harbor anger against him, wondered Jack, or did Kallin's presence explain this behavior? Jini pouted, but camped herself next to Jack. Four security vehicles followed. They drove along the boulevard for about a mile, turned onto a side street, stopped and climbed out. The guards cleared a path, shooing people out of the way. Maya's presence reassured Jack. For the first time since leaving the estate, Jack found himself in a situation not fully controlled by Kallin. It felt both liberating and threatening—good to be in territory where, for all intents and purposes, all were equal, but at the same time, maybe more dangerous.

Before long, the street abruptly changed its character, becoming filthy and full of trash. A flood of humanity greeted Jack. And what a deluge! None of the inhabitants measured taller than four feet, some with limping bodies contorted into grotesque shapes, many with missing eyes, arms or legs. But worse, the sullen despair and depravity smoldering in their eyes frightened him. Enduring the worst forms of exploitation, knowing of no better life, they accepted ceaseless torment as their normal condition. They shuffled hungrily out of the way on crippled, twisted legs. Given a chance, Jack surmised, they would treat each other with the same viciousness that they endured at Kallin's hands.

Across the corner, at the beginning of the next block, a restaurant with large glass windows stood in a small square building having a sunny, yellow roof. Red brick buildings with flat roofs crowded the other sides of the intersection. Open gutters and dusty sidewalks lined the streets.

A bright red sign reading 'McBaby's' nestled above the entrance to the fast food emporium. Inside, Jack noticed a large metal counter against the back wall, five attendees in striped red uniforms and, behind them, lighted signs detailing the menu. The place, featuring cheap gray cement floors and dark red brick walls, displayed a dozen black tables, each surrounded by four red plastic chairs. With the few loitering Raks cleared out, two soldiers guarded the entrance while other officers stood in different parts of the establishment. Jack, Kallin, Jini and the national security advisor sat at a table at the back while Maya and the three Numbers huddled at an adjacent one.

"Who wants burgers?" questioned Maya.

They all raised their hands. Some requested condiments and all wanted soda pop. Maya took it all down, walked to the counter and busied herself calling in the order.

Kallin turned to Jack. "So, are you enjoying your visit to the capitol?"

"It's very interesting." He picked up what the others learned long ago—to wisely keep on Kallin's safe side,

140

taking advantage of his good moods by currying his favor, but avoiding his temper. "Thank you so much for bringing me."

"Yes, yes. The more you learn about us, the more you'll be amazed how brilliantly things are set up. A guy just can't lose."

Maya returned with two big trays, the burgers piled one on top of the other, the buns perfect brown ovals. She placed one platter in the center of Jack's table with a flourish, and the other at her table. Kallin snatched one while Jini and the national security advisor took theirs in hand and the three Numbers chomped down. Jack's hunger, unnoticed all this time, surfaced with a vengeance. He leaned over and seized a burger.

About to take a bite, he stopped, his hand midway to his mouth, and stared at Kallin. Something seemed strange about the manner in which he ate his burger, the way he chewed it, the sound it made when bitten into.

"Look!" shouted Jini, opening her bun open and peering excitedly at its contents.

"What is it?" questioned Jack.

"My burger's got blue eyes!"

Kallin peered into Jini's hamburger and laughed. Jack leaned over. There, lying on a bed of lettuce, covered with mustard, relish, pickles and smothered with special sauce, lay a tiny human fetus. An electric shock of revulsion jolted him. He collapsed into his chair in disbelief. Did his eyes lie? Was he mistaken? He got up and peered again at the horrifying hamburger. It was true! A tiny human being lay on that bun, its hands curled into tiny fists, its legs folded up.

He sat down, his heart beating wildly. His face turned pale and his hands clammed up. Jack nervously pushed his hair back across his head.

"What is this?" he exclaimed, the disgust in his voice apparent. Everyone turned their eyes on him. Kallin frowned.

"They're McBaby burgers," laughed Jini, feebly attempting to deflect the situation. "They're made from baby Raks."

Jack couldn't believe her attempt to make light. "Where did they come from?" He scowled at Maya. She hastily plunked her uneaten burger down. Kallin glared at her.

"Why, silly," crowed Jini. "They come from the cabbage patch, of course. Where else do burgers come from?"

Kallin laughed at her quick wit. His merriment a cue, the Numbers hooted loudly, slurped their soda pops and dove in for seconds, chewing noisily and with great relish.

"Is this what you people eat?" shouted Jack.

Maya attempted to calm him down, her voice wavering with fear. "We always have eaten this. There is no other food."

"What do you mean?"

"We only eat a few types of meat."

"How about vegetables?"

"Vegetables and fruits disappeared since the biotech disasters, hundreds of years ago."

"How about grains like wheat or rice?"

"Same thing," answered Maya. "None left."

Jack couldn't believe it. He picked up a bun. "What is this?" he demanded. "What is it made of? What about the lettuce? The pickles?"

"Plastic and garbage. What do they taste like?"

"Listen, you little punk," interjected the Hand of God. "We've been eating Rak meat for the last three hundred years. Without it, we would have starved to death. Even the Raks would have died without Rak meat. Rak meat is the best type of meat."

"I can't believe it!" shouted Jack. "You're all cannibals!"

Kallin's face turned red. "What the hell are you barking about, you dog? You don't like our food?"

"No," Jack yelled back. "I don't."

A deathly quiet descended. Maya raised her shaking hands to her face and her mouth opened, but no sound escaped. A great anger built up in Jack's stomach and hardened into a tight knot. He wanted so badly to slam his fist into Kallin's arrogant face. Who was afraid of the Hand of God or any other stupid thing he called himself?

Jack threw his burger down on the table. "I'm getting the hell out of here," he yelled and jumped out of his chair.

"Get him," roared Kallin, furious, his face red with anger. The two soldiers guarding the front entrance ran up.

Suddenly, without warning, a loud explosion rocked the little restaurant. The windows exploded and blue streaks of pulsating energy slammed into its walls.

Chapter Eighteen

Kallington, End of Kali Yuga

"It's the rebels," screamed the national security advisor. As shattered glass showered down, they immediately dropped to the floor. The first volley of shots hit the two soldiers at the entrance and they dropped dead, black wounds burning on their torsos.

A jolt of green energy slammed into the wall behind Jack. Heat scorching the bricks radiated upon his back and he, along with Jini, Maya, and the national security advisor, quickly crawled behind the counter. Kallin joined him, on hands and knees, shivering, his legs shaking. More shots screeched around them.

The remaining soldiers quickly threw tables and chairs into a sort of barricade and fired at the unseen enemy. The three Numbers, caught in the no-man's land between the soldiers and the rebels, ran around in panicked circles, screaming in terror and within seconds dropped dead, briefcases in hand, as thin wafts of smoke curled out of their ears.

"Help me," whimpered Kallin, shivering with fear, "please help me!" Jack's stomach turned with disgust.

Outside, pure pandemonium reigned. Shots poured in at all angles while hundreds of Raks scattered in fear. The soldiers fired wildly into the crowd, not caring who they hit. Dozens of Raks fell, some dying instantly while others writhed around, screaming in pain and agony.

"Call the police," Kallin shouted. The national security advisor got on his phone. More green pulsing energy beams came streaking in. Suddenly, a huge explosion shook the entire building and bricks, loosened by the blast, tumbled on their heads. Maya screamed. Jack lay flat on the floor, hands covering his head. The smoke, the high-pitched whizz of the energy beams, the thunderous claps exploding on the walls, the screams of the injured soldiers, the falling bricks and the sheer unexpectedness of the attack panicked him. He breathed deeply, just barely controlling his fear. More detonations came, jolting him from head to toe. Obviously, the rebels were attempting to bring the whole structure down and kill the occupants.

Suddenly, five rebels jumped through the front window. They fired their guns into the cluster of tables. A fierce battle ensued. Three guards got shot in the abdomen. They grunted, screamed, writhed uncontrollably, and died. The remaining security men crawled out from behind the barricade and shot back, flashes of energy zipping relentlessly, killing all the rebels.

Only two guards survived the attack. *At this rate*, thought Jack, *we'll all die very quickly*. Undoubtedly the attackers were regrouping. Another assault and they would be finished.

Suddenly, a loud whistle rent the air. Jack had heard it before. It radiated from a flying police vehicle and, quickly, others followed, and then many more. Several pounding explosions shook the area. Jack peeked over the counter. Brilliant flashes, like thick purple and red lightning screamed straight down from the sky and exploded into the ground, throwing up stones, dirt and pieces of pavement, as the entire neighborhood rocked under the violence of the counter-attack. Raks screamed and dozens dropped dead. Small arms fire rattled all over the neighborhood, followed by more retaliatory blasts. Then suddenly, all noise stopped. Jack waited with baited breath. Seconds later, several pairs of boots thumped into the restaurant.

"Police," shouted a voice. No one moved. Kallin still cringed on the floor beside Jack. More boots pounded the floor.

"Police!" repeated the voice. "Is anyone here?" The two remaining guards staggered to their feet.

"Yes," one said. "We are President Kallin's security detail."

"All clear," said the policeman.

"President Kallin," said the guard, walking over, "The perimeter is secure. It is safe for you to come out." Kallin staggered up, his legs shaking.

Jack stood, wiped his face and breathed deeply. The rebels had devastated the restaurant, smashed its windows and broken its walls. Smoke, smelling of burnt paint and flesh, filled the air and black and purple stains seared the still-hot floors. The restaurant personnel lay draped over the counter like macabre decorations or rested on the floor like crumpled rag dolls, dead as the meat they once served.

The police saluted and shouted, "Victory to the Hand of God!" Kallin's face darkened and his hands shook badly. Maya rushed to his side but he pushed her away. He scratched his beard angrily as General Contog walked in.

"What the hell happened here?" shouted Kallin, his voice as red as his mood. "Why did you take so long to get here? Your men are supposed to be at any emergency in five minutes."

"You were attacked by the rebels, sir. We couldn't start our defensive operations until we were absolutely sure of your location."

"Yes, yes," agreed Kallin, mollified. "Let's go outside."

Jack walked shakily behind them and leaned his back against a remnant of the restaurant's wall. Though mid-afternoon, the sky turned dark and low black clouds rumbled menacingly. A hard red tint colored the horizon and a cold wind blew in from the west, bringing a billowing dust that swirled into his eyes.

The intersection painted a picture of horror. Fragments of the eatery's roof lay shattered on the sidewalk. Nothing of the restaurant's front escaped destruction and its walls remained in name only. Hundreds of dead Raks, rebels, and burning vehicles littered the streets. Soldiers picked up the dead and threw them to the edges of the street, their blood flowing in myriad streams into the open gutters. The screams of incapacitated Raks filled the air, but the uncaring soldiers threw them on top of their dead comrades.

Several thousand soldiers created a ring around the restaurant and the intersection, and a huge sea of Raks gathered just behind them. On the flat rooftops of the low brick buildings overlooking the scene, more collected, silent for the moment. Hundreds of noiselessly floating police vehicles, their blue and white lights silently circling into the black clouds, their spotlights illuminating the ground, hovered above. Soldiers sat in the open bays, observing everything. Far from the scene, about a mile away, airborne vessels shot enormous bolts of purple into suspect buildings, the explosions echoing like muffled thunder.

The national security advisor ran up to General Contog. "Has this area been secured?" he asked.

"Yes, completely."

"What about those Raks?" he asked, pointing to the assembled crowd.

"We have screened them all fully."

An eerie quiet blanketed the scene. Kallin walked to the center of the intersection, surrounded by a group of police. He stopped, bade the men to step aside and, taking a weapon from one of them, blasted green electric flames high into the sky. The crowd instantly recognized him.

"Victory to the Hand of God!" shouted the mighty multitude. Kallin fired his weapon a second time. "Victory to the Hand of God!" they screamed, from the streets, the rooftops and the circling aircrafts. Kallin fired his weapon one last time. "Victory to the Hand of God!" thundered the vast crowd a third time, their voices crashing against the buildings like a tsunami against a defenseless shore. Kallin raised both hands in acknowledgment. They roared. After exulting in their approval for several minutes, Kallin walked back to General Contog.

"Now," he said grimly, "let's take care of the prisoners." Thirty rebels crouched on their knees on the dusty street at the left side of the intersection, near the sidewalk, their eyes blindfolded, their arms handcuffed behind them. They painted a portrait of utter and total defeat, squatting in the dirt, their heads hanging low.

Knowing Kallin's unexpected and violent disposition, Jack watched the proceedings with a queasy stomach.

"Is that the lot of them?" demanded Kallin.

"Yes, President Kallin," affirmed the chief of police. "The rest, about seventy, are dead."

A dozen green-smocked technicians went from one prisoner to another, examining the back of their necks, extracting blood samples and inserting them into handheld devices.

"So what is it?" demanded Kallin. The national security advisor joined him.

"Sir, they have removed their DNA implants," replied General Contog. "But we have discovered their identities. Many of the rebels are originally from Kallington. Some have spent time in Central Prison on various charges such as robbery, thievery and tax evasion. But some, sir, are ex-military. This takes the fight to a whole new level."

"God damn them," spat the Hand of God darkly. "I pay them, feed them, train them to use weapons and they turn against me. I give them everything and this is how they pay me back." Kallin seemed genuinely hurt.

"This explains their ability to use weapons and to engage in combat, and being ex-military, they may have stolen the weapons and ammunition from their bases."

"We'll show these dogs gratitude," growled Kallin. With weapon still in hand, he walked in front of the nearest prisoner and pulled off the blindfold.

"Look at me." The prisoner blinked his eyes rapidly. "Who am I?" shouted Kallin. The man kept quiet.

"I am the Hand of God," shouted Kallin angrily, with fiery, piercing eyes. "I have given you everything. What would any of you have if it wasn't for me? Aren't you ex-military?"

The man nodded his head. Beads of sweat formed on Kallin's shining red forehead and slid down his neck.

"I am the Hand of God. I am the one who is chosen by God. I am put here on earth by God to be his Hand. God works through me. Only me. No one else. There is only one

Hand of God, there will always only be one Hand of God, now and forever."

Jack shivered. Kallin was completely crazy.

"Admit that I am the Hand of God or die."

"You're the devil," spat the rebel.

Kallin whipped the weapon up against the prisoner's head. He pulled the trigger. A purple pulse shot out of the weapon and exploded, blowing his head off and freezing his face in a grotesque mask. Kallin laughed maniacally, pointing at the disembodied cranium as it rolled around. The enormous assembly, excited by the action, shouted loudly, their voices like the roar of a storm.

"I will send you all to hell," screamed Kallin at the rebels, his eyelids twitching, and his face blood red. The soldiers jumped up and surrounded the rebels as he walked back to the front of the ruined restaurant.

"Weapons on first level," ordered Kallin. The soldiers put their guns to stun.

"Aim."

The prisoners trembled, shouted and screamed, some prayed feverishly and others vomited on the ground.

"Fire!"

The rebels keeled over, stiffened and gasped for breath, writhing in agony as green bolts spun around their bodies. The crowd of Raks screamed in delight and picked up rocks and stones and hurled them at the prisoners. The wheezing rebels grunted as the missiles hit them. Running out of rocks, the people picked up bits of metal or pried loose pieces of pavement, while Raks on the rooftops hurled shards of broken glass. Each time an object found its mark and blood spurted, they howled in excitement.

The violence shocked Jack. Didn't these people know their real oppressors? How could they be so stupid as to attack those who fought for them? He then understood. These people, so oppressed, so tightly controlled in every aspect of their lives, found their only escape in this bloodlust. The violence and gore constituted not just a reaction but a moment of liberation, an opportunity to display all their feelings of pent-up rage, hate and weakness without being arrested or controlled by a pitiless system that daily ground them into dust. No wonder the crowd bayed so loudly for blood.

"What do we do now?" asked General Contog.

Kallin looked around at the mob. "Let 'em at them."

The soldiers guarding the perimeter stepped aside and the horde rushed into the intersection. They jumped on the rebels and the dead and dying Raks on the sidewalks and, with bare hands, tore apart the flesh and stuffed it into their hungry mouths. Some cut open the bodies with pieces of glass and pulled out bleeding livers which they ate raw. The orgy of blood drove the Raks uncontrollably mad. They ran around with clumps of flesh in their hands, yelling hoarsely. Jack watched with increasing horror, overwhelmed by the stark public display of insanity. He doubled over, staggered a few steps, fell to his knees on the sidewalk, vomited and crouched there, utterly weak and nauseated, unable to move.

* * *

The Hand of God, followed by the national security advisor and the chief of police, strode into the restaurant. He first saw the three Numbers, dead on the floor, their briefcase handles clasped stiffly with white knuckles. Kallin kicked the bodies out of the way.

"A complete waste of three perfectly good Numbers," he grumbled uncaringly. "And how the hell did the rebels know I came here?" he demanded.

Contog lowered his voice. "Either pure luck or someone tipped them off." Kallin slammed his fist in his hand and swore.

"Who have you been with today?" asked the chief of police.

"After leaving the International Legislative Exchange, with Jini, Maya, the national security advisor, and Jack, that sniveling little idiot."

"Whose idea was it to come here?"

150

"Maya's." Kallin scowled and scratched his beard.

"It might be her or someone else," clarified the general. "We can't be sure until we have definite proof."

"General, we talked about this before, but now there is no doubt. We have a mole in our midst. There is no other way that a hundred rebels could have gathered here unless they knew my habits."

"That sounds like a reasonable conclusion," replied the general.

"Did you to get any information from the rebels?"

"No, sir. Whoever instructed them very cleverly hid his or her identity and location. The rebels work in completely independent cells, each unknown to the others."

"General, you are dismissed," he roared. "I want you to find out who the mole is. I don't care what it takes. I want this person found and brought before me." General Contog saluted and walked out.

"The other issue is that we may have is a mole who doesn't know he is a mole," the national security advisor said softly.

"You mean Jack?" asked Kallin.

"Yes. This was our fear from the beginning. On this, the first day you've spent with him, the rebels attacked. They may be using him to get near you, in ways not yet clear. I think it's time for us to use him to uncover what's actually going on."

"And how do we do that?"

"Let him go."

"Just let him go?"

"Yes sir. The trick is to be patient. Sooner or later, the rebels will get in touch with him. We have the technology to sniff them out."

"Excellent," replied the Hand of God. "He may even allow us to uncover the entire rebellion." The national security advisor nodded his head.

"What about Maya?" asked Kallin.

"I don't think she has anything to do with this, but she serves no purpose anymore."

"Don't worry. I'll get rid of her."

A soldier grabbed Jack by the collar. "Get up," ordered the man. "President Kallin wants to see you."

Jack stood gingerly, his stomach still queasy. How long had he lain there, next to his vomit? With the carnage on the street almost over, only a few Raks wandered about, chewing the bare bones of the dead rebels like hyenas scavenging after a lion's kill. Jack followed the man into the restaurant. Bits of tables and chairs, jagged pieces of glass, twisted metal, shattered bricks and burnt plaster lay around. Kallin was shouting loudly as Maya cried.

"Come here, you stupid ass," yelled the Hand of God. Jack walked over, meekly looking down, but seething with disgust and anger. What a pig!

"But I don't know anything about this attack," sobbed Maya.

"Then why did you suggest having lunch here?"

"We've stopped here so many times before! I only suggested it because I know how much you like the food here."

Kallin slapped her hard on her face. Maya staggered.

"Please," she begged. "Please believe me! I don't know anything. I've been your faithful mistress for so many years."

Jini jumped in. "Familiarity breeds contempt." She faced Kallin. "Oh Hand of God, why do you believe her? What use is she to you now? Don't I serve you better?"

Maya jumped up, her eyes flashing. "Don't you see what she's doing?" she demanded, unable to keep her temper bottled. "She's a conniving witch. She's only using you to get power and money. How can you trust her?"

"You're talking about trust?" Jini sneered. "You almost killed us all. You're a snake in the grass. Oh Hand of God, this woman is old and dried up. Make me your number one and I'll show you what I can do."

152

The Hand of God turned to Maya with scorn. "My mind is made up," he stated, looking directly into her eyes. "Jini is now my number one."

Maya fell to the ground and held his arm. "No, no," she pleaded. "Please give me another chance."

"Get lost," yelled Jini. "Is there anything more pathetic than a washed up old hag?"

Maya jumped up and slapped Jini's face. "I'm going to show you, you stupid blonde," she screamed. She grabbed handfuls of Jini's hair and pulled hard. Jini yelled. She extricated herself and ran up to Kallin, tears streaming down her cheeks.

"Look what she did! She tried to kill me! Aren't you going to protect me?"

"Enough," roared Kallin.

Maya fell to the floor weeping. Kallin ignored her. Jini beamed.

"But I gave given you my entire life," cried Maya.

"This didn't happen overnight. I got tired of you some time ago. I've been looking for someone else and Jini came along when I needed her." Kallin paced the floor. "Go to my estate and pack your things. You can take a couple of weeks. After that, you have to leave." He turned around and glanced at Jack with blazing eyes.

"And take that loser with you. I don't want to see his ugly face anymore."

Chapter Nineteen

On Pilgrimage, Satya Yuga

Three weeks into the pilgrimage, Steve became familiar with the routine, a schedule carefully considered and implemented, an exercise well known to all. He'd wake in the dark, early morning. A quick immersion in the cool waters of the river, followed by a vigorous rub with a cotton gamcha got his blood rushing and instantly refreshed the mind. After this came his sadhana, his individual spiritual discipline. Steve naturally followed Shanti— sometimes they practiced yoga, starting with the asanas, then *pranayama*—the regulation of the breath—followed by *dharana*—the controlling of the mind—all parts of the *ashtanga yoga* system.

On other occasions, Steve and Shanti practiced japa meditation, the chanting of sacred mantras, which cleansed the mind and transport the practitioner to higher states of purified consciousness. He found japa meditation difficult in the beginning; now he loved these early morning sessions.

In the evenings after dinner, their favorite part of the day, the pilgrims built campfires, brought out musical instruments and the entire group, sitting around the fire, sang *bhajan*, spiritual song, or kirtan, a call-and-response type of chant where the lead singer sings a musical phrase which is repeated by the audience. Not ordinary singing but rather a joyous spiritual exercise, a prominent aspect of bhakti yoga, it transported the singer and audience to clearly defined spiritual states.

"Whenever I hear kirtan, I feel lifted out of my body. Can you explain what I am experiencing?" Steve asked Shanti.

"There are three elements to kirtan—*raga*, *rasa* and *bhava*."

154

"What is a raga?"

"A raga is a melodic structure determining the mood of a composition. For example, early morning ragas are generally contemplative, whereas evening ragas are livelier and deeper in emotion."

"And what is a rasa?"

"A rasa is described as a transcendental relationship. Five principal rasas, or relationships, having their origin and resting place in the Divine, are mentioned in the shastras. The first rasa, called *shanta rasa* is a neutral or passive relationship, *dasya rasa* indicates a master-servant relationship, *sakhya rasa* is the fraternal relationship, *vatsalya rasa* specifies the parental relationship and finally comes the conjugal relationship, called *madhurya rasa*."

"Can you explain further?"

"Relationships in this world are reflections of the original divine rasas and, just as there are many emotions in earthly relationships, rasas too have their bhavas, emotions. The kirtan leader's duty is to explore these emotions through her singing and lead the chanters to mystical states of spiritual relationships."

"Experiencing a spiritual emotion, which you call a bhava, in a certain musical mood, or raga, develops spiritual relationships, rasas, with the Supreme. Is that right?"

Shanti agreed. "Kirtan is one way to open the heart. It is very important part of bhakti yoga." She, the daughter of a *Gandharvi*, a celestial singer, many times led kirtan. Her beautiful, melodious voice slowly transported listeners from one transcendental state of emotion to another until the entire congregation felt their hearts filled with rapture.

Many times she sang songs evoking the bhava of *vipra lambha*, that is, the emotion of separation of the Beloved from the Lover, of the Devotee from God, of Radha from Krishna. These songs of separation evoked feelings of both love and longing. Steve sat beside her, not intellectually understanding the intricacies of the raga, rasa or bhava, but yet captured by the emotions brought out by Shanti's sweet and moving voice.

One day, in the late afternoon, Steve went with Shanti to collect firewood. A particularly demanding day, the trail became especially difficult in the steep foothills. Steve knew, despite Shanti's protests, that she undoubtedly welcomed his help with the unusually taxing chore.

They entered the forest on a hill above the camp. Large trees grew at considerable distances from each other in the expansive woodland and it took quite a while to collect enough dead branches or dried bushes. They separated the gathering into two bundles and Shanti tied them with grass ropes. She took one bunch, placed it on top of Steve's head and, keeping her back and neck straight, set the other one on her head and commenced walking. Steve, having not yet mastered the delicate exercise of carrying wood, followed closely behind, imitating her movements. The trick involved keeping the back stiff and the head level, with the eyes looking straight ahead while naturally moving the arms.

Suddenly, the load on his head slipped. Instead of trusting to keep his head upright, he had made the mistake of looking down on the trail. His bundle crashed down and he fell forward, right on Shanti's back. She gasped as both she and her load tumbled.

"Shanti!" he shouted. "Are you all right?"

She sat up, straightening her sari. "Yes, I'm fine."

Steve held out his hand. Shanti looked away for a second and then took it. He helped her up and they stood for several seconds holding hands. Shanti blushed. Steve realized that, for the first time, he was actually touching her. He examined her strong, yet small and delicate hands. On the side of her palms and along each finger, ran an intricate pattern of flowers done in *henna*, a plant whose paste left a red coloring on the skin. Large scarlet rounds adorned the middle of her palms while the tips of her fingers also showed crimson.

The evening sun, full and resplendent, shone behind her, creating an aura that sparkled orange and gold around her head. Her sari covered her hair and her green eyes shone lustrously. He looked deeply into her eyes and she gazed into his. A strong stirring of love delighted his heart and moved into his arms and into his torso. He trembled, breathed deeply and reached for her other hand. It came willingly. They held hands for a few seconds and Steve clasped her strongly in his embrace. She gasped, her body quivering like a captured bird. He held on strongly until she relaxed, her breath softened, and he felt her slowly surrender as she inhaled deeply, calming her shivering heart. His strong arms reassured her and she gently nestled her head upon his right shoulder.

Closing his eyes, he smelled the sweetness of her hair and inhaled the salty scent of her skin. In deep embrace they stood with eyes shut, their hearts beating in rhythm, oblivious to the world, unaware of the passage of time or circumstance.

They finally released, seemingly after an eternity, but in reality was only a minute or two. Quickly collecting themselves and once again gathering their loads, they walked back to the camp holding hands but saying nothing.

That evening, Shanti brought out her harmonium and led kirtan. She sang about the divine love of Radha and Krishna, the Eternal Lovers, a song of both the love and longing Radha feels when apart from Krishna. That night her voice soared, clean and strong and full of color, and deeply moved the chanters' souls. After the kirtan, the young pilgrims rushed to her and remarked on the power of her voice and the elders all smiled, knowing full well what stirred in the heart of this beautiful, sweet, young woman.

Chapter Twenty

On Pilgrimage, End of Satya Yuga

They were now 'officially' a couple as no reason existed to hide their obvious attachment. Despite the liberties Parvata Rishi allowed, Shanti remained an obedient daughter, knowing full well her father's expectations.

Steve spent as much time as possible in her company. They ate together, did chores together, walked together and sang the evening kirtans together. With their relationship open and accepted by all, their connection grew deeper and their affection manifested in a natural and unhindered manner. Steve felt his fondness grow deeper, unlike anything he had ever felt before. He had girlfriends and loved them, but this time he fell deeply in love. Maybe, he reflected, for the first time, he allowed himself to truly love.

They had traded the cows and oxen for provisions a few days back and, now, each carried a bundle. They ate was what they brought, supplemented with fruits, roots, berries and nuts found in the forests. The river rushed rapidly and the path proved harder to follow. Sometimes, the waters suddenly turned or fell from high cliffs, forcing a circuitous and difficult climb. Shambala, still some distance away, hid in the stately peaks now looming large. The real test began; the weeks of journey so far, a prelude.

* * *

Just a few soft clouds wreathed the silver mountains and teal-colored skies painted the beautiful sky. Trekking in the high cliffs on a path only a few feet wide, Steve and

Shanti, though starting the morning at the head of the column, found themselves well at its end by noon.

As they traversed a bend, the trail unexpectedly opened up into a twenty-foot wide promontory sticking out over the plains. A large boulder sat invitingly at the far edge of the overhang. Steve slumped on it, dropping his cloth-covered bundle on the ground. He looked over the green forest, stretching unendingly, with the river cutting through it. The distance traveled surprised him and he searched for Mahavan, but it remained too far away to be visible.

Shanti dropped her pack and sat next to him. She wore a light brown sari with a cream-colored top, black sandals, a small black bindi on her forehead and she breathed fast, the trek being difficult, and the load, heavy.

Shanti started the conversation; the American lifestyle being so foreign and, yet, so intriguing to her. He amazed her with his descriptions of mechanical contraptions and she intrigued him with her portrayals of the various *siddhis*, attainments, which yogis achieved through their sadhana. Steve spoke many times about growing up in Kansas City and riding his bike near the river, while she detailed the journeys made to the different holy *tirthas*, places of pilgrimage. Their experiences, while so different, served not to distance them, but instead formed a source of continuous fascination. Yet, for Steve, the natural simplicity and deep satisfaction of Satya Yuga felt far more meaningful.

"You grew up in Kansas City with your mother, didn't you?" she asked.

The mention of his mother brought a touch of sadness. He waited a few moments and let it pass. "Yes."

"And you also studied there?"

"Yes. The university was close to my home."

"It's good that you lived with your mother while you studied."

"No," he laughed. "I didn't stay at home. I rented an apartment near the campus."

159

"Oh!" replied Shanti, shocked, unable to comprehend not taking care of elders. "Why?" she questioned. "Why did you leave your mother all alone?"

"Well..." started Steve, uncertainly. "I needed the space to study. And...I had girlfriends."

"Girlfriends?"

Steve hesitated. How could he explain this? Shanti would have a hard time comprehending the cultural difference.

"Yes. In America, the custom is to have boyfriends and girlfriends."

She reflected for a few seconds, trying to grasp the concept. "So after you get a girlfriend, you get married?"

"Something like that," he responded, smiling nervously as she contemplated his answer.

"So why didn't you marry any of your girlfriends?"

Steve stopped. He was treading dangerous ground. He said nothing. Shanti looked straight at him with intense green eyes.

"Well?"

"It's not that simple. That's not the way it happens."

Shanti's eyes gleamed. "Oh really? And how does it work."

Steve sweated under his kurta. "Shanti," he finally explained, "American culture is completely unlike yours. The way things function there is very dissimilar. A girlfriend means something completely different."

Shanti looked him up and down with steely eyes. "Maybe you can explain it to me."

Steve opened his mouth, but no words came.

"Am I your girlfriend?" she demanded.

"Yes!" he exclaimed. "I mean, no...!"

Shanti's face flushed red. She spun around furiously, her back turned to him. "So what am I?" she challenged, not looking at him. "Who am I to you?"

Steve breathed in deeply. The confusion in his mind cleared. He understood the need for honesty. He reached for her arm and gently turned her around. "I love very much and I've never loved anyone more than you," he

160

declared with shining eyes. "I want to be with you for the rest of my life."

Shanti glanced hesitantly for a couple of seconds, reached forward, held his hands and smiled. None could doubt her heart. Steve sighed with relief. That was close. He changed the subject.

"You're very attached to your father, aren't you?"

"Of course! Since I was a baby he's been both a mother and a father to me. I would happily serve him for the rest of my life." She gazed up at the sky. "But I have no one else. What is it like to live with someone my age, I wonder?"

"Like me?" suggested Steve. Shanti blushed and turned away. She piqued his curiosity. He saw his opportunity to ask her some questions. "Did you ever date anyone?"

"What does that mean, date?" she inquired, innocently enough, brushing her dark hair behind her ears.

"Dating means going out with boys your age."

"Of course not!" she exclaimed, surprised. "Why would I do anything like that?"

Obviously, dating was not their custom. He hemmed and hawed. "So do you have arranged marriages in your village?"

Shanti jumped off the rock and turned away.

"So you do have arranged marriages!"

Shanti avoided his gaze, slowly nodded her head and backed up the trail. Steve jumped off the rock and followed her.

"Are you promised to someone?"

Shanti scurried up the trail.

Laughing, he followed her. "Are you already given to someone?"

Shanti, practically purple with embarrassment, hurried even more quickly, holding her hands to her ears.

"Is your marriage already arranged?" he shouted, half-jokingly, half-tauntingly.

Shanti stopped, turned around and faced him. Her cheeks burned bright as embarrassment radiated from her face like heat from a flame. Her nostrils flared. She drew herself up, her arms taut by her side and held her chin strong and high.

"No!" she cried. "Do you think that I would allow you to touch me if I was already promised to someone?"

Steve bent over, laughing hysterically.

She gathered herself and, with all the strength and courage she could muster, faced him down.

"And," she yelled. "I will marry the man my father chooses for me!"

She spun around and ran up the hill as fast as her legs could carry her. Steve stood grounded, watching his beloved running away, disappearing around the corner.

He jumped up and clapped his hands happily. Her words made his spirit soar. Sure, he had embarrassed and maybe even angered her, but he knew in his heart that she too loved him. Why else would talk of marriage evoke such a strong reaction? The world felt new and fresh and life full of promise. He peered up the path. Shanti had long disappeared.

He went back to the rock and picked up the bundles. Catching up with her and the rest of the pilgrims would take some time. He smiled and walked quickly, drinking in the pure, sparkling mountain air, striding ever closer to the mysterious white-capped peaks crowding the horizon.

Chapter Twenty One

On Pilgrimage, End of Satya Yuga

One day, in the fifth week of the pilgrimage, they stopped at a small rocky clearing, deposited their loads and set up camp. The river coursed its way more urgently, dashing among rocks and down steep declines and every once in a while, found respite in valleys or lakes hidden between high hills. Shambala lay not far away.

Steve and Shanti never strayed far from each other. The long hours spent together made him truly appreciate her character. Though still full of childlike innocence, she proved to be fiercely loyal to her duties, ever ready to sacrifice her comforts for her near and dear ones. She would make a formidable wife and mother, he thought on more than one occasion.

As usual, Shanti's chores included the search for firewood. He joined her, knowing it to be a difficult task in these high mountains as pine trees and short shrubs replaced the broad-leafed deciduous forest.

They walked up the slope above the camp, following the passage of the river for about a quarter of a mile, until Steve spied a small waterfall, about ten feet high, where the river rushed thick and green, roaring as it tumbled over the edge of a valley and smashed onto the rocks below. Climbing up the side of the hill to the top of the waterfall, they discovered a clear, cold lake measuring three stone's throws across, lying nestled between high hills on the far side and a small gravel beach on their side. Giant rhododendron trees with red and white flowers grew on the opposite shore, their long leaves casting reflections upon the water. The cool air shimmering above the waters lent a touch of the celestial to the already amazing setting.

They walked for about a quarter-mile as Shanti pointed out many dead branches at their feet, washed up from innumerable spring floods. Hard and dry, they made ideal firewood. She bent down and picked up several branches before noticing it. Shielding her eyes, she looked across the waters.

"What is it?" asked Steve. A flock of water ducks, their electric red and green plumage giving a surreal quality to the already colorful setting, swam along the opposite shore and, in the water around them, grew several large lilies and lotuses, their large pan-like leaves floating languidly on the surface.

"Don't you see it?"

Steve strained his eyes. He saw nothing out of the ordinary, or rather out of the extraordinary, in this already astonishing setting. "No."

Shanti lifted her arm and pointed at a clump of lotuses directly across. "Look. Right there."

Steve knotted his eyebrows. "What's so special about them? We've seen so many, much better, ones."

"No!" she exclaimed. "The one in the middle. Look at its color!"

At the very center of the thicket, framed by the white and pink blossoms of the ordinary lotus flowers, and bathed in the orange and gold sunlight of the late afternoon, sat a large blue lotus, like a king attended by his courtiers or a dancer surrounded by ballerinas. Its size, color, and position suggested mystery and beauty, like a regal peacock among common sparrows. No botanist, yet he recognized it as something extraordinary.

"It's certainly wonderful," agreed Steve but, still, Shanti's extraordinary, all-absorbing interest surprised him.

"Don't you understand what this is? Don't you know what this means?"

He shook his head. He wanted to share her excitement but couldn't follow her thoughts.

"A lotus is compared to a spiritually elevated person," she explained. "It grows in the common water and sprouts from the lowly mud. Yet, like a yogi, who withdraws his senses from the world while yet living in it, it always keeps its head above the murky waters."

164

Steve had heard the analogy. The symbol of the lotus, the emblem of transcendence, sprang often in conversations among the villagers. "But what is so special about this one? No doubt it is very beautiful, but other than its color, it's just another lotus."

"No!" Shanti said emphatically. "What does its color remind you of?"

Steve dumbly shook his head.

"Blue is the color of the raincloud that moistens the earth and gives life to all things. It is the color of the infinite sky, of space, that stretches on forever. Blue is the color of the Supreme Lord, the origin and the destination of all souls."

Of course! He immediately remembered seeing paintings of the blue-skinned Krishna holding, in many instances, a long-stemmed blue lotus. Certainly, this flower was not of this world!

He took off his kurta, exposing his bare chest, slipped off his sandals and, making sure to firmly secure the dhoti around his waist, jumped into the water. He gasped. The unexpected coldness startled him.

"No! Stop!" shouted Shanti. The destination lay only a hundred yards away and Steve swam with fast, strong strokes. A natural swimmer, he displayed grace and strength as his powerful strokes propelled him through the water. As he swam, his breathing regulated by years of experience, he wondered whether to get Shanti just the blue lotus or the whole bunch. He looked up and found himself in the middle of the lake instead of being a lot closer to the other shore. Wondering briefly, he put his head down and doubled his efforts. The cold sapped the strength from his arms and legs. He pushed harder, turning his body expertly, breathing the air rhythmically, focusing his energy along his arms and into the tips of his fingers.

He looked again. Not only had he not approached the opposite shore, he had drifted further downstream, away from his target. He turned his head around and saw Shanti shouting frantically. A cold fear jolted him. He immediately realized the situation. An undercurrent had caught him! And it pulled him toward the waterfalls.

Steve turned around and headed back towards Shanti. The undercurrent's cold blue tentacles swirled between his legs and pulled him, imperceptibly but inescapably, toward the roaring cascade. His thigh muscles, already thrust to the limit, cramped and the cold bunched his calf muscles into painful knots. He put his face down and pushed grimly ahead, coming up for breath after only four strokes, instead of the customary two.

He saw Shanti scampering over the rocks, running alongside as fast as she could, frantically crying out to him. Desperate, he kicked his cramped limbs, pushing them beyond the limit of pain. He heard the dull roar of the falls.

The current sucked Steve, struggling helplessly like a leaf caught in its thick green waters, and tossed his body onto the jagged jumble of black rocks below.

* * *

Steve felt a crackling heat. He opened his eyes and saw a small bonfire burning on the gravel beside him. A bed of green reeds lay beneath him. He recognized it as Shanti's handiwork; she must have laid him there. A throbbing headache crashed in his brain and his whole body felt raw and wounded. A grinding hurt shot up both legs and his bruised ribs pounded. He turned around to look but the effort brought a shooting pain up his neck and into his head. He quickly straightened and lay on his back.

"So you're finally waking up!" she exclaimed, her face framed by long dark hair. She sat next to him and mopped his head with a wet cloth.

"How long was I out?" he asked weakly.

"Long enough to frighten me half to death."

She lifted him by the back, helping him to a sitting position. Steve winced, but the soreness felt reassuring. He checked his legs, moving his hands down the limbs, squeezing the joints. At least he suffered no broken bones.

166

"Are you all right?"

"Yes," he replied bravely, mostly for her benefit.

She took a deep breath. "Why did you do such a thing?"

Steve looked down, feeling as dull and stupid as the throbbing in his temples. "I did it for you. I wanted to get that lotus for you."

Shanti turned away, covered her face with her sari, and wiped away her soft tears.

"Why are you crying?" he gently asked.

"I...I almost lost you. I don't know if I would have been able to bear that. When I dragged you from the water, all bruised and bleeding, I thought you were surely dead."

He looked up and followed the water running from the waterfall towards their sitting place. So he had floated about twenty feet before Shanti rescued him! The water splashed playfully at the bottom, misting the mosses on the rocks. It did not look so menacing now.

He painfully got up and put his arms around her. His heart thumped as he held her tight, and a deep love and gratitude overwhelmed him. He knew, at this moment and with all certainty, that she had truly and fully conquered his heart.

Shanti wiped the tears from her eyes. "I didn't realize how close I've become to you. When I pulled you out of the water, I thought you were dead. I would have rather died myself!"

They sat for a long time, in each other's warmth, in close embrace, feeling their hearts beating. After some time, something dark and big and not clearly visible bobbed in the eddies, capturing Steve's attention. He got up, his whole body aching from the effort, and walked towards it with short steps. Reaching the lapping waters, he immediately recognized it. It was the blue lotus!

He looked back at Shanti gathering her firewood. He hid the flower behind his back and walked up to her. She stopped, straightened and looked expectantly at him. The heat from the fire brought a reddish glow to her face, the golden moon shone through her long wet tresses and her eyes sparkled. He held his breath. She never looked more like a woman. He bent down on his knees and brought the majestic flower in front.

"Shanti," he asked. "Will you marry me?"

Shanti smiled broadly. She put her hand on her chest to calm her beating heart. "Yes!" she exclaimed. "Yes, I will marry you!" Laughing with happiness, she reached down, accepted the lotus flower, smelled it deeply and held it to her bosom. "And I will talk to my father. He knows what's in my heart!"

Chapter Twenty Two

Kallin's Country Estate, End of Kali Yuga

Jack sat on the bed next to Maya in her room at the country estate, back from the enormously straining day at Kallington. A soft light glowed on the night table beside them. Maya wore a long, green, nightgown and not much more.

"What's going to happen to me?" she sobbed, barefoot and inconsolable. "Where am I going to go?"

"Don't worry," he reassured her. "You'll be fine."

"You don't know anything about this society! If you fall, you fall all the way down. What value am I to anyone now?"

"Maya, I've had enough of Kallin, the International Legislative Exchange, the DNA implants and the whole rotten, evil system. I want to get out of here." A product of her society, she knew of nothing better. He had to make her comprehend. "You're in this state precisely because you trusted Kallin all these years. You must have known that he was going to betray you, that he was going to dump you eventually, didn't you?"

"I don't know." Tears fell down her face. Her blindness infuriated Jack.

"How stupid can you be?" he yelled. "He's thrown you out like a piece of trash and you still don't see it?"

Maya gathered her breath. "You're right. Deep down, I knew it would happen, sooner or later."

"Don't you see that Kallin is evil, that everything he does is evil?"

Maya nodded her head. "I guess so. Don't you think I know his mood swings, his violence? I never knew what he would do from one moment to the next."

"What gets me is his Hand of God thing. He actually believes he is the Hand of God, whatever that means."

169

Maya shushed him. "Don't ever question that. It really sets him off."

"I don't care," declared Jack. "To me, he is just a towering religious hypocrite. More than that, he's plain crazy."

"You may be right, but there's nothing we can do about it."

"I'll do something. I won't hang around until he gets rid of me too."

"What will you do?"

"I want to find out about the rebels."

She knotted her eyebrows. "Why?"

"I know Kallin has no use for us, but the people fighting him would surely be interested. You know everything about him, what to speak of me? I'm not even in the system anywhere. I'm sure the rebels will find some value in us."

"You're really reckless, aren't you?" she asked, alarmed, her hands held tight. "You are the most impulsive, rash person I've ever met!"

Jack got off the bed and faced her. "Maya, join me in the rebel's cause."

"Do you know what you're saying? If Kallin finds out, we'll be dead."

"Maya," he implored, shaking her by the shoulders. "In a couple of weeks, you'll be kicked out of here. Who else do you have now besides me?"

She wiped her eyes. "You're right. I have no one else. But why get involved with the rebels? Do you know anything about them?"

Jack shook his head.

"I once heard General Contog mention something about the ancient ruins," remembered Maya. "That the rebels sometimes go there."

"Yes!" interjected Jack excitedly, "When the police first brought me to General Contog, he mentioned the ancient ruins! Do you know where they are?"

"Slow down," answered Maya, laughing. "Of course I know where they are."

"Go ahead."

"They're a huge area out in the desert near the Eastern coast, full of broken down buildings, streets and stuff like that. No one knows how old they are and how they got to be like that."

"Do the rebels live there?"

"I don't know. From what I understand, they sometimes show up at the ancient ruins. It is a sacred place for them, a past paradise. They believe that if society is taken back to the way it was, all problems would be solved."

"Really?" questioned Jack, with great excitement.

"At least that's what I heard. People believe in all kinds of crazy things."

"I have to go there!" cried Jack, jumping up, his eyes wide with exhilaration.

"Why?" asked Maya, shocked.

"I need to understand who I am. General Contog thought I was from the ruins. Maybe the rebels will give me a clue about my origins."

"Do you know what you're saying?"

"Yes! First, I don't trust Kallin. He'll do the same thing to me he's done to you. Secondly, from everything I've seen, it very clear that I'm not from here. I want to get away from Kallin, the Raks and everything else. If at all possible, I want to go back to where I came from."

"If Kallin ever found out...."

Jack stood up with great eagerness. "No, Maya. My mind is made up. I have to go. I will go to the ancient ruins. And I want you to come with me."

"No!" she replied. "It's too risky."

Jack rubbed his forehead with frustration. "I'm going whether you come or not," he said finally. "It's up to you."

Maya wrung her hands. "Either way I'm dead."

"No. If you stay here, you will be dead for sure. If you come with me, I can protect you. You'll be safe."

"I don't know..."

He held her hands. "Maya, I know what the problem is. You're still attached to Kallin. Even though he kicked you out the door, you can't let go." He gazed deeply into her eyes. "You have to choose between him and me. If you trust me, come with me."

Maya looked at him in askance. "The only reason I survived so long is precisely because I trusted no one. And you're asking me to trust you?"

"Yes. Believe in me."

Maya sighed. "Well, this may be the end of me, trusting a man. In two weeks' time, when I get kicked out of here, I'll end up in a Rak slum with nothing to my name, picking at bones to eat. That is, if I don't get eaten first. If I die, let me die quickly, not at the hands of a hungry Rak."

She walked to the dresser, opened it, and withdrew a small knife. She handed it to Jack and bent her head down.

"Here," she said, touching her finger to the top of the neck, just below her skull. "Cut there. You will find the DNA implant. Remove it." Jack fingered the point. He barely felt a tiny bump under the skin.

"Make a small incision only," she instructed, "and squeeze it out."

Jack made a tiny, barely visible cut. A drop of blood emerged and dripped down her neck. Using his thumb, he pushed the implant slowly out. Silver-colored, it measured the size of a grain of rice and not much to look at. He dropped it into Maya's hand.

"Can you believe that this little thing controls all our lives?" she exclaimed. Jack shook his head at the power of this insignificant-looking object.

She opened the drawer next to her bed and pulled out a small container the size of a thimble. She offered him her right arm. "Now, cut me here."

"Why?" exclaimed Jack.

"Just do it," she insisted. Jack took the knife and made a small but deep incision. A small stream of blood rolled out. She collected it in the container, dropped the implant into it and turned the cap, tightly sealing it.

"We can reinsert it when we come back. Now they can't follow our every move." She slipped the container back into the drawer and sat on her bed. Jack joined her. He brushed back her red hair and looked into her sultry eyes.

"You don't belong to Kallin anymore."

She nodded her head. "You're the only one now. I have no one else."

Jack smiled. Her loneliness matched his. He had no reason to waste the moment. He squeezed her with his strong arms and kissed her passionately.

She gasped and surrendered. "Come, I am now completely yours."

* * *

The Ancient Ruins, End of Kali Yuga

The land turned dryer the further east they drove. Ten days had passed since their banishment. The first week with Maya felt flush with desire and excitement. They spent the days in each other's arms and beds, exploring the limits of their senses. Her appetite surprised him. Once she lowered her guard and opened up, she held nothing back. He realized the situation: forces beyond their control had thrust them together. It had been easier than he expected.

But in the last three days, the feelings changed. He no longer felt connected to Maya. Once he conquered her, he lost interest. They both understood the deal—a forced dependence on each other and nothing to do with real feelings. They shared only a carnal connection and once momentarily satisfied, he felt awkward, almost alienated, until the next time. By the end, he sensed that they both were going through the motions. He felt restless, as if needing to escape the situation. The sensation seemed familiar.

He pushed the thought out and gazed at Maya. She peered into the darkness, hands resting on the wheel. They had left the estate quietly under cover of early morning darkness. The sandy-colored two-seater hovered along dusty country roads and over flat scrub for several hours, avoiding the highways and towns until it entered a level

173

desert of fine brown sand further east, toward the ocean. The dark and the monotonous countryside lulled him into a deep sleep. A couple of hours later the sun slowly crept above the horizon.

"Look!" shouted Maya. "The ruins!"

Jack woke up and peered keenly out of the window. At first, he saw nothing as the sun shone directly into his eyes but a couple of minutes later, spied some low objects on the eastern horizon. Almost indistinguishable and hardly impressive, the ruins barely jutted above the ground. However, Jack realized, upon entering, that this low, immense field stretched into the desert as far as sight allowed and contained thousands of abandoned edifices, broken down and defeated, half covered with sand. The quiet, flying automobile sped to the center of the ruins and came to a sudden halt in the middle of a large, sand-driven square enclosed by the wrecks of many buildings, their innards lying around in large heaps of brick, concrete, and stone, upon which dust devils spun about incessantly.

"Here we are!" announced Maya, her eyes dancing. Jack shivered as he stepped out, though it was not cold. A sense of foreboding, defeat and despair hung about this place like a fog permeating into his bones. His legs dragged heavily and his brain moved as slowly as his feet. Far at the northern edge of the desert the black sky filled with silvery streaks of lightning and thunder resounded softly in the distant gloom.

A mile to the east, the ocean hid in the haze and the soft rumble of its waves caught his ears and the smell of salt tingled in his nose. Somehow, despite the bleakness of this enormous plain, the sea sparked some hope in his breast. A shimmering mirage of water floated in the air above the breakers as if detached from the despondency of the desert, existing on another plane as a hope to grasp, transcendent to the surrounding desolation. Jack looked up at the illusion and breathed the wild wind deeply. A little bit of courage returned.

"Well, what shall we do?" asked Maya, observing him keenly. "You wanted to visit the ruins and here we are. What do you think?"

Jack only shook his head. Unrecognizable, the ruins meant nothing. "We need to see if the rebels are here."

Maya dragged out a hamper full of food. Dressed in rough, ragged clothes so as to make themselves more approachable to the rebels, they walked down the windy square until they came upon a cluster of large broken buildings. She opened the hamper and spread the assorted meats out in the open and they moved into the shadow of one of the structures. The sun shone brightly and the breeze carried the scent across the ruins. It did not take long for the rebels to appear. At first, a shuffling noise sounded in one of the buildings. Jack didn't see anyone. They sat still for another half hour and just when Jack's patience almost quit, three insurgents straggled out. They walked hesitantly, keeping to the shadows, skipping from one building to another and finally stopped about fifteen feet away, waiting in the dark.

"Come," said Maya to the rebels. "The food is for you." The men jumped on the meat. Jack watched quietly as they satisfied their hunger.

Finally, one of them spoke. "Who are you?" The man's face, sunburned, almost black, betrayed a life spent outdoors. His long hair and beard, completely white, came down to his chest. His long grey shirt and short dark pants, fashioned of long strips of plastic woven or tied together, probably salvaged from the sea-shore, hung low on his knees and his feet sported a pair of sandals created of crushed plastic bottles, tied down with yellow plastic rope. Light blue eyes stared shockingly out of his hard, dark face.

"We're from Kallington," replied Jack. "We want to join the rebellion."

"You're not like the usual Raks who join us. You came in that fancy car."

"No, we're not Raks," admitted Maya. "But we can help the rebellion. We have information that could be useful. Before that though, we need to know a bit about the rebellion."

"Like what?"

"We'd like to understand more about the ruins and why they are so important to you."

The men talked amongst themselves for a while. "Okay," replied the white-haired leader. "Everyone should know about this. Come." Accompanied by the two other insurgents, similarly dressed, both gaunt and with downcast eyes, they walked east.

"These ruins are sacred," proclaimed the old man.

"Is that so?" inquired Jack.

"Yes," he replied, without hesitation. "This place is paradise."

Jack scratched his head. The desert wind picked up and blew the sand fiercely around them. "There are only ruins here."

"Yes, now. But at one time a godly civilization full of beautiful, happy people with just, benevolent rulers and endless prosperity existed here, with absolutely no hunger and never any dissatisfaction."

"Do you have any proof of that?"

"Come. Let me show you."

They walked a quarter-mile south along a wide but broken road that hugged the coast, the blacktop cracked into thousands of pieces in a spider-web design, covered with pieces of plastic, weeds and blowing sand. They finally spotted a bunch of ruined brick and cement buildings on a high bluff, huddled together like gnarled sea pines against the incessant winds, surrounded by drifts of sand. Above these buildings stood a large number of billboards, like ghostly sails on broken shipwrecks. Most had withered away, ground to nothing by the effect of sand and wind, but some withstood the ravages of time fairly well. The letters, the messages, and the colorful models still smiled down on them after the ages, ossified by a thick layer of translucent salt. Jack ran toward them, eager with anticipation, leaving the others behind. He arrived at a billboard advertising a soft drink. A young woman, smiling

176

seductively, all white teeth and shiny red hair, leaned over him, touting some long-forgotten secret formula of sugar, water, color and fizz, the crystallized salt sparkling in the sun, the colors mummified by the dry air.

Jack looked in stunned silence. He shook with excitement. The image, familiar, bubbled up from his sub-consciousness, like a genetic memory from a past life. I'm beginning to remember, he thought. Maya and the others caught up to him.

"Look at that godly woman," stated the old man, pointing to the billboard.

"What do you mean?" asked Jack.

"Look at how happy and beautiful she is. She's no doubt an angel from heaven."

Jack scratched his head. Even if he didn't fully remember the past, the old man's perception didn't seem quite right. "I don't know if she is an angel exactly," he objected hesitantly.

The old man waved off his comments. "Of course she is. Who else but an angel would be so happy?" He walked a few more steps and pointed to another billboard. "Look."

Above them, in large bold letters, the word 'WHISKY' appeared, illuminated by sunlight, and beneath that word lay a sultry platinum blonde with sleepy green eyes and a skimpy black dress smiling invitingly at them. "Happiness does come in glass bottles," reassured the message at the bottom of the billboard.

"Another godly woman," stated the rebel, pointing at the blonde.

Jack shook his head and looked at a building across the street. An outdoor sign hung in the air, perched crazily on one steel leg, featuring a smiling, handsome young doctor. A stethoscope hung around his neck in a professionally casual manner. 'SCIENTIFIC STUDY REVEALS THAT 97% OF PEOPLE AGREE: THE ROAD TO HAPPINESS LIES IN....' The rest of that eternal scientific truth would never be known as the blowing sand had permanently erased it.

He finally saw it. The golden arches, the clown with orange hair, fat lips, yellow suit and red nose, smiling toothily at him from across the street. He held a burger in his hand and below was written: BILLIONS AND BILLIONS SERVED. Jack reeled. His memory jolted, hit him with full force. It all came back. He knew exactly who he was—a native son, and this was his native land! These billboards could have lined any highway intersection, small town or neighborhood in America. Inescapable relics of his past, of his childhood, and during his life, hardly noticeable because of their daily reality, they now punched him in the gut.

Jack fell on his knees and pounded the sand with his fists. Goddammit! They had blown it! He remembered almost everything now: growing up in middle-class, middle-America. He looked up at the billboards and winced, remembering the days and evenings spent casually with girlfriends, the all-night parties with school friends and the uncounted meals at fast food joints, never giving thought to the damage caused to himself, to others, to the earth. The unabated consumption, the environmental destruction, the incessant meddling with genetics—and this is how it all ended up!

He clearly saw what happened. It probably didn't take long, maybe a generation or two before the genetic mutations started to appear. Did humans fall victim to the disruption to nature that quickly? He remembered his biology texts. Genes, busy little things, responded, and quickly, to environmental factors. What humans attempted to destroy came back to harm them. And it ended like this, with Raks, mutant cows and all! No wonder this society fixated itself on genetics! They had no choice—they had to deal with this historical reality.

Jack got up and kicked the sand. He spit on the ground and glared at the stupid, smiling clown. His stomach knotted. He wanted to punch that joker right in his big, fat nose. He let out a long howl of rage and frustration. Maya and the old man regarded him with alarm.

"What's the matter? Are you crazy?" demanded the old man gruffly. "Can't you see the greatness of God?"

It took several minutes for Jack's disgust and anger to settle down. An unexpected blast of cold air from the sea hit him. He shivered. He closed his eyes and breathed deeply. *For once*, he decided, *I'll keep my mouth shut.* How would they react if he told them of his origins in this place, from that time?

"I'm fine," mumbled Jack.

"How come you're not happy?" demanded the old insurgent. "This place always cheers me up."

Jack looked up at him in surprise. "What do you mean?"

"Look at their faces, their smiles," he said, pointing to the ghostly images. "They're so happy."

Jack stared quizzically. It took several seconds to grasp the train of thought. "You think these people are actually joyful?"

The rebel looked at him, puzzled. "Of course. How can you say they're not?"

Did the man actually think that these models displayed real emotions? Or that they themselves were real? "But don't you understand that they're up there only to give a message?"

"Yes! The message is that if we truly believe in God and paradise, we can make the whole world happy once again. These ruins prove that at one time, many, many years ago, humanity lived a godly life and God blessed us with unlimited food, drink, beauty, and happiness." He continued with conviction. "And if we fight against evil and defeat Kallin, God will re-establish his kingdom on earth and the world will once again become paradise."

Maya clapped her hands. "Oh, you are a great prophet! Thank you for giving us the truth!" She looked at Jack happily. "Isn't this wonderful news?"

Jack looked at her in amazement. She gazed back with a perfectly serious, level stare. A realization dawned on him. The message implied on the billboards, that consumption equals happiness, seduced many people, many

179

countries, many cultures in the past and it drew people even now, long after the greedy society it represented consumed itself long ago. 'Greed is good,' his economics professor once taught him. 'It's good for the greedy,' Jack had remarked at that time.

"You can't really mean that," he could only say.

The old man scratched his head impatiently. "Why not? Look at these people. How can you say they're not glad?"

Jack stood silently. What evidence did he have to contradict the endless smiling faces shilling myriad products for the insatiable senses? He decided to turn the tables. "But how can you prove that these people were happy? Just because they're smiling doesn't mean anything. You need scientific proof."

The old revolutionary looked at him in disgust. "What's the matter with you? Look at that." He pointed to the 'SCIENTIFIC STUDY REVEALS THAT 97% OF PEOPLE AGREE' billboard. "You want science? There it is."

Jack looked uncomprehendingly at the billboard. The sand had erased the crux of the billboard's meaning. The old rebel had missed the whole point. He tried again. "But this study…"

"What difference does it make?" interrupted the man. "This study or that? Science is science. You can take any scientific study you want. We all know what they mean." Maya watched the man intently, moving her head up and down in obvious agreement.

"But what about the three percent who disagreed?"

"What the hell is the matter with you?" roared the white haired rebel. "Those three percent are liars. Criminals. Idiots. They ought to be blindfolded and shot!"

Jack jumped back. For the rebels, the word 'science' gave legitimacy to anything attached to it. He understood the old man's fury: he had questioned the creed of a true believer.

"But the truth…." he started and then stopped. He didn't know how to continue. They looked at him blankly.

"The truth?" questioned Maya. She obviously hadn't heard of the word before. "What do you mean?"

"You know, what really happens. You know, reality." Maya frowned.

"Reality!" the old man exclaimed. "What the hell does reality have to do with our lives?"

"Oh, I know what reality is," said Maya, skipping up and down.

"Go ahead," said Jack.

"What really happens is that the person with the most money and power gets his way. That's reality!"

"But it doesn't change the truth," protested Jack. The old man swore. Maya rubbed her forehead and tugged Jack's arm. He felt depressed, defeated. There had to be some way to show them something greater than their suffocating, narrow vision.

"What about God?"

Maya smiled with relief at the change in subject. "I want a church just like the one he lives in," she remarked, pointing to a billboard of a minister and his large, brand-new, stained-glass church. "With a big bedroom in the back."

Jack smiled. He knew what Maya was thinking. "Sex and religion?" he questioned.

She nodded her head. "God will come and God will go, but sex will be here forever."

Jack guffawed. Maya, in her silly way, broke his gloom. She looked at him, fluttering her eyelashes suggestively. He laughed. "Not here, Maya. Not now."

"Okay," she said, wagging her finger. "But you owe me one." They walked for a few more minutes before the man stepped out in front.

"Well?" he demanded. "You wanted to see the ruins and I brought you here. So what do you think?" Jack's mind spun as a surreal feeling overcame him. Standing amongst the remains of what once composed a part of him but which now inspired only disgust, compounded by these people who blindly worshiped the worst parts of it, sucked

181

the energy out of him. But it would be foolish to antagonize them. He stood in their land and needed to respect that.

"These ruins are magnificent. I…I'm sorry to have doubted you. I appreciate your kindness. I understand the sincerity of your beliefs and I'm sure that your faith will be rewarded."

The old man breathed deeply and smiled at the validation of his creed. "Do you believe?" he asked. The two other rebels looked with baited breath.

"Yes, I believe."

The rebels hugged each other. "I forgive you," pronounced the old insurgent. "After all, you are a newcomer. You can't understand everything right away. Please stay here." He walked over to his two comrades and talked to them in hushed tones.

"I'm so excited," exclaimed Maya. "I understand everything this man is saying. How stupid I was all these years!" She kissed Jack full on the lips, an ardent lover's kiss.

He turned away.

"What's the matter?"

Jack felt black, alienated. Not just from this world— from the rebels, the ruins—but also from Maya. *Why am I feeling this way*, he wondered. *What has come between us?* He desperately wanted her all this time but now felt empty inside.

"You're very moody today, aren't you?"

He just nodded. He understood Maya's affinity to this place. Psychologically, it afforded her a place to escape. In reality, her life reached a dead end with nowhere to go. The rebellion, despite its crudeness and lack of logic, offered a bit of hope, of faith.

"Kallin had me so brainwashed!" Maya continued. "I can't believe that I thought these people were liars. The rebels have the truth. I want to join the rebellion right now and re-establish paradise on earth and then we can be like the ancient people; happy, beautiful and never having to worry about food, drink or shelter!" She reached over to Jack and hugged him fervently. "And I owe it all to you!"

Jack's jaw dropped. In a matter of hours, she changed from Kallin's heartsick mistress to a true believer. Did he lose her, not to Kallin this time, but to the rebels?

Chapter Twenty Three

The Ancient Ruins, End of Kali Yuga
The old man and the two rebels returned. "We want you to come with us," the white-bearded man said. "We usually don't do this with newcomers, but I want you to see our prophet, Abraham."

"Abraham?" inquired Jack. "I know about a prophet named Abraham."

The old man looked at him in amazement. "You know Abraham?" he asked reverentially.

"Yes," continued Jack hesitantly.

"Tell me more."

"Well, I don't know much. Except that he's mentioned in the Old Testament."

The rebel leader scratched his head. "I don't know what you're talking about, but I will take you to the holiest place for us on earth, the Throne of Abraham."

They walked across the desert until they reached the coast. The sea pounded the light brown sand with unceasing, ten-foot-high blue waves. Pieces of plastic, of all colors and sizes, rolled in and out with the waves and tiny bits of synthetics—black, blue, yellow, red and all colors in between—mixed in with the sand in a thick meandering line all along the water's edge. Far to the south, Jack observed a small building standing in the middle of a shallow tidal pool a thousand feet long and a hundred feet wide. The shrine resembled a ruined Greek temple, fashioned of yellowing marble, its roof blown away, with pieces of marble columns lying about. A sense of déjà vu overcame him as if he had seen, even in his dreams, this building, this scene.

He entered the pool, the water reaching his ankles, the sandy floor speckled with white, shiny stones. Jack picked one up, turned it in his hand quizzically, and understood it to be a piece of marble, rolled back and forth by the sea until polished smooth and polished. Millions of these marble fragments lay scattered all along the beach as far as he could see, shimmering under the sea water, shooting a thousand beams of light, their radiance reflecting off the ripples, the sunlight stinging his eyes. The marble once covered the exteriors, walls and floors of innumerable buildings. He couldn't imagine the violence that shattered all this stone. What could have caused this destruction?

This puzzle from the past only darkened his mood. His previous life quietly uncovered bit by bit, but the slow unfolding of his memory fed a sense of dread in his stomach. He shivered and kept marching.

They waded towards the temple, urged on by the enthusiastic revolutionaries. The sun, now hot, reflected blazingly on the calm waters. He saw no fish, but an occasional small crab darted here or there. The rebels ran after these crabs and, with luck, grabbed one before it dug into the sand. They cracked the shells between their teeth, swallowed the tiny bit of meat and flung the remains into the water, which other, smaller, crabs set upon instantly.

After a lengthy march, they came upon the back of the rectangular, age-stained, broken marble building. In great excitement, the rebels sprinted around to the front side of the structure.

"Come!" shouted the leader. "Come see the Throne of Abraham." The revolutionaries had piled up sand in front of the temple into a square of about a hundred feet on each side, three feet above the waters, and secured its edges with large flat rocks standing up like dinosaur fins. On it, the three men sat on their knees, their hands held up in supplication. A plinth, five feet above the sand, housed a large stone chair upon which sat a huge sculpture of a man, with long legs and lanky arms, a craggy face, short beard and hawk-like eyes staring off into the distance.

"Behold," cried the rebel, "the Throne of Abraham."

Maya fell to her knees and raised her hands in entreaty. "Oh, Abraham! Oh, holy prophet! Please bless the rebellion with victory!"

185

Jack watched with disbelief. This was Abraham all right; not the Old Testament prophet, but good old Honest Abe, the nineteenth president, the Great Emancipator himself. And this was not the Throne of Abraham but the Lincoln Memorial. Or, rather, what remained of it. He stood transfixed, not knowing what to say or do. He felt a tug on his arm.

"What are you doing?" asked Maya. "They're all staring at you." Jack looked around. The insurgents were most certainly observing him, assessing his surrender to their great seer.

"Come," said the leader, "get on your knees. The prophet will bestow his blessings upon you." Jack felt sick to his stomach. If only he could tell them what he knew—that they founded their whole rebellion on a lie, a misunderstanding. He couldn't stand it any longer.

"This is not the prophet Abraham! You all have made a terrible mistake."

The old man jumped to his feet. "What are you saying?"

"This place is not paradise. It never was! And it never will be!" The rebels advanced angrily.

"Please," cried Maya. "He doesn't understand!"

Jack felt a profound restlessness, a sickening of the soul, a type of impatience a caged rat might feel at the end of its hopeless life. No light lingered, none whatsoever. He felt betrayed, angry, at the rebels. The prospect of the ruins had given him some hope, a faith in the future, but the bitter truth was that the rebels, too, faced a dead end. He gritted his teeth. He hated this world, he hated Kallin and now he hated the insurgents.

"You people have no chance," he yelled. "This is a hopeless cause. You will all die for nothing." The rebels, finding their deepest beliefs challenged, held back no further.

"This man is a blasphemer!" roared the white-bearded man. "Kill him!" Jack jumped away but couldn't escape their wrath. Using bare fists and pieces of the ruined monument, they pummeled him with all their might. Jack grunted in pain and fought, hitting back as hard as he could, but the zeal of the revolutionaries overpowered him. He encountered something greater than ordinary human strength; he didn't have the might to fight against their faith in paradise and their prophet.

Maya jumped in. "Please let him go," she begged, pulling at the rebels. They ignored her. She finally got hold of the old man and pulled him aside. He gasped for breath and sweat ran down his cheeks. His eyes looked clouded.

"Is it proper for you to attack someone in front of Abraham?" she demanded. He shook his head.

"Please stop it!"

His eyes cleared. "All right! Enough."

The other two men stopped the attack, panting heavily. Cuts appeared above Jack's eyes, blood flowed down his face and his lower lip was split. He gasped in pain and held his sides tightly.

"Get out," shouted the old man, "and don't ever come here."

Jack held on to Maya shakily as they walked away, the rebels' curses ringing in their ears. About a hundred yards later Jack slumped to the beach, unable to stand. Maya took cool ocean water and washed the blood from his face. The salt stung his wounds. He grimaced, hissing through clenched teeth and sat there for a long time, gathering strength.

"Why did you say those things?" demanded Maya as they began their long journey back to the automobile.

She enthusiastically accepted the rebel's creed; the pull of a paradise, the seduction of a promised future and the romance of a golden past could be very enticing. Only he knew the truth of their theology. Would she accept what he had to say? Jack hesitated. "I will tell you later," he replied.

They walked north following the coast, straggling over sand dunes, each higher than the one before. Two miles later they came to the top of the last dune which dropped about three hundred feet to a large flat beach almost four hundred feet wide and several miles long, covered with a thin layer of water at high tide. An amazing sight revealed itself. On the beach lay a huge dome, constructed of white marble, completely circular, supported by hundreds of pillars. On top of this first dome stood another much smaller circle of lesser pillars, crowned with a cupola, topped by an enormous statue of a robed woman. The building that supported the dome no longer existed, broken into uncountable pieces, scattered along the shore. The beautiful elegant dome lay partly buried in the sand and its top, crested with the stunning statue, rose at a twenty-five-degree angle. Waves washed into its cavernous opening facing the sea. In the afternoon sun, it reflected beautifully in the clear salt water.

Jack stood transfixed by the unexpected sight. He suddenly remembered it: the Capitol Dome, the seat of the legislative assembly in the heart of Washington, DC. He gulped. Though he had never visited the District of Columbia, he remembered seeing endless newscasts using the dome as a backdrop and the image had burned itself into his consciousness. Even though partly buried in sand, it still commanded awe and respect. Chills traveled up and down his spine.

"What is this thing?" gasped Maya. "Who could have built it?"

He shook his head. He couldn't risk telling her the truth. Would her newfound faith cause her to disbelieve him? "I know, but I can't tell you."

"You are a strange man," she exclaimed.

Jack sighed. Could she understand that he came from a time and place where people poisoned the planet, fought countless wars and endlessly exploited the poor? Could he explain to her that the choices that he and incalculable others had made resulted in the society she lived in? He changed the topic.

"It's okay. Don't worry. Let's go explore this thing." They walked down the dune and into the dome's vast opening, the waves washing up to their knees, and explored within, admiring the bas-reliefs that fashioned a frieze all around its base. Slats of sunlight poured in from the many openings on the structure's sides and sand, pushed in by the waves, formed a dry bank about thirty feet inside, upon which they sat. Jack pulled Maya closer. She came willingly and he laid her down on the sand even though he felt completely alone, disconnected even from this gorgeous lover lying next to him.

"Do you think the rebels may be around?" she asked.

"The rebels be damned," he replied, unbuttoning her blouse. They lay in each other's arms for many minutes and then made furious love in the womb of the dome, their voices echoing back and forth off the walls of the monument. Jack's lovemaking was neither peaceful nor satisfying, but a desperate attempt to bond with someone, anyone, in this dark, desolate world. But the harder he tried to connect with Maya, the emptier he felt. His attempt finished as quickly and as futilely as it started.

"What's wrong?" questioned Maya. He said nothing. There was no feeling at all and it was obvious to both of them. He felt even more alone.

Chapter Twenty Four

On Pilgrimage, Satya Yuga
One day the pilgrims came across an enormous black rock sitting squarely in their path. They found no passage through, over or around it. They gathered at its base as Parvata Rishi unwrapped his palm-leaf manuscripts from their orange cloth coverings, placed a white cloth on the ground and sat down.

The blackness of the granite, its glassy smoothness, the roughly triangular shape and the way it sat on the ground—all seemed oddly familiar to Steve. He jumped up. He had seen it before! "Parvata Rishi, I have something to say," he interjected.

The rishi looked up from the shastras. "What is it, my son?"

"I have seen this rock before."

"Really?" asked the rishi, his eyes wide.

"Yes. My brother and I traveled in the Himalayas, just a couple of months before I appeared in Mahavan."

The rishi put down the scriptures. "Tell me more."

Memories of the trip to India, the temple in Badrinath, the meal at the restaurant and the hike through the mountains; all came tumbling back. Did it all happen just a couple of months ago? It seemed so far away, as if in another time and place. But of course it did happen in another time and place. Yet here he stood again.

"My brother and I came here, following the instructions of a South Indian restaurant owner, searching for the Valley of the Rishis, which if I understood properly, lies somewhere past this rock. Unable to proceed further, we turned back."

"I believe that the Valley of the Rishis, as you call it, is actually Shambala, and a good reason existed for your inability to continue."

"What's that?"

"You did not have the spiritual power to do so." The rishi picked up the shastra. "According to this, to gain the *shakti*, the spiritual strength, to solve the riddle posed by this barrier, we need to meditate for the next seven days to achieve *dhyana*, that is, clarity. Only then will we be able to proceed."

The pilgrims nodded their heads. This seemed completely understandable to them. They regarded this as not just a physical passage but a spiritual one as well and, indeed, the further they traveled in the mountains, the more their voyage had become mystical. Following Parvata Rishi's shastras, they had stopped and conducted yajnas, chanted mantras or meditated at specific places along the way. Steve never attempted a week-long meditation, but the others seemed totally unfazed by such a challenge. For the yogis from the forest, a seven-day meditation was hardly worth mentioning.

They rested for the night and the next morning found their places of meditation in front of the rock. Steve sat next to Shanti. She patted his hand and he found comfort, security and resolution by her side. He crossed his legs, straightened his back, stretched his arms out and closed his eyes, fingers touching the ground.

Shanti tapped his shoulder.

Steve opened his eyes. "What is it?"

"Get going."

"What do you mean?"

"It's been a week already. Time to get going."

"What!" exclaimed Steve. "I closed my eyes just a few moments ago!"

"It's Satya Yuga," laughed Shanti. "You're becoming a real yogi."

The rishi walked to where the granite met the mountain. "My meditation revealed a passage through this rock." He pulled aside some bushes.

"Dig," he pointed.

Steve grabbed a flat piece of wood and started excavating, the expectancy of the journey's conclusion fueling his efforts. The soft ground yielded easily. Others, grabbing makeshift shovels, kitchen utensils, or with bare hands, burrowed at the indicated area and, after a couple hours of work, fashioned a trough ten feet deep and four feet wide. They gathered in the pit and the rishi organized an arti, offering the sacred flame first to the rock and then to the pilgrims, who passed their hands over it and touched their heads respectfully. Parvata Rishi bent down and thrust the rock at the bottom of the trench. A small passage, just big enough for the pilgrims to squeeze through in single file, opened up as part of the stone sprung back. Steve gasped.

They gathered large branches, bound them at one end with oil-soaked cotton cloth, lit them and entered the passage. Steve waited until all the travelers passed through the hole one by one, and finally, he, Shanti and the rishi ducked in. He pushed the rock and it snapped back into place perfectly, leaving no trace of its separate existence.

Steve held the torch above. It illuminated Shanti's and Parvata Rishi's faces, shining like buds in a dark flower bed. As they set off into the belly of the mountain, a long thin line of torches flickered in the darkness, going ever downwards. The pilgrims called out their names from front to back and then back to front in military style, their voices becoming muffled the further they receded.

He whooped, his voice echoing five times, on each occasion growing fainter and more indistinct. The exclamation points of flames stopped moving as their bearers turned around, and shining eyes and flashing smiles reflected back, growing smaller and smaller all the way down and then quickly disappeared as the torches turned back around and the travelers continued their trek. He sighed deeply, inhaling in the unexpected, exquisite scene, the indelible image sending chills down his body.

After a while, he lost track of time in the darkness. They could have walked for an hour, maybe three. The total lack of any reference points made it hard to tell not only time but also distance and direction. The passage led steeply down for about seven thousand steps, where it opened up into a large cavern. Steve waved the torch above his head and the light sparkled back from the roof of the grotto. They sat down to eat a quiet and quick lunch of bread, water, and dried fruit, as no one wanted to waste time.

From this part on, Steve, Shanti, and her father started at the beginning. A slight wind blew into the cave and they decided to walk towards it, hoping to find an exit. The passage did not now so steeply decline but still tilted downwards. Steve breathed in the humidity and relaxed his body; his skin, nostrils and lungs exulting in the moisture after weeks of dry mountain air. After some time, Steve realized that wetness splashed under his sandals. An inch of water flooded the cave's floor and he scooped a handful to taste the sweet liquid. They were heading in the direction it flowed. He looked back. The line of flickering lamps went deep into the darkness, twinkling high on the cavern's ceiling.

The muffled sounds of names being called bounced off the walls in the back recesses of the cave and echoed past him in the dark, warm, moist womb of the mountain. He marched and marched, quietly and resolutely, hour after hour, in the thick darkness, the humid air becoming warmer. The water slowly increased in volume, coming up to his ankles and many thousands of determined steps later, reaching his calves. The wind whistled in his ears, but he saw no sight of the exit. The weeks of walking and the closeness to their destination filled Steve with both great impatience and heavy exhaustion.

After hiking in the dark, unknowing of the passage of time, seemingly like forever, but yet maybe a half a day, the water flowed knee-deep and the trek slowed. The roof of the cavern, now a tunnel, could be touched by extending both arms. The darkness, warmth, and dampness gave him the impression of passing through the mountain's birth canal, of being pushed out of its side. If this was a birth, he reflected wryly, it certainly was a long, painful and difficult one.

Steve's feet ached from exertion. The muscles in his legs bunched, making each step an exercise in agony. Finding footholds under the rushing water further complicated the situation. Each step required care. He looked back. Parvata Rishi panted for breath and every once in a while stopped to gain strength. Shanti clasped on to her father, breathing heavily. They reached the limits of endurance but had no place to stop or rest, as the water, now a river, flowed strong, fast and cold around them.

Suddenly, a pang of fear entered Steve's pounding heart. Did they take a wrong turn? He froze, unable to move his feet in the grimly pulling waters.

Shanti saw it first. "Look!" she exclaimed. "That must be the light at the entrance to the cave."

Steve peered anxiously. A slight paleness, like a purple stain on a black cloth, appeared in the distance.

"Yes! That's it!"

A great cry arose from the pilgrims. A new energy enthused Steve and he redoubled his efforts. The pale patch grew more obvious the closer he came, until there was no mistaking it. Sunlight shone ahead!

The last part of the march, however, proved to be the most difficult. The wind blew fast, warm and moist against his face but the bone-numbing water, now waist deep, drained his energy and slowed his movements. He had to exercise care: any slip or fall risked meant being swept away by the cunning current, and with his load to carry, proved to be an especially arduous task.

Just when he thought he could go no further, when the waters reached up to his chest, when his shaking, cramping legs refused to budge, the passage widened and riverbanks appeared. He scrambled out and dragged himself onto the pebbly shore. Others followed. The ones porting loads threw them down, shivering and gasping in exhaustion. After resting his cold body for several long minutes, Steve once again got up on trembling legs, the exit less than a thousand footsteps away. A roaring sound from outside filled the air.

Not caring for the others, he ran until he escaped into the sunlight which crashed into his eyes, blinding him. He crumpled on the rock, curled up, shivering, trembling, gasping in huge lungfuls of air. His skin felt wrinkled, leathery and slippery from the long exposure to the water and he let out a strange little cry, almost a whimper, a small baby sound.

Many minutes later Steve's eyes focused. The lip of the cave jutted out of the mountain for about thirty feet and down its center raced the river, twenty feet across and six feet deep, thundering into the valley below. He kneaded the knots in his legs, yelping in pain as the muscles straightened out. Steve turned on his stomach and crawled to the edge of the rock. The spray created an intense rainbow that hung in the air, not fifty feet away. The entire valley came into view. From his high perch, it appeared so small, so exotic and so beautiful that it almost seemed to be a painting, the canvas delightfully alive with hundreds of sparkling colors. The water, boiling white and blue, fell far below onto a jumble of white rocks and gathered itself into a picturesque river which meandered all the way through the lush, enchanted land until it disappeared into the ground at the mountains at the other end.

The valley, long but narrow, measured not more than a couple of hundred square miles and lay perfectly hidden, encircled completely by seven ranges of mountains, like an emerald surrounded by diamonds. The sheer granite wall across from where he lay seemed almost close enough to touch, but he knew, stood much further away. Large eagles and hawks floated lazily in the late afternoon haze near those cliffs and the sun sent brilliant shafts of golden light to the valley floor. The scent of wild grass and pine forest floated up, and he relished deeply their inimitable fragrance. A large verdant meadow rested in the valley on the near side of the river, while a forest of pines, rhododendrons, and fruit trees grew on the other. He stood up and looked above. Drops of melting snow fell cold on his now warm face.

"Steve," came a voice from inside the cavern. It was Shanti! He hobbled back inside. She held on to her stumbling father. He jumped between the two of them and with his strong hands, dragged the struggling pair into the open. Parvata Rishi fell on the stone, completely drained, his eyes blinking uncontrollably.

Shanti joined Steve, her face beaming with excitement and relief. Shambala at last! He embraced her, swinging her round and round, too excited for niceties, as she screamed with pleasure. They had traversed for weeks through jungle, over seven mountains ranges, and for many exhausting, grinding hours through underground caves to reach their destination.

Steve walked to where the ledge met the mountain. A narrow path, only two feet wide, gently twisted down. Shanti went first and he, with his strong right hand holding her father, came next, while the rest followed, and they arrived at the meadow within an hour, where, on the grass and under trees, stood the shelters of earlier arrivals. The pilgrims of Mahavan set up camp and the air filled with sounds of joyous laughter, greetings of old friends and much storytelling. Steve dropped his load and ran laughing as far as his legs could carry him, arms stretched out, through the long green blades, past clumps of yellow marigolds, blue buttercups, and white daisies, drinking in the warm sun and inhaling the tang of pine trees. His legs trembled, his arms tingled with delight and he dropped in the lush grass, closed his eyes and fell asleep.

* * *

Shambala, End of Satya Yuga

After three days in Shambala, Steve and Shanti finally sat down with Parvata Rishi near the river, where the sun warmed the grass, sparkled above the stream and shimmered on its fast-moving waters. Parvata Rishi called it the *Sarasvati*, the great watercourse so often mentioned in the Vedas, the mighty mythical river with its origin in the spiritual world, on whose banks the great yogis practiced their sadhana. Without doubt, meditating on its banks and listening to the pleasant sound of the flowing waters induced the most calmful of contemplations.

The peaceful river served as an ironic setting to the anxious pair. Tranquility did not describe Steve's feelings. He gripped Shanti's left hand tightly, butterflies in his stomach, his palms clammy and cold, shaking slightly with apprehension. Shanti nervously fidgeted with the border of her cream colored sari. Anxiety radiated from her face.

The rishi sat bare-shouldered in the crisp air, wearing a Brahmin thread—a loop of cotton string draped over his left shoulder, crossing his chest, circling his right hip, and coming up over his back.

Parvata Rishi turned to Shanti. "Well, my dear, what is it?"

Shanti looked up shyly. "Father, we're here to request your blessings for our marriage."

"Marriage?" enquired the rishi. "You mentioned it to me, but our young friend has said nothing."

Steve managed a quick smile and opened his mouth, but no words escaped his lips. His mind went blank. An awkward silence fell among them.

"Well, son," encouraged the rishi, "speak."

"I...I want to marry Shanti," Steve stammered.

The rishi gazed at the mountains, toying with his Brahmin thread for several long seconds. "Why do you want to marry my daughter?"

The question threw Steve for a loop. He certainly hadn't expected to give justifications for the proposal.

"I love Shanti very much," he finally mumbled.

The rishi smiled. "That is certainly a good reason for a marriage." The sun glistened on his white hair and shone on his bronzed shoulders. "But as a father, I am anxious to see my daughter properly taken care of. Do you understand?"

Steve slowly nodded his head, but his eyes showed bewilderment.

"I mean, how will you support her, and later on, a family?"

Steve turned white. The idea hadn't crossed his mind. "Well, I suppose I can farm or take up some trade. I am sure I'll learn something in a little time," he countered bravely.

"I'm sure you will. But here's my question—are you are ready to marry my daughter?"

"What do you mean?"

"How old are you?"

"I'm twenty-eight, that is, twenty-eight in Kali Yuga years."

"In other words, you are past the age by which most men marry."

Steve slowly nodded his head. In Mahavan, most of the young people married in their early adulthood. Their culture demanded it. But he had another explanation. "I didn't marry, I suppose, because of my mother and brother. As the older one, I had to take care of them after my father died. They needed my help."

"So what has changed?"

Steve didn't know what to say. He kept quiet and looked at the grass. "I do feel an obligation to my brother," he agreed finally. "And though my mother is gone, I made a promise to her."

"And what is that?"

"I gave her my word that I would help Jack, and in some ways, look after him."

The rishi observed him gravely. "Since this obligation is important to you, are you ready to marry Shanti?"

The observation flabbergasted him. "Of course I'm ready! I want to marry Shanti no matter what!"

"What if you discovered that your brother is in Kali Yuga? After all, you did come looking for him, didn't you?"

Steve nodded his head hesitantly. "I imagine so."

"What would happen to Shanti if you went to Kali Yuga? Or for that matter, anywhere else? Would you leave her behind while you searched for your brother?"

Steve said nothing. Parvata Rishi was right. The last many weeks spent with Shanti in the blush of love pushed questions about Jack into the background. He hadn't thought things through properly.

"And what if you have children?" continued the rishi. "The real question is this—are you ready to make a commitment when you have these unanswered questions in your life?"

Steve sat silently. He felt as if the bottom had dropped out from under him. "I haven't thought about it like that," he blurted.

"You both understand that marriage is a big step. A major commitment?"

"Of course," replied Steve and Shanti simultaneously.

The rishi addressed his young daughter "My dear, I'm not here to tell you what to do or to come in the way of your love. I just want the best for both of you."

Shanti nodded her head.

"Therefore I will not tell you what decision to take. The future is yours to decide. But both of you need to be sure that you are ready. The choices you make now will have consequences throughout your lives. So think through this seriously."

Steve had to admit that Parvata Rishi, as usual, understood the situation clearly. The questions that had haunted him at his arrival in Mahavan returned in full force. How could he marry Shanti when his dilemma remained unresolved? Maybe he was not ready for marriage. He needed to be completely honest and fully committed. Anything less would not be fair.

"You have given me a lot to think about," he admitted. He smiled at Shanti hesitantly but also reassuringly. "We need to discuss all things."

The old man got up and touched him on the shoulder. "Yes, you do. A marriage begins with a million words. You both need to talk about this and all other things thoroughly. I cannot do this for you."

199

Steve nodded his head. Things didn't go as expected, but a lot of reflection lay ahead. They got up and walked to their tents to attend to their daily chores.

Chapter Twenty Five

Kallin's Country Estate, End of Kali Yuga

Jack and Maya didn't return to the estate until well past midnight. They entered his room and she climbed into the bed, pillows propping her up. They both fell into dire straits, having shelter neither in Kallin's society nor with the rebels. The Rak slum appeared to be their likely destination.

He paced back and forth. He hit the bottom of his palm against his forehead. He had stupidly alienated the rebels. Even if he proved them wrong, they were his only shelter. Foolish and reckless again. This time he risked not just his life.

Maya yawned. "What are you doing?"

"Nothing. Just thinking."

"Walking around isn't going to help. Just come to bed." He ignored her and continued pacing.

"What's gotten into you?" she questioned. "You've been in such a bad mood all day."

He stopped. He couldn't tell her that he wanted to get out; that he wanted to leave her, that he lost the connection. Another bit of memory returned. Of course! He felt like this several times before! At first he experienced passion but, after establishing a relationship, he would quickly lose interest. Crying, anger and insults followed and, finally, an ex-girlfriend rushed out the door. He hated to be a jerk, but he couldn't help his feelings. He started walking yet again.

"Okay," sighed Maya. "I'm tired of this. You can't sleep and neither can I." She got out of bed and sat on one of the two chairs next to the nightstand. "Tell me what's going on."

"Nothing," he replied glumly. She trusted him, literally, with her life.

Her eyebrows knotted and frustration showed on her face. "I'm not stupid. Since yesterday, your attitude's changed. It's not the ruins or Kallin or the rebels. It's you. You're different, as if you don't want to be with me anymore."

"It's not like that."

Maya's eyes flashed. "No! It's exactly like that! You think I can't tell? When you're nice, you're charming, you're funny, you're cute. Now you're as cold as snow. I deserve an answer!" She slammed her hand on the night table. "I demand an answer!"

Jack nodded. Yes, she required an answer. But where could he start? "It...It's happened before."

"What's happened before?"

"With girlfriends."

Maya observed him keenly. "What do you mean?"

Jack sighed. "I don't know. After a while, I just lose the connection, the attachment."

"And that's how you feel about me?"

He always found this hard, where he hurt others. But nothing could be done. "I'm sorry," he stated stoically. "I don't love you anymore."

She met his declaration with deep laughter. "We never had love. I won't flatter either you or me to say so. We both know what it was, and love it wasn't."

Jack's eyes widened, bewildered.

Maya pointed to the chair next to her. "Come sit down. I've been around men all my life. Nothing you say or do can surprise me. You asked me to take you to the ruins and I did. I trusted you, not out of naïveté, but because I had no other option."

He tried again. "I'm sorry, it's not you. I just get bored quickly. It's not just girlfriends, it's my whole life. I lose interest and move on."

Maya laughed sarcastically. "You get bored huh? Did you think that maybe it's something other than boredom?"

"What do you mean?"

"Like, maybe, fear of commitment?"

He thought for a second. "I guess you could say that. But it comes to the same thing."

"No, it doesn't. If it is boredom, then maybe I'm boring. But if it's fear of commitment, then it's your fault."

"Yeah, you're right. It's my fault."

"And if it is an inability to commit, it makes sense that it is not just women, but other areas of your life, whatever they may be."

Jack had to agree. She hit the nail on the head, but he couldn't stick to one place, do the same thing, all the time.

"What did your family say?"

"I got the same lecture from my mom and my brother. Be responsible. Go to college. Get a job. Get married." He paused. "But that's just not me."

"So you're saying that they're wrong?"

"Listen," he protested. "It's my life. I can do what I want."

"Even if you keep hurting everyone?"

"If I hurt you. I'm sorry. But I'd rather be truthful."

"I'm not talking about me. I'm talking about your mother and your brother. In fact," she continued, "I don't think there's anyone you haven't hurt."

"I haven't hurt my family!" he exclaimed.

"Are you serious? If you can do this to me, I'm sure you could do the same or worse to them."

Jack sat dumbfounded. How could she say something like that?

"So I have commitment issues," he admitted finally. "So what?"

"You're missing the big question."

"What's that?"

"What happened to you that makes you this way?"

Jack straightened. "I...I don't know. I've never thought about it like that."

"Look in your life," continued Maya. "The answers are there."

Her approach startled him. She wasn't one of college girls he had dated. She saw through him, but the darkness still remained. He didn't want to be with her. "Okay. But it doesn't change the situation between us."

"Well then," shouted Maya, "how different are you from Kallin?"

Jack winced. "I can't believe you are comparing me to him."

"Really? Both of you used me for what you wanted. And you both got rid of me when you didn't need me anymore."

"It's not like that at all!" he protested.

"It's exactly like that! I've had enough. I can't stand you!" She jumped up. "I hate you. I'm going back to my room." She walked out the door and slammed it behind her.

Jack shook his head. The memory of Laura, his last girlfriend, came to mind. He vividly saw her doing the same thing. He went to bed and lay down, wondering about what Maya said. That he hurt everyone he knew? How could she say that? To look in his life? That's something he'd never done, being too busy moving from one thing to another. He stopped. A feeling of not remembering something overcame him. Something in his gut told him she was right about hurting his family, but the memory lay hidden.

The rawness of Maya's situation became clear; caught in a bind, she had no escape. Everyone in her life had abandoned her. He felt bad, guilty. She didn't lead an ideal life, in fact, she became the mistress of a man she felt no love for but, despite that, she wasn't jaded at all. A sudden tenderness toward her overwhelmed him and touched his heart. He turned the light off, covered himself with a blanket and lay awake, thinking.

* * *

He knocked on her door. The day just dawned. Maya opened the door.

"What do you want?" she asked icily.

"I...I want to talk to you. Can I come in?"

"You can tell me what you want from right here," she stated, not budging. He understood her hostility.

"I came to apologize," he ventured, "and to talk with you."

She hesitated for a moment before letting him in. She wrapped her robe tightly around her and sat on a chair.

"I've been thinking about what you said last night. Maya, I owe you an apology. I've done some very stupid things and behaved like a complete jerk. I'm really, really sorry."

She looked at him with startled eyes. "Okay, this is different."

"You have the right to be angry at me but, in fact, you gave me the best advice—to look for answers in my life. I thought about it all night. For that, I sincerely want to thank you and hope you can forgive me."

Maya's jaw dropped. "This is the first time you have shown some sincerity."

"I want to make it up to you."

"How?"

"Let's go back to the rebels. Right now, that's the only option."

"But the rebels hate you!"

"Yes, but they don't hate you. I may have spoiled everything for myself, but you might still find a place with them. At least you can save your life, even if I can't save mine."

Her eyes widened. "You would do that for me?"

"Of course. I don't like who I am, how I dealt with you. I want to be better than that. Let's leave this morning right after breakfast."

"You know, this is the first time you've been considerate of me, of my feelings. Actually, this is the first time any man has shown me some consideration. I really appreciate that."

She got up, smiled, embraced and kissed him, a deep closed-eyes kiss. No sense of separation but just sweet union. Is this bliss? Is this love? Jack felt these questions but did not ask them. Consciousness returned, and for the first time, he made a true connection with her, something not fleeting, but real. He breathed deeply and beamed. He wanted to be with her again.

She ran her index finger over the cuts on his face. "Does it still hurt?" she questioned. Jack grimaced. His wounds still pained, but the discoveries of the previous day caused more agony. He visited the ruins to learn the truth of his antecedents and what he discovered left many questions unanswered. Could he go back? And did 'back' still remain? *Let me try,* he thought, *let me share my secret with her.*

"Maya, I need to tell you something."

She sat on her bed. "Go ahead."

He joined her and held her hands. "I don't know if you will believe me, but I come from the place of the ruins. I lived in that country before the Throne of Abraham, the circular dome, and all the buildings were destroyed, maybe thousands of years ago. I lived there when the images of those beautiful people—those billboards—still stood."

Maya's eyes widened. "You're from paradise?" she probed, her eyes dancing.

Jack rolled his eyes. "If you want to call it paradise, go ahead, I don't care. I want to leave this place and go back to where I came from. I can't explain it but, believe me, I came here by traveling through time." He looked her in the eyes. "I'll find a way back. And when I do, I want you to come with me."

The thought of paradise brought her hope again. She smiled. "I know that some of the things you're telling me contradict the rebels' beliefs, but both of you agree that paradise once existed. The rebels want to bring it to the present and you want to go back to it. That's the only difference."

Jack nodded his head. "That's pretty much it." Even though Maya couched the statements in her own frame of reference, she captured its essence.

"Will you come with me?" he requested again.

She arched her right eyebrow. "You want me to live with you?"

"Yes," he laughed. "We can have a nice home with a garden in front."

"Okay, I'll go with you to your paradise," Maya chuckled. "How do we get there?" she asked, as if the key lay in the drawer next to them, waiting to be picked up.

"I will take you to paradise right now." He pulled her down into the bed and kissed her deeply, tightly holding her body.

* * *

The doors flew open and in strode Kallin, Jini, General Contog, the national security advisor and two soldiers.

"Well, well. What do we have here?" mocked Kallin. "Our two love birds."

Jack jumped up, his face pale and body shaking. Maya screamed and covered herself with a blanket.

"Oh, Hand of God," shouted Jini. "What did I tell you? How can you trust this woman?" She ran over to the bed and pulled Maya to the floor. Maya sobbed.

"Get up," yelled Kallin, stroking his beard angrily. Maya jumped up and stood next Jack, keeping her eyes on the floor.

Kallin walked over to Jack. "You fool, do you think I would stupidly trust you? I know where you've been and who you've talked to."

Jack's color drained from his face.

"Our spy satellites tracked you. We know everything you did and who you spoke to. You're like a rat caught in our maze and you never had a chance." He beckoned Maya to come closer. She shuffled over.

He grabbed her hair, pulled it over her head and examined the back of her neck. "Just as I suspected. She's removed her DNA implant." He hit her hard on the face. Maya gasped. Jack's eyes burned and the hair on the back of his neck stood up. "Look around here for it," Kallin commanded.

It didn't take long to locate it, still sitting in the dresser drawer. Jack quickly glanced at Maya. They had been extremely careless.

"Shoot her," Kallin ordered.

Jack grabbed Maya. "Leave her alone."

Kallin laughed in obvious delight. "How touching! Our golden boy fell in love with the slut."

Jack's face reddened. An electric surge of anger washed over him and his breath came shallow and fast. "Whatever she is, she's better than you."

They all stood still, shocked. No one had ever addressed the Hand of God so boldly.

"What are you doing?" asked Maya quietly. "Forget about me. Save yourself." Jack peered into her eyes. They shocked him. Her pupils looked lifeless, as if nothing existed behind them. Death wrote itself all over her body and the soul seemed already departed.

"No," stammered Jack, "I'm going to protect you. I'm sorry, I caused all this. It's my fault."

Maya shook her head. "It's a little late for that, isn't it? The way you behaved, it was bound to happen sooner or later."

A shiver of self-disgust shook Jack. Maya spoke the truth. He hated himself.

"The fact is, the Hand of God has won, as he always does."

Kallin nodded his head, smiling, enjoying himself.

"And the only reason he isn't getting rid of you is because you have something he wants."

Jack managed only a peek at the Hand of God. Kallin's face hardened. "I haven't proved it yet, but I suspect that you must be the mole. The rebels attacked me the first day we spent together and I also know that it was your idea to visit the ruins."

"But I fought with the rebels," exclaimed Jack.

"I know. But there's something strange about you. A mystery to get to the bottom of."

Kallin pointed at Maya. "Get her."

The two soldiers jumped forward. Jack pushed Maya behind him, shielding her. He swung hard, catching the first soldier flat on his chin. The man slumped to the floor. The second soldier's rifle butt smashed on Jack's forehead. Jack grunted and fell. Blood spurted and flowed down his face. The soldier re-positioned his rifle, ready to shoot. Jack jumped up and grabbed the weapon just before it went off. He kicked hard, hitting the guard right in the face. The man crumpled like a rag doll. Kallin and the others jumped back.

"I'm going to get you," shouted Jack rushing at Kallin.

The chief of police immediately drew a weapon from his belt, as did the national security advisor. Kallin screamed in fear, but just as Jack reached him, a shot of green energy hit him right in the gut. He dropped to the ground shaking, his breathing coming in gasps, and after a few moments, lay stiff as a board, teeth gritted with pain.

Kallin, shaking, scratching his beard in fear and anger, his eyes twitching uncontrollably, kicked Jack's inert body right in the ribs. "You stupid dog," he growled. He looked at Maya. "Arrest her!"

The national security advisor ran over and slapped a pair of handcuffs on her. Kallin reached into his pant pocket and handed him a small golden handgun, about five inches long, with several notches on its stock. The advisor dragged the pale, shaking woman into the garden. A moment later a blast echoed into the room.

* * *

Central Prison, End of Kali Yuga

"Get up," commanded a voice. A switch turned on, filling the prison cell with cold, harsh light. Jack rubbed his face, compelling his eyelids to open. They remained shut.

"Get up," ordered the voice again. Jack forced his eyes to open. A fluorescent bulb burned into his pupils. Jack lay on a cot jutting out of a white-tiled wall. The cell measured about ten by fifteen feet with a steel-barred gate in front and, at the other end, a small bathroom. He placed his bare feet gingerly on the gray cement floor and stood up. A shooting pain seared up his left leg and into his thigh.

"Come on, come on," demanded the voice impatiently. Jack focused his gaze. President Kallin and the chief of police stood in front. The Hand of God wore a dark-red, almost burgundy-colored, suit with an expensive red-striped tie, buffed black shoes, and his eyes, always dark, flashed. Jack shivered. Kallin appeared more menacing than ever. Jack felt extremely vulnerable, as if waiting for his execution, but then remembered the reason for his imprisonment—he possessed something Kallin wanted. Revulsion for the dictator soured his stomach.

"Where am I?" he asked.

"You're in Central Prison," replied Contog.

"What do you want from me?"

Kallin walked around, examining Jack from top to bottom, his shoes clacking loudly on the floor. "So you think you traveled here from the past, do you?"

Jack felt sick. They had recorded his conversations.

Kallin laughed. "There's no use hiding. My scientists traced your ancestry. The last humans with your mitochondrial DNA sequences died out about a couple of hundred thousand years ago. How do you explain that?"

Kallin knew everything and lying served no purpose. "Yes," Jack admitted, "I am from the past."

"Of course. It explains the mystery surrounding you— the DNA, your sudden appearance in Kallington and all the other things that didn't make sense before."

Jack shrugged his shoulders. "I don't know what difference it makes now."

"It makes all the difference in the world," laughed Kallin. "I would have you shot just like your girlfriend if I didn't find out about this time travel business."

"Why are you interested in time travel anyway?"

Kallin flashed a toothy grin and stroked his gray beard excitedly. "You see my boy, there comes a time in every man's life when he examines his existence and asks, 'Is that all there is?' He looks back, measures his

210

accomplishments and demands if is he is satisfied. Do you understand?"

Jack shook his head blankly.

"I rule the entire world and there's nothing left for me to do here. I want bigger, better challenges."

"What do you mean?"

Kallin looked at him with mad, beady eyes. Behind them burned a sick restlessness, a barely concealed feverish exhilaration. They darted ceaselessly, glancing at him, at Contog, across the room and, in his excitement, his eyelids twitched. "I need new realms to conquer. I will go into the past and take it over. I will go into the future and master it as well. I will rule the entire world, not just now but forever. None greater than me in human history shall exist."

The Hand of God cackled, a strange high-pitched peal betraying a wildly agitated mind. Jack's heart beat uncontrollably. Kallin proved to be not just dangerous, but mad.

"My boy, you brought me something no one else has. Do you know what it is?"

Jack shook his head.

Kallin pulled himself up and thrust his hands up in the air, as if grasping the world. "You gave me hope, new trials, new horizons, a chance for untold wealth. I will become, not just a man, but God. All I want is a shot at immortality."

The dictator sharpened his gaze and slammed a tablet in Jack's hand. "What I need from you is the secret for time travel. Write it down."

Jack stood with his mouth wide open.

"Well, come on," insisted Kallin.

"I...I don't know," stuttered Jack.

"How did you come here?"

Jack found himself explaining the details of the Yoga Zapper, the mantra and the intricacies of the ritual. Kallin scratched his beard in exasperation. He pointed at the tablet.

"Write it down. This Yuga Zipper or whatever you call it."

Jack held the device with shaking hands. "I don't remember the mantra. I never expected to memorize it."

"Really? You never committed something as important as time travel to memory?"

"But it's not just the mantra. The stars need to be in proper astrological alignment and God's grace is essential."

"The stars? What bullshit! As far as God is concerned, am I not the Hand of God?"

Jack kept quiet.

"Well?" roared Kallin. "What is it?"

"I don't know," stammered Jack. "I don't remember."

"I'll get it out of you, boy," snarled Kallin, "even if I have to kill you." He eyed Contog. "General, you know what to do."

Contog nodded. "I'll squeeze it out of him."

"Good. Call me when you have the information." He turned around and quickly walked out.

Contog waited until Kallin left. "I'll be back for you soon," he said, scratching his rough, creased face. He slammed the door and left.

* * *

Jack slowly got up and hobbled into the bathroom. It contained a metal toilet, a shower, a single light bulb swinging from the ceiling and a steel mirror on the wall. His face was a mess. Deep cuts furrowed his head, both cheeks were bruised badly, the cut on his lower lip shone raw and red and a huge tender bump rose on his forehead. He touched his ribs and gasped. Jack staggered to the toilet seat, hissing painfully through clenched teeth.

The past, his world, lay shattered in a million pieces. He felt like a caged rat facing a dead end in every direction. If he escaped to the Rak slum, he would surely be eaten alive and if somehow he reached the ancient ruins, the

212

rebels would kill him. And Kallin's police and guards encircled the entire area.

How could I be so immature, he questioned. Ever since his arrival in this world he had acted stupidly, impulsively, and uttered things that cast suspicion and danger on Maya and himself. The agony from his wounds stung, but the torment of losing Maya hurt more. She had warned him many times, but he pursued her until his foolish, immature games led to her death. At the exact time he finally connected with her, he lost her. But did he really love her or was he just using her again? He angrily smashed his fist against his head. What did she say about hurting everyone he came across? He hadn't believed it, but she told the truth.

Suddenly the memory, the thought that escaped him all this time, the painful, deep remembrance returned. The whole episode replayed painfully in his mind. He stood on the steps of the Krishna temple while Steve, his face angry and wet with tears, divulged their mother's passing away. And he reacted predictably to the situation by escaping. His brother accused him of selfishness, insisting that he cared only for himself, that he didn't care who he hurt, that he had wounded Mom, pushing her away at every opportunity. Didn't the same thing happen with Maya? For the second time in his life, he could say nothing. First Mom, now Maya.

Didn't Maya instruct him to search for the answers in his life? *Okay, let me ask a question*, he thought. *Why do I feel alienated from everyone and everything; why do I keep moving from one thing to another?*

Suddenly, the answer hit him. Of course! This started when Dad died! Being so young he did what any little kid would do: he pushed that enormous, inexplicable event somewhere deep and covered it up with an attitude so huge that it never saw the light of day. The insight felt stunning, crystal clear, but another intuition arose. He didn't know how to deal with it, how to make peace with his father's death.

213

He got up, looked at the mirror and felt a great revulsion and loathing for the face staring back. He smashed his fist against the metal and dropped to his knees. Bitter tears rolled down Jack's face, burning into the cuts on his skin.

"Help!" he cried. "Someone help me."

Chapter Twenty Six

Shambala, End of Satya Yuga

In all, two hundred souls assembled at the pasture. Each tribe or community wore their distinctive dresses, ornaments, and decorations—rose coral necklaces gracing their necks, dark *kohl* tracing their eyes, tattoos lining their skins and red and black woolen shawls wrapping their torsos. Some had bodies the color of dark rainclouds, others came from desert lands and wore long robes, several, light-skinned and blue-eyed, appeared from the northern snows and a few, golden-hued with enchanting black eyes, journeyed from the southern seas. Others, copper-skinned and almond-eyed, wore necklaces of blue topaz and red seashells, a few stood tall and thin as young coconut trees, several resembled short and stout baby baobabs while some sported straight black hair, ivory skins, and beautiful fish-like eyes.

The huge havan, well over thirty feet on each side, with logs stacked in its middle, lay in the center of the great meadow. Around it, in front, in the place of honor, assembled the yogis and rishis and behind them, like spokes emanating from a wheel, gathered the different tribes and communities. Parvata Rishi stationed himself at the head of his group, with Steve next to him.

The leaders of each community rose one by one and spoke about their ancestries, the lands of their peoples and their long journeys to Shambala. Upon his turn, the rishi addressed the assembly, introduced Steve and enquired about Jack. Steve's heart sank when none offered any news.

After the introductions, a yogi, tall and dark-skinned, head shaven and robed in the orange cloth of a *sannyasi*, a renunciate, walked up and sat facing them.

215

Parvata Rishi glanced at Steve. "This is the great yogi, Samacharya. We are fortunate to have his darshan today."

"As the yugas progress, from Satya Yuga to Treta Yuga to Dwapara Yuga and finally to Kali Yuga," stated the yogi, "the knowledge of the Vedas, the original spiritual teachings, will gradually diminish and finally be lost. At the end of Kali Yuga, mankind will be in a much-degraded state."

Steve turned to Parvata Rishi. "How is it possible to lose these teachings?" he whispered.

"It is the nature of time that things get dissipated. What is now whole and complete will splinter, diminish and then disappear over the course of time. This is true not only of physical objects and ancient wisdoms but also of virtues such as morality, non-violence, justice, and truth."

Samacharya Yogi continued. "This is the purpose for our presence here. Today we will perform a yajna that will create a *mandala*, a mystical circle, around this place."

Steve looked at the rishi. "What is he saying?"

"Our ritual will create a kind of shell around Shambala," explained Parvata Rishi. "This invisible dome will shield us from the advancement of the yugas and within, we will remain hidden from the world and protect the teachings from the corruption of time. Hidden in this valley, our duty is to act as vessels in which these teachings are stored and, millions of years from now, when Kali Yuga ends, to reintroduce the wisdom of the Vedas, which contain the teachings of yoga, to humanity. If we are successful, Satya Yuga, and thus the cycle of time, will start again."

"One may ask why we should stay here in Shambala," Samacharya Yogi continued. "Let me describe what will happen at the end of Kali Yuga. Here are a few passages from the *Srimad Bhagavatam*, one of our shastras.

"'As the earth thus becomes crowded with a corrupt population, whoever among any of the social classes shows himself to be the strongest will gain political power. Where there is a predominance of cheating, lying, sloth, sleeping, violence, depression, lamentation, bewilderment, fear, and poverty, that age is Kali, the age in the mode of ignorance.

"'Because of the bad qualities of the age of Kali, human beings will become short-sighted, unfortunate, gluttonous, lustful and poverty-stricken. Cities will be dominated by thieves, the Vedas contaminated by speculative interpretations of atheists, political leaders will virtually consume the citizens and the so-called priests and intellectuals will be devotees of their bellies and genitals.

"'Businessmen will engage in petty commerce and earn money by cheating. Even when there is no emergency, people will consider any degraded occupation quite acceptable. Harassed by famine and excessive taxes, struck by drought, they will become completely ruined.

"'Cows will be like goats, spiritual hermitages will be no different from mundane houses, and family ties will extend no further than the immediate bonds of marriage. Most plants and herbs will be tiny, and all trees will appear like dwarf Sami trees. Clouds will be full of lightning, homes will be devoid of piety and all human beings will have become like asses.'"

Parvata Rishi leaned over to Steve. "Actually, at the end of Kali Yuga," he reported, "ordinary citizens will become so harassed that those who can, will flee the cities and hide in mountains and caves. Life will be hellish."

Samacharya Yogi continued reading. "'In the age of Kali, people's minds will always be agitated. They will become emaciated by famine and taxation and will always be disturbed by the fear of drought. They will lack adequate clothing, food and drink, and will be unable to properly rest, have sex or bathe themselves and will have no ornaments to decorate their bodies.

"'Lord Vishnu, the spiritual master of all moving and nonmoving living beings and the Supreme Soul of all— takes birth to protect the principles of *dharma* and to relieve His saintly devotees from the reactions of material work.

217

"*Lord Kalki*, the avatar of Lord Vishnu, will appear in the home of the most eminent brahmana of Shambala village, the great soul Vishnuyasha.'"

"What is an avatar and who is Lord Kalki?" asked Steve.

The rishi bent over. "An avatar is a representation of a higher reality in a lower one. The Vedas declare that Lord Vishnu descends, or should I say, his avatar appears, on this earth from time to time. According to the shastras, of the ten major avatars of Lord Vishnu, a future one named Kalki Avatar will lead the forces of good against evil at the end of time."

Samacharya Yogi continued, "'Lord Kalki, the Lord of the Universe, will mount his horse Devadatta and, sword in hand, travel over the earth exhibiting his eight mystical opulences and eight special qualities of Godhead. Riding with great speed, He will kill by the millions those thieves who have dared to dress as kings, as oppressors.'"

Steve stared at the rishi with trepidation.

"Keep listening," instructed the rishi.

"'When the Supreme Lord, the Supreme Personality of Godhead, appears in their hearts in His transcendental form of goodness, the remaining citizens will abundantly repopulate the earth.

"When the Supreme Lord appears on earth as Kalki, the maintainer of *dharma*, Satya Yuga will begin again and human society will bring forth progeny in the mode of goodness.'"

Steve turned to the rishi. "So a great battle will occur at the end of time?"

"Yes, Kalki Avatar will come to lead good against evil in a war that will consume the entire world."

Steve's face turned ashen. Somehow, suddenly, he knew with certainty that Jack had traveled to the end of Kali Yuga. The insight lay hidden in his subconscious, something his gut told him. A cold wash of fear and anxiety showered his body. The rishi read his mind.

"And yes, your brother's life is in danger."

Steve instantly, finally, connected with Jack. The past couple of months of living in Satya Yuga and his daily yoga practice had purified his consciousness and he finally saw, as the rishi promised, his brother's karma.

An image of Jack rushed to his mind. Jack sat crouched on his knees, clasping his hands in front of him in a cold, dark prison cell. His clothes were torn, his feet were bare and a single light shone above his head. Jack was in danger! Steve gulped rapid, shallow breaths, his eyes opened wide and apprehension contorted his face. Did he dare to go to Kali Yuga and sacrifice everything near and dear to him? He loved Shanti so much. Could he give her up?

"Now let's start the yajna," instructed Samacharya Yogi. "All who remain inside this mandala will be protected from the ravages of time. Those outside, will not." Steve had to go somewhere, anywhere, to escape his terrible bind. The extreme restlessness that had gripped him all morning finally overcame him. He jumped up and glanced at Shanti. Her face whitened and her mouth opened in surprise. Something in his chest twisted and pulled. He turned and ran away from the assembly with all his might, not knowing or caring where he went. Behind him, the yajna began.

Chapter Twenty Seven

Shambala, End of Satya Yuga

Steve ran from the meadow until he reached the stream. He slowed to a brisk walk, his mind vacant, following the river downstream until it broadened, slowed and the grass gave way to pine forest. He came upon a small clearing surrounded by a thick grove of evergreens, where sharp pine needles pricked his bare feet, and lay down. The idle chatter of redbirds echoed around him.

The rustle of the wind sounded like trees whispering secrets to each other. All his life, people repeated riddles in his ears, yet he comprehended none of them. Life's meaning lay hidden under the obvious of the manifest world, lying there for the taking, but somehow he never broke through.

The dense green woods reminded him of something. Of course! The first time he spoke to Shanti, in the forest outside the village. The same feeling of seclusion and privacy enveloped him here. Did he fall in love with her then, the first time they met? What was love anyway? Parvata Rishi had informed him that human love reflected the divine love between God, the supreme soul, and the infinitesimal individual soul; that the perfection of love is the ultimate spiritual understanding. He shook his head. He felt no wiser than before.

He gazed vacantly at the sky, following the movements of small, puffy, white clouds. The river softly swirled, its waters lapping gently on the bank. A flutter of wings suddenly sounded in the trees.

"Well, hello."

Steve got up quickly and turned around. Shanti had located him. He sat up, his hands resting behind him.

"How did you find me?"

"It wasn't too hard. I know you well enough by now."
She sat next to him. "What are you doing?"

"Thinking," he replied vaguely.

"Thinking about what?"

"I...I've been thinking about my brother."

Shanti read his face. Her expression turned serious.

"I can't stop thinking about him. I feel paralyzed. I don't know what to do."

"And what about us??"

"I'm sorry Shanti. Your father may be right. Perhaps I'm not ready for marriage."

She turned away as wetness welled in her eyes. "If you don't want to marry me, that's fine. I'm sure my father will find someone else, if it comes to that."

Steve winced.

Shanti shook her head. "I'm not angry. This is an opportunity to really talk about our feelings. It's something we haven't done in a long while."

"You're right."

"What happened between you and your brother? To me, something always felt not quite right."

Steve sighed. "Our father's death created a co-dependency between us and when our mother died, it broke, shooting us off in different directions." He rubbed his chin. "I never understood that before, but now it's perfectly clear."

"Do you mind if I speak honestly?"

"Of course not."

"The way I see it, the problem is not your brother. The problem is you."

"What do you mean?" he inquired, surprised by her frankness.

"It seems to me that you're stuck and don't know how to move ahead."

"That's exactly the way I feel. I'm caught between my duty to my family and my love for you."

"You're trying to control things beyond your power. Learn to let go."

"You mean do nothing?" he retorted.

221

"Your brother's life is his. You cannot change it. Have faith that he will do the right thing."

Steve laughed ironically. "That's the problem, trusting Jack to do the right thing. Since his youth, I've taken care of him, rescuing him from one predicament or another."

"You know who you sound like?"

"Yes," he replied glumly. "I heard it all the time from Jack, 'You're not my father.' But like it or not, I took care of Jack in many ways after our dad died,"

"You don't need to do that anymore. Jack is no longer that kid."

Steve rubbed his forehead. "Maybe what you say is true, but it's just so hard."

"You need to change how you look at Jack. He's grown up and become a man. He may make mistakes or take bad choices but let him deal with the consequences. His karma is his and only he can deal with that."

Steve remained unconvinced. He shook his head.

"Can you let go?" she asked.

"This is really tough. I know I should, but it's difficult for me."

Shanti sighed. "The reason you don't trust your brother is because you don't trust yourself."

Steve looked at her quizzically. "What do you mean?"

"When you first arrived, you were so afraid of believing in yourself that you wrote everything down but, slowly and surely, you opened up and listened to your feelings, your emotions. A lot of it is the yoga, but it is also the love we share. Steve, if you really trust yourself, you will trust others, especially those close to you."

"But what if you lose the ones close to you?"

Shanti straightened her sari. "Let me try again. As a brother, you can do your best, but you can't take away Jack's independence. He needs his freedom. Otherwise how can he change?"

"I can understand what you're saying in theory, but I am not convinced."

"We grow by making commitments. If you don't cross the bridge, you'll never know what's on the other side."

She got up and looked at him. "I have to go back to my father and the ritual. I can't help you anymore. The realization needs to come from you." She turned around and headed back.

Steve watched her disappear. A great deal of wisdom resided in what she said. Going to Kali Yuga remained a long shot: he could try, but the Yoga Zapper required many things to work. For the first time, Steve realized he could do nothing to help Jack.

He remembered his last conversation with his mother. Of course! She kept telling him that he needed to go on with his life while he insisted on looking after Jack. In fact, his mother didn't ask for it at all!

Maybe Jack needed to fail to grow up. By rescuing him, by protecting Jack from himself, he had contributed to Jack's immaturity and irresponsibility. What did Shanti say? Learn to let go? He never thought of detachment as being a part of love—of love being based not on need, but on respect for each other.

Steve's face turned red. Was he that blind? Now, forced to be away from his family and learning to devote his emotions elsewhere, everything became clear. Maybe both needed the separation—so that Jack could see his own weaknesses and that Steve could move on with his life.

He thought about Jack's karma; the vision of him in the dark cell. Instead of imagining the worst, he decided to change the image. Jack's boldness and courage would be the keys to his salvation. Instead of seeing a bleak outcome, Steve chose a different ending. He imagined Jack having a secret friend, a co-conspirator as it were, and somehow or other escaping prison.

As soon as this vision took hold, Steve felt much better. Whatever Jack's destination, he wouldn't direct negativity towards him but send only positive, hopeful thoughts. After all, negative energy attracts only negative consequences. *Jack*, he thought. *I am sending you my support. Don't worry, you'll be fine.*

Steve felt a great burden lift off his shoulders. He closed his eyes and inhaled, the sweet air filling his lungs and energizing his mind. Somehow the whole world changed. He felt reborn.

He glanced at the beaming sun overhead. *Oh my God,* he thought. *I have to return to the ritual before it ended, or risk being outside the shelter of the mandala!* He ran back as fast as his legs could carry him.

He arrived just in time. The participants, offering grains to the sacred fire, chanted 'Svaha'. Gasping for breath, he rushed over and sat down next to Parvata Rishi, who, relieved to see him, gave him some of his grains and spices to offer to the fire.

After the ceremony ended, Steve went over to Shanti. She looked up expectantly.

He pulled her up. "Come."

"Where are we going?"

He put his finger against her lips and shook his head. Her eyes widened and she laughed delightedly. Holding her hand, he led her to the river, their feet swishing through the tall grass. Stepping in and out of the water, they strode silently along the gurgling river until they reached the waterfalls. A path of flat rocks led from the shore to the thundering torrent. Steve peered closely and spotted an opening behind the cascade. They grasped hands, skipped across the stones and jumped through the curtain of water into a small cave, becoming thoroughly drenched. He gasped, tingling from head to toe as his feet tracked on thick green moss. Shanti sparkled, her lips smiling.

The cave measured about ten steps long by five deep. Ferns and mosses crowded its walls and drops of water tumbled constantly from the cave's ceiling as sunlight glimmered through the curtain of water.

Steve led Shanti to the middle of this hidden wonder and bent down on his knees. She breathed heavily, her chest heaving, her hands trembling. Drops of water ran down her face, her wet sari clung to her body, and he examined her from her loose, long, shining hair to her open lips, the fullness of her breasts, the strong torso, her round hips and solid feet. Her eyes, beautiful as usual, reflected not just her youth, but a maturity he only now fully saw.

224

Nothing had changed except something in him and she looked very different.

"Shanti," he asked, ready to fully share their lives. "Will you marry me?"

She shone. "Are you sure?"

"I've never been surer of anything in my life."

"Then, of course, I'll marry you!"

Steve jumped to his feet and they clasped each other, a lovers' embrace, long and sweet, beyond time and space.

* * *

Steve and Shanti met Parvata Rishi at their camp. The rishi beamed, relieved to see the two young lovers together again.

"Where did you two go?" he enquired.

"We talked," answered Steve. "And we have...."

"By the way," the rishi interrupted, before Steve could continue, "I have thought of a way to help your brother."

"Really!" exclaimed Steve.

"Yes. I will create a *bija* thought, a seed-thought, and plant it in the ether. Just as an ordinary seed, when planted in the earth, sprouts after a passage of time, this seed-thought will descend and insert itself in your brother's mind at the proper moment. The Vedas teach us that several realms of reality, beyond this physical one, exist. The ethereal realm, more subtle than the material one, is one such reality. In it, the bija thought will stay unhindered by the passage of time."

Steve laughed.

"What is it?" questioned the rishi.

"You won't believe it, but talking with Shanti, I decided to trust my brother's fate to a greater power and look what happened!"

"Don't worry, your brother's life is in God's hands." The rishi winked at his daughter. "Is that all you talked about?"

"Oh, no," exclaimed Shanti. "Father, we've decided to get married!"

"Are you sure?"

"Yes, we're absolutely sure."

The old man, laughing jubilantly, gave his daughter a long kiss on her forehead.

"Father, do we have your blessings?" she requested.

The rishi put his right hand on her head and his left one on Steve's. "I give you both all my blessings and affection. May your married lives be long and happy!"

"Parvata Rishi," acknowledged Steve. "Thank you for giving me good advice."

"You are welcome, my son," answered the rishi. "After all, what are we old folks for?" He paused for a minute. "So when will you get married?"

Shanti spoke up. "I think the next Satya Yuga is the best time."

"What!" exclaimed Steve. "Isn't that like millions of years from now?"

"Yes, but there is a good reason to wait."

"What is that?"

She smiled mischievously. "You will know when the time comes."

"But what will we do till then?" asked Steve, dumbfounded.

"Don't worry," replied the rishi. "My daughter knows what she's saying. Yoga teaches us that we have several bodies, known as the *Pancha koshas*—the five bodies or five sheaths. Besides the physical body, known as the *Annamaya kosha*, we possess the *Pranamaya kosha*, which consists of the *prana* or the vital energy of a human being. The third form is called the *Manomaya kosha*, the mental body, created out of the conscious mind and memory. The *Vijnanamaya kosha* is made of the intellect, the *buddhi*. The final form is the *Anandamaya kosha*, the bliss body consisting of pure consciousness. Each body encases the previous ones and we can transcend, or move, our consciousness from the gross material body to the higher, more subtle ones."

"How is that possible?" queried Steve.

"By control of the breath and meditation we can slow the vibrations of our bodies to such an extent as to move from the physical body all the way to the bliss body. We will, in fact, live in a super-conscious state, where our physical bodies disappear and we exist in pure spirit."

"Why should we do that?"

"Our mission is to safeguard the wisdom of the Vedas and yoga and to reintroduce it to the world at the beginning of the next Satya Yuga. Even in Satya Yuga, we are subject to old age and death, but by remaining in our bliss bodies, we will escape the ravages of time until our reappearance."

"But what about our marriage?" questioned Steve.

"By staying in the Anandamaya kosha, we will be completely unaware of time and thousands, even millions, of years will pass unnoticed until we will wake up safely at the end of this cycle of yugas."

"Do you think I can actually achieve this state?" wondered Steve, his eyes wide.

"Of course. Am I not teaching you yoga? Yoga means moving the consciousness."

The three walked to the river's edge. There, Samacharya Yogi sat, absorbed in deep meditation. The yogi's body shone orange as he moved to the *Pranamaya* state, then a brilliant gold as he gained the *Manomaya* state, an intense green upon achieving the Vijnanamaya kosha and finally turned blue and disappeared completely as he attained the Anandamaya kosha, the state of pure bliss.

"He has stilled the vibrations of his body and mind to such an extent as to be invisible. Only his pure consciousness now exists," declared the rishi. He motioned to Steve and Shanti. "Now sit down beside the mighty Sarasvati, offer your respects to this great river and start your meditations. Before I join you, I will create and embed the seed-thought for your brother."

Offering their respects to the mythical river, Steve and Shanti closed their eyes and entered *Dharana*, deep meditation. Slowly, their bodies took on different hues as they moved their consciousness from one kosha to another, until finally, they disappeared.

* * *

The rishi closed his eyes and focused his mind. "Jack," he whispered. "Jack, listen to me."

Chapter Twenty Eight

Central Prison, End of Kali Yuga

"Jack," came a man's voice. "Jack, listen to me."

Jack shook in fear. He looked around but didn't see anyone. "Please reveal yourself!"

Suddenly a faint ghost of a man with a white beard, dressed in long orange robes, floated in the air above.

"I am your friend," assured the old man. His garments swirled in the darkness, but his face shone brightly. Jack's rubbed his eyes. The apparition hung in the air against the steel walls of the prison bathroom, just out of reach, and a gentle smile lit his face.

"Please, please help me."

"Don't worry, my son. Don't worry. Tell me."

"I just had the most horrible, yet truthful, realization in my entire life. I've been immature, foolish and hurtful, especially to those closest to me and I've been running away, not from places or people, but from myself."

"Do you know why?"

"It...It's hard to explain, but I've been like this since my father died."

"What do you mean?" questioned the apparition.

"I don't think I ever accepted my father's death or even understood it. I became rebellious and alienated from almost everything in my life, and due to this, I hurt many people, including my mother."

"So what is your question?"

Jack looked at the floating figure with desperate eyes. "How do I come to terms with this?"

The floating face glanced caringly at him. "The problem is that your anxiety is paralyzing you."

"You're right. How do I overcome my fear?"

"Make peace with your father."

"How do I do that?"

229

"You think your father is dead, but in reality, only his body is gone. The immortal soul, which is beyond race, color, nationality, sex, and all other material dualities, is our true being. Your father's soul is ever alive and for that you needn't have any fear."

"I can understand that, but I still miss him and have never stopped missing him."

"Jack," said the kindly voice. "He is no longer with you. Accept that his death is not the end and let your father go."

"Let him go?"

"Yes. Talk to him. Take his permission to leave."

"That's all?"

"Yes," chuckled the apparition. "It's as easy as that."

Jack closed his eyes, concentrating on his father. Nothing happened. He tried harder and harder, the effort causing beads of sweat to appear on his forehead, but couldn't break through.

"I can't do it," he whispered. "I'm drawing a blank."

"Think back to when he last appeared. Go back to that place."

After several minutes of deep absorption, his father's image appeared; young, dashing, just the way Jack always pictured him to be, dressed in a military uniform, his dark hair closely cropped, standing in the front verandah of their home. Jack sat in a school bus and, when it stopped, jumped off and ran to meet him.

"Dad!" exclaimed Jack. "I haven't seen you in such a long time!"

His father looked at him with bright eyes. "I'm here."

"I missed you so much. I never thought I'd see you again!"

"Come, let's talk. I have all eternity."

"Where are you?"

"I'm with you, my son. I am always with you."

"How do I know you're with me?"

"Have faith," said his father. "If you have faith, you'll see me and you will find within a fearlessness you never knew you had."

"Faith?"

"Yes, wherever you are, whether in a prison cell or in a castle, know that I'm here. Don't rationalize it. Just feel it in your heart. If you do that, you will know that I have always been with you."

"I have a question. Why can't I commit to anything? Why do I have to keep moving?"

"Why do people move?"

"I guess they are looking for something."

"And you? What are you looking for?"

"Me?" questioned Jack, surprised. "I'm not looking for anything."

"Really? You're not searching for anything?"

"Wait a minute! I've had this dream before, haven't I? That I looked for you all over the house for you?"

His father smiled knowingly. "Yes. So what does that mean?"

"I've been searching for you all this time, haven't I?" exclaimed Jack.

His father nodded his head.

"All these years, the different places I traveled to, the different relationships I had, the different things I tried?" It felt unreal, but, it was absolutely true! He had a hole in his psyche and his attempts to fill it or run away from it led to failure because he never really understood it before.

"You were young," his father said kindly. "Of course you never understood it."

Jack sat on his knees, in tattered clothes and bare feet, silently expressing everything he ever wanted to. He left all his sorrow, confusion, and self-loathing behind and pushed away every other thought, feeling, and emotion as time stood still. He poured his heart out from the depth of his being until he had nothing left to say, nothing left to feel.

After a while, he remembered the old man's instruction: to summon his father's blessings to move on. "Dad, please give me your permission to leave," he requested hesitatingly. He saw his father move closer. He embraced Jack. A deep feeling of love, something he never before experienced, overcame him. He bathed in his

231

father's strong embrace for what seemed to be an eternity until, finally, he felt his father release him. He looked up. His father's uniform had disappeared, his skin looked weathered, a white beard appeared on his face, and his eyes, though old, still sparkled. His father left him only one message before disappearing: 'Go ahead. I will always be with you.'

Jack opened his eyes, wiped the tears away, took a deep breath and inhaled deeply. He felt the dark curtain lift, removing all burdens. Whatever anyone might say, whatever explanations his mind would give, whatever rationalizations he could make, he knew the truth: his dad stood with him, not as an apparition but really, truly, always and forever. His doubt and fear left him, leaving him completely unafraid of the future.

"You know," he remarked, looking for the floating apparition. "My dad almost looks like you...." He stopped. The old man had disappeared. Did he actually see this person floating in the air? A surge of gratitude welled in his heart. You have saved me, he thought. He got up and looked in the mirror. A smiling, happy face beamed back.

* * *

The door clanged open and two guards stepped in. Jack looked up brightly. "I am not afraid of anything this world has to offer. I have faith."

The guards laughed. "We're taking you to the chief of police. When he's finished with you, that's all you'll have left," said one.

They marched him into General Contog's office and deposited him in a chair, saluted and left. Jack remembered the same nondescript red rug and the utilitarian desk. The General, dressed in a blue uniform, black shoes, a military hat, belt, and holster, pressed a button and a low hum filled the room. He walked around the desk and came to the front. Jack stared at the general straight in the eyes.

"Do what you want with me," he stated. "I am not afraid of you."

The general laughed. "I'm not who you think I am."

"What do you mean?"

"Jack, you see me and think I am an evil man. You recognize me as the chief of police, as one who uses his power to control and punish others, but that's not just who I am."

"Who are you then?"

The general put his hands on the arms of the chair, bent over and stared right into his eyes. "I am the mole."

Jack's eyes widened. "No! That can't be true."

"Yes, it's true."

"How could you be the mole?"

"Think. When the rebels attacked the restaurant, I waited as long as possible before sending the police, hoping that Kallin would be killed by the time we came. Unfortunately, that didn't happen."

"How about last night? When I attacked Kallin, you pulled out your gun."

"Did I shoot you? No. I wanted to use the opportunity to kill Kallin, but unfortunately, at that exact time, the national security advisor shot you."

Jack shook his head in disbelief. "But why? Of all people why do you want to overthrow the system? You are one of the few who benefits from it."

General Contog let out a bitter, empty laugh. "Look at me." He put his face right up against Jack's. "Look at my rough skin, my face. What does that remind you of?"

Jack shook his head.

"I was born in a Rak slum. I learned all my hard lessons in life there. All the scratches and cuts on my face came from there. I grew up with nothing to eat, with violence and death all around. I joined Kallin's army to get out my desperate situation, worked hard and made it to the top." He straightened up and took a couple of steps backwards.

"But I never," he declared, pointing straight at Jack, "forgot where I came from."

Jack sat stunned. "How…how can you be a Rak?"

The General laughed. "You think that all Raks are deformed. Actually most of us are, but many of us are also sufficiently able to be productive. We are the Functionals. We perform many of the ordinary tasks that keep this society working. Without us, the Elite wouldn't survive."

He walked around for a few moments. "After a few years at the top, I realized how evil and corrupt the system is. Because of the greed of the few in power, the majority of people live in misery. I became determined to fight it." He went to his desk and pulled out the bottom drawer. "Come here."

Jack walked over and spied the red computer tablet inside.

"I use this to contact the rebels and coordinate their attacks. Without this, the rebels would all have died a long time ago." Contog's amazing, unbelievable, words sunk into Jack's mind as he stared at the computer.

"So why are you telling me all this?" he finally asked.

"Because of what you have been telling us. About how you claim to be from the past. At first, I didn't believe you, but after all that's happened, I'm convinced that you're telling the truth, for all the same reasons that Kallin gave earlier today."

Jack walked back to the seat and sat down. "But I don't believe in the rebels' faith. I don't believe anyone can recreate the past."

"I know that and I don't really care. All I want to do is to end this evil system." The general sighed. "What does concern me is that you may have the secret to time travel. If Kallin gets that out of you, we are all doomed." He walked over to Jack and pulled a gun from his holster. His face stiffened. "I'm sorry, but I have no choice. You have put me in a difficult situation. Being in my position means having to make hard decisions every day. The easiest way for me to make sure that Kallin never finds your secret is to kill you." He set the gun to 'kill' and pointed it at Jack's temple.

A panic rose in Jack's breast, but he remembered his father's words. He smiled. "If this is how I must die, so be it. I'm not afraid."

The General snapped back in surprise. Confused, he strode back and forth, stroking his face. He walked to Jack and pointed the pistol at him again. "If I pull this trigger you will die instantly."

Jack straightened his back. "If I die, my soul will be in God's hands. So what is there to be afraid of?"

General Contog looked at Jack for several long moments. "I think I may have underestimated you," he muttered, shaking his head.

"How so?"

"I thought of you as an immature spoiled brat with very few redeeming qualities."

"You were certainly right. But anyone can change—all it takes is a bit of inspiration."

"You are certainly different from anyone I have met," the general remarked. He threw the gun on his desk, opened another drawer and deposited something on the table.

"These keys operate one of our aircraft, an experimental vessel, one that cannot be observed or tracked by our systems. Take it. Your secret is as valuable to us as it is to Kallin. As it is, the rebellion is barely hanging on."

He walked over to the cabinet and pulled out a small handgun and a white computer tablet. "After the guards remove you from my office, shoot them with this weapon. The tablet contains a map of the prison and will give you step by step instructions on how to reach the aircraft. Upon entering the plane, enter the coordinates given."

"Where will it take me?"

"Right across the globe, near the mountains, where we operate a hidden base. There, your chances for survival are better than anywhere else."

Jack kept sitting on the chair, still stupefied by the general's confession.

"Take it before I change my mind."

Jack grabbed the tablet, the weapon, and the keys.

"Guards!" shouted the general. "Come in."

235

Chapter Twenty Nine

Near Shambala, End of Kali Yuga

Jack strapped himself into the cockpit, punched the coordinates into the console and lifted off in the dark without drawing attention. The autopilot kicked in and, for the first time since his meeting with Contog, he relaxed. The struggle with the guards had been touch and go, but he'd got through it, though his shoulders and sides still hurt. He exhaled, letting go of the exhaustion.

The pyramid-shaped, blue-tinted glass craft through which he observed the terrain below, glided west, silent and tight to the landscape. Not much bigger than him, it gave him the strange sensation of having his legs dangling in the air. What a novelty to soar so quietly and so low to the ground! He sped past homes and roads, close enough to see individual people and surmised that the craft somehow cloaked itself from human sight.

The moon shone luminously on the land. He flew past populated areas on the coast, then over gray hills and deep gorges. After a couple of hours he entered flatlands as far as the eye could see, brown and featureless, with not a single sign of humans, animals or plants. He soared over the interior badlands, made of small, dusty hills—yellows, browns and reds—the colors visible even in the dark and, then further on, past deep canyons, tall mesas and a sparkling burgundy desert. The landscape appeared primal, untamed, and full of gargantuan red monoliths resembling ancient edifices from lost civilizations. Vista after spectacular vista spread out and Jack observed, fascinated.

Several hours later came the ocean, recognizable by long lines of white breakers rolling on the shore, sounding like timeless whispers, promising eternity. The craft rose quickly and within half an hour flew high enough that the clouds themselves looked like tiny white pillows against the sea's blue bed. Jack fell into a deep, restful sleep.

Many hours later, the craft descended and he awoke as sunlight bathed the scene. Beneath him lay a great expanse of yellow, red and brown plains and close by, a series of hills and past them, the unmistakable profile of white-peaked mountains.

Suddenly, an alarm went off on the console. The display showed two airplanes, resembling small dots, approaching from behind. They had discovered him! He peered anxiously below, searching for the rebels' base, but didn't see a thing. A red eject button stared back from the console.

A yellow bolt flashed from behind and zipped off into the blue. To complicate matters, his airplane both slowed and moved downwards, descending, he supposed, toward the rebels' base. The display showed long, sleek, black interceptors, meant for speed, growing larger, and obviously, close enough to shoot him down. Another flash of yellow shot past. Jack tightened the straps around his shoulders and kept his finger on the eject button.

Suddenly, a red blast sheared off one of the craft's corners. It spun wildly out of control, rolling and tumbling. Jack's stomach jumped into his mouth. He gritted his teeth. The side of a high hill came into his view with frightening speed. He closed his eyes and pressed the red button.

The top of the pyramid blew off and he shot out like a cannonball. Jack gasped as the cold mountain air hit him. His abandoned airplane crashed into stone and exploded in a ball of fire as the fighters flashed by with stunning speed. His seat started its downward arc, gently floated into a small flat area between two hills and dropped smoothly to the ground. Jack opened the straps and stood up gingerly, shivering from the cold and his tingling nerves and dived behind a boulder as the pursuing planes made one final pass before disappearing.

He walked back to the seat and, in a compartment on one side, discovered some survival gear: a knife, candles, water, rope, and rations. He cut off the seat covering for use as bedding, rolled the provisions in it, tied the whole thing up with rope, and slung it on his back. Only two options presented themselves: go up towards the mountains or down into the plains. Surely, Kallin would send others to look for him, and as no shelter existed on the flats, decided to hide in the mountains.

He ascended higher and higher, the exercise getting his blood going. After about five hours of rigorous hiking, he came upon a huge black rock, roughly triangular, big, smooth as glass, and sitting on the trail in such a manner as to allow no passage over, through or around it. Jack ran his hands over its shiny surface. It somehow seemed familiar, but he couldn't put his finger on it. Why did it capture his imagination?

He jumped up with realization. Of course! He had been at this same spot God knows how long ago! Dozens of questions tumbled out of his mind, but no answers came. It seemed so long ago, as if in another life. He smiled wryly. It might have been in another life, he had no way of telling.

The land darkened as the sun hid behind a far-off peak. He had to find shelter, and quickly. Jack scanned the bluffs with knotted eyes and spotted a small cave high above, barely more than a dark smudge between two rocks and carefully climbed up, searching for the tiniest footholds, grasping at any available ledge. He found himself at the narrow opening and heaved himself inside.

The cave opened up into a large area that tapered into the mountain. He carefully rolled a few boulders toward the cave's entrance, leaving only a small opening, both to keep out the chilling wind and to hide himself from anyone who may come searching. He moved to the back of the cave, covered himself with the material from the aircraft seat and opened a can of rations. Despite his exhaustion, he couldn't sleep. It would be a long night.

* * *

Kallin's Country Estate, End of Kali Yuga

President Kallin sat at his desk in his office at the country estate. The national security advisor stood next to him. Two pilots presented themselves, tablets in hand.

"Are you sure?" Kallin asked the nearest one.

"There is no doubt sir. We flew over the area twice."

Besides the standard operational reports, the tablet contained a digital video recording of the entire mission. Kallin fast-forwarded it to where they encountered Jack. As the craft exploded, he smiled with excitement.

"This is where it starts," offered the pilot. The video showed the flaming wreckage falling, then veered off the crash site and followed a small mountain pass located behind a strange-looking black hill. After a few minutes, the land dropped dramatically and images of a small, beautiful valley appeared, shining like a green topaz set in a field of pearls. Trees and grass, a sight unseen for hundreds of years, blanketed the hidden valley. A waterfall cascaded out of the middle of a rock wall and the river emerging from it flowed through the valley, disappearing into the ground at the other end. Its beauty stunned them.

Kallin gasped. "Good God, what the hell is this?"

"I have never seen anything like it before, sir," responded the pilot.

"How is it possible for such a place to exist?" demanded Kallin, stroking his chin. "And how did we not know about it?"

The national security advisor shook his head. "It's impossible. Even though it is in an uninhabited area, our satellites or our moon installation should have detected it."

"So how do you explain this?"

"It must somehow be shielded from our sensors."

Kallin rubbed his beard. "Could this valley be connected to the rebellion? Do they have a technology we're not aware of?"

"It's certainly a possibility."

"If so, we have a bigger problem on our hands."

"What happened to the escapee?" asked the national security advisor

"As you saw, he ejected from his craft just before impact," replied the pilot. "He landed in front of a small black hill."

"That dog is still alive," declared Kallin. "I can feel it in my bones." He waved his hand and the pilots saluted and walked out of the room.

He glanced at the national security advisor. "I have asked General Contog to report to me. I hold him responsible for letting Jack escape and I will have his hide for this, but I suspect something is else is going on." He arched his left eyebrow. "I will do all the speaking, but I want you to keep your eyes on that man."

Kallin pressed a button on his desk. In strode the general, with stubble on his chin, his eyelids sagging and the weight of a sleepless night hanging heavy on his face. His eyes sharpened when he noticed the national security advisor.

"President Kallin what can I do for you?"

"I have your report on the escape."

"Is everything all right?"

"Yes, but I have some questions."

"Please go ahead."

"Am I to understand that the fugitive overpowered two guards?"

"Yes, sir. The interrogations of the guards revealed that he possessed a weapon. We checked our inventory and all of our weapons are accounted for."

"So where did he get the weapon?"

"Last night, one of our prisoners—a rebel from the political prisoner wing, a former military man—confessed that he supplied the weapon."

"How did he operate the aircraft?"

"The manner in which the craft moved suggests it was on automatic pilot. Our interrogation revealed that the same prisoner supplied the coordinates."

"Where is this co-conspirator?" he probed.

"Our interrogations are rough, as you understand. He passed away this morning."

Kallin arched his eyebrows. "General, are you satisfied?"

"President Kallin, we are continuing the investigation. If I have any further developments, I will certainly let you know."

Kallin looked into the general's eyes. "Thank you, you are dismissed." General Contog saluted and walked briskly out the door.

"What bothers me is that this happened on Contog's watch," Kallin stated. "I find it hard to believe that these things happened in Central Prison without his knowledge."

"According to reports, Jack met with General Contog the day of his escape," said the national security advisor.

"Do we have any recordings of that meeting?"

"No, sir. He had the electronic cloaking device activated."

Kallin smiled. "How convenient. All these circumstances seem very suspicious, as if designed to leave absolutely no trail."

"But why did Jack go so far to meet the rebels?" queried the advisor. "He could have met them in or near Kallington. I can only assume that he went to meet not just one or two rebels, but a whole group of them, most likely their top leadership."

"Maybe a whole base up in the mountains?" offered Kallin.

"That makes sense. Is there a connection between the valley and the rebellion? Is it the rebel base?"

Kallin rubbed his beard thoughtfully. "How do we find out?"

"There is always a trace. All things point to General Contog's direction. We need to find the base and...."

"And what?"

"If our general is hiding something from us."

* * *

President Kallin sat on a large sofa in the drawing room. About fifty of his top brass, staff and retinue occupied the other furniture. Jini rested on a loveseat next to him.

"Gentlemen," reported Kallin, "we have a situation on our hands." The gathering looked at him expectantly. "We've had a serious breach of security, but more importantly, we have news of a rebel base in the mountains, something much bigger than expected." A murmur swept the room.

"After Jack escaped, a couple of fighters tracked him to a valley in the mountains whose existence was hidden from us. We have determined that a large group of rebels, maybe even a base, is either inside that valley or very close by."

The advisor took the tablet and tapped on it. "This is a visual from one of the interceptors." Scenes of the valley sparkled in the air in front of the group. They gasped. None could believe such a place existed.

"Is this place for real?" asked Jini.

"Yes," answered Kallin.

A man in military garb with short gray hair, a thick white handlebar mustache, three stars on his epaulets and a green uniform sporting row upon row of badges and medals stood up. He held his cap in his hand, straightened his back and spoke in a low, gravelly voice. "If the rebels have the technology to hide this from us, it makes it an entirely different matter." They all nodded their heads.

"That is the reason for the meeting, General Gahal," said Kallin. "We have to decide on our reaction to this development." The room erupted with animated conversation.

Kallin waited several minutes before addressing the assembly again. "So gentlemen, what do we do?"

General Gahal remained standing. "I say we meet them with as much force as possible and put an end to the rebels once and for all."

"What do you suggest?"

"Let's bomb the valley and be done with it," replied Gahal, his eyes glaring and his chin jutting out. "That's the way did it in my day."

The national security advisor stepped in. "But we don't have conclusive proof that the valley is actually the rebels' base. We are also quite certain that Jack is not there. We shot him down about five miles away."

"There is one more matter," stated Kallin. "This is top secret, so it should not leave the room." The gathering leaned forward attentively. "This rebel, Jack, mentioned that he is a time-traveler. At first, we dismissed his claims as pure nonsense. However, recent developments convince us that there may be some truth to his assertions." The room erupted in exclamations.

"What kind of evidence?" questioned General Gahal.

"That information is classified, but it is a very troubling development. Do the rebels have this time-travel technology? If so, we should capture, not destroy it."

"Then let's send a division, maybe ten thousand men," countered the general, stroking his long white mustache. "Let us enter the valley and see if the rebel base is there."

"Good," said President Kallin.

"But we have a problem," revealed the national security advisor. "We have no base; not even a landing strip in that area. It is too mountainous."

General Gahal spoke up. "The video recording shows a hilly area in front of the pass. We can drop some munitions, flatten the area and clear a base for our troops."

President Kallin got up. "Very good, general. You command of our very best soldiers. Take your division and occupy the valley."

Chapter Thirty

Shambala, End of Kali Yuga

BOOM! The shattering noise reverberated through the valley. And again, BOOM! Aircraft dropped large pulses of golden energy on the hills, crushing them, whipping huge boulders around; the explosions creating enormous fireballs, sending shards of rock screaming into the sky in all directions. The blasts destroyed the calm of the valley as thunder rolled from one end to the other.

Steve awoke and rubbed his eyes. As the shockwaves hit, faint outlines of yogis came into view. From under trees and on the banks of the river, they appeared, their consciousness descending from the invisible, topmost stage to visible, mundane reality. Their forms took on different colors: first blue, then green, gold, orange until, finally, they appeared fully. Shanti tapped his shoulder.

"What's happening?" he questioned.

"Time to get up. Shambala is being attacked."

"Why are we being attacked? Isn't that supposed to happen at the end of Kali Yuga?"

"Yes."

"So why is this happening now?" he asked, completely confused.

Shanti chuckled. "We are at the end of Kali Yuga."

"What! Didn't we enter the Anandamaya state just now? Like a minute ago?"

Shanti laughed heartily. "Try hundreds of thousands, maybe millions, of years!"

"That's impossible!"

"In the state of pure consciousness, anything is possible. Let's go meet my father." They walked to the meadow holding hands. The morning coolness quickly dissipated, but dew still hung heavy on the grass, moistening their ankles. Shanti spied her father, ran over, and hugged him. He kissed her on the forehead and embraced Steve happily.

"Father," she exclaimed. "What should we do?"

"Let us wait until the entire community is with us." By late morning, the pilgrims and sages all congregated and despite the uncounted years, looked just as fresh and vibrant as when their meditations started. The elders spoke amongst themselves for quite some time before addressing the assembly.

"Dear friends," announced Vishnuyasha, the pujari. "Let us start with kirtan." Middle-aged, of average height, with fair skin, dark eyes and a serious face, he wore a white dhoti and while he shaved his head and face, a *sikha*, a long pleat of hair, hung from the back of his head. A practitioner of bhakti yoga, his spiritual practices consisted of developing love in his heart for the Supreme. The inhabitants joyously clapped their hands and sung jubilantly, disregarding the thunderous destruction and the roiling red flames shooting high into the sky at the far end of the pass and, after an hour of chanting, felt refreshed.

"These are momentous times," declared Parvata Rishi. "The great battle at the end of Kali Yuga is commencing." A round of murmurs swept the crowd. "If we aren't protected, we will be unable to carry the teachings of Yoga and the Vedas to the coming Satya Yuga and our mission will be defeated." Whispering broke out in the audience, especially among the saffron-clad yogis.

"So what do we do?" questioned Steve.

"The answer is already amongst us," asserted the rishi, pointing to the young son of the pujari. "Come, my boy." The boy regarded his parents before timidly approaching.

"Who are you?" questioned the old man. The little boy, with a mop of mischievous hair, quick shining eyes, a ready smile and bare feet, squirmed shyly. Steve figured him to be hardly eight years old.

"These are my parents," he mumbled, pointing to the pujari and his wife.

"What are their names?"

"My *mata's* name is Sumati and my *pita's* name is Vishnuyasha,"

The crowd buzzed appreciatively. Bewildered by the attention, the boy ran back to his parents as the crowd laughed at his innocence.

"This boy will be our savior," proclaimed the rishi. "He is destined to become Kalki, the tenth avatar of Vishnu, come to protect us."

Steve looked at Shanti. "How is that possible? He's just a little boy."

Shanti smiled. "Don't doubt the Supreme. He can take any form he wants."

"Tonight we will have a full lunar eclipse," continued Parvata Rishi. "Let us all meet at the river at dusk and pray to Krishna, who is the blue-skinned Vishnu Himself, to descend in an avatar form to help us in our struggle against evil and oppression."

The denizens of the valley got up and chatted with each other in great excitement. They now stood at the edge of a conflict that would determine the course of history, but more than that, they received the unique gift, the reward, of associating with an avatar of God Himself.

Evening brought peace as the bombing stopped and the airplanes left. The sun set quickly, darkness fell, and the heavens sparkled with stars.

"When will the eclipse start?" asked Steve.

"At exactly midnight," Shanti replied. "This type of eclipse is exceedingly rare and the position of the constellations is unique." He looked up. Stars twinkled in the inky sky but, being no astronomer, he couldn't ascertain their relative positions. When the moon rode high, the rishi brought out huge oil lamps, each with dozens of wicks burning brightly. The elders stood on the river-bank, offering the lamps to the flowing waters.

"What are they doing?"

"They are offering *puja* to the River Sarasvati."

"What for?"

"They're requesting blessings from Sarasvati Devi to enter her waters and do our prayers."

246

When the moon shone directly above, they all entered the river where it turned and spread out. The cold waters did not deter the worshippers, but instead, they walked with determination until they stood waist deep. Steve looked up. The moon slowly vanished, slice by slice.

The people chanted loudly and with enthusiasm. Vishnuyasha, his wife and their son moved to the middle of the assembly. When the moon finally disappeared and only a faint circle of light surrounded it, the young boy, as if pulled up by invisible ropes, ascended slowly and silently toward the celestial orb. Steve gasped. In the thick darkness, the child became lost to sight in seconds. The crowd continued chanting with increasing vigor, their voices disappearing into the heavens, determined that their prayers be heard.

Suddenly, a meteor exploded in the dark and shot down like a shell shattering in the sky. The crowd cowered for a moment, then peered intently upwards, straining their eyes, holding their breath. An instant later, a large white horse, its wide wings flapping swiftly, appeared at the head of the shooting star and glided swiftly down to the ground. On it sat the son of Vishnuyasha, no longer a small boy, but a powerful and magnificent young man. A chill traveled up and down Steve's spine. He held on to Shanti's hand tightly and she returned his grasp, squeezing strongly in excitement.

The rider and the horse landed on the riverbank and the tall clean-shaven young man, his skin the hue of moonlight, with long black curly hair, a handsome mustache, brilliantly shining gold earrings, and a glowing, gilded dhoti, descended. His strong, muscular body shimmered like a forest fire on a distant hill and in his right hand he held a sword, about five feet long, which emitted an unearthly radiance. When he smiled, Steve, charmed by his beauty, felt unable to move his eyes away.

As, sliver by sliver, the moon reappeared, the pilgrims moved out of the waters and congregated at the feet of the divine Avatar. Parvata Rishi dropped to his knees and clasped his hands together. "Oh dear Avatar," he cried. "I

247

am so fortunate to be in your blessed presence. Just having your darshan is enough to remove the sins of a million lifetimes, what to speak of serving you in person. Please allow me to assist you."

Kalki Avatar benevolently blessed the rishi in a low and strong, yet immensely pleasing voice. "My dear rishi, you and all the devotees have my love and benedictions."

The Avatar dismounted his horse, approached his parents and bowed his head respectfully. "Son," declared Vishnuyasha with tears in his eyes. "This is the happiest day of my life." His mother, beyond words, embraced him.

"My dear parents, I owe everything to you. I pray that I will bring pleasure to your hearts."

"You already have, my son," answered his mother. "You already have."

Steve and Shanti walked close to the Avatar, his exquisiteness attracting them as a lamp draws moths. Steve turned away, unable to bear the luster. The horse, at least six feet tall at the shoulders, with large blue eyes, a magnificent mane, broad back, muscular legs and alert ears, looked splendid, unearthly in its own right. Steve dared not touch it. It carried itself as if it had blue blood, as if it would neither obey nor allow itself to be handled by mere mortals.

Parvata Rishi spoke. "Dear Kalki Avatar. You are alone. How can you defeat the army of the great tyrant?"

"Whenever any avatar descends, we do not come alone. We are always joined by our eternal associates and our paraphernalia."

"I don't understand," said Steve.

"My horse, Devadatta, is with me," said Kalki Avatar pointing to his steed, "along with my sword, a gift from the great Lord Shiva. My eternal associate, Hanuman, who accompanied me when I appeared as Lord Rama in Treta Yuga thousands of years ago, will join me now."

Steve searched around. "Where is Hanuman?"

The Avatar blew into a large pink and white conch shell. As the last notes echoed among the trees, a large red monkey ran out from the forest on his hind legs. Steve

248

jumped back. The enormous simian, with piercing eyes, powerful arms, and muscular tail, measured six and a half feet tall. Gilded armor shielded his chest, a light yellow dhoti covered his legs and a golden crown sat on his head. He displayed a pleasant appearance, bemused brown eyes, and a wide smile. He bounded over to the Avatar.

"My dear Hanuman, our activities are endlessly variegated and eternal," pronounced the Avatar, embracing his devotee. "Here at the end of Kali Yuga, I ask for your service again."

"What shall I do?" requested the valorous monkey.

"The enemy has created a great disturbance. Please climb out of Shambala and into the mountains above. Return with a report so we can properly prepare for the upcoming battle."

"I will explore the entire area," replied Hanuman, scanning the peaks, now reflecting the early morning sun. "And by evening I will return with all the news." He bowed humbly to his lord and jumped out of the valley with one single bound.

Steve, standing with the awe-struck crowd, grasped Shanti's hand. "We are not alone," he murmured. She nodded, smiling faintly.

* * *

Shambala, End of Kali Yuga

Jack crawled to the cave's mouth and hesitantly peered out. The thunderous explosions of the previous day still rattled his head, unease gripped his stomach and pain took hold deep in his sinuses. The awful result of the devastating bombardment, surely the work of Kallin's men out looking for him, came into view. The black granite stone that had halted his progress lay shattered, its smooth, sharp splinters strewn all over, revealing a small path leading between the mountains. He glanced at the darkening sky. The setting sun threw long shadows, covering the land. For the first time, Jack snuck cautiously out of the cave.

249

Suddenly, something gripped his neck! He got pulled straight up and came face to face with an enormous monkey. The massive creature, with a broad chest, long muscular arms, and sharp, intelligent eyes, roared angrily. Jack gulped in big lungfuls of air and his body shook. The monkey frowned and scratched his chin, then picked him up, threw him on his back and, with his tail wrapped around Jack's body, sprung away. Jack had no choice except to hold on for dear life.

Taking enormous leaps, the monkey clambered down the mountain, hurdled over boulders with amazing agility, bounded into the dark pass and, when he came to the edge of a steep cliff, jumped out into the void with all his might. Jack screamed. The monkey landed on a ledge. Jack calmed his thumping heart and peered into a beautiful valley, observing a river, sparkling as it wound its way through jade forests, reflecting the cobalt sky all along its length like a dark-blue crystal necklace. The monkey again descended at breakneck speed and finally landed in the waters with both of his feet. The crash of a waterfall sounded nearby. The creature ran along the river bank and finally stopped at a flat pasture. There, he laid Jack on the grass, moved about ten feet away, and sat observing him.

"Hanuman," came a voice.

A tall, well-built man, with an aura surrounding his body, walked out of the forest. The monkey immediately jumped over and bent down, touching his feet. The man pointed at Jack and though the simian replied in an unknown language, Jack easily deduced that they were talking about him.

The man motioned and the monkey picked Jack up and entered the forest. A campfire burned under the trees where a few humans cooked food. Left slumped up against a nearby pine tree and too exhausted to move, he fell, within minutes, into a deep sleep.

* * *

Steve rubbed his eyes. *Could it be? The profile was unmistakable!*

"Jack!" he shouted. The figure on the ground got up and groggily looked around.

"Steve? Is that you?"

"Yes! It's me."

Jack scrambled to his feet. Squeezed by his brother's strong embrace, Steve felt himself lifted being off the ground. He yelled. It was incredible! How could Jack be here? "I'm so happy to see you!" he exclaimed.

"Me too!"

Jack looked somehow different, seemingly more centered, more his own person. Still, Steve felt a twinge of ambivalence. Had Jack really changed? Steve didn't want to get entangled in the previous patterns of their lives. Could he trust his brother? The thought of their mother and the scene at the temple came to mind. He flinched. While genuinely happy to see Jack, unfinished business remained.

"Where am I?" questioned Jack.

"When you did the ceremony at the Krishna temple, I had no idea you went to Kali Yuga. I jumped in and ended up in Satya Yuga."

"So how did we end up in the same place and time?"

"That's a long story," replied Steve.

"Tell me. I need to know!"

They talked of their various adventures, the upcoming war, their dilemmas and their realizations as the moon rose above. A beautiful young woman came by and served them meals on leaf plates. The fire's embers glowed on her black hair and her white teeth shone as she smiled.

"Thank you," Jack said, uncertainly.

"Jack, this is Shanti, my fiancée."

"Your fiancée!"

"Yes," exclaimed Steve. "There's a lot of things yet to discuss!"

"We have the rest of the evening!"

Shanti sat by amused while the brothers talked and gesticulated excitedly until the moon moved directly overhead, exhaustion overwhelmed them and they reluctantly had to call it a night.

Chapter Thirty One

Shambala, End of Kali Yuga

The stress of the past many days caught up with Jack and he awoke only when fully refreshed. He joined Steve and Shanti at the meadow.

"Are you feeling better?" questioned Steve.

"Much better, now that we're together."

Jack suddenly jumped up to his feet, pointing at a small group of villagers near the trees.

"That man!" exclaimed Jack. "Who is he?"

Steve looked around. "Which man are you...?"

Jack didn't wait. He ran over to the group and fell, on his knees once again, in front of Parvata Rishi. The villagers looked on in wonderment.

"Who are you?" Jack asked, his eyes glistening.

"My son," replied the old man, speaking English with a strong, but pleasant accent. "I am Parvata Rishi."

"You saved my life! I have no idea who you are, but in my darkest hour you came to help me."

"You may not know me, but I know you. I understood full well your dangerous situation and created a seed-thought which lay hidden in the ether to appear when you needed it."

"Thank you! Ever since you appeared on that dreadful, yet wonderful, day I have been thinking of you."

The rishi laughed. "I am happy to have helped."

"Dear Parvata Rishi," stated Jack earnestly. "Is there any way to repay your kindness? Please tell me what to do."

The rishi reflected for a moment. "If you can aid us at this time of need, it would be greatly appreciated."

"Of course! I will help you in whatever way possible to help win this war." Jack felt unworthy to have received the request, but did he have it in him to make this kind of commitment? After all, being a warrior entailed great responsibilities. The lives of his fellow soldiers, what to speak of Steve, Shanti and Parvata Rishi, would depend in some way on his actions on the battlefield. In a crisis, would he evade the situation as always had? He took a deep breath and calmed himself. He was not the old Jack. A lot had changed. *I have to have faith*, he reminded himself, *if not in myself, then in the Rishi.* After all, Parvata Rishi had saved his life.

"Come. I am just now going to speak to Kalki Avatar," said the rishi. Steve and Shanti joined them. The Avatar and Hanuman sat near the cooking fire, soaking in the warmth. Smoke curled straight up into the atmosphere as no wind disturbed the peaceful valley.

"Yes," said the Avatar, speaking with Hanuman, as they joined him. "Your proposal makes good sense." The Avatar turned to the sage. "We have decided to battle the enemy on the plains that lie several miles away at the other end of the pass."

"But will we be safe?" protested the rishi. "Your presence here drives away all danger."

"My refuge is always available to the sincere, but Hanuman gave a very sensible alternative. We cannot fight here. It is too dangerous. If the rishis and yogis are killed, who then will teach the Vedic philosophy to humanity? On the plains where the enemy is amassed, we can use all our weapons, exploit the space to engage our troops, defend the entrance to the pass and thus protect Shambala."

The rishi agreed. He pointed to Jack. "This young man is Steve's brother. He escaped from the enemy." He nodded to Jack. "Speak. I will translate."

"The tyrant we are up against is named Kallin and he has a very large army and many powerful weapons," started Jack. "He seeks immortality. He wants the secret to time travel and will stop at nothing."

Kalki nodded. "Tell us more." Jack revealed all he knew about the society, the rebellion, Kallin's armies, the great cities and the Raks. When he finished, Parvata Rishi became grave as the scope of the threat became clear.

"And I want to join the battle," concluded Jack.

Steve jumped in. "I will do the same." Shanti looked at him wide-eyed, but said nothing.

Their declarations pleased the Avatar. "Of course, let us meet at the meadow in an hour."

They returned to their camp. "How did Parvata Rishi speak to me in English?" asked Jack.

"After I arrived in Satya Yuga, the rishi insisted that I teach him English. Believe it or not, he picked it up in a week."

"I'm going to have to learn their language," countered Jack. "After all, I want to be able to communicate with everyone, not just you and him."

"I'll teach you," offered Steve. "Besides, with the rishi's help, I'm sure you'll pick up Sanskrit in no time at all."

Shanti questioned Steve. "Why are you entering the battle?"

"The yogis and rishis have to protect the sacred teachings. I don't. It's the least I can do, to protect you and your father, what to mention the rest of the community."

"What about me?"

"Be brave. You have your duty and I have mine."

* * *

Doubts arose in Steve's mind as the community gathered in the meadow. He approached the Avatar. "What will we do now? Certainly, many enemy soldiers will come. But the yogis? They don't know how to fight."

"The rishis and yogis are here to preserve the wisdom of yoga. That is their only duty." He turned to the monkey king. "Hanuman-ji," he said, addressing him affectionately. "Please gather your army and let us fight against evil and for justice and truthfulness."

"May victory be yours," shouted Hanuman, his eyes blazing with excitement. He gestured toward the forest with his right arm and roared loudly. As Steve watched in

255

amazement, countless robust monkeys in shining gold armor, holding assorted weaponry—rifles, swords and maces—and dressed similarly to Hanuman, marched out of the pine forest.

"Call the bears," ordered the Avatar.

Hanuman cried piercingly and an army of enormous bears, each nine feet tall, powerful and fierce, helmets covering their heads and walking on hind legs, trundled out of the woods, led by Jambavan, their king. Dressed in splendid silver armor, they shone beautifully in the sun, their hands skillfully retaining glittering armaments. The monkeys and bears fell into formation, saluted the Avatar and roared bravely. Their leaders held colorful flags—purples, yellows, blues, oranges and blacks—streaming in the wind. Steve observed the proceedings with wonder. Indeed, the shouts of thousands of soldiers, accompanied by kettle drums and horns, the army in strict formation, the different companies' insignias floating in the air—all made a splendid sight.

"Let's march to the plains to meet the enemy," commanded Kalki Avatar. With that, the magnificent army strode out to combat.

Shanti shivered. "The war seems so real now."

Steve held her by the shoulders. "Yes. This is it."

Chapter Thirty Two

Shambala, End of Kali Yuga

"It is wonderful that you procured these garments from your father," Kalki Avatar told Hanuman. Jack, Steve, and a hundred monkeys stood next to the great warriors on a reddish-brown hill extending out of the mountains and into the plains. The late afternoon sun winked on the scene through low clouds, dappling the ochre steppes below as far as the eye could see. It made for a beautiful battlefield.

"Thank you," replied the monkey king. "My father, Vayu, the demigod of the wind, helped happily. With these, we can fly through the air." The gossamer shirts, thin as onion skins, sparkling purple and gold, extended well below the waist, with curious, small, wing-like appendages at the bottom. The pants, of the same material, reached the calves.

"I have something too," continued the Avatar. He carefully emptied the contents of a large brown bag. A hundred swords, each three feet long, fashioned of a clear crystal, tumbled out, and a hundred small shields made of a purple glassy material, each roughly two feet in diameter, joined them.

Jack regarded the swords and shields with bewilderment. "What are they?" he asked in broken Sanskrit.

"These are gifts from Indra, the demigod of storms," answered the Avatar. "We have enough for a hundred warriors."

Jack picked up a sword and, as he did, millions of points of light, atoms and molecules, suddenly swirled into view, bubbling and boiling, until the blade shone brightly. He swung it.

"Stop!" shouted Kalki Avatar.

Too late, a terrific thunderclap sounded over the flatlands as an enormous bolt of lightning burst out of the sword's pointed end and shattered a nearby boulder into smithereens.

"I'm sorry," apologized Jack, thoroughly shaken.

"These are weapons of the demigods," warned Kalki. "They cannot be taken frivolously. And be careful. The swords are very brittle." Chastened, Jack gently deposited the weapon with its brethren. Steve stared at him in askance, but said nothing.

"Look to the right from where we are standing," said Kalki Avatar, as Steve translated for Jack. Another hill, shaped like a camel's nose growing out of the face of the mountain and composed of nothing but huge boulders, jutted out of the cliffs and gently descended to the plains. Between the two hills lay flat land where stood about a quarter of Kallin's troops, preparing to enter the pass leading to Shambala, while the rest extended beyond, on the steppes. In their middle stood an old, grey-haired general with three stars on his helmet, long white mustaches and green fatigues.

"Some of our troops are hiding behind this hill and the other one, while the rest are guarding the pass," continued the Avatar. "Our plan is to cut off part of the enemy's army by linking the two hills with our soldiers, surrounding and destroying them. The idea is to divide the enemy and defeat him, piece by piece."

"A good plan," remarked Hanuman. Jack nodded his head thoughtfully. If it succeeded, the soldiers would have no escape.

"Hanuman, shall we start?"

"Of course," replied the monkey general, his eyes flashing. "May victory be yours!"

When Kalki Avatar blew heartily into his conch shell, two brigades, of about seven hundred bears and simians each, ran out from the hidden sides of both hills and charged straight into Kallin's army. The enemy jeered at seeing the red-haired simians and brown-furred bears. Their taunts reached Kalki's army, but they paid no heed. The monkeys, roaring like lions, armed with rifles spouting balls of golden fire, never missed their mark. The bears worked their own weapons, emitting steel darts at immense speed which pierced many an enemy's heart.

"Wow!" exclaimed Jack. "What a battle!" Indeed, the enthusiasm of the Avatar's army was admirable to behold. The bears fought as if all fear of death abandoned them and the great monkeys seemed even more spectacular, running ahead of the bears, overpowering the enemy before they had time to even aim their weapons. Kallin's troops never before encountered such a courageous and enthusiastic army and, within half an hour, the Avatar's soldiers reached half the way through on each side.

"This is when the battle will be decided," cautioned the Avatar. "The two sides need to join as quickly as possible. If we give the enemy unnecessary time, they will regroup. After all, theirs is a much larger force." Indeed, the enemy soldiers on the plains, as if guided by an unseen observer, turned and started pushing against the containing arms of the Avatar's army.

Fighting back, the two parts of the Avatar's army met, strengthened in number and surrounded the soldiers in a thick circle of bears and apes. The cries of the doomed men rent the air. The old general, outside the area of containment, did not meekly accept the destruction of a quarter of his troops. He roared loudly and fired his revolver in the air, the shots burning like red flares. His men turned and flooded up against the dam holding back their compatriots.

The battle turned. Jack immediately saw the danger. If the enemy broke through the formation, the two arms of Kalki's army would separate, be surrounded and destroyed. "Look, we are getting beaten!" he exclaimed.

Suddenly, dozens of black spots flew in from the west. The old general had called aircraft into battle!

"Quick," shouted the Avatar. "Into the flying garments! Take the swords and shields, and off to battle!"

Jack and Steve removed their clothing and slipped into the shining garments which shrunk to fit the contours of their bodies like second skins. The purple and gold patches suddenly came to life, humming softly, as if stirred by a million microscopic butterfly wings. Tiny puffs of air brushed Jack's face.

Jack pointed his sword into the sky and immediately shot upwards like a bullet from a rifle. His heart jumped into his mouth, his blood drained into his legs and the wind screamed in his ears. He shrieked. He kept jetting upwards, but as soon as he spread his legs, slowed down. He pointed his arms to the right and headed in that direction. He brought his legs together and his speed increased. He got the hang of this.

Lying spread-eagled, he looked around and saw Kalki Avatar pull on the reins of his transcendental steed as it took to the air. The Avatar hovered over the battlefield, shining luminously, a dazzling silver aura surrounding him. Upon seeing this mystical vision, the enemy soldiers stopped, unable to remove their eyes from the rapidly descending divine angel of death. The horse's wings flapped rapidly, resembling a small, furious white cloud moving quickly over the battlefield, and the Avatar's sharp sword flashed like bolts of lightning, never missing its mark, cutting off the heads of the enemy soldiers.

Monkeys, glittering in their garments, joined the air battle. They presented a magnificent sight, purple and gold, with glittering helmets, streaking at breakneck speeds all over the theater of operations, engaging the enemy aircraft in deadly duels. Indra's swords worked their magic and hundreds of thunderous blasts shook the air above the battle.

Suddenly, a small golden sphere raced towards Jack. At the last second, he instinctively raised his shield and got jolted ten feet to the right while the pulse glanced harmlessly away to the left. The thought occurred that if he caught the shots straight on, he wouldn't be pushed aside.

A black pyramid whipped by, emitting flashes of blue energy. He deflected the shots with his shield, let the craft go by and followed it, zipping by dozens of flying monkey soldiers, careening around other black aircraft in the air. He did not dare use his sword: if he missed, the blast could hit an airborne monkey or smash down into the Avatar's army. Suddenly the black plane shot straight up and, as it did, Jack swung his sword. A terrific thunderbolt sounded, shaking him from head to toe as white lightning escaped his weapon and smashed into the hapless fighter. It exploded with a mighty clap and burst into thousands of pieces, none longer than a man's little finger.

The back sides of the flying warriors remained their weak point. If Kallin's aircrafts shot at them from behind, they had no chance. Soon, simians fell out of the sky, dead. Jack flew around, looking for Steve and spotted him, high in the air, hiding behind a small peak, swinging his sword at passing planes. Unnoticed by Steve, one of the enemy crafts swung around from the other side of the mountain. Jack flew down and just as the craft completed its maneuver and came at Steve from behind, let forth a strike of lightning. It exploded ear-splittingly.

"Thank you!" exclaimed Steve, shaking.

"You're welcome. You almost died!" A shadow darkened Steve's face and he suddenly turned away.

"What is it?"

Steve said nothing but left Jack puzzled. It was like Steve to not communicate his feelings. He glanced at his brother and their eyes met momentarily. Jack immediately realized what had happened. This concerned their mother! So Steve still harbored some bitterness! A sinking feeling weighed down his stomach. He gulped. I can understand why doesn't fully trust me, thought Jack. How could he make his failure up to Steve? To Mom? He had no idea. He looked away silently and flew off.

A furious hour-long struggle finally destroyed all the enemy aircraft. The white-haired general understood the situation: the Avatar had gained the upper hand. The old warrior retreated to the base of the hills and ordered his troops into a thick square, their weapons pointed outwards like thorns on a bush, firing into the sky. They became sitting targets. The bears climbed up the cliffs and started shooting. The flying monkeys picked up huge boulders and dropped them on the heads of the hapless soldiers.

The enemy had no chance. Within minutes, they were decimated. The general ran from the scene of devastation but eventually stopped to catch his breath. He looked back at his once proud formation, now totally destroyed. He removed his hat, slowly procured his service revolver from its holster, sat on one knee, aimed the weapon at his temple, sighed, closed his eyes and pulled the trigger. A pulse of energy shot out of the gun and instantly detached his head from his body.

Chapter Thirty Three

Kallin's Estate, End of Kali Yuga

Kallin's face looked gray, ashen. General Gahal dead and ten thousand men gone. The commanding officers sat in their seats with morose faces.

"General Contog," asked Kallin grimly. "Can you get a recording of the battle?"

"Yes sir. We'll get a feed from one of the satellites." He picked up his tablet, made a connection, a beam of light shot forth and images formed in the air. At first, the pictures looked grainy, as if filmed through a layer of cloud. Seconds later, the scene came into view. The moving objects, though small, were clear to see.

"What the hell are those?" demanded Kallin.

"Monkeys and bears!" exclaimed Contog.

"But they've been extinct for thousands of years!" cried Jini. "Look! Look at that man on the flying horse!"

"Who is he?" exclaimed the Hand of God. "How did the enemy get so strong? Where did they get the weapons to compete with us?" Kallin's face flashed with anger. He slammed his hand on his desk. "I want answers!" he shouted. "I want to know what the hell happened up there." Spurred by Kallin's demands, the assembly started discussing things, but the sheer unexpectedness of the turn of events stumped them all. The conversations died down.

"What the hell is going on? Can anyone of you give me answers?" No one spoke.

"They all seem to come from the valley," Jini answered timidly.

"Yes," said Kallin. "Go on."

"Maybe the valley hides species we're unaware of, species been driven to extinction everywhere else."

The national security advisor glanced at Kallin. "Like a land lost in time?" he asked.

Kallin shook his head shrewdly. "Gentlemen, what we're seeing is something extraordinary. This is much bigger than a rag-tag bunch of dissatisfied Raks. Jack undoubtedly has a connection with the valley. If he isn't a time traveler, why would he head there? The monkeys and bears must also come from a former age. It's logical to conclude that the valley has something to do with time travel."

He thoughtfully rubbed his beard. "But this is an extraordinary opportunity as well. I want to find out the secret of time travel and if I do, nothing can stop me!"

"Then we shouldn't attack the valley directly. We need to capture, not destroy it," pronounced the national security advisor.

"Yes. Let us gather all our troops at the plains and head to battle. We will destroy this raggedy-assed bunch of monkeys and bears and seize the valley." His gaze circled the room. "And I want every one of you idiots on the battlefield." They squirmed in their chairs. "What the hell are you waiting for?" He pointed to Jini. "She has more brains than the rest of you put together." Jini beamed. The group scattered.

As Contog was about to leave, President Kallin stopped him. "General, come here."

Contog marched up slowly. "Yes sir. What can I do for you?"

President Kallin smiled thinly. "You have been quiet. You usually have some ideas to share with us"

"I'm sorry sir, I was totally stumped."

"Do you know something that the rest of us don't?"

"What do you mean?"

The president glared at him. "Are you sharing everything with us?"

Contog's eyes narrowed. "You have everything—all my reports, my data."

President Kallin glanced at the national security advisor. "Do you have it?"

The advisor opened a briefcase and pulled out a red tablet. Contog's face turned white.

"Can you tell us what this is?" demanded the Hand of God.

Contog stared down at the floor resignedly. His life just ended.

"I will have your head for this," shouted Kallin.

Contog raised his head and stared fearlessly at Kallin. "Do what you want. I am prepared to die."

Kallin laughed. "You think I will let you off so easily? You will be shot only when I am finished."

"What can you want from me? You already know everything."

"Except for one thing—your connection with that traitor Jack. What do you know about time travel? What is the secret of the hidden valley?"

"I know nothing about that."

Kallin slammed his fist on the desk. "You're lying. When you spoke to Jack you always turned on the cloaking device. Where did he get the coordinates for the rebel base, if not from you?"

"It is true I gave him the coordinates, but I don't know anything about time travel or the valley."

"How convenient that the rebel camp is so close to the valley?" Kallin addressed the national security advisor. "Give us a live feed." The advisor swiped a tablet and images of the base in flames came up. "As we speak, all the rebels on your database are being sought out and executed. Your puny rebellion is over. By the end of the day, there will be nothing left of it except for you."

Kallin got up and grabbed the pale general by the jacket. "This is the fate of all rebels. When I'm finished with you, you will end up the same way." Growling, tore the stars off his epaulets, ripped the ribbons from his uniform, snatched the cap off the general's head and crushed it with his boot. "Guards, throw him in jail."

* * *

Kallin angrily scratched his beard. "I want to have the secret for time travel! I want it now!"

"So what are you going to do?" questioned the national security advisor.

"I want all our armies, every airplane, every soldier, to go into battle and take control of the valley once and for all."

"Is that wise? There are dangers. We need troops here."

"I don't care," raved the Hand of God. "I want to have this power—it's the only thing I don't possess. I will have it and I don't care what it takes. Get my personal aircraft ready. I am going to finish this job myself."

* * *

Shambala, End of Kali Yuga

The brothers looked out on the plains, silent in the early morning sun. Only six hundred monkeys and bears remained of the Avatar's once proud army.

"The enemy will return," mentioned the Avatar to Hanuman, "and in greater numbers. Fortunately, we avoided defeat. Strangely, as the evening progressed, the stronger they became."

"So what will we do?" questioned Steve, his voice expressing concern. The two hardened warriors laughed. Kalki Avatar blew into his transcendental conch shell and as the long notes echoed back from the hills and reverberated into the pass, a huge army took shape on the plains, as if they had always stood there, invisible to the eye, waiting for a signal to materialize. Steve's jaw dropped. Were they real? How did they appear out of nothing?

Kalki laughed at Steve's surprise. "Look—do you see the great heroes—Dristaketu, Dristadyumna, Jayatsena and the others?" Tall, imposing figures stood in front of their armies, surrounded by their generals. "Just like Hanuman, these soldiers are my eternal associates," he continued, "and are never separated from me. They helped the previous avatars and they will appear in the future."

The armies of the Heroes, in total a million soldiers, dressed in the colors of their nations, with weapons in hand, their pennants flying in the air, appeared like an immense, colorful human carpet on the brown dust of the steppes, their beautiful gilded armor shining like jewels in the sun. The Avatar raised his arm and the armies fell silent.

"Illustrious Heroes," he announced. "Your presence here at the end of Kali Yuga is greatly auspicious and brings the assurance of victory." The armies sounded in approval, their voices like a million lions roaring.

"With righteousness, morality and the blessings of our elders, the enemy is already defeated. All you need to do is act. But our adversary is proud and arrogant. He hasn't thrown his full force against us and, in his madness, believes he can defeat us and overtake Shambala. His goal is to learn the secrets of the yogis and the rishis by force."

Laughter flooded the armies.

"This dictator wants to foolishly become a yogi by violence. To acquire the secrets of the yogic siddhis, he only has to learn humbly at the feet of the gurus, devoid of all personal motives and free of bad qualities such as lust, greed, envy, and anger. But unfortunately, these men, whose consciousness is corrupted, will never have a peaceful mind, the first requirement in the practice of yoga.

"But be warned. The enemy has mighty armies, powerful weapons and will use everything he possesses. So let us occupy the land in front of us, let us dig entrenchments in the valley and let us fortify the high places. When he attacks, we will be ready."

Upon hearing this message, the prodigious army cheered wildly and set forth to prepare for the great battle.

"Maybe we aren't in such bad shape after all," Steve said to his brother.

For once, Jack remained speechless.

* * *

In Shambala, Parvata Rishi paced nervously. The lovely sunrise did not bring him peace.

"Father," asked Shanti, "what is it?"

The old man glanced sorrowfully at his daughter. "Shanti, in my mind I see the enemy bringing forth an even greater army, their numbers and weapons far too many to count. I am afraid that we are in for a severe test."

"So what should we do?" exclaimed the young woman.

"Let us help the Avatar." He went into his shelter and returned with one of his texts. "This is the *Vaimanika shastra*. It describes flying craft called *vimanas*, which are created and controlled by the mind."

He went to the meadow near the river, the scene of their previous yajnas, while his daughter corralled the rest of the community. Four yogis sat at each cardinal point, about fifty feet from each other and engaged in deep meditation. The other sages circled them, chanting the Vaimanika shastra, while the rest of the community sat listening in an outer circle. The sound purified the place, creating an invisible shell of intensity and softness above and around them where their thoughts would manifest into reality. The power of their tapasya, their austerity, created an intense heat that escaped from their minds and filled the sacred space above while the drone of the mantras took this energy and created out of it seven types of vimanas.

Shanti's jaw dropped. Flying craft, from the smallest to the largest, floated at seven levels above. Their extraordinary beauty captured her admiration. Several hundred vimanas, looking very much like enormous soup bowls, made of shiny purple ceramic, each about four feet wide and two deep, moved in a wide circle above, almost within grasp. She laughed. They almost looked like flying toilets.

A few dozen vimanas, elongated flower buds with large petals in shades of red and yellow, entwined with large green leaves, floated twenty feet above. Each measured nine feet long and Shanti giggled out loud at their appearance; their strangeness and beauty unlike anything she ever saw. A hundred feet above them, vimanas resembling large fragile bubbles materialized, full of colors, spinning rapidly. Suspended in the blue sky, spinning at incredible speed, they hardly resembled war vessels but rather innocent soap bubbles at children's playgrounds.

A hundred feet further up, several dozen vimanas, looking like floating balls of liquid mercury, rolled in the wind and changed shapes like amoebas, glinting in the sun. Each craft appeared more fantastic than the one before. A half dozen of the fifth type, solid giant crystals of some unknown mineral, each about three hundred feet long, resembling cylindrical obelisks with pyramid-shaped heads, sparkled a brilliant rose-red as the sun shone through their monolithic, gem-like structures.

Several hundred feet above these flew the sixth type of vimana, appearing like huge metallic birds the size of large houses, with brilliant plumage, big shiny beaks and wings gliding out of their bases. At least a hundred of these giant vimanas glided high in the sky, flapping on thin, shiny metallic wings.

The last type of vimana, of which only one appeared, resembled a heavenly palace a mile in radius, floating high above all the rest, too big to be anywhere close to the valley. Shanti couldn't make out much of its features, though she observed a wall all around it and an immense gold pyramid in its middle extending far into the sky.

"Father," she exclaimed, "they're all beautiful!"

"And deadly, too."

Shanti eyed her father. "I want to pilot one of these vimanas."

"It is too dangerous," objected her father.

"If my future husband can go to war, should I not be by his side?"

"But have you thought of the consequences?"

Shanti's eyes narrowed with determination. "Yes. And I want to go."

The sage saw no point in arguing with her. His daughter had never contradicted him. It was a bittersweet moment. Despite his pride in her determination and maturity, the understanding that his girl belonged to someone else still stung. Her heart had gone elsewhere. Everything had changed.

Shanti realized her father's feelings. Tenderness for her father shaded her eyes and she quickly embraced him. "Don't worry. I will always love you. But please let me go." He nodded his head sadly.

A hundred young men and women gathered around Parvata Rishi. The old man dipped his head gravely and handed out slips of parchment with verses written on them to Shanti and the others. "Some of these vimanas need no pilot, but others do. Reciting these mantras will create energies in your brain that guide these ships. Any thought will automatically transform into action—that is, actions of these flying craft. Once absorbed in these incantations, you will be instantly transferred into the ships."

* * *

"What is that?" shouted Hanuman. "It resembles rain clouds descending in the monsoon season, drenching the earth for months on end." A cloud of dust two hundred feet high smudged the distant horizon.

Lord Kalki stroked his chin gravely. "Hanuman, that is our enemy. And surely the land will be soaked, not with life-giving water, but with the blood of brave soldiers on both sides. How much destruction can one man's ambition cause?" He shook his head. "Truly, materialistic desires always end in defeat."

Slowly but surely, a vast army of several million foot soldiers, battalions of mechanized armor, gigantic guns capable of firing shells across vast distances, rockets and fearsome black howitzers headed toward them across the flat lands. Beyond them, their lights blinking in the sky, flew hundreds, if not thousands, of airplanes. The sight of this magnificent, unparalleled, army took Hanuman's breath away.

"Hanuman-ji," asked the Avatar. "This is the army we have to face. Are you feeling any fear?"

"Lord," replied the great monkey general. "Let them come. If I die, I will take a million of them with me. I will make them taste death, by your mercy." Kalki Avatar swelled at his devotee's bravery.

As he peered into the distance, Hanuman noticed a strange sight. A large platform, about a hundred feet on each side, floated in the air above the enemy army, accompanied by black, silent helicopters, three above, and an equal number on each side. On it stood several dozen officers and crack troops, weapons in hand pointing outwards. Twenty feet above, on another stage connected by a ladder to the first one, stood a solitary man in green dress uniform, his jacket covered with assorted medals and ribbons, his head boasting a helmet decorated with six stars.

"Who is that?" questioned Hanuman.

"It is the dictator!" exclaimed Kalki. "He has taken an unnecessary risk. His avarice has gotten the better of him!"

"Good," exclaimed Hanuman. "Let him die on this battlefield, murdered by his greed."

* * *

When the sun positioned itself high over the battlefield, Steve observed a group of men, obviously Kallin's generals, drive in front of their troops. They raised their binoculars and spied on Kalki Avatar's army. Steve wondered at their thoughts. Did the strength of the forces arrayed against them surprise them? Did they hesitate upon seeing the mighty Heroes? Did they recognize the divinity of the Avatar?

An alarm like an air raid signal wailed and Kallin's army came to life. They cheered loudly, waved weapons in the air, shouted in excitement and rushed headlong into battle.

Across the divide, Kalki raised his prodigious conch shell to his lips. The sound started slowly, increased in volume and length until finally, it swelled in the valley and resounded to the mountain tops. The great Heroes followed suit and the wonderful sound of a host of conch shells blowing simultaneously filled the air. A great roar escaped from the throats of the multitudes, their voices flying across the plains. With remarkable energy, the monkeys and bears rushed into the fight, followed by the armies of the Heroes, flames spouting out of their deadly weapons.

Steve scanned the horizon, and sure enough, the sky filled with hundreds of black spots, approaching rapidly. If they attacked the Avatar's troops unhindered, surely all would be lost. Still wearing flying clothes and flashing swords, he shot up into the air, followed by Jack and the others, shooting straight at the advancing aircraft, swinging his sword. The airplanes came at them, their cannons blasting. Suddenly, this looked like a lost cause.

Unexpectedly, the aircraft veered off into different directions, scattering like a flock of doves when confronted by a hawk. Steve stopped in mid-air, confused. He turned around and saw some of the most fantastic craft possible lined up behind him. The flower vimanas, with their brilliant red and orange petals, crested over the mountain tops, swept down to the plains and hovered over the enemy army. As Kallin's soldiers gazed in enchantment, the beautiful flower craft spit out small black seeds. The men picked up the seeds inquisitively, and scoffing, threw them down. As soon as the seeds touched the ground, huge vines sprouted up and instantly entangled the soldiers; so tightly that they couldn't move a single muscle. They died on the vines, asphyxiated in no time at all. To the pilots of the other vimanas, a part of the battlefield appeared as a pitch of thick green weeds with occasional faces of Raks, contorted with fear, looking up through the greenery like small pink buds in dark flower beds.

The enemy aircraft set upon the flying flowers with great fury. The vimanas shot back with small pods which, upon contact, sprouted thick stems with huge thorns, immediately entwining the opponents' craft. Within seconds, they resembled flying bushes and when the thorns pierced their fuselages, they crashed into the ground, exploding upon contact.

As Steve lay spread-eagled in the sky, dozens of bubble-shaped vimanas, accompanied by many bowl-shaped ones, sped past. The iridescent bubble craft floated over the battlefield and he laughed at the incongruity between their beauty and the horror below.

"Steve!"

The voice was unmistakable. He looked around, shocked.

"Steve! I'm down here!"

Shanti, just ten feet below, piloting a bubble-shaped vimana, floating in its middle as if lying on a bed of air, waved to him. It spun round at inconceivable speed, changing its shape from a sphere to a cone as it traveled through the sky.

"What are you doing?" he shouted.

"Same thing you're doing," she retorted. "I am protecting the *dharma!*"

"This is dangerous."

As he spoke, a shot bounced right off Shanti's whirling bubble, slowing its rotation for a fraction of a second. "I feel like I'm falling!" she screamed.

Indeed, Shanti dropped just a bit, but in less than a hundredth of a second, the craft resumed its rotation, safely sheltering her again.

"Go back. You'll get shot down."

"No. If we are serving Kalki Avatar, why should we be afraid?" She had a determined look about her.

"Then let us join forces," he finally agreed.

Jack flew over. The brothers took positions on each side of Shanti's bubble, Steve looking forward and Jack guarding the rear. Suddenly, two pyramid-shaped enemy fighters approached, spitting sharply spinning balls of energy at them. The bowl-shaped craft, protecting all the vimanas, immediately jumped to intercept the red, purple, green and yellow energy pulses, which flew around inside them for a moment and disappeared. As the enemy zipped by, Jack swung his sword. The fighter exploded with a mighty bang while the second one whipped right past.

"Let's go after it," shouted Shanti and they shot off after the second attacker. It engaged in desperate maneuvers, shooting straight up, turning on a dime, flying behind other craft and diving down. The three of them, along with the bowl-shaped craft, followed close behind at enormous speed, bobbing and dodging other vimanas, striking at passing enemy craft, fashioning a trail of destruction through the skies. Steve shrieked with excitement, dipping, weaving and diving at enormous speed, warding off enemy shots with his shield, zipping behind other craft and firing bolts of lightning with his magical sword; the enemy craft exploding in front of him, their broken parts zinging off into the sky.

Suddenly the hunted craft slowed as it approached the cliffs. Shanti, using her mind, let go a stream of small bubbles. They hit it dead on. A thin film coated the fighter and it struggled to escape but within seconds, the covering hardened, rendering it immobile and the doomed craft fell to the ground, exploding in a ball of fire.

"Wow!" screamed Steve as they stopped to observe the destroyed aircraft. He held his hand up, saluting her victory and Shanti confidently raised her fist. She didn't resemble the shy, young woman he first met but revealed a lot more; things like courage and sacrifice.

"Go ahead," said Jack suddenly, saluting his brother. "I want to try one of the other vimanas."

"Wait!" Too late, Jack had left. Steve steamed. How could Jack fly off leaving them alone? He understood Jack enjoying the battle's adventure, but to leave Shanti unprotected on one side? He turned red and shook his head.

"What are you thinking?" asked Shanti.

"How thoughtless Jack can be. Same old Jack. If he stayed with us, we could continue fighting, but now, one of your flanks is unprotected."

"So what do you want to do?"

"Let's go back to Shambala. We can keep an eye out for any enemy vessels that may come there."

"Are you sure?"

"Absolutely!"

"Okay," sighed Shanti. "Let's go back."

* * *

Jack reappeared in a liquid mercury vimana which stretched and moved like a floating amoeba. He saw everything on a silvery screen that sometimes stretched and bent like the mercury his craft was made of. His airship had no rigid structure and he felt as if he was swimming, as it sometimes bucked and heaved like a mechanical bull, pulling him from one side to the other at incredible speed.

The enemy laughed at its stretching itself into odd shapes, moving herky-jerky above the plains, and shot at it. The craft instantly stretched, throwing Jack to one end while the bolts of energy passed harmlessly through the liquid mercury at the other side. Obviously, it couldn't be destroyed in the usual manner. He guided it low over the battlefield and stopped over the enemy. Instantaneously, hundreds of rifles escaped the soldiers' grasps, flew straight up and stuck to the vimana's outside skin. His jaw dropped. Seconds later, the metal, transformed into thousands of pellets of shot, hurled back down, killing hundreds. The survivors ran away as fast as their legs could carry them.

A shell flew right over Jack's vimana and exploded near the hill where the Avatar stood. He traced it back to a group of mortars at the other side of the battlefield and guided his craft over to the cannons, not really knowing what to do. Two other mercury vimanas floated over. A strange thing happened. The three craft came together and joined seamlessly, creating one giant mercury ball roughly fifty feet in diameter. The two other pilots joined him in his cabin laughing and gesturing excitedly.

The now-large vimana descended. To Jack's amazement, one of the cannons slowly lifted off the ground, stuck to the craft's exterior and melted into it. The vimana lifted a hundred feet up into the air, changed hue to a milky white and spit out hundreds of spears, which, traveling at immense speed, impaled the fleeing soldiers. Seeing this demonstration brought a chill to his heart.

Once he destroyed the battery of mortars, Jack bade farewell to his companions, popped out of the top of the liquid mercury craft and flew into the sky until he had a view of the entire battlefield. He looked around unsuccessfully for Steve and Shanti. He shook his head questioningly. Strange. Did they leave for Shambala already?

Jack landed on the hill next to Kalki Avatar. The Avatar pointed to a long tangerine-colored flying obelisk vimana. "Watch. This vimana is guided by my mind and targeted with my eyes."

The vimana inverted itself, its pointed top facing down, and positioned itself above the battlefield, its insides glittering with the reflections of the sun's rays and, after several minutes, blazed from top to bottom like an enormous exclamation of fire in the sky. Suddenly, a hundred-foot-wide beam of intense blue light, like a million lasers, shot out from the vimana's peak and scorched to death every soldier unlucky enough to be under it. The hot blue light devastated the enemy and melted all metal it shone on. As the obelisk crisscrossed the battlefield in several measured sweeps, the men ran away shouting and Kallin's platform moved discreetly away to a safe distance.

The battle possessed a strange beauty. Jack had to remind himself that behind the muffled, distant explosions, the whine of ordnance zipping by, the small puffs of white smoke in the blue atmosphere, the pillars of fire floating in the sky, the purple and gold flying monkeys, the iridescent bubbles, the yellow and orange shell-bursts, the shiny mercury craft which reflected the sky above and the battle below, the black fighter planes flitting like flies and the strange floating flowers, a deadly war unfolded and when evening fell and the fighting slowed for at least a while, the air would be rent with the cries of the injured and the agony of the dying.

* * *

The battle lasted for days and immense was the slaughter on both sides. The armies of the Heroes were decimated by the coordinated attacks of the Functionals, who seemed to anticipate the movements of Kalki Avatar's men. The army of the Heroes retaliated, killing millions. Finally, the victor emerged, but at what a cost! The vimanas worked their magic and, with the help of the bears, monkeys and the army of the great Heroes, destroyed the enemy army and most of Kallin's air force. Kallin swiftly retreated from the battle scene on his flying platform, his entire army decimated, with not a single soldier left alive. On Kalki Avatar's side, only a few thousand remained to celebrate the bloody victory.

Chapter Thirty Four

At the Battlefield, End of Kali Yuga

"What are we going to do?" questioned the national security advisor. "Some of our aircraft are saved, but the army is totally destroyed."

The floating platform moved slowly in the early morning over the previous night's battlefield. A strange, burnt electrical smell, mixed in with the stench of coagulating blood, filled the air. On the plains, as far as the eye could see, lay the bodies of soldiers, many of them staring into the sky with wide-open eyes. Heads, arms and legs lay scattered about.

"I will never give up," proclaimed the Hand of God wrathfully, oblivious to the carnage. "I will get the power of time travel, even if it means sacrificing every single person on this planet." He scratched his white beard. "Gather all the Raks you can find and bring them. Use whoever is left of the police to round them up."

"Untrained Raks! How can they fight? They are not army material. They're all deformed. The only Raks we've used so far are the Functionals!"

"It doesn't matter. When injected with the military grade DNA implants, the Raks will be controlled automatically."

"But sir, isn't that dangerous?"

"Stop arguing with me," yelled Kallin. "From now on, I'll make all the decisions around here. Bring every Rak you can by tomorrow night. Get going!"

* * *

With the decimation of Kallin's troops, Steve, Jack, Hanuman and Kalki Avatar flew back to Shambala, joining

Shanti, Parvata Rishi and the rest of the community under the trees.

"Congratulations on winning the war!" announced Vishnuyasha, beaming at Kalki. Though they destroyed the enemy, none felt any happiness, but sadness at the loss of almost the entire army of the Heroes and of the poor, miserable enemy soldiers, by whose misfortune they served an evil master. Yet, relief arrived with the fight's end.

Suddenly, a small pyramid-shaped airplane appeared at the far end of the valley, flying silently, close to the ground, while being hunted by two other craft. Making desperate maneuvers to escape its followers, it weaved and bobbed all along the valley, dodging its pursuers until hit by a shot of cannon. A seat ejected and drifted into the jumble of rocks near the waterfalls, as the fighters climbed up and flew away. The seat's back remained visible and the occupant lay hidden. Jack ran towards it, joined by several young men, and pulled it over.

"Jack, is that you?" inquired the man. Jack jumped back in surprise. A familiar face, square-jawed, with brown skin creased like sandpaper, stared back.

"General Contog! What are you doing here?" blurted Jack.

"I escaped from Kallington."

By now, the rest of the group arrived. "He's our friend," reassured Jack, "not an enemy." Exclamations of surprise sounded all around.

Contog unstrapped himself and stood up. His face showed the weariness of days of imprisonment and the strain of escape, but his eyes gleamed merrily at the prospect of liberty. He breathed deeply. "Ah!" he exclaimed, "the sweet smell of freedom!"

As Contog and his rescuers returned, Kalki Avatar invited him to sit down. Jack came to the front and introduced the general to the assembled personalities in simple Sanskrit, detailing their previous encounters and the help the general had offered.

"Dear general," questioned the Avatar, after Jack's lengthy history. "Please give us news of the enemy."

"I have heard of the great battles fought here. I offer my heartiest congratulations to all of you for your brave struggle against the supremely evil Kallin."

Jack smiled. "It is only by the blessings of Lord Kalki, not to mention Hanuman and the Heroes, that we defeated the enemy."

Contog nodded, but concern flashed across his face. "The enemy is by no means finished. He is gathering a huge number of Raks at the plains not far from here."

Kalki stroked his majestic mustache. "Is that so? Please tell us more."

A hush fell over the gathering as the general described Kallin, his heartlessness and his ambition, of the great cities, the vast slums, the degraded lives of the Raks, the corruption and the greed of the Elite. The simple inhabitants of the valley could only shake their heads in disbelief. So this evil violent system confronted them!

"General," requested Kalki Avatar, "do you have any suggestions as to how to overcome Kallin?"

"Yes, but I don't know if you will be able to do it." Contog pulled a small metal object out of his pocket, the size and shape of a grain of rice. He gave the DNA implant a small twist and out of its top shot out a dozen extremely thin wires, each about three inches long and fine as spider strands.

"What is this?" exclaimed Jack.

"This is a military-grade DNA implant, his ultimate weapon. It performs all the functions of the regular implants, plus a few more. Not only does it measure the DNA and the proteins in the blood, it also sends tiny electrical pulses into the brains."

"For what purpose?"

"These implants receive transmissions, sent from the moon installation, which travel along these metal wires and into the soldiers' brains. By this, their moods are controlled, with the goal being to make them follow orders unquestioningly." All shook their heads in amazement. "You have destroyed his army, most of his armaments and aircraft, but Kallin's installation on the moon, which controls everything, still remains. It scans the battlefield continuously and transmits information to every single soldier by way of the implants and moves them in coordinated ways. If this system is destroyed, you have a good chance of vanquishing Kallin. Otherwise, his men will descend upon you like flies and overwhelm you with their incalculable numbers and uncountable weapons."

A stark silence enveloped the assembly. For a long while, no one said a thing.

"What do you suggest?" asked Jack finally.

"Destroy the moon-base. It is not easy. Not only is it far away, it is also extremely well-guarded. I don't know how you will do this. You don't have much time. As we speak, Kallin is organizing for the final battle."

"Why hasn't he attacked Shambala directly? We are such a small valley. If he bombed us, we would be finished."

"This is Kallin's mad greed. He is convinced that the means to travel through time lies here. He wants immortality and he wants absolute power."

The sages shook their heads. The shastras clearly stated that lust, greed, anger, envy and illusion are the greatest enemies of the spiritual seeker. One who fell prey to these can never advance in consciousness, but the question was, would Kallin take them all with him to destruction.

Kalki Avatar walked to the middle of the gathering. "It is absolutely correct that we need to destroy the moon installation."

"I would be happy to help," declared Jack, his eyes shining.

"And so would I," added Steve.

The Avatar laughed. "Good. We need brave young men. But those decisions can be made at the proper time. First you need to get out of harm's way and ascend to the grand vimana. This place has become too dangerous. Even if the dictator doesn't directly attack Shambala, he could occupy it."

"But I love this valley," objected Shanti. "I don't want to leave!"

Kalki smiled. "I appreciate your attachment to Shambala but imagine, after the war, when the whole world will be like this valley."

Shanti agreed. The villagers, with the strength of their years of sadhana, chanted mantras softly under their breaths and were transported to the largest vimana, the one that floated highest in the sky.

* * *

General Contog observed the dictator standing on the platform. Kallin wielded a cable of some kind, lengthy enough to come to about twenty feet from the ground.

"What is that?" inquired Kalki Avatar. He, along with the brothers, Hanuman and the remaining warriors stationed themselves at the entrance to the pass, which the Avatar felt was easier to protect. As they peered, the dictator snapped the cable and out of its end emanated a stream of flashing electrical pulses, striking the unfortunate Raks below who screamed loudly enough to be heard across the battlefield.

"My God!" exclaimed Contog. "He's whipping his troops!"

Kallin moved back and forth, mercilessly flogging the Raks, laughing, thoroughly enjoying the sadistic experience. Each swing from his whip produced pulses that cut into the bodies of a hundred, maybe two hundred soldiers at a time. They howled like dogs, driven mad with pain, and rushed towards the pass. Already distressed by deformities, the Raks hobbled on misshapen legs, crying in agony, their eyes red, their twisted spines bearing the brunt of the terrible whippings, being nothing but worthless fodder for Kallin's insane ambitions.

The first wave of combatants clambered up the tight path. The monkeys, high on the mountain sides, uprooted huge boulders and sent them crashing on their heads.

282

Hundreds of Raks lay crushed under these rocks, further constricting the pass. Kalki Avatar's soldiers, though hugely outnumbered, fought bravely, without fear of death. The enemy came in waves, threatening to burst the dam created by the narrow pass, but just as the Avatar predicted, the bottleneck slowed the prodigious army.

Suddenly a rocket, two hundred feet long, screeched through the late afternoon's dimming sun and struck one of the flying obelisks dead on in a thunderous, bludgeoning blast, smashing it into a million pieces which scattered straight up into the sky, resembling orange marmalade through which the sun crackled and sparkled.

"Hide yourselves!" shouted the Avatar. Steve and Jack jumped behind a rock as the Avatar's army hid under their shields. The orange sky descended and millions of shards of crystal showered down, impaling hundreds of thousands of unfortunate enemy soldiers. They fell, screaming in pain as the translucent stones embedded in their heads, faces or torsos. In quick succession, the missiles destroyed other obelisk vimanas, which in turn sent even more knife-sharp crystals bombarding the enemy, causing uncountable causalities.

Kallin adjusted to the strange battle. He brought in large, slow-moving planes that set upon the flying flowers with great fury, pounding them with a strange dark venomous powder until they fell softly to the earth, poisoned, their once great orange and red petals turning a morbid brown.

The enemy shot exploding rockets, dozens at a time, shattering the bowl-shaped vimanas, and purple ceramic pieces, by the thousands, littered the ground. Other strange vessels took off from the enemy base. One, composed of two large, black carbon tubes, each about a hundred feet long, stuck together with a small cabin on top near the back, meandered slowly across the sky. Steve, fascinated, surveyed one of these absurd-looking craft with its hollow tubes and unwieldy appearance, slowly hunting, like a snail would a slug, a stretching and rolling mercury vimana in a herky-jerky motion. The chase looked comical, but the intent remained deadly. Blasts of fire shot out of the two barrels of the enemy machine. Hanuman watched with horror as the vimana turned red, gold, blue and boils appeared on its skin. It exploded in a ball of white gas; the mercury vaporized by the intense heat.

A similar fate befell the bubble vimanas. The enemy fetched large transparent balls filled with a clear liquid, loaded one into a howitzer, and before Hanuman understood what happened, shot it at a flying bubble. The round exploded just as it touched the vimana and drenched it with the liquid. The bubble instantly melted, dissolved by nothing more than sea water! Soon bursts of salt water filled the sky as the bubble vimanas disappeared.

Slowly but surely, Kallin pushed the Avatar's soldiers back as the fighting became fiercer. The Avatar was correct about one thing though; the enemy aircraft provided little useful assistance, the pass being too narrow and his soldiers too well shielded. Kalki Avatar looked up in the sky, his thoughts moving to the rishi and the others in the grand vimana. It had disappeared with the dimming sun.

* * *

Standing on a rampart on the wall encircling the floating island, Steve examined the grand vimana. It contained marble palaces, their walls detailed with bas-reliefs of ancient battles and fantastic creatures, their golden spires reaching high into the air; pavilions with roofs in the oriental manner composed of a multitudes of eaves; small gardens of fruit trees with rounded bridges under which flowed flower-filled streams; pools with huge, red koi fish and courtyards paved with colored stones. In its middle rose a fantastic temple three hundred feet high, wide at the bottom and tapering at the top like an elongated pyramid, built with huge gold-grey stones, looking like a miniature Mount Meru which stands at the center of the universe. Small openings appeared at its top, one on each side. Gigantic doors opened in the front while enormous sculptures of lions stood on each side.

The setting sun, a large orange globe, shone low from the west and poured pure, strong light all over him while the atmosphere glistened a dark blue in the crisp, clear air. Dozens of large bird-shaped vimanas, piloted by young men and women, flew all around the floating island, their iridescent plumage sparkling, splintering the setting sunlight into a million multicolored shards, ready to join the battle below. Shanti appeared in a bubble vimana, while one of the few remaining obelisk-shaped craft followed her. Steve waved her a kiss and she did the same. He would have joined her, but he and Jack had a more important mission.

He glanced below. The mountains danced in shades of white and blue, with large patches of ochre where they gave way to the plains. A smudge became visible at the entrance to the pass. Did they fight the battle there, he wondered. He watched the tableau, spellbound, until it darkened and tiny spots of lights started winking below, understanding them to be bursts from the infantry's ordnance. Even in the gathering dusk, the battle raged! Occasionally, larger bursts of light flashed, either when a howitzer round exploded or when a mystical weapon from the Avatar found its target.

"Steve, come here," shouted Jack. Steve rushed down to the courtyard, joining his brother and eight other young men, just as Parvata Rishi started speaking.

"These young men will help you destroy the moon-base," Parvata Rishi informed him with a sweep of his arm. Steve inspected his accomplices. In keeping with the nature of the community, they displayed diverse backgrounds, origins, and races. All stood proud and strong. He shook his head at their bravery. Most of them would not make it back.

"Are you ready for your mission?" the rishi asked the brothers.

"Of course," replied Jack.

Steve hesitated. An unexpected tightening of the chest, a catching of his breath occurred. His face reddened and he averted his eyes from the rishi.

"What is it, young man?" questioned the rishi.

Steve didn't know what to say. An awkward moment followed. He hated to bring things up, yet he had no choice. How could he explain his feelings about Jack? This was a serious mission, where they all needed to depend on each other. Jack spent his life running away from responsibilities and, despite claims to the contrary, he hadn't seen much to contradict his opinion. Could he trust Jack with his life?

"I hope my brother is equal to the mission," he replied softly, looking down on the ground.

Jack eyed him, shocked, the color draining from his face. The words cut him. He questioned Steve with knotted eyes.

"There is a lot at stake here," said Steve matter-of-factly, glancing at his brother. "At the battlefield, you flew away, leaving me alone to protect Shanti. It really upset me."

Jack gulped. "I'm sorry Steve. I screwed up again. All I can say is that I can do better. I'm trying to change, but obviously it doesn't come easily. But I promise you, I'm not going to run away from anything."

A crease formed on Parvata Rishis' forehead. "Steve, are you sure you want to go ahead with this mission?"

Steve slowly nodded his head. What choice did he have? "Well, let's go."

"My sons," the rishi instructed the ten young men. "You are entrusted with a most important task, a feat that will determine victory or defeat. Kallin's power is dependent on his moon-base where his machines collect information that lead his forces to victory. Your objective is to destroy this base." He looked gravely at the young men. "This is a dangerous task and chances are some, if not most, of you may not return."

None moved.

The rishi produced some maps. "This will give you the location of the base. According to our General Contog, the

286

machines are hidden deep within a cave in this particular area of the moon," he said, pointing to the southern part of the satellite. "You have to destroy it as soon as possible. Now please ascend to your craft."

Ten large bird-shaped vimanas slowly ascended to the moon.

* * *

"Sir, we have reports from our satellites that several airships lifted off that huge station in the sky," remarked the national security advisor.

"What?" exclaimed the Hand of God. "Didn't our reports say that it was unoccupied?"

"It looks like a group of persons relocated there just recently and that no one remains in the valley."

"Interesting. Why would they move from the valley to the flying station? Maybe we're getting too close to them."

"But who are they? Why do they not engage in battle? Why would they need protection?"

Kallin stroked his beard. "Maybe we've had this wrong the whole time. Maybe the secret isn't in the valley, it's with those people."

"Of course!"

"I will send ships to occupy the flying station and take them prisoner."

"And what about the escaping vessels?"

"I'll send my interceptor satellites to handle them," remarked Kallin, smiling.

* * *

"Are we there yet?" asked Steve. Over twenty hours had passed.

"Almost," replied Jack.

In space, the wings of the bird-craft spread out enormously, sparkling brilliantly, billowing, looking like enormous butterflies, collecting radiation from the sun and flying at inconceivable speed towards the moon.

Steve looked at his map on the console. "We should be at the moon any time now."

Suddenly, beams of high energy streaked by. They stopped.

"Where did they come from?" demanded Steve.

"They look like spaceships," exclaimed Jack peering at the console, "Coming to shoot us down."

A dozen rectangular enemy satellites, the size of trucks, bristling with cannon and rockets pointing at all directions, moved at them with great speed and incredible agility. They fired at all angles and at several targets simultaneously. Six surrounded the leading vimana and pummeled it with shot until it fell, a flaming wreck, to the moon's surface.

The vimanas responded by shrinking in size. Their huge wings retreated into their bases in the bottom of the craft, their necks shortened considerably until they only jutted slightly out and their fuselages shrunk to half their original sizes. The vimanas, with their reduced dimensions, almost matched the enemy craft in agility and speed.

A fierce battle ensued. Steve followed an enemy craft, shooting rays from the wings of his craft, but it turned on a dime and his shots flew harmlessly into space.

"Jack," shouted Steve. "Let's do something quickly. Otherwise, we'll all be shot down in no time at all." Indeed, another explosion thundered as a second vimana shattered.

"Stay in one place and I'll chase an enemy ship towards you."

"Are you sure? It sounds dangerous."

"We need to do something before we're all destroyed." Indeed, the space battle turned against them. Enemy spaceships buzzed around a third vimana, surrounding it, aiming to overpower it with their numbers.

Jack flew towards the besieged vimana and chased one of the enemy craft, shooting at it. The trick worked. It flew right into Steve's line of fire and exploded as bolts of energy hit it. The others caught on. The battle evolved into

288

a giant cat and mouse game, with the vimanas chasing the enemy from one to another, while the enemy flew off in bunches to set upon a solitary vimana like a pack of wolves.

They finally won the battle, but what a cost! Four of the vimanas were shot down, their brilliant wings torn off, their heads blown away, their remains lying on the moon's surface, looking like dead dragonflies on the drab lunar dust.

But they received one bit of good news—the cave where Kallin hid his moon-base came into view, not more than twenty miles away. Steve studied the map again. It showed a large crater and on its bottom, along the eastern side, a large black spot circled in red.

He slowed down as the crater's wall came into view. He stopped his craft and the other vimanas collected around him.

"Do you see it," he asked Jack. A dark hole showed on the far side of the crater, just as the maps detailed. An installation of some sort, like a fortress, along with satellite dishes and several long metal buildings appeared at its entrance, probably providing living quarters, engineering shops and the like, deduced Steve.

"What should we do?"

"Let's spread out. That will give us a chance to escape if attacked."

"Yes, that makes sense."

They slowly approached, not more than five miles away, lined up like a bow, with Steve and Jack at each end, and four others between them. The formation looked beautiful, the six vimanas sparkling with color, their thin shiny butterfly wings slowly beating, suspended in the blackness of space, the harsh sunlight glinting at them from behind the grey, colorless moon.

Suddenly four rockets escaped from the long buildings below. "Look out!" shouted Steve, veering sharply away. Jack broke off, but it was too late for the four vimanas in the middle. They exploded.

289

Steve fell in shock. Everything happened so quickly. He knew these young men, their mothers, fathers and siblings since Mahavan, and their remains now became smashed into uncountable pieces, flying away into deep space, never to find a resting place. His hands shook and his knees felt weak.

"I can't go on," he stammered.

* * *

No vimana remained guarding the island. The rishi anxiously scanned the horizon, his eyes filled with tears, looking for his daughter. The afternoon brought with it a dark mist, and just behind, thick black clouds.

The rishi's face suddenly dropped. Four enormous black ships, each a thousand feet long, four hundred feet high, emerged unexpectedly from the thick clouds. He shook his head. They had no way to resist. Others saw these giant craft and raised the alarm. The monstrous craft pulled alongside the grand vimana and thousands of soldiers boarded the flying island, jumping off the top of the hulls and onto the vimana's parapets, looking like an invasion of tiny poisonous mites on the petals of a beautiful golden rose.

"We need to find shelter," cried Parvata Rishi. Those left—the rishis, yogis and maybe forty others—ran inside the great temple, shots blasting around them. They strained and pushed the enormous doors shut just as the enemy soldiers pumped thousands of rounds into the wood. The rishi gasped, beads of sweat collecting on his forehead, as they gathered at the middle of an octagonal-shaped, marble-inlaid hall.

The aircraft commenced firing rockets at the great structure, causing huge square stones to crash down and thunderous explosions to fill the hall. The very foundations of the vimana shook as rockets crashed into it. At this rate, the whole structure would come tumbling down in no time at all.

"What should we do?" cried Vishnuyasha.

"I will invoke *Durga devi*, the embodiment of material energy, to help us," cried the rishi. Within seconds, an incredibly beautiful, six-armed goddess wearing a red sari with a gold border, sitting cross-legged, her fingers held in various *mudras*, hand gestures, emerged out of thin air and floated a dozen feet above. Her skin resembled antique ivory, her hair the tint of the dark night, her light brown eyes looked half open and her incomparable beauty didn't allow Parvata Rishi to keep his eyes off her. Her smile graced the small gathering.

The rishi brought his palms together and bowed his head in honor of this most beautiful, most merciful, goddess. "Oh Durga Devi, Mother of the Universe, shelter of the weak, great Compassionate One, please protect us in our hour of need!"

"As you wish," agreed Durga. "I will transform into my terrifying shakti, my most frightening energy, known as Kali Devi and destroy the enemy on this vimana."

Durga Devi slowly changed into her most fearsome form as Kali Devi. Her skin turned black and her eyes and lips, vivid red. She opened her mouth and a large, bright red tongue dropped out, extending down to her breasts. Her dark hair fell around her neck and shoulders and she held her six arms around her. She looked at once exceedingly beautiful and exceptionally horrifying. She floated to the top of the great temple, flew out of one of the openings on top and, hovering above the pyramid, expanded to the size of twenty men. Kali Devi shut her eyes and eight expansions of her form manifested immediately and floated in a circle above the tip of the pyramid. Upon seeing them, the dictator's men stood frozen in fear and shock.

The nine Kalis swooped down, opened their mouths, and let forth ear-splitting shrieks. The men dropped their weapons and held their palms to their ears. The original Kali pierced the chest of the nearest soldier with a spear. He shrieked in pain and surprise. Using the chopper in one of her other hands, she lopped off his head. As it rolled off, two other hands caught the head and tied its hair into a knot while the body fell to the ground, spurting blood from its neck. The last two hands held a needle and thread, which she slipped through the knot of hair. The entire process took less than a second. Kali spied the next soldier, pierced his heart with the spear, repeated the procedure, and his head ended up on the thread next to the first one.

Kali Devi sped up the process. Within a very short time she created a wreath of decapitated heads, cut the thread, secured the knot and threw it around her neck like a macabre garland. The eight other Kalis attacked the army with unbearable screeches, mowing through them like a scythe would through a field of wheat, each creating the horrifying wreaths of heads. Some soldiers hid behind rocks, in pavilions and in pools, and as they did, huge tigers, the animal associated with the goddess, jumped out from behind blocks of stone, snatched the unfortunate men with fearsome jaws and shook them like a terrier would a rat. Soon, hundreds of tigers, all snarling fiercely, their mouths dripping blood, filled the floating island.

Kallin's remaining soldiers, looking at the apparitions with unbelieving eyes, dropped their weapons and fled, many jumping to their deaths off the parapets of the vimana. Not a single enemy soldier remained standing and the enormous abandoned ships floated away like grey ghosts, disappearing into the black clouds, following the air currents, and when they ran out of energy, turned belly up and hurtled to the ground.

Chapter Thirty Five

The Moon, End of Kali Yuga

The sun came back from the dark side of the moon while they hesitated. They had run out of weapons, out of craft, out of time. Steve's heart hurt. Tears ran down his face. What had happened at the grand vimana? Did Shanti survive? Had Kallin won? Was all lost?

Jack and Steve, piloting the two remaining vimanas, had retreated and spent several hours discussing possible choices. But a solution escaped them. They were alone and out of ideas.

"We have only one option," uttered Jack finally.

"What is that?"

"It's called a kamikaze mission."

"What do you mean?"

"I mean we ram ourselves down the throat of the cave."

"You know what you're saying?" inquired Steve, shocked.

"Yes. We came quite close to the installation, maybe less than five miles, before they started firing."

"So?"

"If we backed up and came at it at our fastest speed, there's no way they could stop us before we hit it."

"But what about the missiles? Couldn't they strike us before we reached the target?"

"Maybe," replied Jack. "But if you're worried about that, let's fly one behind the other. That way, even if they hit the first craft, the second one will certainly strike the installation."

"I guess."

"And at the speed we'd be going, there's no way we couldn't inflict maximum damage."

"You're right, but do you really think we should do this?"

"We need to continue. Parvata Rishi, Shanti, Kalki Avatar, Hanuman and all the others are counting on us. I know how much you love Shanti. You need to take responsibility for her and for her father, what to speak of saving humanity from the clutches of a madman."

The brothers lifted themselves to a distance of about two hundred miles above the moon's surface and spread their wings as far as possible to gather energy, resembling sails on ships navigating the cosmos to eternity.

"Let's do it," stated Steve, as he turned his craft to face the gray orb.

"I'll go first," volunteered Jack, bringing his craft to the front. He waited for a moment. "Are you sure you want to continue?"

"Yes, but I'm worried about Shanti."

"Do the right thing and don't worry about the results. That's the best you can do. In fact, it's the only thing to do."

"But is there a way we can do this without getting killed?"

"We may die, but we need to continue the mission. If we don't, Kallin will win."

"Will we succeed?"

"Don't worry about success or failure. We can die at any time. It may be now, it may be tomorrow, it may be years from now. Instead of worrying about death, let's act with honor—that is, do the right thing, no matter what the circumstances."

Steve arched his eyebrows. "Where did all this courage come from?"

"I'm done running away, Steve. It's a hard lesson I had to learn."

"What changed?"

"Myself," came Jack's simple reply.

"You know, someone wise once told me more or less the same thing."

"What's that?"

"That we grow by making commitments. That we won't know what's on the other side of the bridge until we cross it."

"Hey!" remarked Jack, starting his descent, picking up speed by the second, his brother following close behind. "We finally agree on something!"

"Does that mean we're both finally grown up?" questioned Steve, laughing grimly.

"Yeah, I guess it does."

"So let's get this thing done. Brothers forever?"

"Brothers forever!"

Chapter Thirty Six

The Battlefield, End of Kali Yuga

Egged on by the Hand of God, the Raks reacted in rage against the Avatar's forces. Kalki Avatar and his army found themselves in a dire situation, pushed half-way down the pass. Where once his army numbered in the millions, now only a few hundred remained: monkeys, bears, the rest, human. Exhaustion became as big an enemy as the Raks.

"Oh Lord," shouted Hanuman. "How long can we keep fighting?" The situation turned desperate. The enemy, though decimated, outnumbered them heavily and at this rate, they would be overwhelmed at any moment.

"We will keep fighting until the last man," roared the Avatar.

* * *

"How can we stay here on the grand vimana?" asked Vishnuyasha. The airborne island's pavilions were destroyed, the trees and gardens uprooted, the courtyards scorched black, the great pyramid's sides blasted through, and the red fish floated belly up in the waters. The entire vimana, unsettled by the bombing, started to shake.

"We will have to get off," cried Parvata Rishi.

"Where can we go?" questioned Vishnuyasha.

"There is only one place to go; Shambala."

"What? Didn't we leave Shambala because it was too dangerous?"

"This vimana has suffered great damage. If we stay here, we will surely be crushed by the falling temple or, if the vimana breaks apart, fall to the ground. If we return to Shambala, we will be protected by Kalki Avatar, for however long that may be." The rishi raised his eyes. "Our real delivery will come only when the brothers destroy the moon-base. That is, if they are still alive."

Another ominous rumble shook the floating island. "Come, let's leave this place," he yelled. They all rushed together and held hands. The old man chanted the mantras and instantly, they found themselves back in Shambala.

* * *

"Those people on the station in the sky made our job easier," yelled the Hand of God. "They have returned to the valley. We got them exactly where we want them!"

Indeed, not much hope remained for Kalki Avatar's army. In the space of a few days, they went from what they thought was certain victory to facing overwhelming odds. Pressed up against the pass, the only access to Shambala, their numbers were decimated. Kallin brought in over a million men; the Avatar had just a few hundred left.

"I can taste victory! And when I occupy the valley, the power of time travel will be mine! All mine!" Kallin looked at his troops below. "Time to get these dogs off their asses. Time for the final push."

* * *

Hanuman gasped. The battle raged for days and the enemy, though decimated, came at them inordinately. He saw the silver orb rising in the west as dusk fell. If the brothers did not destroy the moon-base shortly, Kallin's army would be unbeatable. Pushed back to the narrowest part of the path close to Shambala, only two hundred soldiers remained of Kalki's once million man army. The enemy would break through at any moment, gain free passage to the valley and their mission would fail. His body was bloody, shot at many times, cut by shrapnel. He barely stood. "Oh, Lord, I can barely fight. I am about to fall!"

The Avatar heard his desperate cry. "Great warriors, we need to bear the unbearable, fight to the finish. Though battered and bruised, victory is certainly ours. Please keep struggling. Do not lose hope!" Hanuman raised high his bloody head.

"This is it!" continued the Avatar. "Now is the final test!" He turned his horse around to face his soldiers. "If we die, let us perish with weapons in our hands. For warriors, there is no greater glory than to die on the battlefield. We cannot wait for the moon to rise. At night, our foes are practically unbeatable. Let us all gather, prime our weapons, and for one last time, push the enemy back."

A great cheer went up. The soldiers girded themselves and held their weapons high. Every last one of them prepared himself for the hereafter. They prayed to their ancestors and made ready to meet them in the other world. Kalki Avatar, on his horse's back, rose to the air in front of his soldiers, his luminous body glowing in the dark like an avenging angel, reflecting on the somber cliffs on either side.

"Charge!" he commanded, holding his sword high.

With smiles on their faces, lightness in their hearts and mouths chanting victory, the brave two hundred rushed forth from their lair with weapons blazing and headed into the gaping maw of the enemy. Their foes came at them from every direction and dozens of valiant warriors dropped at the charge. Hanuman's eyes brightened. There is everlasting glory for those who die fighting for a just cause.

* * *

"Stop!"

"Stop," came the voice again.

"Shanti! Is that you?" Steve looked at the console questioningly. It showed two objects: a large cylindrical one and a small bubble-shaped craft. His heart jumped into

298

his mouth. She had entered a dangerous situation—much more perilous than she may have realized.

She pulled up next to him in her bubble-shaped craft. "I'm guiding the obelisk vimana right into the installation," she said. The brothers immediately stopped, not more than fifty miles from their target. As they did, the obelisk shot by with enormous speed, sparkling with the energy of the sun, glowing brightly like a pillar of fire. Several rockets immediately shot off the structures at the entrance to the cave. Steve and Jack rushed down, intercepted the missiles and destroyed them with bolts of white lightning. The obelisk proceeded at enormous speed, heading straight for Kallin's moon installation.

"Let's get out of here!" screamed Jack. They turned around and flew away as fast as they could. The obelisk, its lasers blazing, drove itself through the installation, crashing right into the cave at enormous speed, disappearing like a needle into the moon's body.

An enormous explosion shook the lunar surface. The shockwave reached the escaping vehicles and they wobbled, picked up by the blast and thrown forward for fifty miles. A huge, roiling fountain of fire, over ten miles wide and a hundred miles high, escaped out of the target and shot straight out into space, nipping at the heels of the desperately fleeing vimanas.

Steve gasped. It was a near escape. They turned around and looked. The whole east rim of the crater had been pulverized and huge explosions rattled all along its bottom. Enormous chunks of stone flew off in different directions, dropping miles away, creating new craters on the moon's already pocked surface. A large cloud of black dust and balls of red fire collected over the point of impact and flew out into space, trailing from the site of the impact like dark blood streaming out of an open wound.

Chapter Thirty Seven

The Battlefield, End of Kali Yuga

Suddenly, the shots stopped. The enemy soldiers dropped their weapons and looked at each other, bewildered, as if realizing for the first time where they were.

The Avatar looked up at the moon. A small pinhead of orange blossomed in the southern quadrant of the satellite; surely explosions caused by the brothers! They had finally destroyed the moon-base! But at what cost! Of his army once numbering over a million, only two dozen warriors were left standing.

"Victory at last," shouted Kalki Avatar. A cheer went up. The ferocious enemy that had fought as one now reeled in total disarray. They turned their weapons on their comrades and, killing them, cut off pieces of flesh and started eating. The discipline enforced on them by the pitiless system vanished and they reverted to barbarism. A picture of hellish savageness unfolded—it would have been safer to wade into a pack of rabid wolves than to try saving these unfortunate Raks. By the end of the day, very few, if any, would be left standing. The enemy aircraft veered off and headed back west, for what purpose no one knew.

"Where's Kallin?" asked Contog. The platform had disappeared.

"He's escaped!" exclaimed Hanuman. "We need to find him."

General Contog face lengthened. "If he returns to Kallington, he can try to regain control. A great tree is most dangerous when it is about to fall."

* * *

Kallin's hands shook and his left eye twitched uncontrollably. His unkempt face sagged and his eyelids hung heavy from a lack of sleep. The bunker, a thousand feet below the International Legislative Exchange, contained a bedroom, a living room, a bathroom and a security control room lined with monitors, computers, and controls. The unadorned concrete walls, illuminated by bare fluorescent lights, displayed no paintings, curios or knick knacks. On the bed lay Jini, her blue eyes open, staring into infinity, her blonde hair spread out like a fan on the pillow. A round, red hole showed on her forehead and blood dripped from her hand to the floor. On the living room sofa sat the national security advisor, a handgun in his hand, his head blown off.

The Hand of God sat on a chair in the security control room. A picture came up on one of the monitors. Directly above him, flames engulfed the enormous oval building. A huge mob murdered everyone escaping the conflagration, while looters ran out with computers, furniture and anything they could grab.

"This is serious. Now how the hell will I collect my taxes?" mumbled Kallin. Other cameras confirmed the worst. Airplanes bombed Central Prison and criminals took to the streets. The Raks knew well their tormentors. In huge numbers, they overran the city, destroying any emblem of the elite, killing whoever they caught and everywhere, turned on each other with knives, guns, and metal rods; smashing, cutting and shooting, just to taste blood and flesh.

He slammed his fist on the desk. "This is the end. If I can't have it, no one else can. The Raks will get what they deserve, as so will those savages in that valley. No one can ever take what belongs to me. Never." He punched in some instructions on the keyboard.

* * *

301

At first, the explosions sounded indistinct, like distant thuds, barely heard above the rushing waters. After a while, the sound became more distinct, like a bass drum sounding far in the distance. Kalki Avatar first noticed it. He jumped to his feet and cupped his ear, listening keenly to the disturbing sound for several long minutes.

Parvata Rishi came running to the Avatar. "Dear Avatar, what is this sound that comes softly, closer and closer, but echoes like death itself approaching?"

"I will find out," exclaimed the Avatar of the great blue-skinned Supreme Lord. He quickly mounted his flying steed and stayed suspended in the air for several long moments before swooping down breathlessly.

"I saw explosions, dozens of them, in the great distance, covering the entire horizon. Each looked like a dozen suns rising from the earth at once, followed by gigantic clouds resembling trees growing from the earth to the skies, like enormous mushrooms. I cannot imagine what this dreadful weapon is."

Contog stood up. "Kallin must be trapped, with no way out. These terrible bombs will destroy all life on this planet. And he will especially destroy Shambala as he cannot own it."

Kalki Avatar's eyes flashed angrily. He removed his sword from its sheath.

"What are you doing?" asked Contog.

"This is not an ordinary sword," replied Kalki Avatar. "Its handle is courage, its hand guard is justice, one side of the blade is truthfulness, the other side is austerity and the tip is mercy."

"You mean that they represent those qualities?"

"No, the sword doesn't represent those qualities; it is actually those in reality. This sword embodies these qualities in full." The Avatar paused momentarily. "Kallin's heart is lust, his eyes envy, his hands greed, his mind violence and his intelligence, pitilessness. When his body is pierced by this sword, it will destroy not just him, but all his bad qualities."

The Avatar swung his sword with all his might and let it go. It flew like a lightning bolt, illuminating the battlefield like ten thousand suns exploding instantaneously, and even the Avatar's hairs stood on end. It flew straight west, across the sky like a meteor, over the bombed and burned cities on the coast. Kallin's weapons had destroyed everything and not a man nor woman, farm animal, or even a single building stood. The entire earth resembled a scene of utter devastation. The sword flew low over the roiling, churning oceans which hissed and sizzled at the heat of this indestructible weapon. It reappeared at the coast and entered the desert, flying over vast tracts of dry, dead land, scorching the sands black behind it.

It entered the ruined capital of the great dictator's once powerful empire. The deadly sword slowed down over the egg-like Exchange and elevated itself to a height of a thousand feet, right over Kallin's bunker. The Raks looked up dumbly, not comprehending its nature or mission.

Then suddenly, the roaring weapon swooped right down into the ground and the earth around it blew up like an exploding volcano. It blew open the top of Kallin's concrete bunker, entered into the mad dictator's lair, and hung in the air, emanating sparks.

The Hand of God watched the weapon, not comprehending what was happening. He gasped, eyes bulging in his head, sweat rolling down his face, legs shaking, his hands quivering hysterically. For the evil ruler, it came as death itself. He jumped in a futile attempt to escape. In a blink of an eye, the sword descended into his body. The great dictator screamed in agony as fire enveloped him and, within moments, reduced him to ashes.

* * *

Shambala, Beginning of Satya Yuga
The next day, as the community cheered, the two bird vimanas hovered a few feet above, deposited Steve and Jack on the ground, and disappeared. The bubble vimana

descended, slowly stopped spinning, and then popped. Shanti landed on her feet. Steve rushed over and embraced her.

Parvata Rishi walked to the front of the community. "Come, great heroes," he announced, pointing to them. Before they could move, Hanuman ran forward, grabbed the two brothers with strong arms and hoisted them on his broad, right shoulder and deposited Shanti on his left. The community applauded and showered them with flower petals.

Jack examined the smiling faces of the cheering men, women, and children, feeling completely unworthy of their adulation. These simple people made far greater sacrifices than he ever did. Every one of them lost a son, a daughter, a father or mother. They had trekked through miles of harsh terrain, over endless mountains and caves just to get to Shambala. They remained the great personalities; they carried in their hearts, minds, and in their sadhana, the secrets of Yoga and the Vedas. They would reestablish spiritual culture in the coming age, whereas he only destroyed some paltry installation. Tears moistened his eyes. He reflected on the irony: praise usually goes to those who least deserve it and comes from those who most earn it.

Hanuman, roaring with happiness and pride, brought them in front of Parvata Rishi and, lifting them off his shoulders, dropped them on his feet.

"Brave warriors," shouted the monkey king. "All three of you deserve the greatest honor we can give. You have saved Shambala!" The rishi embraced them and in his hands he held three garlands fashioned of beautiful blue, yellow and red wildflowers from Shambala's forests.

"Come," he said, motioning to Steve and Shanti. They stepped ahead and reverently lowered their heads. The rishi slipped the garland over their necks.

He motioned to Jack. "Now you come." The final garland adorned his neck.

Jack shook his head. "My dear Rishi," he started, speaking in passable Sanskrit, "I am completely unworthy of your praise. I have led a useless life and done all manners of sinful things. So many heroes greater than me exist, like those brave young men who accompanied my brother and me to the moon, who gave their lives so we may all be saved, and all of you who lost a loved one in this war. You are the real heroes." Tears flooded the eyes of the villagers as they remembered their terrible losses.

"One more thing," said the rishi. "Let us honor not just the living, but also the dead." He paused. "From both sides."

Jack felt nonplussed. "You mean the enemy?"

"Of course," said the Avatar, joining the conversation. "All of them. The enemy soldiers, the Raks, the generals, and even Kallin."

"How can you say that," retorted Jack, his hackles raised. "That man created so much destruction, so much pain, so much death!"

"All souls are equally precious to me, even Kallin's. From the perspective of this life only, you see a very evil man. But I see all of his lives, just as I see all of yours. From my point of view, from the point of view of the absolute, I see the world as a stage, with actors from both sides. But the real world is the spiritual world, not this one. There is no doubt that Kallin is a very evil man and he will pay the price for that. He will have to work through his karma, but in the end, his soul's place is in the spiritual world as are all others. No enmity, no quarrels, occur there. All souls in the spiritual world exist only in loving relationships with the Supreme Lord. God doesn't play favorites. To him, all are equal."

Jack nodded his head. It made sense. "I need to do one more thing." He turned to the rishi. "Can I have a blank piece of parchment?"

"Of course," replied the old man, surprised. Jack tore the page in half, picked up a piece of charcoal from the cooking fire, and started sketching. Steve looked at him curiously as the rest of the community gathered around.

"This is Maya," said Jack, hanging the portrait on a tree branch. He removed the garland from his neck and placed it around her picture. He winced, remembering the hurts, the betrayals and the sexual games he played that brought pain to both of them. The arrogance, the bitterness, the regret, the wounding passions—he had enough of it.

Jack took the other part of the parchment and, with fingers moving quickly, drew the outline of another woman. Steve eyes knotted questioningly. He stared as the sketch filled with detail, until it showed the familiar curls, the warm eyes and the round glasses. Jack got up, found a tree stump and rested the portrait of his mother on it.

Then a wonderful thing happened. The other villagers brought out their own parchments. Soon, small portraits of loved ones adorned tree stumps, hung from branches or stood on stone surfaces.

Steve took his garland and invited Jack to place it around their mother. It encircled the portrait and hung in front on the stump. The rest of the community came by and, one by one, offered a petal, a blossom, or a flowery vine to the memorial.

Jack stopped and wiped his eyes. "Mom, I appreciate everything you've done for me and I always will. I never had a chance to say bye to you. But I want to tell you that I have always loved you and that you will be with me forever. And I hope that I will become the man you always wanted me to be."

Epilogue

Shambala, Beginning of Satya Yuga

For several months, Jack and the remaining survivors of the terrible war struggled with their sadness not just for their fellow travelers but for all the victims on both sides. The few dozen of them were the only humans left on the planet. Every single other person—whether villager, Rak, soldier, monkey, bear, Hero and even Kallin himself—went to the other side where no earthly differences are remembered.

A great sadness descended upon them and during the customary morning gatherings under the trees, many recited heart-rending stories of loss. Steve's eyes moistened upon hearing the agony of bereaved parents and separated lovers. Shanti joined him, her eyes wet, with great despondency in her heart. But also, tales of countless heroic deeds, of supreme sacrifices and unparalleled bravery were recounted. The elders remained stoic, knowing the material world to be a place of suffering, where no one escapes death, but their hearts still grieved for the young ones. Yet, the end of the war brought relief.

Kalki Avatar, Hanuman, and their companions left soon after the war's end. The small band of survivors became broken-hearted upon the departure of their kind benefactors and protectors. Jack felt especially sad to see Hanuman go. He came to appreciate the loyal monkey's valor and devotion. But the Avatar's work on this planet had ended and he traveled to another place, in this universe or another, always engaged in his lilas, his eternal pastimes. The survivors offered prayers and fire yajnas for their dear departed ones and offered penances for their benefit. Yet, sadness remained.

* * *

But the sun rose every day and life had to go on. It was, after all, the nature of reality that all things must pass and, after many months, the sorrow dissipated. The earth, refreshed, sprouted grasses, flowers, and trees. Jack wandered through the pastures, letting go of hurry and anxiety, savoring the aroma of the renewed land. The guilt and despondency he felt about Maya's death slowly lifted as Satya Yuga gently poured its benevolent waters over him and, while it removed the self-loathing, it also helped him see clearly his follies and his responsibility in the heartbreaking affair. He learnt well his hard lessons. The karmic aspects of his actions became clear and he determined to never again put himself or others in a similar situation.

He imbibed the spiritual practices of yoga and meditation, of living in the moment, of doing his duty and leaving the results to a greater power. The seasons changed and the earth, with the burden of sinful men and their karma lifted from her breast, once again became a happy place. As Satya Yuga began, it brought with it longevity, peace, and contentment.

The residents of Shambala smiled again, joyful and satisfied to live in their intimate spiritual community, taking care of each other in their simple, sweet lives. They re-established their rituals—those of waking at the Brahma Muhurtha hour, yoga, meditation, japa and puja, performing their duties, gathering wood, cooking and singing the evening kirtans—finding in this both solace and structure. It helped them endure their pain and loss and brought them back to the present.

* * *

Finally, the day arrived when the community moved on. Parvata Rishi consulted his sacred books and on the day the constellations provided their benign blessings, the young members of the community got married. The beautiful spring day sparkled beautifully, the sun rose high, the firmament shone a perfect blue and a soft wind caressed the faces of those gathered for the ceremony.

Twelve young couples, each from a different community, representing the different peoples from all parts of the earth, gathered for their weddings. They sat around the havan, chanted mantras, cast grains into the sacred fire, circumambulated the flames and promised the seven great vows that all wedded couples make.

Jack observed his brother and his sister-in-law. Shanti looked impossibly radiant. The sun sparkled on her hair and her face glowed golden. She wore a red sari and adorned her hair with scented blue blooms from Shambala's forest. The flower of womanhood blossomed into a fullness and freshness that shimmered on her face and on her body. Steve stood next to her and, when the time came for husband and wife to circumambulate the sacred fire, tied the end of her sari to his white dhoti. As they strode around the fire repeating their vows, Lakshmi Devi, the goddess of material and spiritual abundance appeared in eight forms above. Each of these four-armed female divinities sat on large white lotuses, circling a hundred feet in the air above the yajna, and sprinkled flower petals on them and the other lucky couples. Steve and Shanti looked up and tendered their respects to the heavenly guests with palms pressed together before offering their obeisances to Jack.

"Good going!" he declared. "Congratulations!"

Shanti looked a bit young. Jack made her out to be eighteen at the most but, obviously being meant for each other, the age difference would only narrow after time. And none could deny their love. Steve would make a good father—he had that sense of duty, that sense of loyalty.

He viewed the rishi. Mischief sparkled in the old man's eyes. What joke, what piece of humor crossed the old man's mind? Parvata Rishi caught Jack's eyes for just a second, long enough for the secret to be transmitted.

Of course! Jack realized it right away. "Wait a minute! None of this happened by chance, did it? That I ended up in Kali Yuga? That Steve got married?"

"No, it didn't," admitted the sage laughing. "It took me some time to realize it, but now it's perfectly clear. There's no doubt that Steve's destiny is to be a *Prajapati*."

"What is a Prajapati?"

"A Prajapati is a progenitor. At the beginning of every Satya Yuga, several progenitors are necessary to repopulate the earth. All these young couples you see here are Prajapatis for this age."

Steve's jaw dropped. "How long have you known my destiny?"

"I wondered about my daughter's future for a long while. I prayed for a suitable husband and when you appeared in Satya Yuga and the two of you fell in love, I have to admit, it surprised me. So many other fine young men live in our village and in the neighboring ones. Yet God found it in His desire to send you. Certainly, you will make a fine husband for my daughter and a good father for your children."

"That's how I ended up here!"

"Yes," said the rishi, still smiling roguishly. "We can say, truly, that you are a divinely chosen couple."

"And we…we're going to have children?"

Shanti interrupted. "Yes," she revealed, clasping his hands excitedly, "we'll have nine thousand, four hundred and eighty sons!"

"Nine thousand, four hundred and eighty sons!" gasped Steve.

"And they'll all look like you," she exclaimed happily.

"And how many daughters?" asked Jack.

She screwed up her face with disappointment. "Only three thousand, three hundred and twenty-seven."

"How are you going to find the time to do all this?" asked Jack, laughing.

Steve turned red.

Parvata Rishi answered. "This is Satya Yuga. One can easily live for a hundred thousand years. My dear son-in-law, your descendants will inherit the earth. This is your destiny."

Steve looked stunned, unable to fathom what had just happened. Jack watched his brother walk away with his bride. Though utterly charmed by Shanti's sweetness and modesty, he himself felt in no way touched. No thoughts of marriage or even women entered his mind. How empty were the glories of the flesh! He wished his brother the best, but his path lay in a different direction.

"And what about me?" he questioned. "By what design did I end up here?'

"You were a surprise," admitted the old man candidly. "I never had an inkling of your showing up. But I have studied you carefully and now realize who you are."

"Who?"

"My dear son, you have a great destiny ahead of you. You are the incarnation of Gautama Rishi, one of the greatest rishis who ever lived. Your arrival here is of great auspiciousness."

"Me, an incarnation of a rishi? How is that possible? I was born in America." He swung his arm around. "I had no knowledge of any of this."

The rishi nodded. "At first, it perplexed me. But our understanding is insignificant compared to that of the Divine. Your destiny is to become a great yogi and you will be known in history as one of the carriers of yoga to the next Satya Yuga. Just as I am, for this age."

Jack's head spun. "I don't know if I can believe any of this. It's too far-fetched!"

"Don't worry, it will be revealed to you in time."

"Now that your daughter is married, what will you do?" Jack asked, already knowing the answer. He felt a kinship with this old man. After all, despite the age difference, nothing of family, of material life, remained for them.

"I'll pick up my solitary spiritual practices again. It is what I've always wanted to do but since accepting the responsibility of taking care of my daughter, something I had to put aside. I'm very grateful for Shanti. I've learned a

311

lot from her. But from now on, sadhana will be my sole occupation."

He pointed to a cave high in the hills. "I will spend the rest of my days there, engaged in yoga and meditation." Jack regarded Parvata Rishi with great affection. His kind, fatherly expression left him no doubt that he wanted to spend the rest of his days in his company. He bent down on his knees once again.

"Can you please teach me?" he requested. "I really want to understand who I am. I need your spiritual instruction."

The rishi smiled. "You are welcome to come with me, my son. I am your spiritual father. When I pass away, you will carry on for me. That," he chuckled, "is my destiny." He lifted Jack up by his arm. The old man and the new renunciate walked slowly up the path toward their place of meditation.

"Come," said the old man, "let us practice yoga."

The End

The Story behind the Yoga Zapper

The legend of *Shambala* is well known in the East, whether in India, China or other oriental countries. James Hilton, in his travels in the Orient, came across the legend of ancient beings with extremely long living in a hidden place in the Himalayas, and subsequently wrote <u>Lost Horizon</u>, mentioning Shangri-La, a variation of the original Sanskrit word.

Several years ago I came across a book titled <u>On the Way to Shambala</u>, written by Dr. Edwin Bernbaum, who holds a doctorate in Asian Studies from the University of California at Berkeley. He writes about visiting a Buddhist temple in Nepal and coming across a scripture which described a passage to the mythical valley. Intrigued, he requested a couple of the monks from the shrine to accompany him on a journey of discovery. They followed the instructions contained in the text and after a month-long trek, after crossing seven ranges of mountains, came across a perfectly hidden valley.

He describes descending into this beautiful valley, with its pristine forests and a small river running through it. His guides confirmed that this was, indeed, Shambala. He enquired as to why he didn't see any sages mediating under its trees and was informed by the monks that, they were there indeed, but he didn't have the spiritual vision to see them.

In my studies as a Hindu Vaishnava priest, I had previously learnt of this legend in a scripture named the *Srimad Bhagavatam* (also known as the Bhagavat Purana) which mentions Shambala in connection with a larger story: that of the degradation of humanity at the end of Kali Yuga, the appearance of the tenth avatar of Vishnu named Kalki, and his role in defeating the forces of evil at that time.

In my conversations with yoga practitioners, I sensed a deep curiosity about the traditional narratives of yoga. Yoga is not just a grounded physical practice (though it can be taken as just that,) or a deep spiritual philosophy (which adds depth to the practice,) but also has its own legends and mythic origin stories—a view of humanity's future (and past), of society's moral evolution and a history of yoga's own rise, diminution, demise and eventual rebirth—all wrapped up in an exciting and engrossing tale.

The narrative has all the elements of a potboiler—a dystopian future, deep spirituality, yogis meditating for uncountable years, fantastical weapons, flying vimanas and a great war between the forces of good and evil at the end of time.

The idea of presenting this engaging story to the modern reader by way of a page-turning fantasy novel immediately came to me. The key was not just to recite the ancient legends, but to let them be seen through the eyes of modern protagonists who would not only have their own engaging stories to tell, but also act as the eyes and ears for the western audience.

I have tried to be as authentic to the original scriptures as possible. The Srimad Bhagavatam describes the end of Kali Yuga in detail as a cannibalistic society with a wicked world ruler, deformed Rakshasas, environmental degradation, and oppressive taxation. The characters (except for those taken from scripture such as Kalki Avatar and Hanuman, among others) and the plot are my inventions, but rest is not; they are the product of many years of study of the original sources.

The Srimad Bhagavatam which I used is the excellent edition published by the Bhaktivedanta Book Trust (www.bbt.com). While vimanas are mentioned in the Ramayana and the Mahabharata, the two major epics of ancient India, there is some question regarding the Vaimanika shastra, which some claim to be of more recent origin. Some current commentators have taken vimanas to be ancient, extraterrestrial flying objects. As well, there is some discussion about the time lengths concerning the yugas. Some recent movements within Hinduism claim that the cycles of time are much smaller—in the hundreds of years—while a few groups even claim that the end of Kali Yuga is just around the corner!

In the Buddhist tradition, Shambala is described as a kingdom in the Himalayas and instead of Kalki Avatar, it is a future Bodhisattva, the Maitreya Buddha, who arises to lead the battle against the invading tyrant.

The elements of yoga spirituality, such as the different limbs of ashtanga yoga, the koshas, rasas, bhavas, and others have been presented faithfully, however fantastic they may seem. The descriptions of the various Deities, as well, have been accurately replicated.

Is there really a scripture like the Yuga Zapper that allows one to travel through time? Not to my knowledge, but in the yoga tradition, eighteen major yogic siddhis, as well as numerous minor ones, are mentioned, of which one, namely, the power of traveling at the speed of the mind, could be construed as the ability to travel through time. The world of Satya Yuga is obviously idealized but yet remains true to the flavor of the original descriptions. Kali Yuga, however horrifying, is as described in the Srimad Bhagavatam: a place of anxiety, forgetfulness, and violence.

So is there really a Shambala? Are there really yogis and rishis, in an invisible state, meditating there? And will Kalki Avatar visit us in the distant future? These questions are obviously not a matter of fact, but of faith. One may accept them or not. But the ultimate goal of this book is to entertain and educate. If you, dear reader, found yourself gripped by this tale, moved by the characters, intrigued by the concepts, and at the end, had your curiosity piqued and considered more questions than when you started, then my goal has been reached.

GLOSSARY

A

Achha—Yes. Also "achha?" as in "yes?"

Agamas—Sanskrit texts which delineate aspects of worship of Deities.

Angrezi—literally "English"; generally any Western person.

Apsara—a heavenly maiden; beautiful, supernatural female beings who are youthful, elegant, and superb in the arts; they are often the wives of the Gandharvas, the court musicians of Indra.

Arti—worship of Deities, consists of offering the Deities a flame in a lamp, incense, flower, water, cloth, and a whisk made with hairs from a yak's tail.

Asana—a body position, typically associated with the practice of yoga, originally identified as a mastery of sitting still. In the context of yoga practice, asana refers to two things: the place where a practitioner, yogi (male,) or yogini (female) sits, and the manner (posture) in which he/she sits.

Ashrama—a) a spiritual hermitage. b) a spiritual stage in life. The four spiritual ashrams in life being:
- Brahmachari, Brahmacharini (female)—a celibate student.
- Grihastha—A married person.
- Vanaprastha, Vanapransthi (female)—a retired person.

- Sannyasi, Sannyasini (female)—a renounced person.

Ashtanga Yoga—also known as Raja Yoga, a yoga tradition. See **Patanjali**. The eight limbs of Ashtanga Yoga are:
- Yama—code of conduct, self-restraint.
- Niyama—religious observances, commitments to practice, such as study and devotion.
- Āsana—integration of mind and body through physical activity.
- Pranayama—regulation of breath leading to integration of mind and body.
- Pratyahara—abstraction of the senses, withdrawal of the senses of perception from their objects.
- Dharana—concentration, one-pointedness of mind.
- Dhyana—meditation (quiet activity that leads to Samadhi.)
- Samādhi—the quiet state of blissful awareness, superconscious state. Attained when yogi constantly sees Paramatma in his (jivaatma) heart.

Avatar—a descent of God into the material world. The avatars of God are mentioned as innumerable, but the ten most prominent are:
- **Matsya**, the fish, from the Satya Yuga. Lord Vishnu takes the form of a fish to save the sage Manu from a flood, after which Manu takes his boat to the new world along with one of every species of plant and animal, gathered in a massive cyclone
- **Kurma**, the tortoise, appeared in the Satya Yuga. When the devas and asuras were churning the ocean in order to get the nectar of immortality, the mount Mandara they were using as the churning staff started to sink and Lord Vishnu took the form of a tortoise to bear the weight of the mountain.
- **Varaha**, the boar, from the Satya Yuga. He appeared to defeat Hiranyaksha, a demon who had taken the Earth, and carried it to the bottom of what

is described as the cosmic ocean. Varaha carried the Earth out of the ocean between his tusks and restored it to its place in the universe.

- **Narasimha**, the half-man/half-lion appeared in the Satya Yuga, with the body of a man and head and claws of a lion.
- **Vamana**, the dwarf, appeared in the Treta Yuga
- **Parashurama**, Rama with the axe, appeared in the Treta Yuga. He is son of Jamadagni and Renuka. He received an axe after a penance to Shiva. Parashurama is the first Brahma-Kshatriya in Hinduism, or warrior-saint, with duties between a Brahmana and a Kshatriya.
- **Rama**, or Ramachandra, the prince and king of Ayodhya, appeared in Treta Yuga. Rama is a commonly worshiped avatar in Hinduism, and is thought of as the ideal heroic man. His story is recounted in one of the most widely read scriptures of Hinduism, the Ramayana. While in exile from his own kingdom with his brother Lakshmana and the monkey king Hanuman, his wife Sita was abducted by Ravana, the demon king of Lanka.
- **Buddha,** Gautama Buddha or Siddhārtha Gautama Buddha, also called Sakyamuni, was a sage from the ancient Shakya republic, on whose teachings Buddhism was founded. He is also referred to as "the Buddha."
- **Krishna** is the eighth son of Devaki and Vasudev. Lord Krishna is the most commonly worshiped Deity in Hinduism and an avatar in Vaishnava belief. His name means 'dark' or 'attractive', and he appeared in the Dwapara Yuga alongside his brother Balarama, and is the central character of the *Bhagavad Gita*, the most published Hindu canon. He is mentor to Arjuna, delivering him the Gita at the Battle of Kurukshetra. Some traditions consider him to be an avatar of Vishnu, whereas other Vaishnava

traditions (such as the Gaudiya Vaishnavas- i.e. the Hare Krishnas) state that Krishna is the source of Vishnu, and that the other aspects of the Godhead are either Krishna's expansions, energies, or his avatars. Lord Krishna, in the Bhagavad Gita, is described as the Supreme Lord, the source of all the Avatars. Lord Krishna is termed as Svayam Bhagavan since he is the purna-avatara (full incarnation.) He is the object of devotion in the Bhakti yoga tradition, and is considered the Supreme Lord.

- **Kalki** is a future incarnation of Vishnu, foretold to appear at the end of Kali Yuga, our present epoch. He will be atop a white horse and his sword will be drawn, blazing like a comet. He is the harbinger of end time in Hindu eschatology, and will destroy all unrighteousness and evil at the end of Kali Yuga.

B

Badrinath—a temple town in the Himalayas

Bhagavad Gita—literally "the Song of God"; a sacred scripture of Hinduism, which discusses the Yogas. It is in the form of a conversation between Lord Krishna and Arjuna, his disciple.

Bhakti yoga—a yoga tradition that focuses on devotion to God. The nine processes of Bhakti yoga are:
- śravaṇa ("listening" to the scriptural stories of Kṛiṣhṇa and his companions),
- kīrtana ("praising," usually refers to ecstatic group singing)
- smaraṇa ("remembering" or fixing the mind on Viṣhṇu)
- pāda-sevana (rendering service)
- arcana (worshiping a Deity)
- vandana (paying homage)
- dāsya (servitude)

319

- sākhya (friendship)
- ātma-nivedana (complete surrender of the self)

Bhava—a spiritual emotion

Bija—literally "seed"

Bindi—a dot on a woman's head in Vedic cultures; a red dot signifies a married woman, a black one signifies a single one; other color dots are used for decorative purposes

Brahma Muhurta—the early morning hours between four-thirty and seven, reputed the best time for spiritual practices.

Brahmanas—priests.

D

Dahi—yogurt.

Dharma—The true nature of things, such as "the dharma of fire is to burn." Also used to describe the nature of reality, as in belief or faith.

Dharmashalla—a pilgrim hostel.

Dhoti—a single cloth, 4 feet wide and 16 feet long, worn by men.

Dosa—a South Indian dish resembling a large crepe, made of ground rice and urad dahl.

G

Gamcha—a thin cotton towel.

Gandharvi—an inhabitant of **Gandharva loka**, one of the heavenly planets, reputed for their skill in vocals and other arts.

Ghee—clarified butter; can be stored for long durations.

Guru—a spiritual teacher.

H

Hanuman—an ardent devotee of Rama, one of the incarnations of the Supreme Lord; a central character in the epic *Ramayana* and its various versions, and is mentioned in several other texts, including Mahabharata, the various Puranas and some Jain texts.

Hatha Yoga—a yoga tradition that focuses on asanas.

Havan—the place of the yogic fire ritual.

I

Iddli—a South Indian steamed rice cake or dumpling.

J

Jantu—a) a sentient being, whether human or animal. b) a citizen.

Japa—a meditative process, consisting of chanting a prescribed number of mantras, usually on a mala, a rosary.

Ji—yes.

K

Kali—the goddess associated with empowerment, or shakti; she is the fierce aspect of the goddess Durga (**Parvati.**)

Kalki—a future Avatar of Vishnu, who appears at the end of Kali yuga. See **Avatar**.

Karma Yoga—a yogic process; means doing work for the sake of God or his devotees, or work without the expectation of personal benefit.

Kartik—the autumn season, the post-harvest period.

Kirtan—spiritual song, usually the repetition of the names of God.

Kohl—an ancient eye cosmetic, widely used in South Asia, the Middle East, North Africa, the Horn of Africa, and parts of West Africa as eyeliner to contour and/or darken the eyelids and as mascara for the eyelashes.

Kosha—literally "sheath"; one of five coverings of the soul according to Vedic philosophy. The five Koshas are:
- Annamaya kosha, food or material-body.
- Pranamaya kosha, the life-force body.
- Manomaya kosha, the mind-body.
- Vijnanamaya kosha, the wisdom or intelligence-body.
- Anandamaya kosha, the bliss-body.

Kurta—a long shirt which comes down to the thighs.

L

Lake Manasarovar—a freshwater lake in the Tibet, about 940 kilometres (580 miles) from Lhasa. The word "Manasarovara" originates from Sanskrit, which is a combination of the words *manas* meaning mind and *sarovara* meaning lake. According to the Hindu legend, the lake was first created in the mind of the Lord Brahma after which it manifested on Earth.

Lakshmi Devi—the wife of Lord Vishnu. The goddess of prosperity and wealth.

Lila—a pastime or play; specifically used in conjunctions with God's activities, which are beyond karmic reactions.

M

Mahabharata—a text which recounts the story of the **Pandavas**, five legendary brothers, and of **Krishna**; one of its chapters contains the **Bhagavad Gita**.

Maha mantra—A) literally "the great mantra"
B) The Hare Krishna mantra:
"Hare Krishna, Hare Krishna,
Krishna, Krishna, Hare Hare,
Hare Rama, Hare Rama,
Rama, Rama, Hare Hare."

Mahavan—literally "the great forest"

Mala—a rosary used in Hinduism and Buddhism, composed of 108 beads, made of a sacred wood, such as Tulasi.

Mandala—a sacred circle.

Mantra—a sound, syllable, word, or group of words considered capable of creating spiritual transformation; its use and type varies according to the school and philosophy associated with the mantra.

Mata—mother.

Mitochondrial DNA—the DNA material found in the mitochondria; organelles found within cells.

Mount Meru—a mythical mountain, composed of gold, which exists in the middle of the universe, in Hindu, Jain and Buddhist cosmology.

Mridanga—a terracotta two-sided drum used in India for accompaniment with devotional music. The drum is played with palms and fingers of both hands.

Mudra—a hand gesture with symbolic meaning.

P

Padmasana—the lotus **asana**, one of the yoga postures.

Pagal—crazy

Patanjali—the compiler of the Yoga Sūtras, an important collection of aphorisms on Yoga practice, circa 200 B.C.

Pita—father.

Prajapati—a progenitor. At the beginning of very cycle of yugas, several Prajapatis are required to repopulate the earth.

Prasadam—literally "mercy," refers to anything offered to God, especially foodstuffs.

Puja—worship, especially as delineated in the **Agamas**, manuals of worship.

Pujari—a priest.

Puri—a fried bread, made of whole wheat, rolled thin and fried in oil or ghee.

R

Radha—the embodiment of the internal energy of Krishna; his consort.

Raga—literally "color, hue" but also "beauty, melody"; is one of the melodic modes used in Indian classical music. A raga uses a series of five or more musical notes upon which a melody is constructed. However, the way the notes are approached and rendered in musical phrases and the mood they convey are more important in defining a raga than the notes themselves. In the Indian musical tradition, rāgas are associated with different times of the day, or with seasons.

Rakshasa—a cannibal, a mythological race of humans.

Rasa—a Sanskrit theological concept specific to Krishna-centered bhakti traditions, such as Gaudiya Vaishnavism. It is believed Rupa Goswami developed, under the direct guidance of Chaitanya Mahaprabhu, an incarnation of Krishna who appeared in 16th century Bengal, the articulated and formulated theology of rasa as "the soul's particular relationship with the divinity in devotional love." The five principal rasas are:
- Shanta rasa - a neutral relationship of the soul with God.
- Dasya Rasa - a master-servant relationship.
- Sakhya rasa - friend-friend relationship.
- Vatsalya rasa - parent-child relationship.
- Madhurya rasa - beloved-lover relationship.

Rishi—a seer, a carrier of the Vedas; the Seven Rishis (the Saptarshi) are often mentioned in the Brahmanas and later works as typical representatives of the pre-historic or mythical period; their names are Uddālaka Āruni, Bharadvaja, Vishvamitra, Jamadagni, Vashista, Kashyapa, and Atri. There are also records of female rishis (in the Rig

Veda): Romasha, Lopamudra, Apala, Kadru, Visvavara, Ghosha, Juhu, Vagambhrini, Paulomi, Yami, Indrani, Savitri, and Devajami.

S

Sadhana—a spiritual practice,

Sambar—a type of lentil soup from South India,

Sankirtana Yajna—the **Yajna** (sacrifice) which is mentioned by Bhakti traditions to be the public chanting of God's names.

Sannyasi—the life stage of the renouncer within the Hindu scheme of *ashramas*. It is considered the topmost and final stage of the ashram systems and is traditionally taken by men or women over fifty or by young monks who wish to renounce worldly and materialistic pursuits and dedicate their lives to spiritual pursuits. People in this stage of life develop *vairāgya,* or a state of dispassion and detachment from material life, renouncing worldly thoughts and desires in order to spend the remainder of their lives in spiritual contemplation. A member of the *sannyasa* order is known as a **sannyasi** (male) or **sannyasini** (female.)

Sarasvati—a) an ancient holy river in India. b) the Hindu goddess of knowledge, music, arts and science and companion of Brahma, also revered as his *shakti* (power.)

Sari—the traditional clothing of women in Vedic culture.

Savasana—the "dead man's" yoga posture; see **Asana.**

Shakti—sacred force or empowerment, it is the primordial cosmic energy and represents the dynamic forces that are thought to move through the entire universe

326

in Hinduism. Usually represented as a female Deity.

Shambala—In Hinduism, a mystical village in the Himalayas where yogis and rishis, in an invisible state, exist for thousands of years. Also the appearance place of Kalki Avatar. In Buddhism, a mythical kingdom hidden somewhere in Inner Asia. It is mentioned in various ancient texts, including the Kalachakra Tantra and the ancient texts of the Zhang Zhung culture which predated Tibetan Buddhism in western Tibet. Whatever its historical basis, Shambhala gradually came to be seen as a Buddhist Pure Land, a fabulous kingdom whose reality is visionary or spiritual as much as physical or geographic.

Shastra—scripture.

Shrivan—the "forest of plenty or opulence" used for harvesting of medicinal herbs and foodstuffs.

Siddhi—a Sanskrit noun that can be translated as "perfection", "accomplishment", "attainment", or "success."

Sikha—a tuft of hair on the back of the head

Srimad-Bhagavatam—also known as the *Bhāgavata Purāṇa* literally meaning *Divine-Eternal Tales of The Supreme Lord)* is one of the *maha* (Sanskrit: 'great') Puranic texts of Hinduism, with its focus on *bhakti* (religious devotion) to the Supreme, primarily focusing on Krishna. It includes many stories well known in Hinduism, including the various avatars of Vishnu and the life and pastimes of his complete incarnation, Krishna or *Svayam Bhagavan.*

Svaha—a) whenever fire sacrifices are made, svāhā is chanted; it is said that the gods to whom offerings are being made through yajna refuse the offerings unless the word 'svaha' is uttered during the sacrifice. b) the wife of Agni, who is the presiding Deity of fire sacrifices.

T

Tapasya—In the yogic tradition, tapasyā may be translated as "essential energy", referring to a focused effort leading towards bodily purification and spiritual enlightenment. It is one of the Niyamas (observances of self-control) described in the Yoga Sutras of Patanjali. Tapasya implies a self-discipline or austerity willingly expended both in restraining physical urges and in actively pursuing a higher purpose in life.

Tapovan—the forest of austerities; in Vedic times, the forest where the yogis and rishis went to perform their spiritual practices.

Tirtha—an object or place of pilgrimage.

Tulasi—an aromatic plant in the family Lamiaceae which is native throughout the Eastern World tropics.

V

Vaimanika shastra—shastra on the topic of vimanas; sometimes also rendered *Vimanika,* regarding human made flying structures. See **vimana**.

Varnashrama dharma—an ancient social system, based on the four **Ashrams** and the four *Varnas*. The Hindu caste system is a corruption of the original Varnashrama system.

Vedas—The original books of wisdom, they are a large body of texts originating in ancient India. Composed in Vedic Sanskrit, the texts constitute the oldest layer of Sanskrit literature and the oldest scriptures of Hinduism. The Vedas are *apauruṣeya* ("not of human agency"). They are supposed to have been directly revealed, and thus are called *śruti* ("what is heard.")

Vimanas—flying craft mentioned in the Ramayana, the Mahabharata and other epics.

Vipra lambha—one of the bhavas, or spiritual emotions.

Y

Yajna—a ritual of offerings accompanied by chanting of Vedic mantras derived from the practice in Vedic times; ancient ritual of offering and sublimating the *havana sámagri* (herbal preparations) in the sacred fire.

Yuga—an 'epoch' or 'era' within a cycle of four ages; the four ages are: Satya Yuga, Treta Yuga, Dvapara Yuga, and Kali Yuga.

About the Author

Mohan Ashtakala is an initiated Hindu Vaishnava priest and has lived in yoga ashrams across India. His goal is to expose the authentic narratives of the yoga tradition through the medium of modern, page-turning novels. He edited and published a community newspaper in Denver, Colorado for thirteen years.

Mohan lives in Calgary, Canada with his wife Anuradha, son Hrishi, daughter Gopi, and Lila, the family's Boston Terrier. He can sometimes be spotted absent-mindedly chanting mantras in the city's parks.

www.yogazapper.com
www.facebook.com/yogazapper

CPSIA information can be obtained
at www.ICGtesting.com
Printed in the USA
FSOW03n0509270116
16160FS